A CONQUEST IMPOSSIBLE TO RESIST

A CYNSTER NEXT GENERATION NOVEL

STEPHANIE LAURENS

ABOUT A CONQUEST IMPOSSIBLE TO RESIST

#1 New York Times bestselling author Stephanie Laurens returns to the Cynsters' next generation to bring you a thrilling tale of love, intrigue, and fabulous horses.

A notorious rakehell with a stable of rare Thoroughbreds and a lady on a quest to locate such horses must negotiate personal minefields to forge a greatly desired alliance—one someone is prepared to murder to prevent.

Prudence Cynster has turned her back on husband hunting in favor of horse hunting. As the head of the breeding program underpinning the success of the Cynster racing stables, she's on a quest to acquire the necessary horses to refresh the stable's breeding stock.

On his estranged father's death, Deaglan Fitzgerald, now Earl of Glengarah, left London and the hedonistic life of a wealthy, wellborn rake and returned to Glengarah Castle determined to rectify the harm caused by his father's neglect. Driven by guilt that he hadn't been there to protect his people during the Great Famine, Deaglan holds firm against the lure of his father's extensive collection of horses and, leaving the stable to the care of his brother, Felix, devotes himself to returning the estate to prosperity.

Deaglan had fallen out with his father and been exiled from Glengarah over his drive to have the horses pay their way. Knowing Deaglan's wishes and that restoration of the estate is almost complete, Felix writes to the premier Thoroughbred breeding program in the British Isles to test their interest in the Glengarah horses.

On receiving a letter describing exactly the type of horses she's seeking, Pru overrides her family's reluctance and sets out for Ireland's west coast to visit the now-reclusive wicked Earl of Glengarah. Yet her only interest is in his horses, which she cannot wait to see.

When Felix tells Deaglan that a P. H. Cynster is about to arrive to assess the horses with a view to a breeding arrangement, Deaglan can only be grateful. But then P. H. Cynster turns out to be a lady, one utterly unlike any other he's ever met.

Yet they are who they are, and both understand their world. They battle their instincts and attempt to keep their interactions businesslike, but the sparks are incandescent and inevitably ignite a sexual blaze that consumes them both—and opens their eyes.

But before they can find their way to their now-desired goal, first one accident, then another distracts them. Someone, it seems, doesn't want them to strike a deal. Who? Why?

They need to find out before whoever it is resorts to the ultimate sanction.

A historical romance with neo-Gothic overtones, set in the west of Ireland. A Cynster Next Generation novel—a full-length historical romance of 125,000 words.

OTHER TITLES BY STEPHANIE LAURENS

The Elusive Bride

The Brazen Bride

The Reckless Bride

The Adventurers Quartet

The Lady's Command

A Buccaneer at Heart

The Daredevil Snared

Lord of the Privateers

The Cavanaughs

The Designs of Lord Randolph Cavanaugh

The Pursuits of Lord Kit Cavanaugh (April 30, 2019)

The Beguilement of Lady Eustacia Cavanaugh (July 18, 2019)

Other Novels

The Lady Risks All

The Legend of Nimway Hall – 1750: Jacqueline

Medieval (As M.S.Laurens)

Desire's Prize

Novellas

Melting Ice – from the anthologies *Rough Around the Edges* and *Scandalous Brides*

Rose in Bloom – from the anthology *Scottish Brides*

Scandalous Lord Dere – from the anthology *Secrets of a Perfect Night*

Lost and Found – from the anthology *Hero, Come Back*

The Fall of Rogue Gerrard – from the anthology *It Happened One Night*

The Seduction of Sebastian Trantor – from the anthology *It Happened One Season*

Short Stories

The Wedding Planner – from the anthology *Royal Weddings*

A Return Engagement – from the anthology *Royal Bridesmaids*

A CONQUEST IMPOSSIBLE
TO RESIST

A CONQUEST IMPOSSIBLE TO RESIST

Copyright © 2019 by Savdek Management Proprietary Limited

ISBN: 978-1-925559-17-0

Cover design by Savdek Management Pty. Ltd.

Cover couple photography and photographic composition by Period Images © 2019

Savdek Management Proprietary Limited, Melbourne, Australia.

www.stephanielaurens.com

Email: admin@stephanielaurens.com

The names Stephanie Laurens and the Cynsters is a registered trademarks of Savdek Management Proprietary Ltd.

❀ Created with Vellum

CHAPTER 1

MARCH 24,1851. NEWMARKET, ENGLAND

"*I*t looks like I've stumbled on a real prospect. Finally!" Prudence Cynster strode, skirts swishing, into her family's breakfast parlor. Her gaze on the letter she held in her hands, she advanced on the table. "Or perhaps I should say"—she glanced again at the signature and title at the end of the second page—"a potential prospect has found their way to us."

She halted by the head of the table, met her father's blue eyes, and held out the letter. "What do you think, Papa?"

Her father, Demon Cynster, set down his knife and fork and took the two sheets.

Pru nodded a good morning to her mother, seated at the foot of the table, and to her aunt Patience, currently visiting, who occupied the chair on her mother's right, then circled the table to her usual place on her father's right, between her brother Nicholas and their father.

Nicholas nodded at the letter. "When did that arrive?"

"Just now." Pru shook out her napkin, then reached for the teapot. "Gilbert was sorting the mail as I passed."

"Who's it from?" Toby, Pru's younger brother, was, as usual, sitting opposite her.

"The Earl of Glengarah, of Glengarah Castle in County Sligo, Ireland." Pru took a long sip of her tea and slanted a glance at her father's face. A slight frown tangled his sandy brows. A good sign? Or the opposite?

While her father, now in his sixties, remained the titular head of the Cynster Stables, Pru, twenty-nine years old and his eldest child, ran the breeding program, while Nicholas, not even a year younger, managed the day-to-day affairs of the racing stable. Toby, now twenty-five, was an able second-in-command to them both, although his talents and interests aligned more closely with Pru's.

"Glengarah writes," her father rumbled, "that his late father had amassed a collection of horses purely for his private satisfaction. Apparently, the late earl's guiding principle was to acquire horses that embodied the strongest and clearest features of the various bloodlines. The current earl wishes to inquire if we have any interest in examining the collection with a view to an arrangement of mutual benefit." Her father humphed, then folded the letter and laid it beside Pru. "He's included a short description of three horses as an indication of what the collection holds. However, he hasn't mentioned the size of the collection beyond that it's large, and he gives no specifics as to bloodlines."

"True," Pru conceded. "But given I've spent the last twenty and more months combing the length and breadth of the British Isles in an until-now largely fruitless search for horses that will allow us to reintroduce the features of the foundation bloodlines back into our bloodstock, thus reinvigorating the most desirable features, then I view the chance that Glengarah has in his stable at least one useful horse as a possibility too good to pass up."

"Not fruitless," Toby corrected. "You found that Barb stallion in Scotland last year."

"Last June," Pru admitted. "But that's the only one, and we need a great deal more if we want to lift the quality of our horses."

She'd journeyed all the way to Perthshire following a tenuous rumor of a beautiful bay horse owned by an eccentric Scottish lord. She'd tracked down the horse and, eventually, the lord. She'd bargained hard and had secured an exclusive license to breed from the stallion; that was her first and, to date, only success in her patently necessary quest.

Nicholas tapped Pru's elbow and pointed at the letter. She handed it over.

While Nicholas read, Pru glanced at her father, who was frowning abstractedly and slowly tapping one finger on the tablecloth, then she looked down the table at her mother, whose dainty features wore an expression of faint frustration. "Do you know anything about the Glengarah horses?"

Her mother sighed. "All I ever heard were rumors that Glengarah—the late earl—had become a recluse obsessed with collecting particular horses. I never heard what sort of horses."

"I'd heard the same." Her father met her mother's eyes. "And that Glengarah wasn't interested in showing off his horses. I can't recall hearing of a single person who's managed to view his stable."

"Do you mean to say that nobody actually knows what's in the Glengarah stable?" Toby's incredulous expression matched his tone.

Pru's reaction mirrored Toby's; those involved in horse breeding were notoriously proud, curious, and gossipy. She glanced at Nicholas and saw interest kindling in his eyes, too.

But caution was Nicholas's middle name; he grunted and refolded the letter. "I thought you checked the Irish entries in the General Stud Book."

Toby reached across the table, fingers waggling, and Nicholas surrendered the letter.

"I did," Pru said, "but of course, I studied the most recent edition. If the late earl was reclusive to the point of maintaining isolation from the horse-breeding world, then what are the odds he never bothered reregistering the horses he acquired, and consequently, they've been written out of the active record?"

Toby was scanning the letter. "It sounds as if the late Earl of Glengarah has created something of a Pandora's box—you won't know what's inside until you open it." He met Pru's eyes, grinned, and waved the letter. "The amazing thing is that you've received an invitation to visit and lift the lid."

"Exactly!" Pru's enthusiasm took flight. "I definitely have to go over and take a look." She reached for the letter, and Toby handed it over.

From the end of the table came a long-suffering sigh. "I had hoped," her mother said, "that you would come to town for one last Season."

From where Pru sat, she couldn't see her sister Margaret—Meg—who was seated on Nicholas's other side. Meg was the only member of the family who was not horse mad; she rode well, but her opinion of horses was that they were beasts of transportation, possibly elegant accoutrements, but nothing more. Now twenty-four, Meg humored the rest of the family and their avid interest in horses with good-natured tolerance while steadily pursuing her own interests, which, to date, centered on enjoying as much of society and ton events as her birth, station, and parents allowed.

Pru smiled understandingly at her mother; despite Pru's advanced age, her mother had never given up hope of her making a suitable match. "You'll have Meg to show off, Mama, and you have to admit that having an older sister forever present at the same events will only hamper her chances."

Meg leaned forward and flashed Pru an encouraging and grateful grin.

But her mother shook her head at Pru. "You can't hide away from society forever."

I can try.

Despite being born into a family deeply entrenched in the haut ton—the glittering world of the highest echelons of society—Pru had never been drawn to the balls and parties. The hunting, the riding, the horses, yes, but the rest she found intensely boring.

Galloping on a powerful horse and feeling the wind fresh in her face was her idea of pleasure.

"I'm not sure one would class a trip to Glengarah Castle as hiding from society." All eyes swung to Patience, the wife of her father's older brother Vane and a firm favorite of the family. She was also much more actively engaged with the ton, spending months at a time in London by the side of the family's matriarch-in-the-making, Honoria, Duchess of St. Ives.

Patience met Pru's gaze with a fond yet shrewdly understanding expression. "The current earl is Lord Deaglan Fitzgerald. That's an Irish version of Declan." Patience pronounced the name as Declan with a *g* in place of the *c*. "The story is that he had a falling-out with his father—the late horse-obsessed earl—and was banished and came to London... That must have been about five years ago."

Pru frowned, trying to recall the man; surely she'd met him during one of the Seasons she'd been unable to avoid? Her mother, she noted, was frowning in similar fashion.

"I doubt you would have encountered him." Patience looked from Pru to her mother. "In the main, Lord Deaglan Fitzgerald avoided ton events and, instead, set about raising hell. He'd inherited wealth from his mother and a great-aunt and, consequently, didn't lack for funds. While to the ladies of the haut ton, his activities in London were cloaked in shadows, I understand he was widely known in less-elevated circles, and that his reputation, apparently well-earned, painted him as a licentious rake."

Pru quickly pointed out, "Luckily, I'm only interested in viewing his horses. And if Lord Deaglan is in London, chances are I won't even cross paths with him."

Although he is the one who wrote...

Patience smiled, faintly smug. "Ah, but he's no longer in London. The instant the news of his father's death reached him, he returned to Ireland —to Glengarah Castle. Indeed, the speed with which he decamped left many of us speculating that his wild behavior had been in reaction, as it were, to his banishment. In support of that conclusion, he hasn't subsequently ventured off his estate—at least not to any social engagement. Nor has he invited any of his erstwhile peers from London to join him. What word has filtered out suggests he's devoting himself to rebuilding the estate in the wake of the famine."

"That," Toby said, "could be the reason he's written. He might want the money from a breeding license to plow into the estate."

Her father nodded. "From what I've heard of the situation in Ireland, that could well be the case."

"Be that as it may," Patience continued, "now Deaglan's the earl and somewhere in his mid-thirties, his refusal to re-engage with society on a more appropriate level is—as one might expect—causing considerable angst among the matchmakers on both sides of the Irish Sea."

Nicholas frowned. "I would have thought his reputation would see him crossed off the matchmakers' lists."

The affectionate look Patience bent on Nicholas was a touch condescending. "The Fitzgeralds are one of the older Anglo-Irish families. The earldom is ancient, the estate—while possibly under stress at the moment —is extensive, and Deaglan is known to have significant funds in his own right. All things considered, there are many in the ton willing to overlook an earl's past in order to gain a foothold in his future."

Pru heard Patience's words, but distantly, too busy considering the logistics of traveling to western Ireland. "We need to act quickly. If Glengarah's collection contains even one gem, we can't afford to have the earl assume we're uninterested and invite one of the other breeding stables to cast their eyes over his horses." She glanced at the letter she'd set beside her plate; every word was already etched in her brain. "He didn't say whether he was writing to others as well."

"We've long been the pre-eminent name in Thoroughbred breeding," her father said, not without pride. "Unsurprising if he thought to write to us first and test the waters."

Nicholas nodded. "In his shoes, I'd do the same. But that doesn't mean I wouldn't later solicit interest from others."

"We can't risk that," Pru stated. They were currently in a five-way tussle for the title of best Thoroughbred breeder, which was assessed on the racing successes of the offspring produced. The effectiveness of the breeding program underpinned the performance of the racing stable, which in turn was the cornerstone of the family's prosperity. She picked up the letter. "I need to get over there and ensure that, if there are any diamonds to be found in the Glengarah stable, we get first chance to license them. I wouldn't want the Cruickshanks or Dalgettys getting there first."

She eased back her chair. "I'll reply immediately. I should be able to leave the day after tomorrow. With any luck, I'll be there in a week's time."

Her father's expression had progressively darkened. Now, he growled, "Toby can go. Jauntering about the wilds of Ireland isn't something a daughter of mine needs to do."

Pru inwardly sighed; she'd hoped to avoid this argument—one they'd had regularly over the past years. "I'll be perfectly safe. As usual, I'll take Horricks and George, as well as Peebles and Suzie." The four—her wily and experienced coachman, vigorous and intelligent footman-cum-groom, dragon of a lady's maid, and quick-as-a-whip younger maid—made up what Toby called her entourage; with them around her, she would, indeed, be safe—even from licentious noblemen. "Not even you, Papa, can imagine any harm befalling me—it didn't through all my journeys through Scotland, and that was through country far wilder and less populated. And on that occasion, I couldn't even say where I was heading. This time, I have a definite destination."

"And," Toby said, meeting her gaze, "it has to be Pru, Papa. I'm not in her league in spotting bloodlines, and I can't shoulder the responsibility at that level—not yet."

Pru grinned with relief and in gratitude for what was a borderline lie. It was true she had the best eye in the family when it came to bloodstock, but although Toby was still learning, he wasn't that far behind.

Nicholas, too, weighed in on her side. "We do need fresh bloodstock —none of us can argue that—and given how many hours Pru has already sunk into her search, and for only one stallion thus far, the Glengarah collection is an opportunity we can't afford to let slip. And while going with Pru might help Toby learn more, with the spring races upon us, I need him here. At present, we're all hands on deck."

Her father grunted. The racing stable was his first love, professionally speaking; anything that threatened its success was unlikely to meet with his approval. "I still don't like it." He frowned at Pru. "You would be better employed going to London with your mother and sister, at least for a few months." He looked down the table, transparently inviting the support of his wife and sister-in-law in forbidding Pru to venture so far afield as the west coast of Ireland.

Pru, Toby, and Nicholas looked at their mother and aunt, too, waiting to see which way their votes would go.

The ladies had had their heads together, whispering while Pru and the others had been talking of horses. Now, her mother and aunt sat back and exchanged a long, wordless—distinctly weighty and meaningful—look.

In her lap, Pru crossed her fingers; despite her mother's wish to see her married, her mother had always supported her in her burning ambition to manage the Cynster breeding program. Although her mother had never been lauded as the premier horseman in all of England, as her father had been, in her day, Felicity—Flick as she was known—had been a superb rider, with a way with Thoroughbreds that Pru had inherited.

Pru prayed that both her mother and aunt would accept her disinterest in marriage. Heaven knew, after the recent spate of Cynster weddings— those of Pru's second cousins, the Duke of St. Ives's children, all three of whom had married in the space of four months, culminating with Louisa's wedding to Lord Drake Varisey only a week ago—even the Cynster ladies' legendary thirst for family nuptials ought to be assuaged, at least for a few months!

Focusing on her aunt's face, Pru suspected that, as Patience knew something of the current earl, he with whom Pru would need to negotiate, in this instance, Patience's view was likely to be the deciding factor.

Yet it was her mother who spoke first, her blue eyes resting with fond shrewdness on Pru. "This seems a situation too promising to pass up." Her mother shifted her gaze to her husband. "I really don't think Pru will be in any danger, and who knows? At Glengarah Castle, she might well find what she's been searching for."

"Indeed." Patience nodded decisively. "I concur. On all counts, it seems advisable that Pru goes and as soon as possible."

Pru looked at her father to see him frowning in a puzzled way. She knew he hadn't given up hope of seeing her married to some suitable gentleman; he'd expected her mother and her aunt to support his stance.

In leaning forward to listen to her mother and aunt, Pru had noticed Meg, as usual sipping her tea and nibbling her toast and thinking faraway thoughts of balls and dresses and dancing while the rest of the family argued around her. With a clink that drew everyone's attention, Meg set down her teacup and airily said, "I'm really looking forward to the Season this year."

Pru could have hugged her sister. In Meg's apparently artless way, she'd just reminded her father that he had two daughters, not just his firstborn.

Along with everyone else's, her father's gaze had gone to Meg. After a moment, he grunted, then he looked at Pru and sighed. "All right. I give in. You may leave for blasted Ireland as soon as you wish."

Pru beamed, pushed to her feet, stepped to her father's side, draped her arms about his shoulders, and hugged him. "Thank you, Papa. You won't regret it."

He patted her arm and gruffly barked, "Make sure I don't."

Pru dropped a kiss on his graying hair, then returned to her chair to rapidly finish her toast and drain her teacup.

The instant she had, she picked up the Earl of Glengarah's letter, rose, and hurried off to write her reply, then make the necessary arrangements to travel to Glengarah Castle.

~

Lord Deaglan Fitzgerald swung up to the back of his gray stallion, then looked around and whistled for his dogs. The red-and-white Irish setter, Molly, raised her head from the stony bed of a nearby brook, looked, and obediently came trotting, but Sam, the Kerry beagle, was more interested in some trail—most likely that of the wily old fox that hunted the area.

"Sam!" Deaglan didn't wait to see if the dog followed—he could easily catch up; he wheeled Thor and tapped his heels to the horse's flanks. Thor surged, happy to be moving again, even if it was in the direction of the castle stable.

Deaglan tried not to think of what awaited him at home. Yet more papers, information on investments, letters from his bank in London, and the never-ending scourge of invoices and accounts. Being the Earl of Glengarah was not the easy, idle life most in society would imagine. Not that, over the past five years, he'd entertained any illusions as to how hard he would have to work—to battle—to get the estate up to scratch once the title and its attendant responsibilities landed on his shoulders—once his father had died, bringing an end to the long period of his willful neglect.

Admittedly, Deaglan was doing exactly as he wished, but the

constant, unexpected calls on his time—such as the summons to give his approval to the line of the new fence being erected across one of the horse paddocks—stretched the task before him until at times he felt as if he'd never see its end.

If it wasn't a fence or similar issue, it was problems with foaling, lambing, or calving, or a rockslide that had blocked one of the main internal lanes—that was last week—or the damn fox taking someone's chickens. All of which were preferable to having to evict the pine marten that had taken up residence in old Mrs. Comey's shed.

Some things he could foist onto others, but Mrs. Comey had known him all his life—she'd been a nursemaid at the castle when he'd been born—and he never felt comfortable sending someone else in response to her latest complaint.

Still and all, he was slowly progressing in his self-appointed—also admittedly self-serving—task. Step by step, he was moving the estate onto a more stable financial footing while simultaneously reforming farming practices so that, in the years ahead, his farmers would reap the greatest rewards from their efforts.

His goal was to steer the Glengarah estate into smooth and secure financial waters and anchor it there, so that no matter what storms the future brought, the estate and its people would survive.

They'd weathered the recent famine only by the skin of their teeth— and by the blessing of him having established the kennels as a going concern before he'd left. If it hadn't been for the income from the sale of the highly rated Glengarah gun and hunting dogs that, even from afar, he'd been able to direct to assist the families dependent on the earldom, the estate's population would have been decimated, and as was now the case on so many Irish estates, Glengarah would have been left without the manpower to pull themselves back into shape now the famine had at long last eased its hold.

Sam had caught up, and he and Molly now flanked the cantering stallion. To the rhythm of Thor's hooves thudding on the thick, emerald-green sward, Deaglan gave thanks that this corner of the country—the pocket including his home—had been spared the worst of Ireland's national disaster. Despite his father's depredations, he'd been able to ensure that the majority of those on the estate had survived and stayed. Now, he was working to ensure that everyone thrived.

Ahead, the castle came into view, its twin towers and crenellated battlements in dark-gray stone standing solid and tall above the surrounding greens of paddock and meadow and scattered pockets of woodland. The castle's lead roofs added a deeper shade of gray, their slopes running this way and that, breaking the otherwise rigid lines and hinting at the multitude of extensions that had been added within the outer walls over the generations.

The holder of the title before his father—not Deaglan's grandfather but a distant cousin of his father's—had modernized the castle, at least to his time, an act for which Deaglan offered profound and frequent thanks. His father would never have bothered, too fixated on his obsession, but thanks to the previous earl, Deaglan and his younger brother, Felix, had grown up in a house that had been the epitome of comfortable.

To Deaglan, his home exuded comfort; it always had and always would. To him, the castle was simply home, a place steeped in every nuance that word could convey.

Thor carried him swiftly toward the gray walls. The big stallion needed no direction to veer for the archway in one towering wall that gave access to the side court and the stable yard beyond.

They cleared the arch, and Deaglan reined Thor to a walk. His gaze went to the stable, and as always, he felt the addictive tug—the siren-song lure of the horses inhabiting the stalls beyond those used by the hacks and carriage horses.

That very addiction—his father's complete surrendering to it—had led to their falling out. Nothing else. It had been something shared, something Deaglan had innately understood—that passionate love of horses. But while Deaglan placed people higher in his scales, his father had seen only the horses.

Having set up the kennels and successfully developed them into a commercial concern, having confirmed the financial benefits as well as the satisfaction derived from such an endeavor, Deaglan had hoped to do the same with the horses.

His father had disagreed.

Vehemently.

His sire hadn't cared for anything beyond his horses, even in the face of the looming famine and the estate's potentially dire need.

Furious at such blind intransigence—and frustrated by his helplessness to change it—Deaglan had left Glengarah. Since returning, other than to fetch Thor, he hadn't ventured deeper into the stable, to the stalls in which his father's prizes were housed.

Later, he'd told himself. Eventually.

Only once all else on the estate was fixed.

He trotted Thor into the stable yard, and a groom came running.

Deaglan glanced at the maw of the stable entrance and opted to rein in and dismount. He handed the reins to the groom with instructions to rub the horse down well and treat him to a small measure of oats. After bestowing a last pat on the stallion's long nose, Deaglan turned toward the castle's side door.

Crossing the cobbled side court, he ran through his mental list of the tasks he'd yet to complete in his program of rectification and, somewhat to his surprise, realized the list was considerably shorter than he'd thought.

He was halfway to the castle, the dogs trotting on either side, when the side door was hauled open, and Felix rushed out. His gaze locked on Deaglan, and relief visibly rolled through him, then he lowered his chin and determinedly strode to meet Deaglan.

Deaglan noted that Felix was carrying a letter in one hand and slowed. *What now?* He'd only just noticed his list of tasks shortening; how many were about to be added?

The first words out of Felix's mouth, "I've a confession to make," did nothing to ease Deaglan's mind.

Deaglan waved his brother back toward the house. As Felix fell in beside him, Deaglan uttered a bland, unthreatening "Oh?"

Felix drew a deep breath, held it for a second, then said, "What we've been discussing about commercializing the stable... I know you intended putting it off until you're ready to take up the reins again, so to speak. And God knows, I can understand that. You're constantly busy, and you've resumed overseeing the kennels, too— sensible, given how critical they are to the estate's coffers."

During the years of Deaglan's banishment, Felix had stepped in and overseen the kennels and, since their father's death, had watched over the stable as well. Wondering whither his brother was leading, Deaglan cast him a measuring glance. "You did well enough with the kennels."

"Only because you wrote and told me what to do."

True, yet Felix had proved himself capable of acting in Deaglan's stead—acting as Deaglan's eyes, ears, and voice.

"But this is about the horses." Felix waved the letter.

Deaglan quashed the urge to seize the missive and read it; whatever it contained was Felix's to reveal. Despite the five years between them, he and Felix were close, and Deaglan saw no reason to step on his brother's toes.

They reached the side door, and Deaglan pushed it wide and strode through, into the cool dimness of the corridor that led to the front hall.

From long experience, Deaglan knew there was no value in trying to rush Felix—he would only lose his train of thought, tortuous though it might be, and have to start at the beginning again. Calling on oft-used patience, Deaglan walked on and waited.

Felix came up beside him, displacing the dogs, who disgruntledly fell back. "We discussed the direction in which you were thinking of taking the stable—about our best bet being to form some sort of an alliance with one of the major English breeders so we get access to their expertise as well as a leg-up via the association. I know you wanted to hold back until you were free to re-immerse yourself in the collection, but I thought, as that time can't be too far away, perhaps I could help by testing the waters." Felix hauled in a huge breath, then let it out on the words, "So I wrote to the Cynsters."

Deaglan blinked. They'd reached the front hall; he halted in the middle of the black-and-white tiled floor and stared at Felix as his brother swung to face him. "The Cynsters?" Felix had gone straight to the top of the tree. The implication of the letter Felix was carrying slammed into Deaglan. "And?"

"And"—unable to contain his delight, Felix brandished the letter —"they replied!"

Felix thrust the letter at Deaglan, and he all but snatched it. He read... then realized that the letter was addressed to him—to the earl.

"Ah...yes. That was the major part of my confession," Felix said. "I thought it would be better if I wrote in your name."

His eyes tracking the lines of the Cynsters' reply, his mind scrambling to absorb their meaning, let alone its significance, Deaglan grunted. "No matter."

He reached the end of the letter, then looked at Felix—and smiled. "This is wonderful!" He felt his smile widen to match Felix's. "Well done!"

Deaglan returned his attention to the letter. "It seems this P. H. Cynster is definitely interested in casting his eyes over our horses." Timing-wise, Felix might have jumped the gun a trifle, but not by much, and the result of his attempt to help couldn't be better—eliciting the immediate interest of the Cynsters was nothing short of a coup.

Speaking of timing… Deaglan looked at Felix. "When did you write to them?"

"I posted the letter twelve days ago."

Deaglan calculated the time for delivery, then checked the date of the letter in his hand. "They replied virtually as soon as your letter reached them."

"Yes. They must be quite keen."

"What did you tell them?"

"I kept it vague," Felix assured him. "I told them of the principle the pater followed in creating the collection and gave them descriptions of three horses, but I didn't mention anything specific regarding bloodlines —only that the pater purchased with an eye to that."

"What about the number of horses in the collection? Did you tell them that?"

Felix grinned. "Just that there was a large number."

Deaglan grinned back. "Good."

He looked again at the letter, trying to read between the formal phrases via which P. H. Cynster had communicated the Cynsters' interest and felt vindication for his stance against his father—for his people— flow through him; he'd been right in thinking there was a real future in breeding from his father's collection.

Glancing again at the signature, Deaglan realized the hand was not the same as the one in which the letter was written. Apparently, P. H. Cynster was wealthy enough to command the services of a secretary. Then again, the man was a Cynster, and when it came to anything to do with horses, Deaglan had heard that they did not stint.

According to the words beneath the signature, P. H. Cynster was the head of the Cynster breeding program. For Deaglan's ultimate purpose, there couldn't be anyone better to be on their way to get a first look at his father's horses—now his.

He looked again at Felix. His brother had yet to calm; indeed, Felix seemed to be growing progressively more agitated. "This"—Deaglan held up the letter—"is a hugely encouraging response."

Felix stared at him, then jabbed a finger at the letter. "Did you read the last paragraph? It says he expects to reach here by this afternoon!"

"What?" Deaglan had skimmed over the date. He looked again. March 31st. "Good Lord."

"Yes!" Felix all but shouted. "Cynster's letter was delayed—look at the date it was sent. That storm in the Irish Sea a few days ago—remember? That's why I came rushing to get you. He estimates arriving at Glengarah on the afternoon of March thirty-first, and that's today, and it's already after two o'clock!"

Deaglan stared at his brother and felt his head spin. He hauled in a steadying breath and straightened. "All right. Don't panic." He wasn't sure whether that last was directed at Felix or himself. Possibly both.

"As soon as I read that," Felix said, "before I came to find you, I sent a footman up to the tower to keep watch. I told him to come and find us the instant he spots any visitor bowling up the drive."

Deaglan nodded. "Good. At least we'll have a few minutes' warning." He thought, then said, "Let's go to the library. In what time we have, you need to tell me everything you can about the current state of the stable."

He led the way to and into the library, a large room he and Felix considered shared territory. Deaglan diverted to tug the bellpull, then dropped into the armchair he favored, while Felix made for the one opposite.

The butler, Bligh, a tall, stately individual perfectly turned out in butler's black, duly arrived. "Yes, my lord?"

"Advance warning, Bligh—we're due to receive a visitor, a gentleman from England here to view the horses. He could arrive at any moment. I suspect we should be prepared to put him up for the night."

"Possibly for longer," Felix said. He met Deaglan's questioning gaze. "If he's interested in the horses, from what I've been able to gather, assessing them might take several days."

Deaglan looked at Bligh. "So. We'll know after he gets here. But you might warn Mrs. Bligh and Mrs. Fletcher. Regardless of how long he remains, dinner is likely to be on the cards."

Bligh's eyebrows had risen. He pondered, then inquired, "If I might ask, my lord, of what station is this gentleman?"

"Haut ton, Bligh. Top of the tree."

"I see, sir." Bligh bowed. "In that case, please be assured we will be on our mettle. I will inform Mrs. Bligh and Mrs. Fletcher accordingly."

"Oh," Felix said as Bligh prepared to depart. "In case you're wondering, I sent Henry up to the tower to keep watch."

Bligh nodded. "An excellent thought, sir. I'll away and speak with the staff, then return and keep vigil in the front hall."

The instant the door shut behind Bligh, Deaglan leaned forward. Resting his forearms on his thighs, he fixed Felix with a commanding look. "Now, what do I need to know about how things stand in the stable?"

As Felix rattled through an equine inventory, refreshing Deaglan's memories of the horses, memories he was relieved to discover remained clear and detailed, he found himself prey to the same rising excitement that had patently infected Felix.

The more that excitement built, the more completely he embraced what was occurring—set in train by Felix's action, yet clearly meant to be —Deaglan felt forced to acknowledge that perhaps he'd hung back from resuming control of the stable for too long—that he'd allowed his vow to completely rebuild the estate first to override not just his inclination but also his better judgment.

Clearly—transparently—Fate had decided it was time for him to return to the stable, to face that siren-song lure and conquer it.

Eventually, Felix ran down. After a moment of silent pondering, he offered, "I can't think of anything more you need to know."

Deaglan nodded. "You've told me enough to be getting on with." Neither he nor Felix had for one instant considered that Felix should be the one to deal with P. H. Cynster. Aside from all else, Felix had little experience of the ton; leaving him to deal with a Cynster would be the equivalent of throwing him to the wolves.

Deaglan had no doubt that, if after viewing the horses, P. H. Cynster was interested in a breeding arrangement, the man would ruthlessly push for a deal that favored the Cynsters. Luckily, the past eighteen months of having to deal with bankers and the like had left Deaglan with no qualms whatsoever over engaging in ruthless negotiations.

"I have to say," Felix observed, "that the speed of Cynster's reply is... well, heartening, don't you think?"

Deaglan nodded. "Indeed."

Both he and Felix froze as the sound of pounding footsteps, muted by the thick walls, reached them. Then the footsteps hit the hall tiles and headed their way.

An instant later, a tap fell on the door.

At Deaglan's "Come," Henry, the footman, out of breath and rosy of face, stumbled in and gasped, "Carriage bowling up the drive, my lord." Despite his labored breathing, Henry's eyes lit. "Prime turnout, my lord. Can't say I've ever seen its like. And the horses! Top o' the trees, they be —high-steppers an' all. Beautiful, they are—just beautiful!"

Deaglan arched his brows and rose. He met Felix's eyes as his brother sprang to his feet. "Clearly, given Henry's gushing, this P. H. Cynster likes to travel in style. Those have to be his own horses."

Felix was nodding. "He must have brought them over on the ferry."

That wasn't something many travelers did; relatively speaking, Irish jobbing horses were better than the average. Deaglan suspected that bringing his own horses and carriage said something of P. H. Cynster, but he couldn't quite fathom what.

Deaglan sent Henry to warn Mrs. Bligh. They found Bligh himself standing tall close by the front door.

"I gather the gentleman's arrival is imminent, my lord."

"So it seems, Bligh." Deaglan nodded at the door. "Mr. Felix and I will await our guest on the porch."

Bligh swept to the massive double doors and drew one wide.

"Leave it open." Deaglan walked past to take a position at the head of the steps leading up from the forecourt. First impressions were important in the ton.

Especially if, as seemed entirely possible, he was about to welcome his destiny.

As the carriage bowled into sight, he felt anticipation rise, sweet and heady. The equipage was every bit as eye-catching as Henry had reported, not because it was in any way showy but purely because of its perfect lines. Not even Deaglan had seen its like before; it had to be a recent design. And superbly well sprung; as the coachman drew on the reins, the body of the carriage smoothly responded. As for the four bays between the shafts, they were, indeed, a joy to behold.

Deaglan watched the horses' actions as the coachman drew them to a halt with the sort of understated flourish only an experienced whip could achieve. Although aware of the people on the carriage and inside it—of the shadowed faces behind the gleaming windows—Deaglan couldn't drag his eyes from the horses. Couldn't pull his gaze away from tracing their lines.

From the corner of his eye, he saw Cynster's groom—or was the man a footman? He was certainly tall enough—drop down from the rear of the carriage and go forward to open the door.

"Cynster's even brought his own footman," Felix unnecessarily muttered. "Who does that?"

"Indeed," Deaglan replied, still focused on the horses.

Once the carriage door was opened and the steps folded down, the first to alight was a bright-eyed young maid. She stared up at Deaglan and

Felix, then transferred her gaze to the castle rising behind and above them. Her eyes grew round in a satisfying way.

First impressions.

The next to alight was an older lady's maid—more rightly termed a dresser—clad in black bombazine with her hair pulled tightly back from her face and an expression that remained set in forbidding lines even as she gazed at the castle.

Not so impressionable.

Deaglan was about to return his attention to the horses when the oddity struck him. Why was Cynster traveling with a lady's maid? Let alone two maids?

Then the footman reached into the carriage, and Deaglan saw a gloved hand—a small, slender gloved hand—grasp the footman's as, with all due solicitousness, he handed down a lady...

A lady.

Golden curls framed an arresting face. A touch on the tallish side, with a curvaceously slender figure displayed to advantage in a stylishly cut traveling dress of bright sky-blue, she possessed a complexion the English termed peaches-and-cream.

From this distance, Deaglan couldn't see the color of her eyes, but they were large and well-set beneath delicately arched brows. Her features were supremely feminine—the flutter of feathery brown lashes, a straight little nose, and generous lips the color of the palest pink roses.

His attention was captured, focused, and held in a way it hadn't been for more than eighteen months.

The attraction was visceral and compelling—and very, very familiar.

For long seconds, all he could see was her—all he felt was a rising compulsion to smile seductively, walk down the steps, take her hand, and lead her somewhere private, preferably somewhere with a bed.

He swayed, about to step forward, and only just hauled himself back.

Instinctive alarm flared, and his mind belatedly caught up with events.

Deaglan stared down at the vision gracing his forecourt and tried to make sense of it. Of her.

Cynster had brought either his sister or his wife—his young and gloriously beautiful wife—to Glengarah Castle, to meet Lord Deaglan Fitzgerald, acknowledged rake of the ton, gazetted seducer of willing, usually married ladies.

Why?

Cynster had to know of his reputation. Why bring his dashingly attractive wife to Glengarah?

To distract Deaglan while Cynster looked over his horses and offered a deal?

That, Deaglan had to admit, would work, at least to some degree.

And if the lady was Cynster's sister...

Deaglan had been told that now the title was his, many parents were willing to overlook his past misdemeanors in order to install their daughter as his countess.

He hadn't invited any lady to the castle, not ever. Cynically, he wondered if the Cynsters thought this a way to break through his walls.

Avoiding the snares of a delectable young lady... That, too, would be a distraction.

All those thoughts streamed through his mind during the seconds the lady took to consult with her maids and footman, then the lady raised her gaze and, bold as brass, examined him and Felix as they stood shoulder to shoulder on the porch.

Finally, her gaze lifted to the castle behind them.

Freed of her spell, Deaglan stared at the carriage, waiting for P. H. Cynster to emerge. Was the man ailing that it was taking him so long?

Then the lady turned to the coachman and spoke, and the footman shut the carriage door.

The lady turned to face Deaglan and smiled—confident, bold, and assured.

Then she raised her skirts and started up the steps.

It was her confidence that opened his eyes—that sent realization jolting through him, shattering his thoughts and making his lungs seize, leaving him feeling as if his world was tilting sideways...

CHAPTER 2

$\mathcal{F}$orced to look down as she climbed the steps, Pru hid a cynical smile. She would wager her favorite riding cap that the taller gentleman of the two waiting was the earl. Instead of traveling directly from Newmarket, she'd gone by way of London, stopping overnight at St. Ives House expressly to pick the brain of her father's cousin-by-marriage, Honoria, Duchess of St. Ives. Among other insights, Honoria had shared a comprehensive description of Lord Deaglan Fitzgerald, covering his physical attributes, his personality, and unexpectedly, the impact of his presence; regarding the latter, Honoria had stated that if Pru was to deal with the man directly, she needed to be prepared and appropriately armored.

At the time, Pru had wondered at the exactness of Honoria's observations—surely no mere man was that much of an Adonis, let alone possessed such potent allure. Now, she had cause to be grateful for Honoria's accurate and clear-sighted assessment of the Earl of Glengarah.

She'd been warned. She was armored—as much as foreknowledge could make her.

She still felt it—felt him. The beckoning attraction.

And she hadn't got within a yard of him yet.

As she climbed, she reviewed what awaited her on the porch. A tall man, a head taller than she, broad shouldered and slim hipped, with the long legs and lean, rangy build of a born rider. His face had been described as that of a fallen angel, all chiseled planes and broad forehead under a sweep of crow-black locks that held just the hint of a wave. A strong patrician nose, mobile lips, and a square chin completed the portrait.

Nearing the top step, she glanced up through her lashes. Dissolute he might once have been, but there was no sign of even hard living marring his handsome yet stony face.

She reached the porch, released her skirts, straightened, and met his eyes.

Green—the green of Ireland, an emerald so intense it captivated the beholder.

For a second, she felt as if she was falling into those mesmerizing eyes...then she shook off the entrancement. She was there to see his horses, nothing more.

He returned her regard for a pregnant instant, then, somewhat hesitantly, growled, "P. H. Cynster, I presume?"

His voice was deep and rumbly, the faintest trace of Irish burr softening the gravelly edges.

She smiled and held out her hand. "Yes. I'm Prudence Cynster." Obviously, her fame hadn't penetrated the wilds of Ireland. Equally obviously, he'd been expecting a man, which tipped the advantage between them her way; she hadn't anticipated being handed such a gift and wasn't inclined to squander it. She tilted her chin a notch higher. "I manage the breeding program at the Cynster Stables and was intrigued by your letter inviting us to view your late father's collection of horses."

A gentleman—a nobleman—of Glengarah's ilk would be comfortable and assured dealing with a conventional young lady. Therefore, being her usual unconventional self would serve her interests best.

She let her smile deepen and light her eyes, let anticipation and just a hint of teasing show. "I'm here, therefore, to evaluate your stable."

His lips tightened; his eyes hadn't left hers. Then his fingers closed, firm and strong, about her gloved hand, engulfing it in heat and strength.

For a second, she could have sworn the world slowed while all her senses leapt to focus on his touch. Behind Glengarah's emerald eyes, she glimpsed a whirlpool of powerful emotions, sensed their tug, and felt a glittering sensation of presentiment dance along her nerves, setting them alive, on edge in a tantalizing and unprecedented way...

Then his lashes lowered, hiding those fascinating eyes, and he bowed elegantly, if a trifle stiffly, over her hand.

"Welcome to Glengarah, Miss Cynster." Deaglan straightened and forced himself to release her hand. He hesitated, but felt compelled to probe. "I admit we hadn't expected a lady as the sole representative of the renowned Cynster breeding program."

He glanced down at her carriage, at her people busy unpacking and handing boxes and bags to two of his footmen. Several grooms were waiting to tend to the wonderful horses—all but vying for the job.

From the corner of his eye, he saw Prudence Cynster's alluring lips curve in a smile edged with cynicism. He couldn't resist remarking, "I hadn't thought your father would be so…"

He faced her again, and her blue eyes—the same blue as her gown, that of glorious summer skies—met his gaze levelly. "Advanced in his thinking?" she suggested. Her smile turned wry. "You're correct. He isn't. However, when it comes to horses and the stable he founded, he has always believed in nothing but the best. Although he's arguably the most accomplished rider and the most experienced and successful trainer in Britain, he recognized long ago that my mother had a superior eye for bloodlines. I appear to have inherited that trait, along with my father's riding ability, and I enjoy using my eyes and accumulated knowledge of breeds in furthering our breeding program."

Her diction grew crisp, her words flowing as if she'd recited them many times before. "I've been involved in the breeding program since I was a child, became formally involved over a decade ago, and assumed control of the program four years ago." She met his eyes boldly—directly —in a way few ladies ever had. "So, my lord earl, if you wish for an arrangement with the Cynster Stables, it's me you will need to convince of the quality of your horses."

A challenge, open and direct, one far too much of him was eager to accept. Ruthlessly, he reined his impulses back. "You'll have to excuse our ignorance. I admit I hadn't heard that the Cynster breeding program was managed by a lady." He continued to hold her gaze. "And you did sign yourself P. H. Cynster, thereby disguising the fact."

She lightly shrugged. "So many men squirm over doing business with a female that I long ago adopted the practice of sparing male sensibilities whenever I can. But all the major breeders and anyone involved in the business, or who does business with us, knows who P. H. Cynster is." She studied his eyes, then hers changed, a teasing twinkle sparking into existence, and she dipped her head. "I apologize if I've…discombobulated you."

He managed not to snort; she was damned well enjoying discombobulating him—he who was accustomed to being the source of feminine discombobulation. But it wasn't her catching him wrong-footed that had evoked the sense of impending danger welling inside him.

He tried to tell himself that such an intense, visceral attraction, one so potent it set his senses afire, was only to be expected after an eighteen-months' abstinence. Prior to that, he'd gorged on female companionship, so the sense of a yawning, empty pit hungry to be filled wasn't to be wondered at, was it?

Not even he believed that. He'd never felt such flaring, heated hunger before, not for any woman. That urge to take her hand and lead her off to somewhere private remained, a compulsive beat in his veins.

They'd only just met.

How bad was the compulsion going to get?

How long would she need to stay?

His thoughts churned.

For one instant, he toyed with the notion of handing her over to Felix to deal with and cravenly retreating to the shadows, but ultimately, the horses were his—his property, his responsibility.

His future.

Yet she was going to test him as no other lady ever had. He could see that clearly.

He couldn't afford to allow his baser instincts free rein, couldn't seduce her—couldn't risk damaging the chance of making a deal with the Cynsters and gaining their support in developing the collection into a viable breeding concern.

He continued to be suspicious of the Cynsters sending her to him—even allowing her into his orbit. What were they thinking? They had to know of his reputation, that it had been well-earned. Was this a test of sorts?

Regardless, he couldn't foist handling a lady like her onto Felix. She was not that young—somewhere in her late twenties was his educated guess—and if even half her claims were true, she would be far more experienced in all matters to do with trading and breeding horses than either him or Felix.

And she'd already demonstrated that she was perfectly prepared to exploit any advantage her sex afforded her.

No. It had to be him.

Him and her.

Pru searched the earl's green eyes and knew beyond question that he was weighing up whether to balk at dealing with her—a female. He was certainly arrogant enough—used to getting his own way enough—to push the point.

She wasn't about to allow him the option. Quite aside from the unexpected and remarkably strong urge to learn more about him—such an un-Prudence-like feeling and therefore fascinating in its own right—she wanted to see his horses. In that respect, her instincts were pricking. She hadn't missed the brothers' appreciation of her bays; they knew their horses. They might be amateurs when it came to horse breeding, but horses, they knew—through experience or instinct or, more likely, both.

His attitude, which stood like a solid wall between him and her, a barrier through which she wasn't allowed to reach so she couldn't touch him or his mind and influence either, was a flagrant challenge, whether he meant it as that or not. He should have researched more deeply; it was never wise to challenge a Cynster, male or female.

Pru didn't wait for him to speak but calmly took control. "If I might inquire, have you contacted any of the other major stables regarding your late father's horses?"

Glengarah blinked, then repressively countered, "Perhaps you would enlighten me as to the precise nature of the Cynsters' interest in the Glengarah collection."

She smiled and airily explained, "We are always on the lookout for new bloodstock that carry the foundation bloodlines. How many such horses are in your collection?"

"Several. You must have started on your journey within a day or so of receiving our letter. Are you always so keen to look over prospective horses?"

She narrowed her eyes on his, on his faintly aloof and haughty expression; her smile had grown tight. "We've never been known for letting grass grow beneath our feet."

"Is that so?" His eyes darkened. "And is that the sole reason you beat such a rapid path to my door?"

Her temper sparked—then she realized he was seeking just that.

The brother cleared his throat and all but stepped between them.

Pru blinked and stepped back—only then realizing that she and the damned earl had edged closer. Too close. She'd been lost in his green eyes, drawn in, and hadn't noticed.

She glanced at Glengarah and, from his faintly stunned expression, deduced that he hadn't noticed, either.

She forced her gaze from his face to that of his brother, who, with a hopeful, benevolent expression, was waiting to engage.

Deaglan saw Prudence Cynster's attention deflect to Felix; she regarded his brother as if she'd only just remembered he was there.

Seizing the opportunity, Deaglan stepped farther back and waved at Felix. "Allow me to present Mr. Felix Fitzgerald, my brother."

Felix smiled and reached for her hand, which she surrendered. "Miss Cynster. Might I say what a pleasure it is to welcome you to Glengarah Castle?"

Releasing her fingers, Felix slanted a questioning glance at Deaglan. He returned it with a near-imperceptible nod, encouraging Felix to take the lead.

Felix promptly returned his attention to their visitor. "We hope you will enjoy your time with us. We'll endeavor to meet whatever requirements you have regarding viewing our horses." Felix pointed to the right, to where a corner of the stable was visible beyond the side of the castle. "The stable is over there—I'm sure our stablemen will be happy to assist in accommodating your horses. Meanwhile, might I suggest we venture inside? You must be quite fatigued after your long journey."

Prudence Cynster, Deaglan noted, was now fully focused on Felix. When he waved toward the open door, she smiled sweetly and accepted the implied invitation to stroll into the castle. Felix fell in on her left, leaving Deaglan to follow on her right—a little behind so he didn't draw her attention from his brother.

Felix possessed a gilded tongue; he could flatter and charm and sweep young ladies off their feet. Deaglan had never bothered cultivating the ability—he'd never had need of it—but Felix was a recognized master.

Deaglan ambled a step behind the pair as they walked into the front hall. He paused beside Bligh and, while keeping an ear tuned to Felix's natter and Prudence Cynster's replies, confirmed to a surprised Bligh that their visitor had—unexpectedly—proved to be female. "She's brought a dresser and a younger maid, as well as a coachman and either a footman or groom—he might serve as both. I take it accommodating them won't be a problem?"

"Of course not, my lord." Bligh sounded faintly affronted.

Deaglan's lips twitched, but he had no difficulty keeping them from curving; Miss Prudence Cynster being under his roof was no laughing matter. "In the circumstances, I suggest Mrs. Bligh reconsider which chamber to assign to Miss Cynster. I suspect the room at the far end of the west wing—the one that overlooks the stable—would be most appropriate."

It was also the guest chamber farthest from his own apartments.

Bligh bowed. "Indeed, my lord." He glanced at Felix and Miss Cynster, who had paused in the middle of the long front hall—originally the baronial great hall; their visitor was looking about her with apparent interest and questioning Felix about the family crest displayed on various old pennants hanging on the walls. "If I might suggest, my lord, a tea tray might be in order. I understand the lady has traveled some distance to reach us."

"Indeed. Although I haven't detected any signs of wilting, no doubt tea and cakes would be the civilized thing to offer." Deaglan made a snap decision and smiled to himself. "In the library, Bligh. Bring the tray there."

"My lord?"

Leaving Bligh to his puzzlement over Deaglan's choice of venue in which to entertain a well-born lady, Deaglan sauntered toward Felix and Miss Cynster. He studied her face, expecting to see the usual softening and evidence of her relaxing her guard that interacting with Felix usually produced. Instead, although her features were set in pleasantly relaxed lines, in her eyes, Deaglan glimpsed calculation.

And realized he'd misjudged her. She was immune to Felix's blarney.

She saw him coming and shifted, drawing Felix's gaze. "Tell me," she said, her voice low, "have other stables shown interest in the Glengarah collection? Do any others know of the horses it holds?"

"I..." Felix glanced over his shoulder; relief flooded his face when he saw Deaglan approaching. "I...er..."

"What my brother is attempting to put into words, Miss Cynster"—Deaglan dropped a reassuring hand on Felix's shoulder—"is that we have no way of knowing to whom my father might have shown his horses nor with whom he might have corresponded regarding them."

She met his gaze with the directness he was coming to expect from her. "I see."

Deaglan smiled easily and kept a tight hold on the conversational reins. "I've given orders for your staff to be accommodated, and your bags will shortly be taken up to your room. Our housekeeper, Mrs. Bligh, will escort you there whenever you wish, although I hope you'll consent to take tea with us first."

He waved her down the hall. With a graceful inclination of her head, she accepted the invitation and moved forward. He fell into step alongside her, leaving a faintly puzzled Felix to follow in their wake.

Deaglan continued, "I apologize that my aunt Mrs. O'Connor is not here to greet you. She's presently out visiting, but is expected back shortly." He caught Prudence Cynster's blue eyes. "You'll be pleased to know that my aunt lives here. Consequently, with respect to you residing under this roof, the proprieties will be observed."

The arrested look in her eyes suggested that, in setting out for Glengarah Castle, she hadn't considered that point.

Deaglan smiled thinly, not at all impressed. Her appearing on his doorstep unheralded—at least with respect to her sex—might have created the sort of difficulties he normally took pains to avoid.

He halted before the library door. As he grasped the handle, Felix, having caught up to them, blithely assured her, "Just as well that you can stay here—there's nowhere else suitable that's close enough, not if you want to examine our horses."

Just so. Fleetingly, Deaglan met her eyes, then set the door swinging wide and waved her over the threshold.

She sailed in and, to his surprise, showed no sign of being the least bit discomfited at finding herself in a large and distinctly masculine library.

Pru walked to the center of the long room and halted where a gathering of well-worn armchairs stood angled before a massive fireplace. Instantly, she felt at home, embraced by the ambiance of a highly familiar space. The furniture was of excellent quality, but just a touch shabby, worn to the point of inviting comfort, and sporting magazines—guns, dogs, hunting, and horses—lay scattered over every horizontal surface. The fire was already lit and threw out a gentle heat, dispelling any chill from the thick stone walls. Bookshelves groaning with a hodgepodge of books covered the three internal walls, while down the long fourth side, French doors gave access to a stone-flagged terrace, beyond which lay lawns flanked by garden beds showing the first shoots of spring growth.

She swung to face Felix and the earl as they followed her into the room, her gaze going directly to the latter's face.

A hard-featured face that wasn't all that easy to read.

She conjured up a grateful and somewhat rueful smile. "Indeed, I do thank you for your hospitality, and I apologize if my gender has caused any problems. I admit it hadn't occurred to me that it might."

The earl met her gaze, and she read the words *But it should have* in his emerald eyes.

And in that, he was correct. He was every bit as dangerous as his reputation painted him; she should have realized that staying under his roof might be unwise, yet thankfully, courtesy of his aunt's presence, impropriety had been averted.

She found her chin rising a notch. "I fear I'm somewhat single-minded when the question of horses is dangled before me."

A flicker of amusement crossed the earl's otherwise impassive face, then, prowling closer, he waved for her to take a seat.

She chose one of the armchairs closer to the hearth, not for the warmth but so that she had the widest view of the room and its occupants.

She watched as Felix took the armchair beside hers, and with effort-less grace, the earl sank into the one opposite. Felix, she could easily lead. His older brother, however, was cut from very different cloth; she wouldn't class him as susceptible to anyone's manipulation—possibly not even her cousin Louisa's, and Louisa was an acknowledged expert.

As the men settled, Pru let her gaze wander the room; the comforting ambiance lapped about her, and she allowed a smile of appreciation to show.

Then she realized the earl was watching her with faint puzzlement in his eyes. She nearly laughed. Of course! He'd thought to discompose her by bringing her there; instead, the formalities of a drawing room would have kept her much more on edge.

She wasn't about to tell him that but couldn't resist smiling more broadly and remarking, "This room is so very like the library at our manor at Newmarket, it's almost uncanny." She waved at a nearby table all but buried beneath sporting magazines. "My father and brothers subscribe to all these issues, too, and leave them everywhere." She met the earl's gaze. "I should thank you for bringing me here and putting me so much at ease."

The dark look in his eyes informed her that hadn't been his intention, but beyond a slight tightening about his lips, he gave no other sign.

Surveying his otherwise unrevealing face, she realized that, while she might not know everything about him, he knew next to nothing about her.

His gaze resting on her, he leaned back in the chair. "I'm curious, Miss Cynster—I would have thought that, regardless of your wishes to pursue fresh bloodstock, your family would have herded you to London and the more conventional entertainments there."

She smiled. "They try. Sometimes, they succeed."

"You've had your Season, then?"

"Several." She saw no harm in admitting that; she wasn't a fresh-faced debutante.

"No offers?"

That was impertinent—as attested to by Felix's suddenly in-drawn breath. Not that she cared. "Several of those as well, but none that interested me as much as breeding horses."

One dark eyebrow arched. "Indeed?" He was, she realized, one of those men who could convey a great deal in a glance. The look in his eyes now translated to *Whoever your suitors were, they either didn't try hard enough or weren't very clever.* "So you spend your days at your family's Newmarket stable?"

"Generally, I'm to be found there, but during the past two years, I've traveled here and there, viewing those horses brought to our attention."

"To where have you traveled in your quest?"

That was one question she wasn't prepared to answer; she didn't need to give Lord Deaglan Fitzgerald any inkling of how hard she'd been searching for suitable horses—from there, it was too short a leap to comprehending just how much the Cynster Stables needed new breeders.

She was wracking her brain for some sufficiently witty or impertinent counter-question with which to distract him when the door opened and the butler appeared, bearing a well-stocked tea tray.

The earl pointed to the low table between the armchairs. "Set it there."

"Yes, my lord." The butler placed the tray in position. He cast a curious glance at Pru as he straightened.

The earl caught her eye and tipped his head at the tray. "Would you mind?"

"Of course not." She would make a better job of pouring than either man. Sitting forward, Pru reached for the teapot, poured three cups, then handed one to the earl and another to Felix, both of whom thanked her. Then she picked up her cup and saucer, sat back, and sipped—and very nearly sighed in appreciation. "This is excellent."

"My housekeeper prides herself on the quality of the tea she brings in." Deaglan glanced at the butler, who was on his way to the door. "Miss Cynster's compliments to Mrs. Bligh, and mine as well."

"Indeed, my lord." The butler smiled and bowed himself from the room.

The door had barely shut when a tap fell on the panels.

The earl shot a glance at Felix, who shrugged. The earl called, "Come."

The door opened, and a neatly dressed gentleman walked in. The earl and Felix relaxed.

Pru sipped her tea and, over the rim of the cup, surveyed the newcomer. He was tallish, although not as tall as the earl, and possessed a heavier build. He had curly light-brown hair, and as he neared, she saw he had brown eyes as well. His features were good, even and pleasant, and he was clean-shaven except for the current fashion of side-whiskers, which in his case were curly. He appeared to be of similar age to the earl and was neatly attired in what Pru termed "country clothes"—riding breeches and boots, with an unremarkable waistcoat, simple shirt, and neatly tied neckerchief beneath a brown hacking jacket.

Whoever he was, he was surprised to see her there, sipping tea with the earl and Felix.

"Jay." The earl nodded, then looked at Pru. "Miss Cynster—allow me to introduce my steward and distant cousin, Jervis O'Shaughnessy."

O'Shaughnessy smiled and half bowed. "Miss Cynster. But please— call me Jay. Everyone does."

Pru smiled and inclined her head. "Jay."

"Miss Cynster is here to look over our horses," Felix said, eager admiration glowing in his smile. "She's in charge of the Cynster Stables' breeding program."

"Is that so?" Jay looked at Pru uncertainly, as if unsure what to make of her.

She was accustomed to such reactions and smiled reassuringly back.

"Ring for another cup, if you wish, Jay." The earl waved toward the bellpull.

"Thank you, Deaglan, but no." Jay faced the earl. "I just looked in to ask if you wanted Joe's crew to get started on the bridge repairs next or head over to that fence on the far paddock."

"The bridge," the earl replied. "The spring flooding definitely weakened it, and I don't want to risk any unnecessary accidents."

Pru listened while the men, Felix included, discussed the finer points of how to repair the weakened bridge and used the time to consider what lay before her and which of the three men she needed to focus on most.

On some estates, a steward might be her principal contact, with his master's agreement and signature a foregone conclusion. In other cases... She'd already learned from Felix that over the past five years, ever since

Deaglan Fitzgerald had left the estate after falling out with his father, it had been Felix's role to oversee the stable, and since their father's death, Deaglan had concentrated on everything else, leaving the stable in Felix's care. Logically, it should be Felix with whom she would work most closely.

However, the discussion over the bridge presented her with the perfect opportunity to study the relationships between the three men. And although both Jay and Felix offered their opinions freely, and the earl listened and considered, the ultimate decision patently rested with him.

By the time he issued his orders regarding the bridge, there was no doubt in Pru's mind that, as Honoria had foreseen, it was Lord Deaglan Fitzgerald himself with whom she would need to deal.

That would be a challenge—and not the sort of challenge she normally faced.

Despite his reputation, despite the leaping of her senses, despite their earlier, charged exchange, her highly evolved and experienced instincts detected no overt personal threat from Deaglan Fitzgerald.

If anything, he'd walled himself off from her, blocking any impulses his baser instincts might prompt. He was, quite definitely, holding himself back, not moving toward her. Not threatening her in any way.

Making himself as unthreatening as a man of his ilk could.

Sadly, that didn't make him any less of a cynosure for her senses, much less her unruly imagination. What she saw in him—a combination of powerfully turbulent yet deep waters and the quintessential allure of forbidden fruit—was beyond enticing.

It was easy to stare at him and imagine and speculate…

With his directions to his steward completed, the earl swung his attention back to her.

Pru blinked and mentally scrambled to reassemble her wits—something she'd been having to do often since setting eyes on Deaglan Fitzgerald.

How odd.

Gentlemen did not turn her head. Not ever. Especially not when there were horses to discuss.

Then again, I hadn't previously met the Earl of Glengarah.

Horses!

Before he could speak—and direct the conversation—she fixed him with a mildly inquiring look. "In your letter, you referred to a possible mutually beneficial arrangement. Can I ask what sort of arrangement you have in mind?"

His mobile lips curved slightly—almost patronizingly. "As I'm sure you realize, that was a general statement. It might be more to the point if you would outline what arrangements the Cynsters are likely to propose with respect to new bloodstock for your breeding program."

"There are numerous possible arrangements—which ones we would consider will depend on the type and quality of the horses involved."

"Yet given your prompt response to our query, there must be some specific gap you're seeking to fill."

"Yes and no." She leaned forward and placed her empty cup and saucer on the tray. She took her time, sitting back in the chair and regarding him for several seconds before adding, "We're a large enough stable that we're able and willing to utilize any prime breeding stock that comes our way. Yes, there are specific lines we'd like to strengthen, but in general, we work with whatever prime prospects we find."

That wasn't what he wanted to know, but it was all she was willing to say. She let that decision infuse her eyes and her expression and wasn't surprised when, after he'd studied both, his lips tightened.

He wanted to learn the reason behind the Cynsters' immediate interest, while she wanted to know what had prompted him to send his letter in the first place and why, despite her being a female and the difficulties his reputation might potentially cause, he was, nevertheless, willing to deal with her.

And he was willing, of that she felt sure.

Yet neither he nor she were novices when it came to negotiations; neither were willing to show their hand—certainly not at this early stage.

They stared at each other for several seconds. Felix and Jay both watched from the sidelines; Pru felt their gazes flicking between her and the earl.

Deaglan hid his frustration over Prudence Cynster's intransigence; obviously, there were reasons her family—whom he'd heard described as unrelentingly canny—had sent her as their representative. She wasn't going to budge—to give him the advantage of knowing what she was looking for, much less why.

That being so...

He realized Jay was still hovering and looked up and caught his eye. "Was there something else?"

Jay considered, then replied, "No. I'll take the word to Joe." Jay slanted a glance at their unexpected visitor. "Is there anything else you'd like me to see to?"

A part of Deaglan wished he could accept the offer; dealing with Prudence Cynster was going to try his temper. Following Jay's gaze to her —seeing her listening with open understanding—he said, "No. Let me know what Joe says."

"I will." Jay bowed to their guest. "Miss Cynster." He nodded to Deaglan, then Felix, and headed for the door.

Deaglan waited until the door shut, using the moment to weigh his options. Perhaps it was time to put Miss Prudence Cynster and his late father's horses to the test. He met her eyes and waved at the tea tray. "Now we've dealt with the social niceties, perhaps you would like to run your educated eyes over some of our horses."

Pru managed not to leap to her feet; she rose with regal grace— bringing both men to their feet—and with an entirely genuine smile curving her lips, candidly replied, "I would like nothing better."

She wanted to see the Glengarah horses—even more now than when she'd rolled up the drive.

CHAPTER 3

*P*ru walked beside the earl down a corridor away from the front hall and out through a door that gave onto a large cobbled courtyard. On the far side of the courtyard, about a hundred feet away, lay the arched entrance to the stable yard, and beyond that rose the stable itself, boasting a large arched doorway with thick wooden doors, presently set wide.

Everywhere she looked, all appeared in good if not excellent order— neat, clean, in good repair. All of which boded well for the stable. In her experience, those who kept their property in good condition generally took care of their horses.

As they strolled toward the maw of the stable's doorway, she tried to get some sense of the size and layout of the building; it wasn't a simple block, as most stables were. If the rooflines were anything to judge by, the Glengarah stable comprised multiple alleys of stalls, some leading off others and even doubling back.

Curious.

They were halfway across the cobbled courtyard when two dogs came bounding up. Pru had never seen their like before; her pets might be horses, but she knew dogs, too. One of the pair she recognized as an Irish setter, but the color was russet-red and white, not the customary solid russet-red. The other dog had a sleek coat the color of old gold and a face that reminded her of a bloodhound. The pair fell to cavorting around her and the men—Felix on her left and the earl on her right.

Mouths agape, tongues lolling, both dogs were clearly intent on playing.

Glengarah sighed and halted. "All right." The dogs immediately converged on him. He bent to pat them and ruffle their coats. "But only for a minute."

Felix and Pru halted as well. Felix met her eyes and grinned. "He spoils them."

"They're loyal hounds," Glengarah countered.

Satisfied with the attention received, the red-and-white setter came dancing toward Pru, keen to investigate the new person. She smiled and bent to ruffle the dog's ears. "You are a pretty one, aren't you?"

Glengarah glanced her way. "You're comfortable with dogs."

"Entirely." Pru caught the setter's jaw and tipped its face up to study the dog's eyes—bright and clear. "My cousins in Scotland breed Scottish deerhounds. We often end up with one or more."

Glengarah straightened, releasing the golden-coated dog, who immediately nosed over to Pru.

She stroked the large head, took note of the powerful body and long, strong legs, then glanced at Glengarah. "I've never seen this breed—a type of hunting dog?"

He nodded. "Kerry beagle. They hunt much the same as deerhounds."

Pru realized there were barks and yips coming from another set of buildings set back from the right side of the courtyard. She was so accustomed to the sounds of dogs, she hadn't, until then, registered just how many different animals were giving voice.

Seeing the direction of her gaze, Glengarah hesitated, then said, "We've run breeding kennels for both breeds for over a decade. Many of the hunting packs in Ireland come to us for the beagles, and the setters are gun dogs and in high demand by landowners of all sorts."

The dogs were in superb condition, which augured well for the horses. Pru tucked away the even more pertinent information that Glengarah already had long experience in running a commercial breeding enterprise; although there were significant differences between breeding pedigree dogs and Thoroughbreds, the business basics were the same.

Glengarah looked at the dogs. "We're going to the stable. You can come if you want, but don't expect attention." With that, he waved Pru on.

As he fell into step beside her, Pru saw the dogs dither, then the pair turned and trotted toward the kennels. Smiling, she shook her head. "You have them well trained."

Glengarah softly snorted. "They'll be fed soon—that's why they left."

Pru chuckled and looked ahead. As they passed beneath the stable arch into the stable yard and the doorway to the stable neared, she told herself not to let her hopes get too high. She might be the first person from the horse-racing world to see the horses inside, but there was really no evidence the animals the late earl had collected would be worth her time.

She'd been lured there by the promise inherent in the late earl's guiding principle, the short descriptions of three horses, and the intrigue surrounding a stable no outsider had ever viewed. There was no guarantee of what awaited her inside.

If the horses proved to be of no interest, she could get back on the road straightaway and head south to Ballyranna in County Kilkenny and visit the Earl of Kentland. Russ was Priscilla Caxton's twin brother and, therefore, a connection of sorts, and the Cynster and Kentland stables had traded information and horses for years.

Regardless of what Pru found in the Glengarah stable, now mere yards away, her trip across the Irish Sea wouldn't be in vain.

The stone arch loomed over them, and they passed beneath it into the relative dimness of the stable.

As she'd expected, a long aisle stretched before them, with stalls on either side. She slowed, waiting for her eyes to adjust. She breathed in, calmed by the familiar smells of hay and horses.

Glengarah paused, his gaze touching her face, and waited. When she stepped forward again, he waved down the aisle. "Carriage horses to the right and in the first stalls to the left, then following on the left are the family's hacks. The bulk of the collection are stabled farther on."

Pru glanced briefly at the first of the carriage horses, a strong, powerful gelding with excellent lines, but she wasn't there to view such animals. She progressed down the aisle. As she neared the first of the stalls housing the riding hacks, the horse inside shifted, and a huge gray head appeared over the stall door.

A large, dark eye regarded her with interest, shifted briefly to Glengarah, then returned to her.

Pru halted and stared.

The horse snorted.

Pru almost did the same. "Hack?" She cast a sharp glance at Glengarah, then, offering her hand to the horse, stepped up to the stall door for a better look.

Deaglan slanted a glance at Felix, who widened his eyes back. No point pretending he wasn't impressed by the lady's immediate reaction, purely based on what she could deduce from the lines of Thor's head.

Now she was hanging over the stable door, apparently communing with the big gray while casting knowledgeable eyes over his body and legs. "What's his name, and who rides him?"

"Thor," Deaglan replied. "And I do."

She slanted a glance his way. "He's strong." Her nose tipped up, and she looked back at the horse. "Even for you."

That was actually true, so Deaglan said nothing.

She ran her hand admiringly down the long line of Thor's jaw. "He has to be one of your late father's purchases—a part of the collection."

"He is. Given the horses are here and need to be exercised, all those of the household who ride have drawn horses from the collection for their personal use." He nodded down the line of stalls. "They are the horses I referred to as our hacks."

She humphed in patent disapproval of the label, then unhooked the latch on the stall door and slipped inside.

Deaglan leapt to rescue her.

Only to see his usually irritable stallion standing perfectly placidly as she circled him, examining his lines, then she stepped close and ran both eyes and hands over Thor's shoulders and back and down his long legs. Thor watched her, his huge head swinging to keep her in view, but otherwise remained unmoving—apparently as fascinated with her as Deaglan was.

No—Deaglan wasn't fascinated. He was simply trying to read her, to get some hint of how she rated Thor.

Deaglan wasn't entirely surprised to discover that, at least on that subject, Prudence Cynster had an excellent poker face.

Apparently satisfied with her examination of Thor, she turned and looked over the partition at the horse in the next stall—a mare his aunt Maude occasionally rode.

Prudence Cynster walked out of Thor's stall, leaving Deaglan to latch the door while she went into the stall with the mare. Somewhat distantly—as if her mind was already focused on the mare—she asked, "How many horses are in the collection? You didn't mention in your letter."

Deaglan shot a warning look at Felix, then strolled to the now-open stall door and leaned against the post. And lied. "Fifty-two."

It was an impressive enough number—as witnessed by the arrested look she threw him before she went back to examining the mare—without the addition of the five horses kept in the stable's innermost stalls. He wanted to keep those two mares and three stallions as bargaining chips. He was determined not to lose his head over the Cynster name, much less over the challenge—or the person—of the head of that fabled stable's breeding program.

Any thought she didn't know her business—didn't know horses and bloodstock and bloodlines—had evaporated like morning mist. If anything, her obvious expertise as she crooned to the flighty mare while running her hands over the horse's hocks only put him further on guard.

She—as head of the Cynster Stables' breeding program—was going to make him an offer. That much was already clear, and she'd seen only two of the fifty-two horses he was willing to show her. What offer, he had no way of knowing, and he had little information on which to base any judgment of whatever she proposed. She was the expert in such negotia-tions, and he was a rank novice. He needed to secure and hold on to every possible advantage he could.

Pru was battling to hide her excitement. His hack, Thor, was the most magnificent specimen of Alcock's Arabian blood she'd ever seen. And to top it all, he was one of the rare grays!

She wasn't going to be traveling to Kentland or, indeed, anywhere else for some time. Examining and assessing fifty-two horses—fifty-two! —would take at minimum a week and most likely more.

She couldn't wait to get started, but trying to rein in her enthusiasm and not let her soaring hopes show in any way whatsoever was distracting when she didn't want to be distracted. She wanted to be able to devote every iota of her brain to cataloguing these fabulous horses.

Eventually leaving the mare, she went into the next stall and met a chestnut stallion. After that, she battled to stop herself from going into every stall—she needed to get some idea of the scope of the collection, preferably today. Yet every horse she saw set her horse-breeding heart leaping.

Glengarah was, unsurprisingly, watching her closely. As she progressed farther down the aisle, he murmured, "Like what you see?"

Despite the lock the horses had on her brain, she nevertheless regis-tered the double entendre, even though she would have wagered a sizeable sum that he hadn't intended the second meaning. No, that was purely a product of her senses' awareness of him and the way his low, faintly rumbly voice played over her nerve endings. "I have to admit I've never seen a collection of horses such as this." Two could play with ambiguity. To avoid the further probing she was sure would otherwise come, she said, "You have mares as well as stallions, and so far, I've seen an even number of each." She spared him a glance. "Does that hold true over the entire collection?"

"Roughly. There's a slight preponderance of stallions."

"What about ages? Any over fifteen—mares or stallions?"

He shook his head. "No. My father only started the collection fifteen years ago, and he sold the earliest horses he purchased as he refined his vision and found horses that better suited his purpose. The youngest, a mare, is two, and the oldest, I believe, is a stallion of fourteen."

"I see. So they're all of breeding age—excellent!" It was impossible to keep the joy from her voice.

Lord knew, as they progressed down the aisle and turned in to the connecting building, where the aisle had stalls down one side and was open to a grassy area on the other, she was having a hard enough time simply keeping her feet moving rather than stopping and glorying at every single stall door. Indeed, other than for Thor, the first mare, and the chestnut stallion, the deeper they went into the stable, the higher the quality of the horses became, as if the beasts were organized in order of increasing rarity and perfection.

Curious, she asked, "Who chose which stalls each horse has?"

"My father."

"He had an excellent eye." It cost her nothing to admit that.

"So I believe." After a moment, Glengarah murmured, "In part, that's why you're here."

She said nothing to that, too distracted by the next horse. She'd seen so many strong examples of the foundation bloodlines, she was starting to feel giddy. Literally.

The value and significance of what lived in the Glengarah stable was...almost beyond calculation.

Almost beyond belief.

They finally reached the end of the second aisle. When she turned the corner and saw another long aisle of stalls stretching out before them, she halted. Then she looked at Glengarah. "How many more horses are there to see?"

He glanced back along the previous aisle. "We've gone past twenty-six of the collection, so there's twenty-six more to view."

Twenty-six more! Her head was spinning.

Rather than go forward, she remained where she was; she needed to catch her breath. She swung to face Glengarah; other than answering her questions, he'd remained silent, but had continued to closely observe her, no doubt trying to gauge her reaction. She fixed her gaze on his handsome, annoyingly unreadable face. "Tell me—what was your father's reasoning in creating this collection?"

Wondering why she was asking, Deaglan offered, "Horses were his abiding passion. Originally, he simply wanted to own fine specimens. His first purchases were driven purely by that subjective assessment. However, in his search for horses that, in his eyes, qualified as fine, he bought two stallions at auction—at a creditor's sale—and subsequently in researching their backgrounds, he discovered what he interpreted as links to foundation sires and mares. From that point on, he paid more attention to the bloodlines of the horses he considered acquiring as well as to the physical characteristics he felt defined his notion of 'fine.' Over the following years, he refined his approach and his vision. For the past eight or nine years, he consistently acquired horses and sold none—he'd defined his criteria and adhered to them."

She nodded. "I see." She glanced back along the second aisle, then faced forward and looked to where, at its end, the third aisle turned to the left. "I have to admit that the layout of the stable is unusual to me—I haven't come across such an arrangement of aisles and stalls before. Most stables are simply blocks or multiple adjoining blocks or stalls arranged around a courtyard. This seems to wind around itself."

He wasn't going to tell her why. "The design is partly due to my father having added successive wings—aisles—as he purchased more horses and the collection grew. The original castle stable was much smaller." And it had been, in fact, a single small courtyard with six stalls arranged along each side.

"I suppose that explains it."

When she said nothing more, just continued to stare down the next aisle, he couldn't resist asking, "Do you wish to see more?"

She met his eyes, hesitated, then said, "Yes and no."

Deaglan blinked; that wasn't the answer he'd expected.

Pru looked down the aisle again. "Yes, I do want to complete an initial viewing of all fifty-two horses"—she could admit that much—"but what

with traveling and then having already viewed so many horses, I fear I'm
not in any state to do the rest of the stable justice."

Ordinarily, she would never suggest that she was suffering such feminine weakness, but she needed time to absorb what she'd already seen,
and she seriously doubted her ability to continue to conceal her reaction
to the horses likely to be housed in the next twenty-six stalls. The twenty-
six she'd already viewed had been stunning enough—had tested her
emotionless façade enough; she didn't need to push until it cracked. That
would give Glengarah negotiating ammunition he didn't need. And if
there was one thing of which she was now absolutely certain, it was that
she would be negotiating a breeding agreement with the wild, wicked,
and outrageously handsome earl.

He didn't need any further advantage.

She glanced at Glengarah and caught him exchanging a look with
Felix. She might not be able to read Glengarah's expression, but she had
no difficulty comprehending Felix's flaring concern.

Neither brother knew what to make of her apparently flagging
interest.

Good.

Yet she still didn't know what had prompted Glengarah to write to the
Cynster Stables. Recognizing that she might well be toying with a very
real need—and the last thing she wanted was for Glengarah to imagine
she wasn't interested and write to one of the other major breeders—she
added, "However, I have seen enough to know that, with your approval, I
will need to complete a thorough assessment of the horses in the collection. That"—she glanced at the nearest stalls—"will take about a week.
Possibly more."

She looked back to see both brothers brighten, although in Glengarah's case, the change didn't show in his face but rather in his stance.

Deciding to strike while the iron was hot and hoping she would strike
lucky, she went on, "As part of my assessment, I'll need to take each
horse into your exercise ring to study its paces and gait. Some, I will need
to ride—naturally, I have my saddle with me." She looked from Glengarah to Felix and, resisting the urge to cross her fingers, asked, "Which
of you should I see about taking horses into the ring?"

Felix smiled, reassured and relieved. "I'll be happy to assist you in
any way I can."

Relieved herself, she was about to thank him when Glengarah
rumbled, "I'll assist in the ring."

He caught her gaze as, swallowing her curses, she looked his way. He smiled, apparently innocently, but she wasn't buying that. "They are my horses, after all, and ultimately, it will be me with whom any agreement is struck."

She inclined her head with what grace she could muster and turned to stroll back the way they'd come.

Clearly, it had been too much to hope that he would leave her alone to evaluate his horses. But while she would have preferred him not to be present, as it *was* he with whom she would eventually have to negotiate—and that, face-to-face—then perhaps it wouldn't be such a bad thing to expose her senses to him on a regular basis so that they settled down and no longer responded to his nearness, his voice, his physical presence.

So she would be able to negotiate without needing a fan.

As they walked back to the castle, with Felix chattering about the others she would meet over dinner—Mrs. O'Connor, their widowed aunt, plus a cousin and an ancient uncle who was actually a distant cousin on their mother's side—she tried to shut her mind to the reality of Deaglan Fitzgerald pacing, silent and somehow looming, at least in her imagination, on her other side.

Just as well she was accustomed to large gentlemen who loomed; that, in itself, did not discompose her, although she suspected he was walking just that tad closer than necessary to see if it might.

She tried to dismiss him from her mind and concentrate on mentally cataloguing the horses she'd thus far seen—to no avail. She would have to place her hope in blunting her senses over the coming days.

But for now—for all the times they were not working with horses—she really needed to find some way to distract him from noticing how he affected her.

But how?

As they stepped through the side door and the cool dimness of the castle enveloped them, the obvious answer popped into her brain.

She could distract him from her reactions to him—from any attempt to use them to his advantage—by engaging with him in a way to which she already knew he was susceptible. She could prevent him from focusing on her reactions to him by forcing him to focus on his reactions to her.

She smiled as, with Felix dropping behind, she and Glengarah walked into the front hall.

While he summoned the housekeeper to conduct her to her room, Pru watched him from the corner of her eyes and decided she was not above using her feminine attributes in a worthy cause.

Pru arrived outside the drawing room door, dressed to captivate without being too blatant about it. She was secretly pleased that at least some of the gowns her mother had insisted be made for her, in case she took it into her head to appear in London, looked set to be put to the use for which they'd been designed.

In a rich old-gold shade that not every lady could wear, her gown's luxurious satin lent an understated sensual allure to the fitted bodice with its sweetheart neckline, the clinging elbow-length sleeves, and the full skirts. To guard against the evening's chill, she'd draped a fringed silk shawl in gold, black, and umber about her shoulders.

She drew in a fortifying breath and, with an expectant smile curving her lips, walked through the door the butler held for her.

Judging by the arrested look in Glengarah's eyes as they landed on her, she didn't need to wonder if her strategy would work.

For a second, he stared at her, then, as she glided toward him, his lips thinning, he uncrossed his long legs, rose, and walked to meet her.

Fighting a losing battle not to allow her wayward senses to dwell overmuch on the figure he cut—a dramatically riveting one in his dinner jacket in a green so dark that at first glance it appeared black, plain ivory-silk waistcoat, and stylishly draped trousers—she halted before him, bobbed a curtsy, and offered her hand with a smile and a "My lord."

She could almost *feel* him steeling himself—locking away his reactions—in the second that passed before he closed his long fingers firmly about hers and inclined his head. "Miss Cynster." He released her and glanced toward the others gathered on the sofa and chairs before the fireplace. "Allow me to make you known to the rest of our household."

His words were stilted and formal, nothing like the fire she'd glimpsed in his eyes before he'd lowered his lids.

She told herself the breathlessness that had afflicted her was only to be expected and turned her attention to the three members of the company she hadn't yet met—an older matronly lady, a young lady in her early twenties, and an older gentleman with steel-gray hair who was ensconced in a Bath chair.

The matron and the young lady rose from the sofa to greet Pru as, with Glengarah by her side, she drew near. Then she felt his palm brush the back of her waist and fought to suppress a reactive shiver.

"Miss Cynster"—was it her imagination, or was Glengarah's voice a touch deeper, more burred?—"allow me to present my aunt, Mrs. O'Connor."

Glengarah's aunt was a tall, heavy-boned woman who exuded an impression of stoic strength. She was dressed unremarkably in a navy-blue evening gown finished with silk tassels, and her hair was set in a simple style, drawn back to reveal the strong bones of her face. Her features were pleasant, and her hazel eyes were shrewd yet kindly.

"Maude, my dear." Mrs. O'Connor took Pru's hand in a firm clasp. "I'm a widow and have lived here for an age—ever since Glengarah and Felix's mother died. Someone had to take the pair of them in hand." This was delivered with a pointed yet affectionate look directed Glengarah's way. "I regret I was not here to greet you when you arrived," Maude continued. "You must absolve me of any discourtesy in that." Her gaze sharpened on her nephew's face. "I wasn't informed that we were expecting a visitor."

Visitor, not female visitor—any visitor.

Pru slanted a puzzled look at Glengarah. "I wrote...you must have received my letter."

Glengarah's lips tightened. "We did. Today."

"But I posted it over a week ago."

"There was a storm in the Irish Sea last week. That always disrupts the post from England—your letter only arrived at noon today."

"Oh." Pru turned to Maude and smiled. "In that case, it is I who should apologize—I should have given you more warning."

"No matter." Maude waved her words aside. "It's a pleasure that you're here. We so rarely have company." Another sharp glance at Glengarah accompanied those words, then Maude returned her attention to Pru. "I hope you found your room comfortable."

"Yes, indeed. I have no complaints—it seems most suitable." Pru glanced at her host. It hadn't escaped her notice that her window provided an excellent view of the stable.

"Good." Maude turned to include the younger lady—a pretty, fresh-faced miss with blond ringlets piled artlessly atop her head. "Allow me to introduce my niece, Miss Cicely O'Connor. Her home is in Dublin, but she's come to take the country air and spend time with me for the nonce."

Miss O'Connor bobbed a curtsy, then touched fingers with Pru. "You must call me Cicely. I do love your gown—is it from a London modiste?"

Pru grinned. "I hope you will both call me Prudence." She heard a soft, cynical huff and realized Glengarah had just registered the meaning of her name. Her smile brightening, she continued speaking to Cicely, "And yes, the gown is from London. Not that I've visited recently—my mother orders them in the faint hope that I might be gripped by the urge to reappear in ton drawing rooms. Suffice it to say, that rarely happens."

"Oh." Cicely's soft blue eyes grew round. "But don't you want to dance at the balls and attend all the parties?"

Pru couldn't stop her smile from turning cynical. "I had three Seasons and found that quite enough. Sadly for Mama, I prefer the company of horses."

"Well," Maude said, "in that case, you'll fit right into this household." She threw another quick glance at Glengarah, this one faintly curious, then the heavy clearing of a throat had all four of them turning toward the gentleman in the Bath chair.

He smiled genially at Pru and held out his hand. "Patrick Devereux, m'dear. Delighted to make your acquaintance."

Pru moved to take the proffered hand and pressed it between hers. "I'm pleased to meet you, sir."

"Oh, none of that formality—call me Patrick."

Pru smiled. Patrick Devereux looked to be a little older than her father —late sixties, perhaps. Encouraged by the undeniable twinkle in the old man's eyes, she remarked, "I take it your role here is to exert a sobering influence on your younger relatives."

He laughed, as did everyone else. "Oh, we're all sober enough, at least for being Irish. But I first came to Glengarah when m'sister married Hubert—the late earl—and I've always returned." He peered past Pru and added, "Like a bad penny."

Glengarah shifted out of Pru's shadow. "Nothing bad about you, old man. You've always been the best of us."

Patrick colored and uttered a dismissive "Pshaw!" yet was transparently pleased.

The affection that flowed between the members of the household was palpable; Pru owned herself a trifle surprised. If asked, she would have described Glengarah as a hard man; he'd certainly maintained rigid control over his emotions thus far with her, yet clearly, the emotions were there, and he was freer with them—more open to showing them—with those close to him.

The drawing room door opened, and Felix looked in; he spotted her and smiled. "You found your way."

It hadn't been difficult; the corridor from her bedchamber door ran in a long straight line to the gallery at the head of the main stairs. Pru returned his smile as Felix shut the door and came to join them. "I did. But thank you for checking—it was kind of you to think of me."

Maude buttonholed Glengarah, telling him of the state of the cottages she'd visited that afternoon, suggesting repairs were needed at two.

Patrick asked Felix about some horse race, and Felix replied. Cicely joined them about Patrick's chair and asked a question about the track that surprised Pru, track conditions not being a subject young ladies were wont to advance.

Two minutes of Felix's animated chatter—fueled by both Patrick and Cicely—were enough to tell Pru why, exactly, Cicely was rusticating at Glengarah Castle.

Cicely had her blue eyes on Felix. Although Pru watched Felix carefully, she detected no awareness of Cicely's focused admiration; to Pru's eyes, Felix treated Cicely in exactly the same way he treated Pru.

Hmm.

The talk of the race led to a discussion of the current crop of Thoroughbreds racing on Irish turf, which Pru listened to with half her mind—just in case something was said that she should remember to pass on to her brothers or to Kentland.

Increasingly, however, her attention was drawn to the conversation between Glengarah and Maude. Maude's observations and suggestions painted her as down-to-earth and practical, someone who understood the welfare of her nephew's tenants and was willing to speak for them.

Pru wasn't surprised by that. What did surprise her was the depth of knowledge inherent in Glengarah's replies and his countersuggestions and the solutions he proposed.

Earlier, Felix had told Pru that since their father's death, Glengarah had devoted his attention to everything within the estate bar the stable. What she overheard testified to the truth of that.

Yet Glengarah knew the horses and was definitely more invested in them—in the notion of converting the collection into a breeding stable—than Felix. Felix's interest in the horses was, in comparison, superficial.

Glengarah's commitment ran deep—just as it did with all else on the estate.

Deep waters. Yes, indeed.

She'd reached that conclusion—a potentially important insight in terms of eventually negotiating with the man—when the door opened and the butler, Bligh, appeared and intoned, "Dinner is served, my lord."

"Excellent." Maude glanced around their company. "Deaglan, if you would escort Prudence in, Felix can take Cicely, and I will accompany Patrick."

A footman had slipped into the room and now took position behind Patrick's chair.

Pru turned to Glengarah as he turned to her.

His gaze landed on her chest—on the creamy mounds of her breasts visible above the subtly revealing neckline. Immediately, he jerked his gaze upward, briefly met her eyes, then, his lips thinning, offered her his arm.

Smiling—satisfied that her stratagem was effective—she gracefully dipped her head in acceptance and set her hand on his sleeve.

He turned her toward the door.

As they walked toward it and on into the front hall, she felt the steely muscles in his arm shift, hardening beneath her fingertips.

The effect of his presence so close beside her, close enough that her hem brushed his boots, felt like an invisible hand skating over her skin, leaving a prickling sensation in its wake.

She also sensed, again, the steely wall—impenetrable and cold—that he persisted in maintaining between them, the wall behind which he corralled his reactions to her. To her overactive senses, what lay behind that wall was akin to a dark, turbulent sea.

He was determined not to allow her to goad him into lowering that wall.

She told herself that was what she wanted—him focused on that, on keeping their interactions strictly business and her at arm's length. While his attention remained on ensuring his dam remained unbreached, he was less likely to notice her ploys to learn all she could about his reasons for wanting an alliance with a major breeding stable.

All she had to do was resist the urge to bait him too far.

Her wild side wanted to. Was already whispering in her ear about how satisfying that would be.

But she knew better than to give in to that impulsive side of her that, as her family had frequently lectured her over the years, inevitably sent her careening headlong into danger.

No. As long as she adhered to her plan, she would end with the upper —or at least an improved—hand in their eventual dealmaking, and that was her necessary goal.

She and Glengarah reached the dining room—an impressive chamber, yet, she suspected, not the main dining room in the castle—and he escorted her to the chair to the right of the great carver at the table's head.

He held the chair, and she sat. As the others were distracted, taking their seats, instead of moving to the carver, he leaned over her and quietly murmured, *"Bon appétit."*

Perfectly innocent words, yet his tone somehow made them salacious.

Then a fingertip boldly trailed across the bare skin at her neckline, from her nape to her shoulder, eliciting a sensual shiver so intense she barely managed to suppress it.

Two could play at the game she'd started, and the damned man had realized that.

She refused to look at him, but instead plastered a smile on her lips and directed it at Felix as he claimed the chair alongside hers.

Deaglan managed not to glower at their guest. He knew perfectly well what she was about. He watched as she dazzled Felix—with her inviting smile, her inherent sophistication, and her delectable appearance—yet it wasn't Felix who Deaglan was worried about.

The infernal female had deliberately chosen to poke at him—presumably to distract him and give her an advantage in their dealings.

More fool her, but he seriously doubted she had any idea of what, in provoking him, she was inviting.

Still and all, there was hay to be made while she was limited by the constraints of a dining table.

He waited through the soup course until, over the fish, the rest of the table fell into a discussion of the catch currently being drawn from nearby Glencar Lough and the Drumcliff River that formed the southern boundary of the estate.

"Miss Cynster."

She turned her head his way, her brows rising. "As I've made the rest of your family free of my name, perhaps you, too, should call me Prudence."

Holding her gaze, he tilted his head as if weighing the notion. "I could, although it hardly seems appropriate."

Amusement danced in her cerulean-blue eyes. "Be that as it may, it is my name."

"Does your family call you that?"

"No." Eyes locked with his, she debated, then conceded, "They call me Pru."

He nodded. "Better. Not so misleading. Pru, then. And in the spirit of reciprocity, please call me Deaglan."

"Deaglan." A slight frown tangled her brows; he squashed an impulse to reach out and smooth it away. She tipped her head. "Did I say that correctly?"

She'd mimicked his pronunciation reasonably well. "Well enough for a Sassenach."

She laughed.

"I wanted to ask... Your father is known as the head of the Cynster Stables—their founder and owner. Is he still actively involved?"

She shook her head. "My brother Nicholas—he's a year younger than I—now runs the racing stable in the same way that I run the breeding stable, and our younger brother, Toby, divides his time between the two."

He continued advancing questions, angling to understand why her powerful family had sent her—why they'd allowed her to come to him, alone and unsupported.

Only to discover that she was as adept at verbal fencing as he. She answered his questions, then posed her own—about the estate, about the importance of the collection to him and to the estate—clearly seeking to gain some idea of how vital commercializing the collection was to the estate and, therefore, to him.

He grew absorbed defending against her, then coming at her again, with her moving in counterpoint and neither of them gaining any real advantage.

He forgot about the others, and she seemed to as well, but thankfully, the rest of the table kept themselves amused through the main course and removes and on through the dessert and fruit, nuts, and cheeses.

Eventually, he gave up all subtlety and simply asked, "Why you? Of all your family, why are you—specifically you—here? There's a—forgive the pun—ton-worth of reasons that should have ensured one of your brothers was sent."

She held his gaze, then looked down and laid down her cutlery. She paused, then met his eyes. "If you must know, I'm here because, firstly, I'm hands down the best we have in terms of evaluating horses, and secondly, because this is the role I fought to make mine, and I was not, am not, and never will be inclined to allow social pressures to keep me from it."

He studied her eyes, the set of her lips, and accepted that was the unvarnished truth. He nodded. "Thank you."

"My turn." She fixed her eyes on his. "How important is a deal involving the Glengarah collection to the estate as a whole?"

He held her gaze, then quietly said, "Important enough for me to immediately resume control of the stable and all to do with you while you're here."

She studied him in turn, then softly humphed. "Not, I note, quite the same degree of candor with which I answered your question."

He dipped his head. "That is, however, all I can give you at this point."

She narrowed her eyes at him. "Hmm."

He chanced another throw. "What prompted you to respond to our query so quickly? You acted immediately you received our letter."

She arched her brows, her gaze drifting from his face. "That, in reality, was mostly me. My mother was angling to have me go to London with her and my younger sister. They're there now." Her gaze returned to his face, and she smiled. "I used your query to give me a cast-iron excuse not to go. I pointed out that, as nobody seemed to know what manner of horses might be lurking in the Glengarah collection, then given you'd issued an invitation, we had to respond with alacrity rather than risk you thinking we weren't interested and writing to one of the other major breeders. From our point of view, it was important for us to get first look—to be able to make the first offer if the horses warranted it."

"As they do."

She inclined her head. "Indeed. I am, therefore, vindicated in arguing so hotly that I needed to leave for Glengarah immediately."

He couldn't help but smile. His father's refusal to allow anyone from outside the estate into the stable made her tale plausible, yet he couldn't shake the feeling there was more behind her rapid response than that. But how to probe further... He didn't yet know what questions to ask. On another front, however, he was now seriously curious. "Do you dislike the pleasures of London so much?"

She tilted her head. "It's pleasant enough, yet...not engaging. One achieves so little in a week there. I always feel as if I could be doing so much more at home or, for instance, on trips such as this. A Season in London always felt like so much wasted time."

He had to nod. He'd felt the same about the years he'd spent in the capital, with anxiety over what wasn't being done at Glengarah while he was away constantly gnawing at his bones.

"Ladies." Maude pushed back her chair and rose. "It's time we left our three gentlemen here to their whiskey."

Deaglan rose and drew out Pru's chair for her. She thanked him with a swift, easy smile, then walked to where Maude waited.

Maude glanced at Deaglan, then focused on Pru. "We can go to the drawing room, of course, or as we usually do, we can repair to the library, where the gentlemen will be happy to join us. Which would you prefer, my dear?"

Pru glanced at Felix and Patrick, then at Deaglan, then turned back to Maude. "The library. I was there earlier and found it very comfortable. It reminds me of home."

"Excellent." Maude swung toward the door and started walking, drawing Pru and Cicely with her. Without turning her head, Maude called, "Gentlemen, you heard—we'll see you in the library shortly."

Pru grinned and followed Maude from the room, across the hall, and into the library.

Maude claimed the armchair Pru had previously occupied. Assuming Deaglan would use the same chair he had earlier, she chose the armchair beside it.

Her strategy to distract him was still in play, although they'd both seemed to forget their mutual sensitivity during the heat of their verbal battle. She'd managed to learn a little more without giving away too much, yet her understanding of Deaglan Fitzgerald was still lacking in too many respects for her to feel assured about sitting down to hammer out a deal with him. She'd negotiated many breeding agreements, but never with someone about whose needs and wants and desires she knew so little.

The more she could learn about Deaglan from others, the less she would need to extract from him—and the less chance she would reveal too much about the Cynsters' needs in so doing. Consequently, once Maude had settled, Pru asked, "I gather you've stood as surrogate mother to Deaglan and Felix?"

Maude tipped her head, considering, then replied, "Felix, certainly— he was an infant when my sister-in-law died. But Deaglan is five years older, and as he was the future earl, my brother insisted Deaglan learn all about the estate in a way that my brother himself had not. My brother succeeded our cousin to the title at the age of thirty-three and, not having been groomed for the role, always viewed managing the estate as a burden he was ill-prepared to shoulder."

"So he ensured his son was better prepared?"

Maude nodded. "Needless to say, Deaglan was a serious boy—he felt the weight of responsibility on his shoulders from an early age."

"I see." Pru had difficulty reconciling a serious boy with a man of wild, licentious ways, but Maude's insight was certainly giving her more to think about. She tried another cast. "It must have been difficult being caught in the middle when Deaglan and his father fell out."

Maude snorted. "I wasn't in the middle—I was firmly on Deaglan's side. But by then, my brother had grown so obsessed with his horses, there was no reasoning with him. None at all."

Footsteps approached the door, then it opened, and Deaglan pushed Patrick's chair into the room. Felix followed and closed the door.

Pru stifled a humph; they must have gulped their whiskey. Admittedly, had she been in Deaglan's shoes, she would have done the same thing rather than leave her alone with a source of personal information like Maude.

She glanced at Maude, and the older woman caught her eye—as if warning her not to mention the subject they'd been discussing.

Happy to hide her latest knowledge, Pru looked at Cicely and smiled. "I'm sorry—I don't know how old you are, but have you had a Season in…would it be Dublin?"

Cicely smiled brightly. "Last year and the year before that, too, and I suppose when I go home—to Dublin—I'll get swept up into the rounds of balls and dinners and parties. Our Season is a little later than yours in London."

"I see." Pru deftly steered the conversation to modistes and gowns and the latest fashions while waiting for Deaglan to position Patrick before the large fire now roaring in the hearth, then sink into what seemed his customary armchair beside the one she'd claimed.

Once he had, as soon as she could extricate herself from the frivolous exchange with Cicely—by drawing in Felix and handing over the reins to Maude—Pru turned to Deaglan and asked, "How long have you been commercially breeding your dogs?"

It was a pertinent question, but one she judged he might deign to answer.

He held her gaze for a moment, then replied, "Ten—no, twelve years now."

"And the kennels have been a viable concern for all that time?"

He nodded. "Both breeds are relatively rare and highly sought after. We established strong pedigrees from the outset and have worked to maintain and improve them—we've never had difficulty commanding a good price."

"How are they sold?" she asked. "Via an agent, or is there some central market place?"

"We sell by word of mouth." Deaglan leaned back in the chair, crossed his legs, and answered her next question—on the personnel they employed—with cynical patience. He waited...and sure enough, eventually her observations swung from canines to equines.

He wasn't averse to the change. "So how is the Cynster breeding stable run—what structure of stablemen and lads do you use?"

She blinked, but replied readily enough, and while committing her answer to memory, he managed another question before she wrestled the reins back and asked who he had in the stable at present and whether he would consider appointing them to head any future breeding enterprise.

"Rory Mack is our head stableman. He was born on Glengarah and has worked with our horses all his life. He came into the stable about the time my father started the collection, so has knowledge of all the horses we have. With the right guidance, he could step up to the role of head stableman of our breeding program." He arched his brows at her. "In your opinion, how many lads would he need to manage fifty or so horses?"

"That would depend on the mix of stallions and mares. Of your fifty-two, how many are stallions?"

He held her gaze. "I don't know the number off the top of my head, but I believe it's a little over half the total."

"In that case, I would imagine at least ten lads capable of exercising the stallions. Of course, you and Felix, too, ride, but there's a lot of work involved simply keeping horses in good condition—which, of course, you already know." She fixed her blue eyes on his face. "I've seen your Thor —which of the other horses in the collection do you ride?"

"There's a roan stallion I sometimes take out. What sort of horse do you ride?"

Her eyes lit—indeed, her whole face came alive. "I have a bay Arab mare—she's my favorite. But when I ride to the hunt, or simply want to jump, I ride an older gray hunter. He's heavy and raw-boned, but he'll take any fence I point him at."

Judging from her expression, she thrilled to the chase.

Her gaze refocused on his face. "Do you hunt around here? Is there a local pack?"

He nodded. "Out of Sligo. We provide most of the dogs."

From there, they diverted into an animated exchange on the subject of which breed of dogs performed best in the hunt. He discovered she had insights into several Scottish breeds in addition to the deerhounds she'd mentioned; apparently, she had family connections scattered all over the British Isles.

"Kentland, of course, swears by his beagle pack, although they're ordinary beagles, not like your Kerrys."

He nodded. "Although setters have less speed over short distances, they do better than ordinary beagles in the country around here—too many dips and valleys and clefts. And over our more undulating terrain, Kerry beagles will outlast any other breed, bar perhaps the deerhounds."

Eyes shining, she laughed and recounted a tale of a chase that had ended with a wily fox running a young and inexperienced pack in a complete circle, then vanishing, leaving the confused pack circling on their own trail.

Watching her face, following the flow of emotions as they crossed her features, he was struck by an unexpected sense of comradeship. Companionship.

A connection he'd felt with very few people and never with a lady.

When she finished, he shifted and felt compelled to relate his own tale of a run the local pack had taken north along the flanks of Benbulben. "The way the pack howled, we thought they must have come upon the ghosts of the Fianna."

She tipped her head. "Who were they?"

"Legendary Irish warriors of very long ago. Apparently, they were fearsome, and Benbulben was one of their hunting grounds."

"Did you ever find out what had set the dogs off?"

He shook his head. "No. But the pack refused to go on."

Pru widened her eyes, then tried another tilt to learn more about his horses. "When you ride to hounds, do you and Felix use horses from the collection?"

Deaglan nodded. "We rotate among the older stallions."

The tea trolley arrived. Maude poured, and Felix distributed the cups and saucers, and they settled back and sipped.

While they'd talked, their circle had grown, first with Patrick adding occasional reminiscences and, eventually, Felix and Cicely joining in, while Maude took up her embroidery. But in the main the others listened, leaving the conversational direction to her and Deaglan; whether the others had any inkling of the subtle thrust and parry their questions and answers disguised, Pru had no idea, but that Deaglan was fully aware of the real nature of their engagement she did not doubt.

She felt him watching her over the rim of his cup. Setting hers on her saucer, she asked, "Are there times when your horses are stable-bound?"

He batted that question away.

She continued to angle for more useful information, yet he was as stubborn as she in sliding away from any revelation that might give the other an advantage in any future negotiation.

Yet she managed to learn more about him, and strangely, instead of being bored as she usually was when men talked about themselves, she found herself captivated in a manner she hadn't expected.

She'd never had a chance to interact with a gentleman of his ilk—one patently dangerous to young ladies simply by being himself. She'd never been allowed near such gentlemen—at least, not those unrelated to her—and until now, she'd never felt the slightest wish to engage.

She and he were exchanging opinions on exercise regimens for horses in general when Maude laid aside her needlework and declared, "It's time for me to retire. Cicely?" Maude rose and looked at Pru. "And you must be tired after all your traveling."

Pru suppressed an unexpected reluctance. "Indeed. I'll retire, too." She set aside her empty teacup and, with Cicely, got to her feet, bringing Deaglan and Felix to theirs. She glanced at Deaglan. "I'd like to complete my initial viewing of the horses tomorrow morning. After that, I'll have a better idea of how best to proceed."

He inclined his head. "I'll see you at breakfast."

She smiled and nodded back. "Goodnight." With her gaze, she included Patrick and Felix.

After murmuring their own goodnights, Maude and Cicely joined her, and together, they left the library.

As she climbed the stairs beside Maude, Pru was conscious that, for quite the first time in her life, she would rather have remained talking to the gentlemen—to Deaglan—than fall into her bed.

And he might have felt the same; certainly, as she'd left the library, she'd felt his green gaze lingering on the backs of her shoulders. She'd had to exercise stern control to stop herself from glancing back.

~

Deaglan watched the door close behind the three ladies, then sank back into his chair.

He'd expected Pru's relentless inquisition and had anticipated being relieved to see her retreat. Instead...

"She's quite engaging, isn't she?" Felix remarked. "She seems to know about dogs as well as horses."

"And she hunts." Patrick nodded sagely. "I've always thought ladies who do are easier to converse with. Less flighty."

Anyone less flighty than Pru Cynster was hard to imagine; Deaglan had seen only clear-eyed intelligence, a quick and agile mind, and a steely resolve cloaked in feminine grace.

And he couldn't deny he'd enjoyed her company. Their undeclared battle of wits and wills had been entertaining. Innocuous enough, yet energizing. While crossing swords with her, he'd felt alive—challenged and focused and intrigued.

He let that observation seep into his consciousness. Let the implications register.

He was going to have to be careful around her—careful in dealing with her on every level. "We need to ensure we don't underestimate her. Especially as she's a female." He met Felix's gaze. "When the time comes for negotiations, we have to remember she won't be on our side."

Felix raised his brows, but nodded.

"The Bar Cynster!" Patrick said. "That's what the ton used to call them."

Deaglan frowned. "Who are you talking about?"

"Her father and his cousins. The duke—Sylvester Cynster, Duke of St. Ives—was the leader. There were six of them as I recall."

"The Bar Cynster," Felix repeated. "What does that mean?"

Patrick humphed. "I was never clear about that, but it was the nickname the ladies of the ton bestowed on the group."

Deaglan shifted to face Patrick. "I didn't realize you knew them—her family."

"Not so much knew, as knew of. At least her father and his peers.

They were the darlings of the ton for quite some years. Handsome devils, the lot of them, and wealthy to boot. They cut swaths through the ranks of the bored matrons, don't you know? They were all a bit younger than me, but everyone regarded them as good men to have at one's back in a brawl."

Patrick's eyes took on a faraway look; Deaglan waited and didn't interrupt.

"Wine, women, and gaming," Patrick went on, "not that I ever heard they lost much. They preferred to win. That went for horses, too—they always had an eye for fine horseflesh and appreciated it, what's more. Demon—that's Pru's father's nickname—was the best rider you're ever likely to see. Hands down, no argument from anyone." Patrick paused, then went on, "And then they married, one after the other, like dominoes falling. It was something to watch—it felt like the end of an era in the ton."

Patrick focused on Deaglan. "It's said that Cynsters only marry for love, and with those six, that seemed to be the case. Devoted husbands and fathers they became, every last one."

Felix stirred. "What happens if they marry without love?"

Patrick shook his head. "I only know the whispers—that if they marry without it, bad things happen."

Deaglan considered Patrick; he'd never thought his uncle fanciful before.

Patrick humphed, then waved. "Ring for a footman for me, Deaglan."

Deaglan rose and did. Once the footman appeared and wheeled Patrick out, Deaglan looked at Felix. "I'm for bed. If Miss Cynster—Pru —wants to continue viewing the horses tomorrow morning, I'd better be there, too."

Pru lay curled on her side beneath the crisp sheets on the tester bed in the large bedroom she'd been given and, with her gaze on the moonbeams sliding across the ceiling, thought of the horses she'd seen that afternoon. The twenty-six horses of the collection she'd cast her eyes over in the hour she'd allowed herself.

"Twenty-six!" And there were twenty-six yet to go, twenty-six more horses of steadily increasing quality… She could barely wrap her mind around that fact.

She was so glad she'd come—so very glad she'd followed the impulse that had insisted she travel to Glengarah.

This was a once-in-a-lifetime opportunity—a once-in-a-generation find.

She had, she assured herself, managed well enough in dealing with Glengarah—with Deaglan. She'd managed to keep her welling, bubbling, exuberant excitement inside.

But she had to sleep now. Had to rest her overextended eyes and brain so she could properly view the rest of the horses tomorrow—and continue to conceal her delight.

Determinedly, she closed her eyes and, somewhat to her surprise, found sleep waiting to draw her into its soothing embrace.

Just before she fully succumbed, she realized that her inner sight had focused on something unconnected with a horse.

A pair of brilliant emerald-green eyes drifted across her mind's eye, and their keenly observant gaze followed her into her dreams.

CHAPTER 4

*D*eaglan sat at the breakfast table, sipping coffee and pondering the wisdom of leaving Felix to deal with Pru while she viewed the rest of the horses.

Her questions last night had kept him on his toes; he had no intention of ceding her any unnecessary advantage. But spending more time with her, in her company…he wasn't sure that was wise.

He heard footsteps approaching the breakfast parlor—a breezy, swinging stride that could only be hers. Felix had yet to come down, and the rest of the household habitually broke their fast later.

He steeled himself. Today, he needed to keep her in her place—at a distance and locked out of his head.

She swung through the door—bright and decidedly chipper in a figure-hugging riding habit in blue velvet the same color as her eyes.

Deaglan hauled his gaze upward, met her shining eyes, and inclined his head. "Good morning." He made the greeting as cool as he could.

She smiled brilliantly—open, direct, transparently expecting to be pleased with her day. "Good morning to you." She looked around and spotted the sideboard. "Ah—excellent."

He watched her walk to where Bligh stood and accept the plate the butler offered with a smile and a murmured thank-you.

Deaglan studied her as she progressed along the sideboard, helping herself to various dishes. The skirt of her habit did not sport the customary long train, relieving her of having to carry the extra bulk over her arm. In fact, the skirt appeared to be significantly less full than was normal, hugging her hips and derriere before falling from her upper thighs to her ankles, which were sheathed in well-worn riding boots.

She turned and, unrelentingly bright, came to join him at the round table. Perforce, he rose and drew out the chair next to his.

She set down her plate and sat. As he resumed his seat, she glanced at his already-cleaned plate. "Finished already? You must have risen early."

He'd woken at dawn and hadn't been able to get back to sleep—too exercised by what the day might hold. He shrugged. "It's nearly eight. Felix should be down shortly." He hesitated, then against his better judgment, asked, "Are you always so early?" So cheerful and chirpy.

She grinned at him. "I'm an early bird. I often ride immediately after breakfast."

Did she intend to ride that morning?

"However"—she waved her fork—"this morning, I have horses to view. That comes first."

He took a sip of coffee, then lowered the mug. "You said that after viewing all the collection, you would know how to proceed. What did you mean by that?"

She swallowed another mouthful before replying, "That once I have some idea of the scope of the collection—by which I mean the likely bloodlines present and the degree and variation in the quality of the horses—I'll know how much time I'll need to devote to fully assessing the particular horses that we, the Cynster Stables, might be interested in licensing, either as stallions or broodmares."

"I see." Engaging with her, letting her close—allowing her to draw any closer—was unwise. Dangerous on every level he could think of.

But...

He couldn't leave her to Felix. God only knew what admissions and even concessions she might wring from his unsuspecting brother.

He could warn Felix, but he doubted that would work; she had only to grow enthusiastic—to shine and glow and enthuse over the horses—to sweep away any guard his brother erected.

No. *He* would have to accompany her, at least until he learned how many horses she and the Cynsters might be interested in licensing.

He poured himself more coffee and waited in silence as she ate.

The instant she set down her cutlery—she'd already drained her teacup—he pushed back from the table, rose, and reached for her chair. "I'll accompany you."

She stood and smiled at him. "Excellent."

He bit his tongue, waved her on, and followed her from the room.

Pru walked down the long first aisle, around the corner, and down the next aisle, casting covetous eyes over the horses she'd viewed the day before.

They were just as beautiful, just as noteworthy, although Deaglan's Thor remained the best she'd seen thus far.

But the last horse she'd viewed yesterday, a sleek black stallion that she would swear carried the blood of the Godolphin Arabian, came close to stealing her horse-mad heart.

She paused to stroke the long velvety nose the stallion lowered over the top of his stall door. "Yes, you are a beauty," she crooned. "But now I have to meet the rest of your stablemates." It was hard to keep her eagerness from her voice.

With a last pat, she moved on, highly conscious of Deaglan pacing on her right. Only the first aisle had stalls on both sides; the second aisle and the one she'd just turned in to, which connected at an angle a bit larger than ninety degrees, had stalls only on her left and, on the right, stood open to a grassy area on which the horses could be walked.

She'd wondered if Deaglan would have time to accompany her; from his discussion with Maude the previous evening, she'd understood that he was frequently called upon to deal with matters elsewhere on the estate.

Apparently, not today. No matter. While she might have been able to extract more-sensitive information from Felix, Deaglan seemed to have a better feel for the horses themselves, a better knowledge of their pasts.

Within seconds, she'd forgotten who was with her. The black Godolphin Arab was the first in a string of stallions that left her literally speechless.

Then came a selection of mares, and she nearly swallowed her tongue. Never had she seen such strong examples of the best of the Irish-Hobby-derived foundation lines.

She examined each horse with exacting care, expecting to find fault, yet finding none at all.

Steadily progressing onward into the next aisle, she forced herself to keep her mouth shut and her tongue still, the better to guard against unwise exclamations. Against telling the horse's owner just how incredibly valuable his horses were.

How terribly important she now knew they would be to the Cynster Stables.

She had to—*had to*—clinch a breeding agreement with Glengarah. An exclusive one.

There was no other option.

While she could stop herself from speaking, hiding her widening eyes and the utter amazement that overtook her expression as she walked into the next stall, then the next, became increasingly impossible.

Deaglan paced silently beside her, eyes and senses trained on her, alert to every nuance of her reactions.

Initially, he'd been relieved that she hadn't continued her barrage of questions—continued her probing, trying to learn what had prompted Felix to write to the Cynsters. Although Felix's letter, a rough draft of which Deaglan had read last night, had been as carefully worded as Felix had intimated, she clearly understood that there had to be some reason— some expectation and hope—behind the approach.

She didn't need to know that the estate was only just paying its way, that at present, income barely exceeded expenses. That, as he had always maintained even as his father had denied it, the stables had to start paying their way.

Expecting to have to rebuff her, he'd steeled himself to hold aloof, but she hadn't so much as glanced his way; she'd been too busy trying to conceal her building excitement over the horses.

That, he could have told her, was entirely wasted effort; her appreciation and, yes, joy radiated from her. He could feel it—an effervescent, buoying warmth, a tide of emotion lifting her and, by association, him.

She was utterly captivated with the Glengarah collection.

By the time she was examining the huge chestnut stallion in the last stall of the fourth aisle—the last of the fifty-two horses he'd elected to show her—she was ready to admit defeat.

After standing as far back against the stall wall as she could and admiring the stallion's lines, she heaved a huge sigh, then walked out of the stall, swung to face Deaglan, and met his eyes. "Your horses are, as you well know, utterly magnificent. Of the fifty-two, I haven't found a single one that doesn't merit further evaluation."

He could see in her eyes that she'd dropped all pretense, that her focus had shifted to businesslike certainty. Slowly, he arched his brows. "And?"

Her lips firmed, but she replied, "And I'm certain that the Cynster Stables will be seeking to forge an agreement with Glengarah with a view to breeding from"—she raised her hands, palms up—"any number of your horses. Until I complete a full assessment and confirm their blood-lines and characteristics, I won't be able to say how many or which horses we'll make an offer on."

He nodded. "Very well." Her excitement was infectious. "So what's next?"

She smiled—anticipation glowing in her eyes and face. "I start at the beginning again, but this time, I'll need to work the horses in an exercise ring." She glanced at the sward that curved around the second, third, and fourth rows of stalls. "Or on that grass, if you don't have a ring."

"We have a ring under cover." He tipped his head in the direction of the building opposite the second aisle. "As you guessed, there are winters when we're snowed in for weeks at a time."

Her grin was swift. "I thought so."

He wondered if, in light of her dropping all her screens and her admis-sion that a wide-ranging deal would be forthcoming, he should show her the last five horses who were stabled in stalls around a corner that was concealed behind a non-obvious door; the construction of the stables was an angular spiral that disguised how many rows of stalls there actually were.

But then footsteps came their way, and he swung around to see Felix striding toward them, and the moment passed. Besides, as he'd originally decided, those five horses were the perfect bargaining chips, now more than ever.

"There you both are!" Felix exclaimed. "I was called to the kennels— my favorite setter bitch is close to dropping her latest litter, but it proved a false alarm." Felix halted and looked from Pru to Deaglan and back again. "So how have you found the horses?"

"Amazing!" Pru beamed. "The Glengarah horses are a truly stunning collection. I've grown up with the best of Thoroughbred racers, and I've struggled to take in what I've been seeing." She glanced at Deaglan and smiled self-deprecatingly. "In all honesty, some of the horses have become a blur of wonderful possibilities in my mind. I'll need to take notes as I do my detailed assessments." She arched her brows. "I've never had to do that with any other stable."

Felix beamed at her. "That's wonderful!"

Pru nodded earnestly, and Deaglan had to smile.

"It truly is," she assured him. "You have no idea how many stables I've visited that have nothing more than well-bred nags to show me. That's partly why I'm having such trouble taking in the reality of fifty-two horses at one time."

The solid bong of the luncheon gong reached them, echoing off the castle's stone walls.

"Gracious!" she exclaimed. "Is it lunchtime already?"

Smiling still, Deaglan waved her back along the aisle. "Time flies when one is engrossed."

In total charity with each other, they walked out of the stable and across to the castle's side door. As he held it for Pru, Deaglan asked, "Given what you've now seen, in terms of value, how would you rate the Glengarah collection versus other breeding collections you know?"

She glanced at him over her shoulder, then faced forward. "Until I've confirmed how many of your horses rate highly for the foundation blood-lines and that they carry no marring trait, I can't advance any guess as to that."

Pru smiled to herself as she walked on ahead of the brothers. She wasn't surprised at Deaglan's question; had she been in his shoes, it was the one above all others she would have asked.

Over luncheon, by mutual accord, they discussed anything and everything bar horses.

Pru continued to be curious over what went on in Deaglan's life—what was important to him, what tasks were presently on his plate. She told herself she needed to know what pressures he was under in case those affected how he responded to her eventual offer.

She had cousins—mostly second cousins—who were being trained to manage large estates; some, like Marcus in Scotland, had already taken over the estate they would ultimately own. Others, like Sebastian, still operated under his father's aegis, yet had been given responsibility for certain of the dukedom's far-flung properties. Indeed, during her recent visit, Patience had revealed that her eldest son, Christopher, would step into the shoes of his father, Vane, while Vane and Patience traveled on the Continent.

So Pru had a reasonable understanding of what managing an estate such as Glengarah entailed, at least within England. From all she was hearing, estates in Ireland weren't notably different.

One thing that did strike her as unusual was that the steward, Jay O'Shaughnessy, joined the family about the luncheon table; from the non-reactions of all, she surmised that was customary practice and assumed his distant cousinship lay behind it.

After chatting to Maude about various estate tenants, Jay looked at Pru. When she met his eyes, he flashed her a smile. "So how did you find the horses?" He glanced at Deaglan. "Are we allowed to ask?"

Pru also glanced at Deaglan. When he merely raised his brows at her, she replied, "I've pronounced the Glengarah horses of interest, but I need to properly evaluate them before I can say more."

Jay's brow furrowed. "And what does such an evaluation entail?"

"The next step is to work each horse in the exercise ring, checking gait, lines, and paces." She shrugged. "Once I've examined every horse, I'll decide what more I need to know before making any decision."

"I see." Jay regarded her for a moment more, but when she vouchsafed nothing further, he turned to Deaglan. "Joe and his team have started on repairing the bridge. It would be helpful if you could come and take a look and approve Joe's approach. I'm not entirely certain his is the best way, but..." Jay shrugged. "Your opinion would be useful."

Deaglan's gaze touched Pru's face; she met it with as innocent a look as she could. His eyes narrowed slightly. "Miss Cynster—Pru—will need assistance from someone the horses are comfortable with."

Jay flashed her his easy smile. "I'm sure Miss Cynster"—he tipped his head her way—"Pru, if I may, will understand, and assuredly, she is more than experienced enough to handle the beasts." Jay's gaze flicked to Felix. "And Felix will be there as well."

Deaglan straightened in his chair. "Perhaps, but I'm no engineer, and I have every confidence that Joe knows what he's doing. By all means go and supervise if you think it necessary, but I'll be spending the afternoon in the exercise ring, watching Pru assess our horses."

Pru had wondered if Jay would succeed in distracting Deaglan—from her perspective, not having him watching her wouldn't hurt—but the finality in his tone was absolute.

Jay lightly grimaced, but accepted Deaglan's decision without further argument.

Deaglan turned to her. "What, precisely, do you do when evaluating horses in the ring?"

The question was broad—any horses—and seeing interest in everyone's eyes, she settled to explain her process.

She'd only just begun listing the paces when she saw Maude touch Jay's sleeve, and he turned to her, apparently losing interest in Pru's explanation. As he didn't turn back but continued chatting quietly to Maude, seated at the other end of the table, Pru concluded that Jay, unlike his master, had little interest in the horses of the Glengarah collection.

Good. One more person whose opinion she could safely ignore. And neither Felix nor Patrick wielded any real weight in terms of influencing Deaglan.

That left the erstwhile wicked and potentially wild Earl of Glengarah as the sole focus of her push to secure an exclusive deal to breed from his indescribably magnificent horses.

~

Deaglan had assumed that the afternoon would pass much as the morning had, with him following Pru at a sufficiently safe distance. From his perspective, the morning had held no real danger.

Sadly, the afternoon proved to be a very different experience.

For a start, her notion of working horses in the ring commenced with him—having volunteered as her assistant—holding the horse on a short rein while she circled both him and the horse. That posed no difficulty, but then she stepped close and examined each horse's head, ears, eyes, gums, tongue, and teeth, and that brought him and her very close, and as many of the horses weren't entirely certain of her and were wont to jib, he was forced to keep his attention on them, rather than on avoiding her.

During her examination of the first three horses, on several occasions, he found himself stepping into her or bumping her, causing her to place her hands on his arms or back as she steadied herself.

As far as he could tell, her attention remained unwaveringly riveted on the horses.

His attention, predictably, became riveted on her.

And then there were the times when she reached for the hand with which he was gripping the reins, closing her small, strong, yet femininely soft hand over the back of his, slender fingers lightly gripping to adjust the angle of the rein to shift the horse's head.

With the first horse—Thor—he'd allowed himself to breathe easier once she'd switched to a long rein and, with a light switch, started Thor pacing; he'd stepped back until the shoulder-high plank wall surrounding the ring was just behind him and had concentrated on pushing down the instincts she'd stirred, reminding that side of himself that she was one lady he dared not seduce—only to jerk into motion when, as she pushed the stallion, Thor gathered himself to rear, forcing Deaglan to rush forward, reach around her, and lock his hands above hers on the reins to help her control and calm the powerful horse.

The backs of her shoulders had brushed his chest, while the curves of her derriere had grazed his loins.

The sensation of having her innocently yet seductively shifting against him, all but trapped within his arms, had crashed through him and instantly evoked an uncontrollable reaction.

Torture.

He'd had to grit his teeth and bear it.

And that had been just the first of the first three horses.

By the time Felix, who was watching from outside the ring, brought in the fourth horse, Deaglan was mentally reciting the mantra: Prudence Cynster is one lady I dare not seduce.

It didn't help.

After assessing the fifth horse, Pru paused to make notes on the sheets of paper Felix had fetched for her. And also to give herself time to breathe deeply and steady her giddy head.

All the little touches and brushes were admittedly inadvertent—indeed, inescapable, given their occupation—and something she'd weathered countless times before without being terribly aware of it.

However, with Deaglan Fitzgerald as her assistant, every little touch, every gliding brush of his clothes against hers, set prickling awareness washing over her skin and sent heat flushing beneath it, steadily building to a pervasive prickly warmth that was proving distinctly distracting.

Worse, for some inexplicable reason, she was attuned to him in a way she'd never been with any other man; she was highly aware of the steely wall of control he constantly deployed, sealing off what she sensed were powerful and potent impulses and emotions.

The lure of those deep, turbulent waters was growing.

And her wilder self's curiosity was steadily escalating; she could no longer banish wanton thoughts of what might happen if she breached his dam.

A dangerous temptation, one she was endeavoring to hold against.

She jotted her last note, then handed the papers back to Felix, turned, and watched Deaglan lead in the next horse. Felix, although well-built enough, didn't have Deaglan's height, reach, and strength; she couldn't think of any reason to suggest Felix replace Deaglan. And of course, her inner self was wholly fixated on Deaglan; that side of her all but salivated as her gaze roved over him.

That side of her wanted him closer, not at a greater distance.

Inwardly sighing at her own annoying susceptibility, she reminded herself that she was there to assess his horses, not him. And both he and the next horse were waiting.

Reining in all wayward impulses, she walked over and commenced her examination.

He watched her—closely, intently—following everything she did. Only the fact that she'd performed so many assessments she could go through the process in her sleep allowed her to proceed without any outward sign of distraction.

Keeping her mind on the horses was harder, but she forged on.

She started her initial assessment of physical attributes of the latest horse—a skittish bay stallion she put at a bit more than two years old. They were following the order of the horses from the stable entrance, so while Thor had been first, the mare in the stall alongside second, and the chestnut stallion third, the subsequent horses were, in her view, the weakest in terms of breeding value in the whole collection. But in the young stallion, much of that weakness lay in immaturity; his body had yet to take on the strong lines and accomplished gait he might yet develop.

Deaglan held the horse's head steady, but the stallion's big eyes were rolling.

Standing close beside Deaglan, Pru crooned and stroked the horse's long nose, and gradually, he grew less tense. His ears pricked, then flattened as she lifted his lips, but he allowed her to examine his teeth and jawline and to run her hand over the strong lines of his neck.

"Your head is well-formed," she murmured. "You're going to be a handsome lad when you're fully grown."

"What about his hocks?" Deaglan asked.

Moving slowly, Pru bent and ran her hands down the horse's front leg, then repeated the exercise from shoulder to hoof. "He's got some growing to do yet. Once he's fully mature, he's going to be remarkably strong."

Deaglan grunted. "He's strong enough now."

That, of course, was why he was there, and why Pru hadn't wasted her breath trying to suggest she didn't need his close assistance; having grown up with protective brothers and cousins, she'd recognized the futility. No matter how much she sensed he—like she—didn't appreciate the inevitable and constant abrading of their nerves occasioned by the enforced proximity, there was no way he would leave her in the ring alone with such powerful beasts.

And she was too experienced in examining horses that she was unfamiliar with to be silly enough to insist he did.

She kept her hand on the warm brown hide, maintaining soothing contact as she passed down the horse's side, careful not to startle the beast when she eventually stepped back to study the lines of body and hindquarters. After assimilating all she could, she went to fetch the longer rein from where Deaglan had left it draped on the ring's fencing. "I'll put him through his paces, but he'll need to be reassessed in a year's time."

She carried the long rein to Deaglan, and he switched the reins. He stuffed the shorter rein into his pocket and handed her the long one. "Be careful—he's one of the unreliable ones."

She swallowed a scornful humph and concentrated on making eye contact with the young horse. Deaglan stepped to the side, bent, and retrieved the long switch from where he'd left it, then came to hand it to her.

Without taking her eyes from the horse's, Pru accepted the switch with a nod. "Right, then, my fine fellow—let's see what you can do."

She stepped back and, with a twitch of the reins and a light tap of the switch on the horse's rump, started him pacing. Although at first hesitant —she doubted the horse had been worked in that way before—the stallion quickly fell into the rhythm of the stride she urged him to, and she steadily advanced him through the paces she used in her assessments.

So focused was she on the horse's legs and powerful fore- and hindquarters, estimating the length of his stride and tracking the shift of bones and tendons, the fluid bunching of muscles both in the various gaits and during the transitions, that she lost track of all else.

Even Deaglan.

That shouldn't have mattered, except that, as Deaglan had warned her, the young stallion was unpredictable.

And when her ruffling senses informed her that Deaglan was near, close, and she shifted her gaze from the horse to, from the corner of her eye, glance Deaglan's way, the stallion seized the moment to abruptly swing about.

She reacted to the feel of the rein and instinctively refocused on the horse—just as he swept past her. Too close.

The stallion's rump connected with her shoulder, sending her flying—

Deaglan swooped and caught her, hauling her up from where she'd nearly tumbled to the sandy floor; he had to pull her tight against him to counter her weight and keep his balance.

"I say!"

Distantly, Pru heard Felix scrambling over the fence, dropping onto the sand, then running to catch the trailing reins and calm the now-agitated horse—distantly, because her senses had seized, her gaze captured by the green of Deaglan's.

She was trapped, mentally as well as physically, held captive by the roiling heat she glimpsed in the emerald pools of his eyes.

She caught only a bare flash of that tempting fire before his lids fell and cut off the sight.

Deaglan clenched his jaw, gritted his teeth, and willed down his unruly, far too ravenous reactions.

Prudence Cynster is one lady I dare not seduce.

He felt as if he was screaming the words in his mind.

His every muscle rigid, locked against the impulse to drag her even tighter against him—against his arousal—he forced himself to ease his arms from about her, grip her upper arms, and steady her on her feet. Then he took a deliberate step back and forcibly swung his attention from her to the stallion that Felix had caught and calmed.

Without looking at Pru—at temptation—Deaglan managed to say, "I suggest we call a halt for the day."

He'd lost track of the hours, but it had to be almost time to go in and change for dinner.

Felix glanced questioningly Deaglan's way, and he nodded. "Take him back to his stall." Still without meeting Pru's eyes, he said to her, "Have you seen enough for your purposes?"

When she didn't immediately reply, he chanced a glance at her and, immediately, wished he hadn't. With her head tilted, she was regarding him with open calculation—a feminine assessment he recognized all too well.

Given that context, his question had been poorly worded.

And the expression in her eyes stated she was deciding which option to address in her reply.

Viewing her...he realized she wasn't in any sort of fluster. Surely the last moments should have thrown any well-bred spinster into at least blushes?

He'd long ago mastered the art of keeping his expression impassive. That was just as well, as her lips lightly curved in a disquieting smile, and she airily replied, "We've done well for one afternoon." Her blue eyes quizzed him—whether teasingly or invitingly, he couldn't be sure. "We can carry on tomorrow."

And that was pure provocation. The damned female was...

What was she doing?

He resisted the urge to shake his head—she'd only be encouraged—and resolved to do his damnedest to pretend he wasn't aware of the undercurrent she'd stirred and set swirling around and between them.

Manfully hiding the grimness he felt, he waved her to precede him out of the ring. He followed, and they walked out of the stable, heading for the side door.

While they crossed the cobbled court, he was conscious of her shooting surreptitious glances his way, clearly trying to read his direction.

As they neared the castle and walked into its shadow, he returned the favor.

That evening, Pru descended the stairs and headed for the drawing room, eager to examine and learn about a subject that had nothing to do with horses.

Since returning from the stable, she'd found it impossible to rein in her thoughts—her welling curiosity—over what, exactly, was simmering between her and Deaglan Fitzgerald.

After this afternoon, she knew beyond question that he felt the tug—the lure, the distraction, the temptation to seize the moment and ride without restriction—every bit as much as and possibly more than she did.

But, she felt certain, he had the advantage of knowing what their attraction presaged and to where it might lead, while she'd never been subject to such an engrossing and absorbing distraction before.

Certainly, no other man had ever impinged on her mind and senses the way he did.

She wanted to know why. She wanted to know what her options were for learning even more.

The instant she walked into the drawing room, she saw Deaglan standing by the fireplace, one arm resting along the mantelpiece as he listened to Maude.

His gaze flicked Pru's way, and he straightened as she neared, but although she searched, she detected not the slightest sign of awareness in his face.

He inclined his head to her. "Can I offer you a glass of sherry?"

She'd sampled the sherry the evening before; it was a particularly fine Jerez. She smiled. "Thank you."

He turned away, and she focused her smile on Maude.

Maude smiled back. "How is your work with the horses going?"

She explained that she'd only just started the more detailed assessments.

Deaglan, the glass of sherry for her in his hand, had paused to speak with Felix, Cicely, and Patrick. He came on and halted beside her, wordlessly offering her the glass.

Pru looked into his face and saw absolutely nothing beyond polite disinterest. Willfulness spiking, she met his eyes, held his gaze, and smiled—and reached for the glass, allowing her fingers to trail over his as she lifted the glass from his hold.

His physical control didn't waver; he didn't react by so much as a subdued twitch. But for a split second, some fiery emotion sparked in his eyes, before he doused it.

She lifted the glass to her lips and, her eyes still on his, sipped, then lightly licked her lips and complimented him on the quality of the wine.

If anything, he grew stiffer, more distant—to her, it felt as if the steely wall he'd erected between them grew even thicker.

Then Maude spoke, and Deaglan looked at his aunt and replied.

He and Pru remained standing and conversing with Maude; Pru grasped the opportunity to ask several general questions about the estate.

When she'd drained her glass, Deaglan relieved her of it—and this time, his fingers and palm lazily brushed over her hand.

Her pulse leapt. She glanced at him, but he'd turned to set the glass aside, and when he straightened and swung back to her and Maude, his ridiculously handsome face was unreadable.

Yet he seemed more relaxed, as if he'd changed his mind and was no longer rejecting her expressions of interest.

Then the others joined them, Felix pushing Patrick's chair, and as she and Deaglan shifted to accommodate the others, she felt his hand, hard and hot, lightly touch the back of her waist, then slide suggestively lower, before the sensation of his touch fell away.

Her senses prickled, and awareness raced over her skin.

For the next ten minutes, while they chatted with the others, he grasped every opening to tease her senses.

She had precious few chances to return the favor—a challenge her willful self accepted with glee.

She'd spent an inordinate amount of time deciding on which gown to wear—her stylish spring-green silk—and encouraging Peebles to fluff her curls just so. Her experienced maid had eyed her with faint suspicion; Pru had to admit that fussing over her appearance was distinctly unlike her. Consequently, she'd been a trifle late appearing in the drawing room, and it wasn't long before Bligh arrived to summon them to the table.

Pru turned to Deaglan, and he met her eyes and smiled—a hint of wolf showing. This time, he reached for her hand and, holding it between strong fingers, set her palm on his sleeve.

She gripped lightly and felt the steely muscles beneath the fine fabrics of coat and shirt tense in reaction. Smiling to herself, she held back, letting the others go ahead. Once the pair of them had joined the exodus, the last in line, she allowed her hip to brush Deaglan's hard thigh. He permitted it, then leaned closer, his arm slowly—suggestively—brushing her shoulder.

She was sternly suppressing a too-revealing shiver when he murmured, "You were extremely focused while in the ring, yet unerring over what you needed to do. How many horses have you put through their paces this year?"

Distracted—by the tenor of his voice, by the wash of his breath over the shell of her ear—she opened her mouth, the truth on her tongue, and only just caught herself in time.

She shot a glance at him and caught his eyes...

The fiend was intentionally playing on her senses, hoping to lure her into divulging information she should hold close, at least from a man she would be facing over a negotiating table all too soon.

Rather than letting her lips firm into a line, instead of glaring at him, she smiled sweetly and tipped up her chin. "Quite a few."

His gaze sharpened.

She looked ahead and smiled—and bided her time.

Deaglan escorted Pru to the chair beside his, then continued to the carver at the table's head.

As soon as the company settled, Bligh and Henry the footman appeared with the first course. Under cover of supping his soup, Deaglan surreptitiously studied Pru's face; no hint of suspicion or of resistance marred her lovely features.

When they'd finished the broth and Bligh had whisked away the plates, Deaglan shifted to face Pru, lounging in more relaxed fashion in his chair.

His movement fixed her attention on him; he caught her eyes and smiled easily. "You mentioned your younger brother acts as your second-in-command. I take it he's watching over the Cynster breeding empire while you're here?"

Lips gently curving, she inclined her head. "Whatever supervision the program needs, he'll give, and he has Mama and Papa to ask if he runs into anything unexpected."

"Was there any question of him coming here in your stead?"

Her smile deepened a touch. "Not really." She paused, then added, "He's not experienced enough in assessing bloodlines—he declared as much himself." She met his eyes levelly. "For such evaluations, experience is key."

He allowed something of his underlying interest to color both eyes and voice. "And are you so very experienced?"

Her brows rose a fraction—a teasing lift. "When it comes to assessing at a glance, most consider me without peer."

"I see." Beneath the table, he shifted his leg, letting his knee press lightly against hers. Her eyes widened a touch, and he softly asked, "So how long do you think assessing my stable is likely to take?"

Her breath came more shallowly, but she leaned on one elbow, propping her chin in her palm, and with her eyes fixed on his, calmly stated, "It's hard to know—not every stallion is the same, any more than every mare. And of course, there are those I will need to ride to...verify my understanding of their best traits."

He blinked, and the damned woman pressed her knee to his, then lightly slid the arch of her foot, freed of her evening slipper, upward, tracing the curve of his calf.

His lungs seized; lost in her eyes, he saw the danger too late.

Forcing himself to move, to straighten in his chair, removing his legs from her easy reach, he battled to draw in air.

Before he could think of how to reassert control, Bligh sailed in, leading two footmen bearing the dishes for the main course.

A moment later, while serving himself from the dish Bligh offered, Deaglan felt stockinged toes slide over the arch of his foot and flirt with the edge of his trouser leg.

He shot Pru a dark glare, but she was looking at Felix and didn't see.

What followed was a covert game of teasing temptation that, entirely against his better judgment, he found himself engaging in, tit for tat, in what proved to be a futile attempt to wrest back the reins and reestablish his authority.

Far from achieving that laudable aim, by the time dessert was placed before them, their interaction more closely resembled a curricle racing out of control, entirely unrestrained...

When the meal finally ended and Maude rose, and with a smugly delighted smile just for him, Pru rose, too, he got to his feet, but beckoned the footman to draw back her chair for her and remained before his, unwilling to get any closer to her. He watched as, with a last taunting look his way, she joined Maude and Cicely; when the door closed behind the three ladies, he hauled in a breath and slumped back in his chair.

The footman pushed Patrick into place on Deaglan's left, and Felix moved to take the chair Pru had vacated. Deaglan reached for the whiskey decanter Bligh placed before him, splashed the usual quantity into Patrick's and Felix's glasses, then tipped twice that amount into his own glass, set down the decanter, lifted the glass, and took a healthy swallow.

The burn of the spirit down his throat did little to ease the fire inside.

A conflagration Prudence Cynster, supposed tonnish spinster, had deliberately stoked.

What the devil am I to make of that?

He had no clue and didn't want to think too deeply about the double entendres they'd exchanged. That way lay madness. But as he sipped and let Felix and Patrick's idle conversation drift past, and his brain cooled and, eventually, cleared, he realized what he had to—needed to—do.

When he, Felix, and Patrick joined the ladies in the library, for the first time in his life, Deaglan played safe. He'd used the minutes apart from Pru to lock down every impulse and reinforce his control over any and all reactions.

Of course, that didn't save him from being tested; she all but immediately tried to lure him back into their game.

He resisted, refusing, no matter the provocation, to allow his hands to stray near any part of her anatomy and keeping himself sufficiently apart from her to ensure she couldn't touch him.

Every verbal advance she attempted, he met with po-faced repressiveness, in the vein of a stern and priggish stuffed shirt. That wasn't a role that came naturally, but he clung to it for all he was worth. He had to weather her storm and wear down her stubbornness. Only when she accepted defeat and turned away would he—or she—be safe.

His flat refusal to engage eventually brought a frown to her blue eyes.

When he consistently declined to rise to her verbal baiting, frustration sparked, fleetingly darkening her cerulean gaze and tightening her lips.

Good. With any luck, she would reap the same frustration-induced reward he knew awaited him; as he would have to endure the consequences, so should she.

And with any luck at all, those unavoidable effects would dissuade her from trying to provoke him again.

With that goal in mind, he gritted his teeth and bore with her alluring nearness, with her subtle yet definite invitations to engage, without letting himself react to her in any way at all.

Two hours later, swathed in her nightgown and dressing gown, with her arms crossed beneath her breasts, Pru stood before the window in the bedchamber she'd been given and scowled at the night.

She was irritated—supremely so.

Partly with Deaglan Fitzgerald, but mostly with herself.

What had she been thinking?

What megrim had invaded her brain and prompted her to engage with him in such a manner?

Heaven knew, she'd never flirted with any man in her life. She'd never felt the slightest impulse to do so. Yet after landing in Deaglan's arms that afternoon…something had gone to her head.

That was the only explanation she could find for whatever had possessed her to try to provoke a gazetted rake simply in order to see if she could—to find out what might happen.

Only silly, flighty misses indulged in such reckless behavior.

You were born reckless, a little voice reminded her. *And willful and stubborn, too.*

Her family had long known about her wild side—the side that made her such a fearless rider—but in the main, after reaching adulthood, she'd rarely let that side loose, at least not when she wasn't on a horse.

She needed to rein herself in and focus—unrelentingly—on the reason she was there.

She only had to remember the quality of the horses in the Glengarah stable to feel the weight of responsibility settle on her shoulders—where it belonged, where it would hopefully keep her grounded, with her feet firmly planted.

Never before had she faced such a critical challenge—she had to remember that. Signing an exclusive breeding agreement with Glengarah would catapult the Cynster Stables to the very top of the Thoroughbred tree and keep them there for decades. Not just the breeding stable but the racing stable as well.

Just from her initial viewing of the horses, she knew that—could swear to that.

The thought led to her imagining conveying that to her family. Convincing her parents of the worth of the Glengarah horses wouldn't be that hard; both were so experienced, just a few descriptions of the bloodlines represented would have them prepared to back her in offering whatever was necessary to get Deaglan's—Glengarah's—signature on an agreement.

But Nicholas and even Toby?

It wasn't that her brothers would question her assessment, but both would instantly perceive that any breeding exchange of the sort she was sure Deaglan—Glengarah!—would propose and hold out for would elevate the Glengarah stable to much the same extent as it lifted the standing of the Cynster Stables.

Any deal struck that involved an exchange—and she couldn't fool herself into thinking that Deaglan wouldn't insist on such an arrangement —held the risk of eventually creating a strong competitor, at least in breeding the most valuable bloodstock.

In her own mind, she was certain, regardless of that risk, that gaining an agreement to breed from the Glengarah horses was essential for the future of the Cynster Stables, and she felt sure her parents would think the same.

The idea of passing up the opportunity and leaving one of their competitors to step in and meet Deaglan's terms was simply too horrifying to contemplate.

Staring into the darkness, she considered her brothers' likely reservations and how best to overcome them and persuade Nicholas and Toby to her view and had to admit that she wasn't at all sure who in this engagement was using whom. There was, after all, some reason that had prompted Deaglan to write to the Cynster Stables. She hadn't yet succeeded in confirming precisely what that was, but consoled herself with the observation that, while Deaglan might hope to establish his own breeding program—essentially in competition with the Cynsters—he demonstrably had no interest in racing, nor was his stable set up to support such an endeavor.

That was a point she needed to seed into her brothers' brains from the outset.

Turning away from the window, she drifted toward the bed, a large tester with a deep mattress she'd found blessedly comfortable. After removing her robe, she slid beneath the sheets. She lay back, settled her head on the pillow, and stared up at the canopy.

For several minutes, she mulled over what conditions she could insist on to help alleviate her brothers' wary concerns.

Continuing to keep her mind firmly focused on the Glengarah horses —holding all thoughts of their master at bay—she decided that her first act with respect to forging an agreement with Glengarah had to be to inform her family of the magnitude of her find. That fact alone would underscore that Glengarah was the horse owner above all others with whom they needed to make a deal—an exclusive one—before any other breeder got wind of the incredible treasure he owned.

CHAPTER 5

*P*ru walked into the breakfast parlor the following morning determined to show absolutely no awareness of the covert interaction she and Deaglan had engaged in the previous evening; in her considered opinion, that was the only viable way forward.

Then she set eyes on him—and his emerald-green gaze locked on her.

Her feet slowed. For a second, she hesitated just inside the room, then she forced herself to move; somewhat haughtily inclining her head to him, she continued to the sideboard, belatedly realizing that Jay was sitting in the chair next to Deaglan and was speaking to him.

As she accepted a plate from Bligh, Jay continued his report; she listened while she moved along the sideboard, making her selections from the array of dishes.

Jay was describing the work on the bridge he'd spoken of the day before; he ended by pressing Deaglan to ride out with him and give his approval to something about the structure.

Deaglan had been watching her ever since she'd entered; she could feel his gaze like a tangible touch and could sense the assessment behind it—he was wondering what tack she intended to take regarding their personal and highly private clash.

She heard him question the need for his presence at the bridge, but Jay insisted that Deaglan's approval was essential for the work to continue.

"Joe said he wasn't prepared to make the decision himself," Jay said. "He wants your say-so before he continues."

Pru idled at the sideboard, waiting to hear Deaglan's reply.

It came in a rather terse, "All right. We can leave immediately after breakfast."

Brightening, she turned and, with an easy smile, joined the men at the table, choosing a chair one place removed from Deaglan's left; given the table was round and the seating informal, she hoped only Deaglan would understand the message she was endeavoring to send him.

Bligh drew out the chair for her. As she sat, she smiled at Jay and bade both men a good morning.

They returned her greeting, Jay brightly, Deaglan impassively.

Felix arrived, and a plate clattered on the sideboard. "What-ho, all! It's a glorious day."

Pru glanced out of the window and saw he was correct. When Felix came to sit beside her, taking the chair on her left, she turned to him and said, "I need to post a letter home. I'd like to get it into the post as soon as possible. Is the nearest post office in Sligo?"

Felix nodded. "You should get Deaglan to frank the letter for you—it'll get delivered all the more quickly."

She was forced to glance at Deaglan, to meet his eyes.

He regarded her for a pregnant moment, then said, "If you'll bring it down, I'll frank it before I head off."

"Off to where?" Felix inquired.

When Deaglan said nothing—his attention still fixed on Pru—Jay explained about the bridge.

"Ah, I see." Felix turned to Pru, and with an effort, she swung her attention his way. "If you wish to ride, I'll be happy to ride with you and show you the way."

She smiled. "Thank you. Your company would be welcome. I have no idea where the post office is."

Deaglan listened to Felix expound on the attractions of Sligo and inwardly cursed. He'd already agreed to ride out with Jay, and the estate needed the underpinnings of the bridge, weakened by the floods after the thaw, repaired as soon as possible; too many of his tenants relied on the bridge to cross the stream.

Yet…

But no matter how he juggled his commitments, he could see no way of riding to Sligo. And at least with Felix, Pru would be safe enough; that would have to do.

He'd spent half the night tossing and turning, debating whether, given he was convinced her family were, indeed, the best major breeders with whom to engage, seducing Pru might actually be a clever move—or the very worst move he could make.

He'd fallen asleep without reaching any conclusion.

Her utter lack of encouragement that morning was, he presumed, his answer. Apparently, she'd realized that their drawing closer in a personal sense would be...a complication neither of them needed.

Well and good. At least he now knew where he and she stood. They were back to being representatives of their families, both focused on getting the best result for their side in the upcoming negotiations.

He watched Pru respond with outwardly guileless eagerness to Felix's suggestion that they set out as soon as possible, the better to return so Pru could continue her assessments in the ring...

Deaglan switched his gaze to Felix's face, and his silent curses grew virulent.

While riding to Sligo, Pru would have an unfettered opportunity to drag all sorts of information from Felix—and his brother wasn't up to evading such an experienced angler-for-information as she.

Damn!

Jay cleared his throat. "If there's nothing awaiting you here, we should start as soon as possible for the bridge. Joe's holding back from doing anything more with the spans until he has your go-ahead."

Deaglan gave up cursing; he had to go to the bridge.

He eyed Pru's profile; at least the infernal woman would have to see him before she left to get her letter franked.

As if she'd heard his thought, she reached into her habit's pocket and withdrew a neatly sealed letter. She met his eyes, set the letter on the tabletop, and pushed it his way. "If you would frank that and leave it on the hall table, I'll pick it up on our way out—I wouldn't want to delay you."

He held her gaze for a second, then put out his hand and drew the letter to him. "As you wish."

She looked into his eyes for a second more, then turned back to Felix.

Leaving Deaglan to rein in his dark and stormy mood and do what he knew he must.

Pru intended to extract every possible advantage from the ride. As, with Felix, she quit the castle, she said, "I should use the opportunity to trial one of the horses—there are several I will need to ride to complete my assessment on the potential of the collection."

After leaving the breakfast parlor in Deaglan and Jay's wake, she'd retreated upstairs to have Suzie attach the train to her riding habit, then she'd donned her riding boots, hat, and gloves, and picked up her coin-purse and quirt and headed downstairs again. She'd found her letter residing on the hall table, with "Glengarah" scrawled across the corner. Felix had been waiting, as eager as she for the outing, it seemed.

They passed into the stable, and Felix readily replied, "I'm sure that can be arranged. Which horse would you like to ride?"

"Let me see."

As she continued deeper into the stables, turning corners until she was in the fourth row of stalls, Felix grew increasingly nervous. When she stopped outside the stall of one of the stronger stallions, he was clearly visited by second thoughts. "You want to ride Macbride?"

"Yes." She unlatched the stall door. "My groom brought my saddle down to your tack room yesterday. Could you ask someone to fetch it?"

She didn't wait for Felix to agree but slipped into the stall and spent the minutes until a groom appeared with saddle and bridle communing with the powerful black stallion.

While the groom bridled and saddled Macbride, Pru retreated to wait with Felix.

He shifted anxiously. "Macbride's not always the most amenable of customers." He looked at her hopefully. "Are you sure you wouldn't like to try out one of the mares?"

She smiled reassuringly. "The value of the collection resides more in the stallions than the mares." She patted his arm. "Don't worry—I'm considered an expert horsewoman."

Deaglan walked out of the castle and into the side court to see Prudence Cynster perched sidesaddle atop a seventeen-hands-high mountain of black muscle. He managed not to let his jaw drop, then anxiety spiked and, face setting, jaw clenching, he strode forward.

This was what happened when he let her near his horses without being there to restrain her.

She trotted forward.

He reached up and caught Macbride's bridle, halting the stallion and immediately earning a frown from her. "You're not strong enough to manage Macbride."

The stare she leveled at him would have made a lesser man cringe. "Riding horses is not about strength alone." Both her voice and her expression had retreated into haughty aloofness, forcefully reminding him that she was a descendant of a ducal dynasty.

He glared at her, his jaw clenching even tighter.

Then she smiled—a tight, humorless gesture. "Release him and allow me to show you."

It was an outright challenge, one she'd couched in such a way that he couldn't fail to meet it.

At the edge of his vision, he saw Felix, looking worried, as well he might, trotting out on the strong chestnut stallion he habitually rode; if Macbride got away from her, Felix should be able to ride the stallion down.

Deaglan opened his hand and stepped back.

Pru's eyes flashed as she gathered the reins, then she set Macbride walking—past Deaglan, then in a wide arc, circling him and Jay and Felix on his horse where they stood more or less in the center of the court. She shifted fluidly into a trot, then to a gentle canter—then, with barely a twitch of the reins, she somehow guided the heavy stallion into a complicated series of turns and wheels, weaving and crossing this way, then that, before cantering again, then checking and—amazingly—sidestepping to halt two yards away, facing their little band.

His hands on his hips, Deaglan stared in disbelief at a stallion that, in the past, had proved a handful even for him. Perhaps the horse had mellowed.

Macbride stared back, then snorted and shook his huge head.

And waited patiently, unmoving and, apparently, entirely content to follow the directions of the rider on his back.

Deaglan raised his gaze from the horse to Pru's face.

She was waiting to meet his eyes. Her eyebrows arched. "Satisfied?"

He had to eat his words. He replied with a curt, distinctly terse nod. "But"—he couldn't hold back the protest—"I still think Macbride isn't a wise mount for you."

She met his eyes for a second, then her lips curved in a more conciliatory way. "I'll admit he's a challenge, but I thrive on challenges." She regathered the reins, then added, "I got my first pony on my second birthday. I could already ride unaided. Since then, I've spent a large part of my life a-horse."

With a tip of her head his way, she collected Felix with a look, then, with a general regal wave, set Macbride cantering down the drive.

Deaglan stood and watched her go; the jaunty peacock feather in her cap waved mockingly back at him.

The pair disappeared down the drive.

He stared after them for a moment more, then snorted, lowered his arms, and said to Jay, "All right. Let's go." And strode for the stable.

Adhering to her stated intention, Pru used the journey to Sligo to test Macbride's paces; the roughly eight-mile trip on a reasonably well-surfaced road gave her plenty of opportunity to assess how well the horse moved.

He was, indeed, a potential handful, but in her terms, that was all to the good. He had power, stamina, and excellent carriage, and his stride was perfect for his size. She couldn't wait to see him on a track, but that would come later—after they had an agreement in place. She, like her mother before her, didn't need trackwork to accurately assess a Thoroughbred; they'd developed a method of grading based on the other criteria she now used in her evaluations. That gave the Cynster Stables a distinct advantage in signing up new bloodstock for their breeding program. Trackwork was sometimes difficult to arrange and could give variable results, even with a single horse. The criteria they'd developed were far less variable day-to-day and had proved far more reliable indicators of a horse's potential.

By distracting herself with the stallion, she managed to keep her mind from dwelling on his master. His irritating, yet understandable and increasingly predictable master.

Felix was a much more relaxing companion; when the first houses of Sligo appeared ahead, and she eased Macbride into an easy trot, he asked, "How much did you see of the town on your way through?"

"Nothing, really. We didn't stop. We'd stayed at Longford overnight."

"Right, then. I'll point out the sights as we head to the post office."

He dutifully directed her down through the town and onto the bridge over the Garavogue River. He pointed ahead to the left, at a grassy mound strewn with stone ruins. "That's the old abbey over there. The post office isn't much farther."

The streets on the other side of the river were busier, lined with shops and thronged with bustling people, carts, and carriages.

"Sligo is a major port," Felix informed her. "Many of the ships sailing for the Americas leave from here."

They walked the horses for another block, then Felix drew rein and dismounted before the brick building sporting a sign for the post office. Pru waited for him to steady Macbride before sliding her boots free of the stirrups and dropping to the ground in a practiced way. "If you'll wait with the horses, I shouldn't be long."

Felix nodded. "Mr. O'Leary will help you."

Pru went inside and found the helpful Mr. O'Leary behind a short counter. He accepted the letter, noted the frank on the corner, and assured her that her missive would be on its way to Dublin at noon. "We have special couriers now, for the letters. We'll have this on a ferry bound for Liverpool tonight."

"Excellent." Pru thanked him and returned to find that Felix had moved the horses to where a stone bench provided a suitable mounting block from which she could scramble back into her saddle. She did so, then Felix swung up to the back of his chestnut.

"Would you like to see more of the town?" he asked. Then he grinned. "Or are you keen to get back to your assessments at Glengarah?"

Pru grinned back. "Glengarah. I've only gone through eight of the fifty-two so far. I need to get on with greater purpose, or I'll be here for weeks."

"We wouldn't mind," Felix assured her as they turned the horses and started retracing their steps. "Both Deaglan and I are enjoying helping you work with the horses."

The word "enjoying" threw up a mental vignette—of her in Deaglan's arms, courtesy of a horse. "Enjoying," she decided, was not quite the right word.

As they clopped back onto the bridge, she said, "I have to admit I'm eager to gain a more comprehensive idea of the full gamut of the collection." When they reached the opposite bank and started the horses trotting again, she asked, "Tell me, what prompted your father to start collecting horses?"

"I always thought it was out of boredom. After our mother died, he drew back from society—he'd never been terribly keen on cutting a dash. He'd always had good horses—he appreciated riding good cattle—and he grew fascinated with the beasts, and ultimately, it became, as Deaglan terms it, an obsession."

Before she approached any negotiations, she needed to learn as much as she could about why Deaglan wanted an alliance with the Cynsters— why he wanted to set up a breeding agreement. What did he hope to achieve with such a deal? How much did he need it? Was it merely an interest? Or was his relationship with his late father involved in some way?

"As I understood it," Felix went on, "Papa became fascinated with the physical features of the foundation bloodlines—those you can see in a horse just by looking, as you did in your initial viewing. So he went out searching with an eye to that, for both mares as well as stallions."

Pru leaned forward and patted Macbride's glossy neck. "I've been told that Deaglan and your father fell out and that Deaglan spent years in London. Yet since he inherited and returned to Glengarah, he's remained here, and I've seen how much time he devotes to the estate. Do you think he misses society?"

Felix snorted. "Not he. He only went because—" He broke off, but then lightly shrugged and went on, "Deaglan always thought that, financially speaking, the stable should carry its own weight. Then came the year the Great Famine took hold. He could see what was coming and wanted to ease the burden on the estate that the stable had become." Felix paused, then said, "Sadly, Papa didn't see it that way. The horses were his obsession, and he wouldn't hear of them being used for gain, not in any fashion."

Pru let a moment pass, then, allowing her puzzlement to show, said, "So your father banished Deaglan?"

Felix's lips twisted. "They argued. Rather violently. Things were said. And Deaglan left. He told me to keep an eye on things and walked out and didn't come back, not until Papa was dead."

Pru absorbed that, then ventured, "I've seen Deaglan with the horses —he knows them almost as well as you do."

Felix huffed. "He knows them better than I, even though he's not been working with them that much over recent times. Before he left, he was as involved with the stable as Papa. But Deaglan was raised to take over the estate, and he sees things in a wider perspective. He'd started the kennels and made them a going concern—he'd hoped his success with the dogs would show Papa the way with the horses, but Papa wouldn't hear of it, regardless."

"So the onset of the famine was what prompted Deaglan to push the matter with your father?"

Felix nodded. "Of course, the famine is waning now—essentially over. But Deaglan still considers the stable an unjustifiable burden on the estate, and he wants to change that."

"I see." Pru thought of all she'd heard since she'd arrived at the castle about Deaglan's involvement with the estate at large, about the ongoing repairs to the bridge and cottages. "But he's only recently taken up the reins of the stable."

Felix glanced sharply at her, then looked ahead. "He's partial to the horses, but in light of the past, he vowed to put right everything else Papa had neglected before giving time to the stable again."

Pru smiled. "Well, I'm glad he's reached that point—and that he thought to write to the Cynster Stables first."

Felix nodded and offered nothing more.

While they cantered on, Pru shuffled the pieces of Deaglan's life that had fallen into her hands thus far; her picture was still missing several vital pieces, but at least she now knew why he hadn't moved to do something with the stable immediately on returning to Glengarah. Further, his initial focus on all else on the estate had been deliberate and due to noblesse oblige rather than any lack of interest in the horses.

She didn't know much about the Great Famine, but she knew the people of Ireland had suffered, those on the great estates as much as those in the towns. It seemed Deaglan, at least, had felt a need to do what he could to alleviate his people's state. Despite the famine's waning, she suspected that motive was still at least partly in play in fueling his desire for a breeding agreement to make the stable pay its way.

She was debating how to approach her next question—to see if she could gain any insight into how financially important a breeding agreement would be to the estate and therefore to Deaglan—when hoofbeats sounded behind them, thundering nearer.

Felix glanced at her, then they slowed and looked back—and saw Deaglan, today riding a chestnut stallion rather than Thor, closing the distance between them.

He slowed as he neared; Pru noted approvingly that he directed the heavy horse with his knees rather than the reins. He nodded to them both and brought the horse alongside Macbride—who predictably jibbed, but she'd expected that and immediately settled him, reminding the huge animal who was in charge.

Once the three horses were trotting in a line, she looked at Deaglan and met his eyes. "We weren't lost."

He held her gaze. "I didn't imagine you were."

No—he'd known she would use the time to quiz Felix, so Deaglan had joined them as soon as he could.

Reflecting that in his shoes, she would have done the same, she merely arched an eyebrow and looked ahead.

Felix leaned around her to ask, "What's happening with the bridge?"

"Heavier struts needed," Deaglan replied. "I'm glad I went and took a look. Joe should have it fixed in a few days."

He watched Pru confidently manage Macbride, who was now trotting easily. Her attention, however, had switched to the chestnut he was riding; he'd deliberately chosen another of the stallions from deeper in the stables, and after viewing the bridge and agreeing with Joe's assessment and approving the extra costs, he'd left Jay to get on with his day and galloped through the fields to drop onto the road from Sligo. Luckily, he'd glimpsed Pru—easy to spot in her sky-blue habit—across the fields, realized they'd already passed him, and had turned after them. He glanced at her face. "You didn't spend much time in town." He'd thought they would be just riding out.

She shook her head. "I only wanted to post my letter." Her gaze hadn't shifted from the chestnut. Then she glanced up and met his eyes. "Can we canter for a while?" She tipped her head toward his horse. "I'd like to get some idea of his stride."

In answer, he tapped his heels to the chestnut's sides, and the stallion surged into a long-legged canter.

On a laugh, she followed, bringing Macbride up to pace a yard or so away. Felix, smiling, trailed behind.

As they rode side by side, Pru constantly glanced at the chestnut's legs. After a time, she eased back to a trot and remarked, "He has a very even, easy gait. Quite impressive."

That was more than she'd revealed about any of the horses she'd thus far assessed. Hoping for more, Deaglan reined back the chestnut to trot beside Macbride and nodded at the black stallion. "What of Macbride?"

She smiled and patted the stallion's neck. "He's equally impressive— if I was buying, it would be hard to choose between them. That said, as they hail from different lines, for breeding purposes, they would properly be judged against others of the same line, not against each other."

He hesitated, then ventured, "Papa thought Macbride hailed from the Byerley Turk and that Constantine here was descended from the Godolphin Barb."

She nodded. "I would agree with that." In turn, she paused, then added, "I would class them both as strong examples of those two foundation lines."

The castle wasn't that far ahead. He chanced another leading question. "What do you think of the...scope of the collection, if I can term it that?"

"That"—she dipped her head his way—"is..."

He held his breath.

"Nothing short of amazing." She glanced at him and met his eyes. "Your father had a highly educated eye. He's collected horses of all three major bloodlines and all the major secondary lines as well. In some instances, those are even rarer, yet carry qualities any breeder would choose to have available."

He felt hope bloom. "So from the point of view of Thoroughbred breeding, the Glengarah horses are...a valuable resource?"

She nodded. "Indeed. I've already told you the Cynster Stables will wish to discuss an agreement, although I can't yet say for how many horses, much less which." She paused to draw in a breath, held it for a second, then continued, "And just to be clear, the part I find most amazing about the collection is the spectrum of bloodlines represented and represented at high quality—meaning by animals who are very strong examples of those lines.

"I can think of several breeding stables that have as many high-quality horses—the Cynster Stables for one, and several of our competitors, too —but none have anywhere near as many strong representatives of all the foundation and secondary bloodlines." She met his eyes and smiled. "In many respects, the Glengarah collection is a horse breeder's paradise. That doesn't, of course, necessarily speak to value in terms of monetary worth. But in terms of worth in the broadest sense, there can be no greater testament to your father's acumen than the horses he's assembled in the collection."

Deaglan acknowledged the words with a dip of his head and faced forward as the battlements of the castle hove into view. He'd given her a little information, and in return, she'd told him quite a lot.

As they rode on, he allowed her words to sink in. He'd spent so much time over the last years of his father's life battling to convince his father of the need to at least investigate the case for breeding the collection's horses that he'd lost sight of the collection itself. He'd forgotten the wonder he—and Felix, too—had always felt when his father had brought home a new horse. That wonder had been an emotion they'd shared with their sire—an appreciation that had tied them together.

Until the stable became the issue that had split them irrevocably apart.

Still and all, seeing the collection anew through her eyes left him with an appreciation of what his father had actually achieved. Of what he'd left as his legacy.

The realization had him feeling closer to the man who had sired him than he'd felt in many long years.

They clattered back into the stable yard, and the grooms came running, her groom included, Deaglan noted.

The luncheon gong sounded as they dismounted; his nemesis slid from her saddle to the ground before he had a chance to cross to her and lift her down.

Remembering how she'd felt in his arms the previous afternoon—and his instant reaction—perhaps that was just as well. With Felix, they walked into the castle and headed for the dining room.

Pru felt unexpectedly content with her morning's endeavors. On reaching the front hall, she diverted upstairs to shed the heavy train of her riding habit, then joined the others at the luncheon table. Seated as usual on Deaglan's right, she replied to Maude's queries regarding posting her letter and her opinion of Sligo—limited though her experience of the town had been—then let the general conversation wash over her while she reviewed what the morning had revealed.

Even though Deaglan had cut short her time with Felix, she'd managed to extract enough to feel she was making headway in understanding what was driving Deaglan's desire for a breeding agreement. She'd also gained further insight into his responsibilities and his attitude to those, which, in turn, fed into that desire.

On top of that, a satisfying ride on a new and exciting horse always brightened her mood. Indeed, a ride on the likes of Macbride would lift the heart of any horseman.

She slanted a glance at Deaglan—presently talking with Jay—and wondered if Deaglan or Felix or any of those who lived at the castle truly comprehended how lucky they were to have such horses to ride. She was starting to suspect they didn't—not really. Perhaps they knew it intellectually, but the horses were there, so...

"Well, Miss Cynster."

She looked at Jay.

He met her eyes and smiled. "What's your plan for the rest of the day? Have you completed your assessments?"

She laughed. "No. Each assessment takes time, and as I explained to Deaglan and Felix earlier, all the horses in the collection are worthy of assessment. The late earl chose well."

"I see. So we'll have the pleasure of your company for a while, then?"

She nodded. "For several days more at least."

Deaglan caught her eye. "So what do you have in mind for this afternoon?"

She remembered her new tack—nothing but horses; that had worked well so far today. "I'll continue my assessments in the ring. The faster I can complete those, the sooner we'll be able to get down to discussing an agreement."

She wasn't surprised when Deaglan nodded. "I'll join you."

On her other side, Felix sighed and caught Deaglan's eye. "I'll ride out and see what Mrs. Comey wants, then work on the roster in the kennels." To Pru, Felix explained, "We've several bitches approaching their time, so we try to have at least two hands present around the clock."

She smiled and, as Deaglan rose, pushed back her chair. Everyone quit the table in a group, walking into the front hall, then dispersing.

She, Deaglan, and Felix walked out into the side court and across to the stable. There, Felix asked for a specific mount to be fetched and saddled; with Deaglan, Pru continued down the first aisle and on across the grassed expanse to the exercise ring, which was housed in the building beyond.

With minimal talk, she and Deaglan settled into the rhythm they'd established the previous day. Deaglan left her checking her notes and went to fetch the next horse. When he returned leading a large bay mare, Pru laid aside paper and pencil and turned her attention to the horse.

She'd assessed countless horses over the past decade; she quickly sank into the work—a task she loved. Deaglan did nothing to distract her; he worked alongside her, holding each horse steady for her initial close inspection, then putting the animal on the long rein, handing the rein over, and standing back while she put the horse through its paces.

Some horses took longer for her to be completely satisfied she'd seen all their weaknesses. Or convinced herself that they had none. As most of the Glengarah horses fell into the latter category, forcing her to try harder and for longer in an attempt to expose a weakness that, ultimately, wasn't there, she wasn't getting through the stable all that quickly.

She didn't care, and she doubted Deaglan did, either. She wanted to be thorough, and she suspected he would prefer that she was. Her judging his horses as "without fault"—she'd seen him checking her notes—would, in the end, benefit him and the estate more than anyone else.

After a while, he asked a question, and she answered. From there, his patent interest in her process prompted her to answer his queries—intelligent and apt—and even draw his attention to this indication and that, until the exchange approached that of an instructor and pupil, with her teaching him the finer points of evaluating Thoroughbreds.

She'd almost completed her assessment of the fifth horse of the afternoon when the mare turned abruptly, and she stepped back and stumbled. Deaglan's hand was immediately there, a steely, steadying grip about her elbow. Although heat flashed up her arm at the contact, she found his strength more comforting and reassuring than disconcerting; as soon as she'd steadied, he released her, and she flashed him a quick smile of gratitude before turning back to the mare. Somewhat to her surprise, despite the contact, neither she nor, she sensed, he had jerked from their absorption—their immersion in their shared task.

Good. She told herself she was relieved. Despite their flaring senses, they could work together like two sensible people without letting desire run away with them.

It was the sixth horse that was her—their—undoing.

He was a magnificent roan stallion with a white blaze down the center of his nose, and she was almost positive that he was a descendant of Curwen's Bay Barb.

He was also one of the more aggressive horses; not skittish but rather wanting to dominate. He seemed unimpressed that she was a female—shorter, slighter, less strong—and appeared to have nothing but contempt for her experience. He shifted and jibbed and stamped his feet throughout the close inspection; if it hadn't been for Deaglan's assistance, Pru doubted she would have been able to complete a sufficiently thorough examination.

But once she started the long-rein pacing, the horse settled. Or seemed to. He certainly paced at a rapid rate, perhaps a touch faster than she wished, but well enough for her to study his lines and his stride.

She was impressed by both his strength and his assurance, the confidence and rock-solid firmness with which he placed his hooves. She would have to see him ridden to be sure, but the raw power rippling beneath his glossy russet hide promised a stayer of potentially phenomenal class.

She urged the heavy horse into the final, fastest pace and focused on his hooves, gauging how perfect the line between each thudding placement was.

Without warning, the horse turned the wrong way, dragging the reins over his back.

She was a second too late releasing her hold on the ribbons—the reins tightened about her fingers, and she was jerked off her feet.

Into the stallion's path as he wheeled again.

Her breath caught. She stumbled, fighting to regain her balance and swing away.

Deaglan grabbed her, wrapped his arms about her, and hauled her to him. He swung his back to the stallion, who bumped him hard, jarring them both as the horse stormed past.

The instant the horse was clear, Deaglan dragged her to the relative safety of the ring's fence. They slumped against it. With his arms still wrapped around her, they looked across the ring at the stallion—who had halted on the opposite side. The ornery beast regarded them for a moment, then blew a long, gusty, snorty breath, shook his great head and lowered it, and appeared to settle to rest.

Pru was still struggling to breathe; she kept her eyes locked on the horse even as her senses surged. "Did I push him too hard?"

Deaglan huffed out a disbelieving laugh. "I think he got bored and decided he'd had enough."

"Huh." Pru's heart continued to thud. Deaglan's arms remained around her, holding her close. Close enough that her breasts pressed against his chest. She tried to think, but couldn't seem to find her wits, buried somewhere beneath a sea of sensation.

A flush spread over her skin, and she felt too warm, yet her impulses were pushing her to burrow even deeper into his heat. To sink into his strength—to claim it as hers.

She dragged in a breath past the constriction banding her chest and looked up.

She'd intended to laugh—to somehow make light of the moment.

There was nothing of lightness in his eyes.

Desire—stark and hot—darkened the emerald green.

The sight sent her unruly senses surging anew, and wildness—that inner wildness she'd carried inside her for all of her life—erupted. Impulse battered her, pushing, prodding, urging her on.

She couldn't stop her gaze from lowering to his lips.

His arms tensed, hot steel about her, but he didn't draw them from her, didn't loosen his hold, grasp her arms, and set her away from him.

Instead, his arms tightened, locking her against him, pressing her closer still.

Her wildness took that as encouragement. Or at least a sign that he couldn't resist whatever this was that was sparking and flaring between them any more than she could.

That he wasn't of a mind to back away this time any more than she was.

Her eyes had fixed on his lips, his mouth; she stretched up, offering hers, and he dipped his head.

Her lids fell as their lips met.

And melded—fused—in a kiss.

In the instant her lips moved under his, Deaglan knew exactly what sort of kiss this was.

It wasn't tentative; it wasn't shy. It wasn't even innocent.

It was a quest—a search powered by a yearning to know.

He'd wondered how experienced she was, not so easy to guess given her age and self-assurance, but now he knew—she wasn't.

This wasn't the kiss of a lightskirt, much less that of a courtesan, both types of females highly familiar to him.

This was the kiss of a confident woman who wanted to know more—who wanted to explore.

He was very ready to lead the way.

All thoughts of wisdom had fled. As her lips softened under his, he understood what she sought—that she wanted to find out what the undeniable attraction flaring so hotly between them might lead to.

He wanted to know, too—a wanting stronger than any he'd experienced in a very long while.

Perhaps ever.

It was a wanting he couldn't resist—and as she had made the first move, he didn't feel it was incumbent on him to toe society's line.

Not if she didn't wish it.

It was easy to take charge of the kiss, to sup at her lips, then part them. To taste her and her rising passion.

To steer the kiss deeper.

Into dangerous waters, but he was a master at navigating such straits.

Her mouth was a delight, slick and soft; her tongue tangled with his in wanton encouragement—drawing him still further into the exchange.

He sank deeper, and she was with him, her hands rising to frame his cheeks as he pulled her fully against him, molding her soft curves to his much harder frame, feeding his desire, inciting his passion.

Hunger reared its head, then surged and soared, and he was suddenly ravenous, and her blatant, flagrant, urgent response—all heated demand —only drove him on.

A whirlpool of need rose through him; it tugged and dragged—and only then did he realize he was no longer in control.

Nor was she, yet she was intent on driving him—driving them both— into the maelstrom, straight on into full-blown passion.

She wasn't ready for that—nor, heaven help him, was he.

Not like this, with their passions racing unrestrained and desire a tumult in their blood.

He searched for their reins—and couldn't find them.

She slid her hands upward, tangling her fingers in his hair, and held him to the kiss. To the raging, ravenous, rapacious exchange that had claimed them both.

He caught a glimpse of control and desperately lunged for it—only to have her shift against him and rip it away.

For one second, he absolved her—she was the novice here, he the master—only to have her lean fully into him, deliberately pressing into him, cindering any notion that she wasn't intentionally challenging him— here, now, in this arena.

His response was instant and utterly ungovernable—entirely outside his ability to control. He released his hold on her, raised his hands and framed her face, and plundered her mouth.

And still she met him, matched him—drove him on.

Footsteps came striding along the path, heading their way.

Felix.

Desperately summoning the strength, Deaglan tore his lips from hers.

He looked into her face, waited for her lids to rise, revealing eyes brimming with a potent mix of passion and desire. "We have to..."

Her gaze snapped into focus. Then she stepped back and turned away, facing the stallion still standing peacefully on the other side of the ring.

Deaglan hauled in a breath and forced himself to remain where he was.

When Felix clambered onto the railings and looked over, Deaglan was lounging against the fence, his posture relaxed as he watched Pru.

She was still facing away, hands on her hips as she stared at the stallion. She'd picked up the switch she'd dropped and was tapping the end against the sand. "Bad, bad beast."

Deaglan had no idea who that was directed at—the stallion, him, or her.

Or the ferocious mutual passion they'd provoked.

Deaglan was waiting in the drawing room when Pru joined the company. He watched her sweep in and searched for some sign, some indication of her direction.

There were only two ways for her to go—forward or back. There was no chance of dancing around what had happened; the engagement had been far too intense.

Her gaze swept over him, and her eyes met his briefly—too briefly for him to read anything from the glance—before she turned to greet Maude and Cicely.

Tonight, Pru wore a dark-blue silk gown; given her coloring, the effect was dramatic. Eye-catching.

Stirring.

Then again, after that incendiary kiss, he had difficulty keeping his eyes from her anyway, and her being in the same room was enough to stir his interest.

An interest that had lain dormant since he'd returned to Glengarah. That might, he supposed, have contributed in some small way to the intensity of his response to her—to that relatively simple if heated kiss—yet he doubted abstinence was the major cause.

That was something else. She incited his interest in a way no other woman—lady, bored matron, or courtesan—ever had. In a way he couldn't resist.

With all other women, whether to engage had been a decision he'd cold-bloodedly made. With her...his blood was anything but cold, and his rational mind was no longer in charge.

After that kiss, he'd jettisoned wisdom and set aside any notion of safety. In terms of his responsibilities, he couldn't justify pursuing her—potentially risking an agreement with the Cynsters—yet he knew beyond question that, if she beckoned, he would respond.

Turning his back and walking away was no longer an option.

He moved to the tantalus, poured her a glass of the sherry she preferred, and, holding his own as well, carried the glass of Jerez to her.

Experienced as he was, he knew she had to make her own decision, and with all he'd seen of her character thus far, he felt confident she would already have made it; if anything, she was proactive to a fault.

She turned as he approached, a polite, social smile on her lips, her usual engaged expression on her face.

He held out the glass, and her smile deepened as she reached for it. "Thank you."

As she took the glass, her fingers brushed over his and lingered for a second too long. She looked up, and her eyes met his—and he read in the blue her decision, her direction.

His pulse leapt; anticipation spiked.

She lifted the glass from his fingers and turned to address Felix.

Deaglan raised his glass and sipped. And waited for what, he now knew, would come.

He had no idea why she affected him so powerfully, but he was determined to find out.

"How many puppies are you expecting?" Pru asked Felix.

"Four at least, but sometimes we get as many as eight. Sometimes even nine."

"Are they all spoken for? Or do you breed according to some plan and sell whatever eventuates?"

Felix looked to Deaglan for direction; after the ride to Sligo, Deaglan had drawn Felix aside and warned him over being too ready to answer Pru's questions, especially about anything to do with the horses, with their breeding practices in the kennels, or regarding the estate.

Felix had glumly admitted he'd already divulged something of the stable's history, but that was water under the bridge; from now on, Felix would be more careful.

"Mostly the latter," Deaglan replied. As long as they kept their answers general, there would be no sensitive revelations.

They continued chatting about the dogs and the anticipated litters, then Patrick asked how Pru was getting on with the horses.

Pru smiled and returned a vague answer, but when, with a sidelong glance at Deaglan, Maude asked how long she might be staying, Pru confirmed that her assessments would take several more days, perhaps even a week to complete.

Maude, Patrick, and Cicely brightened at the news; Pru didn't need them to say the words to know that they enjoyed having a lady visitor, especially one from England.

Then Maude asked Felix how he'd found Mrs. Comey. Listening to the exchange, Pru gathered the old woman was something of a local character.

She sipped the sherry, but the drink did nothing to cool the warmth coursing through her. To her senses, Deaglan, beside her—all muscle and size and alluring heat—was temptation incarnate, yet as the company continued to chat over inconsequential subjects, there was nothing in his demeanor or behavior to encourage her one way or the other.

Except that he'd dropped his steely wall; she no longer sensed that between them.

Yet he wasn't doing anything at all to lure her on.

That left her in something of a quandary; while she knew what she wanted, she didn't actually know what to do next.

She'd never participated in a liaison—an affair, a seduction. She'd never been even vaguely interested before and, therefore, had zero experience on which to draw.

She wished, now, that she'd paid more attention to her cousins' whispers, but she'd always dismissed their girlish conferences as a waste of time.

So now, she was out of her depth and floundering, even though she knew what direction she wanted to—needed to—take.

In light of their recent interlude in the stable, she'd reversed her decision to maintain a businesslike distance from Deaglan. Over previous evenings, she'd thought to distract him and had learned that, between them, distraction worked both ways. She now saw his subsequent refusal to engage as entirely understandable; infinitely more experienced than she, he had seen the risk to his own equanimity—he hadn't wanted to risk being distracted by her.

Well and good. They'd ended the previous night adopting comple-
mentary positions, each resolving to treat the other with businesslike
reserve. They'd managed that through most of the day and had been
progressing reasonably well.

Then had come that kiss...

As a revelation—an epiphany—it had been eye-opening. She needed
to know more—*had* to learn more—and she wasn't going to be able to let
that need go.

From the look in his eyes when they'd broken apart—a look that had
tugged at something deep inside her—he'd been as stunned and as
captured by those wild, unfettered moments as she.

To her mind, if pursuing their unexpected connection distracted them
both equally, then surely there could be no undue advantage to either of
them in pushing forward and learning more.

In indulging further.

That was her new direction, and if, in taking it, her wild side was well
and truly in charge, this time, she had not the slightest interest in reining
that side of herself in.

She needed to know what this was between them—what it might
become if they allowed it to grow; that was all there was to it.

Bligh appeared, and in response to his summons, they repaired to the
dining room. Although she strolled on Deaglan's arm, that evening, the
company moved as a group, and there was no moment for any private
exchange.

That situation continued throughout the meal, with the company as a
whole exchanging light, relaxed banter across the board. A pleasant meal
in pleasant company, and if beneath the banter, she and Deaglan
frequently exchanged glances that carried a subtext quite different to that
of the general conversation, neither seized the opportunity afforded by
their proximity to incite each other's senses in any other way.

There were no illicit touches as there had been the evening before.

That didn't stop her nerves from sparking, her senses from leaping,
simply because of his nearness. She'd never before experienced such
anticipatory distraction—tightening her nerves, suborning her senses, and
at times, even her wits.

She clung to a façade of normalcy—or hoped she did.

At one point, she noticed Maude's gaze resting on her, then it moved
on to Deaglan and rested on him measuringly, too.

Pru had to wonder if their covert interest in each other showed, yet as far as she could tell, they were both being careful to hide any outward signs.

Eventually, Maude rose, and together with Maude and Cicely, Pru retreated to the library.

There, she endeavored to contribute to the conversation as best she could, yet she was on tenterhooks, waiting for Deaglan to appear.

Then he was there, and her senses, her wits—all of her mind—converged on him; he was a magnet for every element of her awareness.

He sat in his customary armchair; as usual, she'd claimed the one beside it. They listened and occasionally contributed to the general conversation—a chatty exchange between Felix and Patrick, which drew in Cicely as well, about weather and conditions elsewhere in the country and how the different counties were recovering from the famine and how that was affecting friends and acquaintances.

On her way across the country, Pru had noticed signs she now realized signified recovery from what, apparently, had been near-devastation. She had a passing interest in hearing how other counties were faring; she hadn't visited her connections at Kentland, in County Kilkenny, for quite some years.

Yet her awareness of Deaglan—her interest in him—dominated her mind.

She would have preferred to have remained in the library until all the others had gone, so she and he could address the simmering, senses-stealing, utterly distracting attraction that grew only more potent with every minute they spent in each other's company—until she felt she had to struggle to breathe...

Yet when Maude set aside her embroidery and suggested they retire, Pru smiled, rose, and with Cicely, followed Maude from the room.

Until she figured out what the appropriate next step for her to take was—and she had to wonder why he was sitting back and not even giving her a clue—she was, effectively, stymied.

Deaglan watched Pru go, watched the door close behind her, then rose and poured himself another glass of whiskey. He waved the decanter at Felix and Patrick, but both shook their heads and returned to their discussion, which, now the ladies had left, veered into politics.

Deaglan returned to his chair, sprawled at his ease, sipped, and listened with half an ear while he contemplated the peculiar situation between Prudence Cynster and himself.

He'd never been in such a situation before; every lady he'd previously engaged with had known the ropes—had known how to play this age-old game.

Pru didn't. That much was now clear.

And while he had all the knowledge in the world on which to draw, he couldn't prompt her. At this stage, his prescribed role was purely passive. Honor insisted—and given who she was, in her case more than in any other—that he do nothing to influence her in any way.

He could no longer push her away, and he couldn't draw her to him. He had to wait.

How long he would have to wait he didn't know; given it was her, he couldn't even guess.

None knew better than he that there was only one destination on the path that unexpected kiss had flung them down. He was willing to travel that road with her—if she wished it.

She could still retreat; he would allow her to do so—if she wished.

Given all he'd seen and sensed that evening, he didn't think her exercising that option was at all likely.

She was the sort to throw her heart over any fence—and for her, for the sort of lady she was today, tossing her cap over the proverbial windmill lay well within her scope.

Yet how long she would allow this excruciating hiatus between them to continue—how long she would allow the frustration of passion and desire denied to continue to build—he didn't know and couldn't predict.

He drained his glass, then stared at it.

Experienced he might be, but when it came down to it, she and this situation were entirely new to him.

CHAPTER 6

*T*he next morning, after an unusually disturbed night, Pru arrived at the breakfast table only to have her entire awareness lock on Deaglan with an even greater degree of concerted focus than had afflicted her the evening before.

Keeping her state concealed through breakfast was difficult enough. What followed was worse.

She had to continue assessing the horses, and that meant working with him, often close beside him, for hours on end.

Every tiny, inadvertent touch, each and every unavoidable brush of their bodies, sent her—and him—all but rigid with the effort of holding back their reactions.

It might have been amusing hearing each other's sharply indrawn breaths, their stuttering breathing, the sudden exhales, and glimpsing the near-stumbles and almost-fumbles if the moments hadn't been so highly charged and fraught.

With Felix free to watch and assist as needed throughout the day, she and Deaglan had no opportunity to so much as refer to the steadily escalating, sparking and biting tension between them, much less do anything about it.

At the end of the day, during which, via a herculean effort, she'd managed to complete the assessments of ten more horses, as she and Deaglan walked to the side door, his lips were set in a thin line, and he was casting her dark, aggravated looks, and she was returning the favor.

What was she supposed to do? How was she supposed to—surreptitiously—invite his attention?

She hadn't a clue—and she hadn't had any opportunity to tease or even provoke one from him.

In silence—for there was no saying who might be out of sight yet able to hear them—they climbed the main stairs, heading for their rooms to change. At the top of the stairs, they stepped into the gallery. They paused and looked at each other, then she swung right and strode down the west wing to her room at the far end, leaving Deaglan to head to his room, wherever that might be.

Pru swung open her door, walked in, and shut the door behind her.

Peebles was there, shaking out her spring-green satin. "This one again?"

"No." For some reason, Pru wanted a gown far less eye-catching. "What else have we brought?"

Eventually, she had a disapproving Peebles help her into a bronze silk gown, one she'd recently taken to wearing at home; having memories of her family around her was comforting.

Not that, even if she had been able to appeal to her family, they could have helped her with the conundrum she faced.

She sat on the dressing stool and let Peebles have at her hair—and tried to think of what to do.

She wanted to...

The truth was, she hadn't allowed herself to think of precisely what she wanted—intended—to do. Not in straightforward terms.

She hadn't allowed herself to actually think the words *I want to have an affair with Deaglan Fitzgerald.*

Much less *I intend to become the rakish and notoriously wild Earl of Glengarah's lover.*

At least for as long as I remain at his castle.

Compelled by her first heady experience of real desire, she hadn't thought matters all the way through, had she?

If she did—if she enumerated and weighed all the pros and cons— would it change anything?

She seriously doubted it would.

When her wild side took charge—as it already had over Deaglan Fitzgerald—mere negatives didn't even cause her to pause. The harder the jump, the higher the fence, the more determined she was to clear it.

She'd been that way all her life. She couldn't change herself now.

Aside from all else, she didn't wish to; herself as she was suited her very well.

Yet when it came to it, despite her increasing desire to start racing down the path that would land her in his bed—or him in hers—she still hadn't made the final decision to tap her heels to her wilder self's flanks and loosen the reins.

She'd been staring unseeing at the mirror. She refocused on her eyes and pursed her lips. "Hmm."

"Here." Peebles set a pair of worked gold earbobs on the dressing table's top. "Never seen you so distracted. Lord knows where you've gone in your head, but time's a-wasting, and you're expected downstairs."

Pru reached for the earbobs. "Thank you. I am distracted."

She fixed the bobs in her ears and pretended not to notice Peebles's suspicious look.

"Horses?" Peebles asked.

"Among other things. There!" Bobs affixed, her matching gold necklace straight, Pru stood, turned, and surveyed herself in the cheval glass, then, satisfied, headed for the door.

She knew herself well enough to accept that she wasn't going to back away from the challenge Deaglan Fitzgerald, the wicked Earl of Glengarah, posed. Consequently, she needed to determine how to propel them both down the path that would land her in his arms in some suitably private place.

With luck, the next hours would yield some clue.

Sadly, over the following hours, matters did not fall out as Pru had hoped, and she returned to her bedchamber thoroughly out of sorts. During dinner and the usual interlude in the library, the battle to cloak her reactions to Deaglan had reached epic proportions, while a heretofore unprecedented need to touch and be touched had grown and swelled until it was a prickling, compulsive itch beneath her skin.

Her younger maid, Suzie, was waiting to assist her out of her gown; Pru was cravenly glad the much-older Peebles—who had been her nursemaid and knew her all too well—had ceded nighttime duties to the younger woman. As Suzie's nimble fingers unhooked the closures down Pru's spine, she thought to distract herself by asking, "How have you found the household here, Suzie?"

"It's very nice, miss—comfortable and calm. No panics, and no one yells. They're pleasant people all around. George and Horricks are right at home in the stable, and me and Peebles and Mrs. Bligh and Dulcie— she's Mrs. O'Connor's dresser—and the other maids all get on like a house afire."

"Good." Her people were settled and content, so they wouldn't be concerned if their stay there stretched to a few weeks. None of the four were married or had anyone waiting for them in Newmarket; they enjoyed accompanying her on her jaunts all over the British Isles.

No reason not to engage with Deaglan Fitzgerald on their account.

But once Suzie had helped her into her nightgown, shaken out her evening gown and hung it up to air, bid her a cheery "Goodnight, miss!" and whisked out of the door, there was nothing to keep Pru's thoughts at bay.

She settled beneath the covers, then reached out and turned down the lamp.

Hopefully, a sound night's sleep would revitalize her wits, and on waking, she would immediately perceive some obvious way forward she'd overlooked. Determinedly, she closed her eyes.

Less than a minute later, she opened her eyes and stared up at the bed's canopy.

She'd never felt this way before and didn't understand why the wicked Earl of Glengarah was the only man—nobleman, gentleman, or any man at all—to have evoked such a reaction in her.

A reaction that refused to abate, that only grew stronger with every passing hour.

She could dwell on the possible reasons for his uniqueness for days, but she doubted it would get her any further. It was possible—even likely —that he provoked the exact same response in many ladies, hence his reputation.

She wasn't so naive that she hadn't realized that the powerful, potent, compulsive emotion that had her in its grip was desire. Reckless and wanton sexual desire for a dangerous nobleman.

Had surrendering to her willfulness and seizing the chance to experience his kiss been a mistake?

Even now, with that itch, a persistent prickling beneath her overheated skin, increasingly abrading her nerves, she couldn't bring herself to regret that moment of madness. She would have deeply regretted not grasping the opportunity—not leaping that fence when it presented itself before her

—but now she had, and they'd indulged, and given birth to this wretched, compulsive itch...

She had to go forward, not retreat. Retreat was a concept she rarely embraced; such behavior was simply not in her nature.

Forward, then—no other option existed.

He was waiting, watching—signaling beyond question that this was her decision to make.

In part, that was why she'd dragged her heels over doing something to propel them on; it would have been easier if he'd stepped up and taken the lead, and she'd been able to follow—and perhaps later, take the reins.

She now knew that wasn't going to happen—that between them, she had to take the first decisive step.

Figuring out how to do that had consumed a good part of her mind—all of her mind not devoted to his horses—throughout the long day.

She still didn't know what to do—how to proceed.

Yet...

A small, subdued voice deep in the darkest recess of her mind quietly whispered, wondering if the next fence might just be that one fence too far.

She mentally humphed, but forced herself to consider the possibility, yet she still couldn't see herself bowing to convention and backing away.

Mentally shaking her head, she reviewed her recent thoughts—they resembled a tangled skein. There was no point adding to the mess by tugging at it further. Again, she closed her eyes and sternly told herself to fall asleep.

After five minutes of tossing and turning, she accepted that the thoughts of her and Deaglan that continued to churn in her mind were too unsettling to allow her to relax.

She tossed back the covers, got out of bed, found her silk robe, shrugged into it and belted it, found her slippers and slid her feet into them, then she turned up the lamp she'd left burning low and carried it to the door.

She slipped into the corridor, leaving the door ajar, and treading quietly down the central runner, set off for the main stairs.

She reached the gallery and went quickly and silently down the stairs, then turned toward the library. An absorbing novel was just what she needed; she recalled seeing some of Miss Austen's works on one of the library's many shelves.

The door to the library loomed ahead; she opened it and walked in.

The curtains had been drawn earlier in the evening, leaving the room shrouded in shadows, dispelled only by the light of her lamp and the glowing embers in the hearth.

Quietly, she closed the door and walked down the middle of the room to the far right corner; once there, she played the light from her lamp over the shelves.

There they are. She set the lamp on a nearby table, then bent to examine the titles on the spines lined up along the second lowest shelf.

She'd just pulled out a volume of *Persuasion* and straightened when a sound—a faint creak—had her whirling around.

Her heart leapt into her throat and started to beat in a frenzied tattoo, then she spotted Deaglan—with his cravat untied and hanging about the strong column of his throat, the heavy locks of his hair rumpled, and his eyes glinting darkly in the lamplight—sitting in his usual chair, watching her.

Her heart didn't slow. Her lips formed an "Oh," but no sound came out.

With his gaze locked on her, he raised the cut-crystal tumbler in his hand and drained it—watching her all the while—then he lowered the glass and set it on the table by his elbow.

Her heart started to thud as, mesmerized, she watched him uncross his long legs and rise, then stalk, slowly, toward her.

She searched his face, but could deduce nothing from the arrogantly impassive planes.

Yet his weighty gaze…felt like fire.

As that gaze, insolent and knowing, swept over her—an all-but-tangible, seductive caress—excitement bloomed, and she felt thrilled to her toes.

Caution prodded her to flee, but the rest of her mind was avidly intent on learning what was driving him.

Deaglan watched her eyes flare as he neared.

He halted before her. Without taking his eyes from hers, he reached for the book she was clutching, gripped, and slid it from her grasp, then dropped it on the table beside the lamp.

As the soft thud faded, he reached for her and smoothly, deliberately, drew her into his arms, then he raised one hand, framed her delicate jaw, tipped up her face, and kissed her.

This time, he let his hunger loose. Intentionally lowered his shield so she could feel his desire, could taste it and understand, while he assuaged the ravenous, rapacious need she'd stoked over the past two days.

Under his practiced guidance, her lips parted, and he angled his head and dove within, staking his claim with heat and passion even before her tongue tangled with his.

He didn't take—he ravaged and conquered; this was no gentle seduction but a deliberate plunge into searing waters. He wanted, and he took, and relished the taking; only after he'd slaked the sharp edge of his hunger did he ease back and let her come up for air and steady...

He fully expected her—a well-bred spinster, older than the usual young lady perhaps, yet, he would wager, a virgin nonetheless—to be rattled by the force and power, the sheer unadulterated passion he'd allowed to pour through the kiss.

He waited for her to come to her senses and draw her lips from his.

Instead, her arms slid around his neck and tightened, her lithe body pressed closer, and she kissed him back—every bit as greedily as he had kissed her.

No—*more* greedily. He, at least, had some notion of degree; she seemed to have none short of wholehearted, unrestricted, unrestrained ardor.

She kissed him with a naked desire that made him reel; through the fiery kiss, she lavished on him passion so evocative it set his blood on fire.

He crushed her to him, and she set him alight.

Pru reveled in the moment, wholly immersed in the whirlpool of desire and need he'd unleashed. It was consuming, all-absorbing; she couldn't get enough, couldn't *feel* enough, even as her nerves overloaded and her senses sang.

Then she felt his hands slide from her face, felt his palms, strong and hard, caress her breasts, her waist, her hips, and heat welled and poured through her; flames rose and cindered any nascent reservations, and something inside her all but purred.

She pressed herself more fully against him in blatant invitation, then his hands returned to her breasts, closed and kneaded, and she gasped as her senses spun.

As on a wave of sensation, her body came alive in a way, in a fashion, she hadn't known was possible. Hadn't known existed.

This was passion. This was desire.

She wanted more of both.

Her fingers tangling in his hair, she clutched his head and held him to the kiss as she pressed that truth upon him, with lips and tongue telling him plainly what she wanted, before forging on.

Freed.

Freed of all restraint, free of all convention and expectation.

This was her—the true, unfettered her, the fearless rider who flew over fences others didn't dare attempt.

Within her, passion flared, then roared, tempting her to surrender to the conflagration swelling between them.

Abruptly, he wrenched back from the kiss. His hands left her breasts to grasp her upper arms in an unforgiving grip and forcibly hold her still as he stepped back—stealing away his heat, his passion, and holding hers at bay.

Stunned, with her wits and senses whirling, she stared at him.

His eyes burned with green fire, a telltale sign of his desire, yet his hold on her only grew steelier while his face hardened to a granite mask.

"Last chance," he growled, and his voice had descended into roughness and a darkness edged with violence. His chest swelled as he drew in a breath. "If this happens again—and it will if you stay—our next encounter is going to end in a bed with nothing between us but naked skin."

Deaglan lowered his head so he could better meet her eyes and willed her to listen, to understand. "If that's not what you want, you need to call a halt to this—and the only way to do that now is for you to leave Glengarah."

He was trying hard to save them both. He searched her eyes, the blue darkened by passion, but could find no hint of retreat. She stared at him still, but if anything, there was calculation surfacing in those lovely eyes. He swallowed and made one last bid to send her running. "I can promise you—absolutely and without a shred of doubt—that if you wish to leave Glengarah Castle virgo intacta, you'd better be prepared to finish your assessments tomorrow and leave before evening." He tried to think through the tumult in his brain and failed. Straightening, he added, "We can negotiate by letter."

He released her and stepped back.

As if freed from some hold his closeness had imposed on her, her gaze sparked to full awareness, then sharpened as her eyes narrowed. "You're telling me I have to leave?"

No—I'm begging you to leave for both our sakes.

But he'd learned enough of her not to utter those words. "I'm telling you that you should."

He fought down the urge to rake both hands through his hair—a show of weakness she might recognize.

Never in all his years of bedding females had he ever not been in control. But he wasn't in control of this—wouldn't be able to keep control of this. Not with her. Not with her challenging him—both intentionally and unintentionally—every step of the way.

That, more than anything else, prompted him to try one last time to scare her off.

He made his face and his voice as forbidding as he could. "You can choose to spend tomorrow night safely tucked into bed at the Castle Hotel in Sligo, or spend the night here in bed with me—your choice."

He didn't wait for her answer, knowing full well that she would only argue. With one last, forceful look, he swung on his heel and stalked to the door.

He opened it and went out without once glancing back.

Pru stared at the door as it clicked shut. Her lips still throbbed, her skin was on fire, and her flesh ached in a way it never had before.

For long moments, she didn't move—just breathed as her body calmed and her wits and senses realigned—while she replayed every second of what had just passed between them.

A full minute ticked by, then another. Then she picked up the book, returned it to the shelf, lifted the lamp, and headed for the door.

Unhurriedly, she climbed the stairs. Now she knew where she stood, where he stood, and knew beyond question what she needed to do—now she'd made the decision he'd been waiting for her to make and was absolutely certain she'd decided correctly—she wouldn't have any trouble falling asleep.

CHAPTER 7

The following morning, Pru walked into the breakfast parlor in a sunny and confident mood. She bestowed a cheery smile on Deaglan and Felix, already at the table, then helped herself to the dishes arrayed along the sideboard.

She ensured her inner smirk over the wary watchfulness in Deaglan's eyes didn't make it to her lips.

When she approached the table, Felix rose and drew out the chair between his and Deaglan's.

She rewarded him with a bright smile. "Thank you." Setting down her plate, she sat.

When she flashed her smile Deaglan's way, he met it with a stony expression and a rather stiff nod.

Felix resumed his seat on her right. "Watching you perform your assessments in the ring is fascinating. I'm seeing so much more in our horses than I did before. I had no idea such examinations could be so revealing."

She inclined her head. "From our point of view, they have to be. Without a sound notion of the quality of the horses, formulating a breeding agreement—which, let's face it, always carries an element of risk—becomes even more a case of buying a pig in a poke. A sound assessment ahead of negotiations means we all know what quality of horses we're talking about."

"Do you always take as long as you have been with each horse?" Felix asked.

"Yes and no. The close physical inspection is much the same with every horse, but the scoring of gait, paces, and overall movement takes longer the higher the quality of the horse."

Deaglan shifted in his chair. "Why is that?"

She turned to him and, suppressing a grin, explained, "Because the scoring is based on weaknesses, and to be certain a specific type of weakness isn't there, it's necessary to give a horse plenty of opportunity to display it. Hence, the time spent on the long-rein assessment lengthens." She returned her gaze to Felix. "During my initial viewing, I realized that, barring the horses selected for personal use and brought closer to the entrance, all the horses in the collection are stalled roughly in order of increasing quality. I understand your father organized the stalls."

Felix nodded. "He insisted that the horses had to be housed in a particular order. I think it was the order in which he kept them in his head."

"That makes sense." She resisted an impulse to look at Deaglan. "So the deeper I go into the stable, the assessments will take progressively longer, although I won't need to take quite as long with the stallions we rode on the day we went to Sligo because I've already seen them in action. That said, I've only completed twenty-two assessments to this point—I've thirty horses yet to examine."

She picked up her teacup, sipped, and slanted a surreptitious glance at Deaglan.

A definite frown had formed in his eyes as the realization sank in that pressing her to leave this afternoon with her assessments incomplete wouldn't be in his best interests. Luckily for him, she had no intention of running away from the castle, the stable—or him.

He lifted his coffee mug and drank, then lowered the mug and looked at her. "How many more days do you think it will take for you to evaluate the remaining horses?"

She met his eyes, hard and unrevealing, and arched her brows. "I did ten yesterday—five each in the morning and afternoon sessions. Realistically, that rate will fall—with the last third of your stable, I wouldn't expect to manage more than three in a session. So the next thirty horses in this particular stable... I wouldn't expect to have the assessments completed for at least four more days." She paused, then, her eyes steady on his, added, "Possibly as much as a week."

He was silent for several seconds, then somewhat tightly asked, "That long?"

What did he think she was telling him? "At least." To underscore her point, she continued, "The Cynster Stables aren't in the habit of making snap judgments—our decisions are always carefully considered." Holding his gaze, she sipped, then added, "Calculated, even."

She saw the muscles in his jaw clench and couldn't hold back a smile.

Deaglan stared at her, his expression as rigidly uncommunicative as he could make it. The damned woman was baiting him...no, it was worse than that. She was signaling her clear intention to toss her cap over the windmill and fling herself into his arms.

Willfully tumbling them into a bed.

Heaven help him! How had he got into this situation?

Reining in his own carnal desires was bad enough. Restraining hers as well...

No matter her reference to calculation, he couldn't believe she'd thought this through.

When she pushed back her chair and rose, he got to his feet and tossed down his napkin; he needed to seize the first chance that offered and talk some sense into her. She and Felix had both intimated they were heading directly for the stable. Deaglan followed them into the front hall.

As Pru and Felix neared the side door, it opened, and Jay walked in. He nodded to them both, then, seeing Deaglan walking behind, Jay waved him down. "Just who I wanted to see."

Without taking his gaze from Pru, Deaglan waved Jay off. "Later."

He was aware of Jay's surprise. Jay glanced at Pru, who was stepping through the door Felix was holding open. "But it's—"

"Not as important as the business I need to discuss with Miss Cynster. Immediately." Deaglan stalked on and followed Felix and his nemesis into the side court.

Leaving Felix to fetch the next horse to be examined, Deaglan trailed Pru into the exercise ring. He stalked to her side and halted—close.

Close enough that her eyes widened slightly as she turned and looked up at him with questioning interest tinged with just a hint of wariness. At last! He could work with wariness.

"What," he ground out, his voice low, "do you think you're doing?"

One delicate eyebrow arched. She studied him for several seconds, then evenly replied, "Calling your bluff."

Exasperation geysered. "I wasn't bluffing." He heard heavy hooves approaching.

So did she. A pleased-with-herself smile flirted about her lush lips. She raised a hand, placed her soft palm against his arm, pressed reassuringly, and murmured, "I know."

He stayed where he was—battling a nearly overwhelming urge to raise both hands and clutch his hair—as she moved to accept the reins of the horse Felix led into the ring.

What the hell am I supposed to do?

What was the right thing to do now?

Slamming a mental door on his roiling reactions, he spun on his heel and strode to where she was holding the horse—a black mare—on a short rein and crooning to settle the beast.

With grim determination, he forced himself to ignore the constant distraction provided by his nemesis and his own inner demons and, instead, fall into the rhythm they'd established over the past days, with him helping her manage the horses through the various stages of her assessment.

While watching her work—acidly noting that she seemed to have less trouble ignoring him than he did ignoring her—he spent long minutes considering whether there was any way to speed up the undertaking, only to reluctantly conclude that there was not. He needed her assessments to be accurate—to properly identify the breeding worth of his late father's horses, now his—if he wanted to wring the best possible agreement from the Cynsters or anyone else.

He'd finally come to fully appreciate the bind Fate had landed him in; Prudence Cynster leaving Glengarah without any agreement being struck wouldn't reflect well on the Glengarah horses—wouldn't help him establish any sort of breeding concern to alleviate the drain on the estate the stable had become, much less generate anything like the supportive revenue the kennels already provided.

When the sound of the luncheon gong reached them, she was in the final throes of her examination of only the fourth horse of the day.

And he had accepted that, as she was, apparently, obstinately set on her path, there was absolutely nothing he could do to sway her. More, earl though he was, for some ungodly reason, he was powerless to deny her, to avoid the looming destination on the path she was intent on racing them both down.

She...had it in her to fracture his control. To challenge it and prevail.

Why that was so, he didn't know, but he wanted her with a ferocity he'd felt for no other, and no matter how hard he pretended that wasn't so, she'd already seen enough to feel confident that, if she issued an invitation, he would accept.

And he would. He knew himself well—enough to know that fighting this attraction in the face of her active encouragement would be a complete waste of time. His fall, when it happened, would only be the harder.

And her triumph all the greater, which would make her even more difficult to manage.

No. Given where they now stood—given the gleam in her blue eyes as she waited for him to join her at the entrance to the stable—the only viable option open to him was to fall in by her side and allow her to race them headlong into intimacy.

As he'd informed her, it was her choice to make. And clearly, she'd made it.

All he could do now was go along, keep the reins firmly in his hands, and ensure she didn't run them off some cliff.

As he closed the last yards, he read the question—the personal question—in her eyes. With a dip of his head and an elegant wave toward the house, he gave her his answer. "Shall we?"

Pru couldn't restrain her smile. As she fell into step beside him—Deaglan Fitzgerald, the wicked Earl of Glengarah—a frisson of expectation lanced through her; he'd agreed, and she was finally going to learn everything she'd increasingly wondered about over recent years from a nobleman widely held to be a past master in that sphere.

In terms of finding a partner with whom to explore all the experiences she'd been barred from indulging in courtesy of her unmarried state, she doubted she could have done better.

And it wasn't as if he was truly reluctant; after that scorching exchange the previous night, he could hardly pretend to be uninterested.

Indeed, as he held her chair for her at the luncheon table, then straightened and moved to claim his own, unseen by the others, his fingertips trailed across her nape, eliciting a delicious shiver.

She reached for her water glass and, as he settled in his chair, met his eyes.

He sat back and held her gaze levelly—and she realized he was remembering their recent interlude. Looking into those mesmerizing emerald eyes, she recalled—relived—those moments, too, and it felt as if he'd thrust a flaming brand into their embers and set them smoldering red-hot again.

She had absolutely no doubt of the rightness of her decision. Of her direction.

He wanted her, and she wanted him, and as far as she was concerned, that was all the permission either of them needed.

As the company helped themselves from the platters laid before them, then settled to eat, she retrod the arguments that underpinned her resolution.

She wasn't a young lady; she was twenty-nine years old and, with calculated deliberation and all due consideration, had turned her back on marriage. Marriage would restrict and restrain her; living the rest of her life within the conventional confines society stipulated for ladies of her birth and station wasn't a future she was prepared to accept. Consequently, she'd embraced spinsterhood as her lot.

However, from the time of her first Season—after which she'd decided a conventional life was not for her—she'd longed to explore the pleasures of the flesh without the drawbacks of the wedded state. She was a Cynster, after all, but being female had restricted her opportunities.

Until she'd come to Ireland, to the far west coast—to Glengarah Castle.

Home of the wicked Earl of Glengarah—sinful temptation incarnate.

From the first, she'd seen no reason to resist the temptation he embodied, yet thoughts of unbalancing their business relationship had intruded. But in reality, enjoying a brief liaison with Deaglan Fitzgerald wasn't going to influence either her view of his horses or his demands regarding any breeding arrangement; both would be dictated by the quality of the horses, nothing more. Indeed, from either of their perspectives, the quality of the horses was such that any other outcome was impossible to imagine.

She sliced an apple with her fruit knife. From beneath her lashes, she slanted a glance at Deaglan, who was still consuming slices of roast beef and listening to Jay, on his other side, describe the progress on the bridge that the estate workers were repairing.

For several seconds, she allowed her gaze to rest on Deaglan's face, then returned her attention to the apple. She'd initially been puzzled by his...not reluctance per se but determined resistance, yet now she'd had time to observe him, she'd realized he wasn't all that different from her father, her brothers, or her numerous male cousins.

Toward ladies, he was inherently, innately protective—very much a creature of his time and station. His reputation notwithstanding, he instinctively operated within society's rules, and one of those rules was that a gentleman, especially one of his standing, should not seduce a well-bred young lady residing under his roof.

Of course, the underlying assumption was that the lady was both young and innocent, and she was neither, yet the existence of that rule and his unquestioning adherence to it was what lay behind his attempt of the previous night to send her fleeing; he'd tried to do what he viewed as the honorable thing.

Your choice. He'd told her so, and from his point of view, he'd spoken the absolute, rigid truth. She felt perfectly certain that he wouldn't so much as kiss her again if she didn't make her wishes beyond plain.

Courtesy of her words and actions that morning, he understood that she intended to do so, but she had no doubt that he would push her to make an even more explicit declaration.

And she would. This evening. Once their work with the horses was done for the day, and they were alone.

Until then…

She popped the last piece of apple into her mouth and chewed, increasingly slowly as a corollary of Deaglan being like her father, brothers, and male cousins bloomed in her mind—illuminating a looming danger she hadn't, until that moment, perceived.

She should have; that particular prospect was an outcome she would need to take steps to avoid.

Luckily, that particular hurdle could be overcome easily enough; she would simply have to make matters clear at the outset, before they engaged in any further interaction.

And of course, theirs was destined to be a brief liaison—one with an end date all but predetermined. She would be at Glengarah for at least a week more, possibly ten days, but once they'd defined and reached accord on and signed a breeding agreement, she would return to Newmarket and the Cynster Stables, and he would remain here, managing his estate.

Their liaison would be of limited duration, which, in turn, would reduce the likelihood of any unexpected complications.

"Ready?"

Deaglan's question, in that low, deep voice that set some string inside her thrumming, snapped her out of her planning daze. She looked at him and smiled. "Indeed."

She gave him her hand, allowed him to help her from her chair, then led the way back to the exercise ring.

While she had a horse to concentrate on, she managed well enough to block out the effects of Deaglan's nearness and stop her thoughts flitting down the avenue of what their next engagement would be, thus keeping her unruly senses under some semblance of control.

Yet throughout the gathering in the drawing room, dinner, and the customary sojourn in the library—all of which passed in pleasant and entirely unremarkable amity—her nerves slowly tightened, her senses leapt and sparked ever more sharply, and her breathing grew steadily more restricted until she felt she was on the brink of swooning.

As far as she could, she kept her gaze from Deaglan, yet not even that stopped excitement swelling and expectation welling.

The ratcheting tension had grown well-nigh unbearable when Maude, finally, set aside her embroidery and announced that they should retire.

Pru responded with an anticipatory alacrity she struggled to conceal.

She found Suzie waiting, but dismissed the young maid with a tale of wanting to work on her notes on the horses for an hour or two before seeking her bed. As part of her planning, she'd made sure her gown that evening was one she could remove without assistance, so Suzie wouldn't expect to be summoned later. The instant the door closed behind her maid, Pru laid aside the notes and started pacing, glancing every few turns at the carriage clock sitting on the mantelpiece.

Eventually, in an effort to make the minutes at least appear to tick by more quickly, she returned to her discarded notes and doggedly made a summary of her assessments to that date, then studied the result. "Impressive" was the only appropriate adjective.

She neatened the pile of notes and glanced at the clock. "At last!"

Her heart leapt again. She rose, straightened her gown, then opened her door. She felt as if she was hurrying to join a hunt she expected to be exhilarating as she made her way along the silent wing to the gallery, then went quickly down the main stairs.

All was quiet, all wreathed in shadows.

She hadn't bothered with a lamp—during her excursion the previous night, she'd discovered that the household left lamps burning low at strategic points about the huge house—so when she paused outside the library door, she stood cloaked in shadows. She raised a hand to tap, then realized the door was a fraction ajar. She paused, and the deep rumble of Deaglan's voice reached her, clearly speaking to someone else.

Had Felix, for some ungodly reason, remained behind with Deaglan?

Then she heard Jay say, "I have to own to considerable surprise that the Cynsters sent her, a female, to assess your father's collection. Isn't that an insult of sorts—a slight at the very least?"

Pru's eyes widened as her temper soared, but then Deaglan drily replied, "You wouldn't suggest any such thing if you'd seen her working the horses. She's a natural, and she's an expert."

Pru smiled, and Deaglan went on, "In fact, one could with greater justification say that the implication of the Cynsters sending her instead of anyone else is the very opposite—that the only reason they would allow her to travel all this way is because they'd heard enough of the collection to warrant sending their very best assessor, namely the head of their breeding program."

That was, in essence, correct; if it hadn't been so very important to find fresh, high-quality bloodstock, her parents would have been much less likely to bow to her determination to travel to Glengarah.

"Perhaps," Jay allowed; he sounded unconvinced. "But while she may be an excellent rider, will she be in any position to propose a deal? Or will she return to England and report, and any offer from the Cynsters will come by mail?"

"She is an excellent rider, but that's not why she's the head of what most regard as the premier Thoroughbred breeding program in the British Isles." A certain crispness had crept into Deaglan's tone. "And yes, she is expecting to make an offer once she's finished her assessments, and beyond that, it seems likely we'll come to some mutually beneficial arrangement."

"I see." Jay sounded a touch surprised. After a moment, he went on, "Well, you'll be pleased to have the extra income coming in, no doubt— and I don't suppose any arrangement will change much about the way the stable is run."

Pru inwardly snorted at Jay's naivety; now she'd come to understand how deeply Deaglan's interest in the stable actually ran, she couldn't see him simply allowing the Cynsters to breed from his horses without setting himself up in reciprocal fashion—and that would certainly involve a significantly greater degree of oversight and quite a few changes to the current practices of the Glengarah establishment.

Yet instead of setting his steward straight, she heard Deaglan say, "As we've yet to discuss the details of any arrangement, I really can't say."

"Ah, well. No doubt time will tell. I'll be away to my bed, then—I'll be out to the bridge to check with Joe first thing."

"Good. I'll most likely be in the stable with Miss Cynster should you have need of me."

Pru whisked away from the door, slipping into the denser shadows in the alcove under the stairs. She heard Jay emerge from the library and held her breath as he walked past her, then swung into the corridor leading to the side door.

She listened to his footfalls fade, then distantly heard the side door open and close.

She exhaled, then drew in a determined breath, brought her rehearsed stipulations to the forefront of her mind and fixed them there, then stepped out of the shadows and walked briskly to the library door. She opened it, walked inside, located Deaglan seated behind his desk, then, without taking her gaze from him, shut the door behind her.

His eyes, dark in the lamplight, had fixed on her. The weighty nature of his regard sent a sensuous thrill slithering down her spine.

Moving slowly, he set down the pen he'd been holding and sat back in his chair.

Endeavoring to keep her breathing even and appear unaffected—as if her nerves weren't already taut and her senses dancing with excitement— she crossed toward the desk. When he started to rise, she waved him back, then perched on the arm of one of the chairs facing the desk.

At this point, keeping the width of the desk between them seemed a wise idea. She wanted to make her position plain before he got within arm's reach. Placing her hands in her lap, she locked her eyes on his and, ignoring the vise slowly cinching about her lungs, stated, "Before we embark on further exploration of where our mutual attraction might lead us, I wanted to make a number of points clear."

His eyes searched her face, she sensed with a measure of disbelief. After a moment, he prompted, "Such as?"

"Such as"—she drew in a quick breath—"that we both agree, here and now, that any liaison between us will necessarily be of limited dura- tion." She gestured with one hand. "A few days, perhaps a week, but ulti- mately, only until I leave Glengarah."

His eyes narrowed fractionally. "You mean until we conclude whatever deal we decide on."

She nodded. "Exactly." Before he could say yea or nay, she hurried on, "And from the outset, I want to make it clear that I have absolutely no interest whatsoever in attaining the married state."

No matter how intently she scrutinized his expression, she couldn't read his reaction to that. Compelled to make certain he understood her stance, she added, "To be plain, I do not want you suddenly suffering an attack of conscience and deciding that it's necessary for us—being who we are—to marry in order to protect my name and reputation. You may trust me when I say that my name and reputation will easily weather any whispers that might arise due to a liaison between us."

She couldn't be any more blunt than that.

Leaning back in his chair, Deaglan stared at the confounding female seated before him calmly reciting what conditions applied to him bedding her.

For all his experience, this was a novel occurrence. However, while her words should have had him singing hallelujahs, instead, he felt perversely offended.

And as with so many incidents over the past days, his immediate response to her declaration was a powerful and compelling urge to make her change her mind. Lunacy, in this instance, yet there was no denying she'd just painted herself as a challenge beyond any he'd ever faced...

Good God, what am I thinking?

A willful, obstinate, strong-minded lady was the very last sort of lady he needed as his countess.

She'd keep me on my toes.

Enough! He thrust the strange and disturbing thoughts aside, pushed back his chair, got to his feet, and rounded the desk. He halted by her side; looking down into her upturned face, he arched an interrogatory brow.

She'd tracked his approach; now, she frowned up at him. "What?"

"If you've finished laying down the law...?"

She narrowed her eyes, and her luscious lips thinned, then parted on "I thought—"

He grasped her arms, hiked her up against him, and kissed her ferociously, then broke off to growl against her lips, "Don't think."

It came out as an order, one he subsequently devoted his considerable expertise to ensuring she obeyed.

Pru raised her arms, wrapped them about his neck, and clung as his lips feasted on hers, as his tongue claimed her mouth, provocative and demanding.

As he crushed her body to his, and a firestorm of sensation erupted between them.

Passion's flames engulfed them, setting her flesh burning from the inside out. She sank her fingers into his hair and held him to the kiss—her only anchor in a spinning world.

Thought was far beyond her; whatever reins she might have held had cindered in the conflagration, in the heat that flashed over her skin, then sank deep.

She was caught, beyond fascinated; this was what she'd yearned to explore—this unrestrained plunge into passion and desire.

Her wild self had surfaced and taken over, responding to the moment, to the heat, the sheer excitement, and the unstated challenge. She'd wanted to learn about this side of herself for so long, now the moment was finally here, she flung herself into it with every iota of passion in her soul.

She clenched her fists in his hair, pressed her body to his, and kissed him back, as ravenous as he, as flown on the promise of the flames licking, hungrily, greedily, over her skin.

Flames he stoked, his hands—hard palms and long, strong fingers—sculpting her curves, his touch burning even through the silk of her evening gown and her light stays. One hand drifted lower, over her hip, then he cupped her bottom and molded her hips to his; the evidence of his desire for her pressed against her stomach, an iron rod impossible to mistake.

The kiss turned voracious, a melding of lips that was all hunger and need.

Her wits spun under the twin onslaughts of his passion and her own desperate wanting.

Abruptly, he broke the kiss. His darkened eyes stared into hers, then he grated, "Upstairs. Now."

One of his hands engulfed one of hers, and he led her—towed her—to the door, and dazed, she followed, her head whirling, her breathing shallow, her wits flown.

He drew her down the short corridor to the front hall and the bottom of the stairs; when she tried to step up and half tripped, he swore beneath his breath, then bent and hoisted her into his arms.

Grateful, she latched her arms about his neck as he carried her swiftly up the long flight, then strode through the gallery and on down the west wing.

He paused outside her door, let her legs swing down, then opened the door and guided her before him over the threshold and inside. She'd left the lamp burning on the table by the window; the soft illumination spread through the room. She heard the door snick behind him as she turned to face him.

His gaze, intent as any predator's, locked on her face. He hesitated, then, in a low, grating growl, murmured, "Last chance."

She blinked at him...then his meaning registered, and impatience and temper spiked. Instead of stepping back and bidding him leave, she held his gaze and stepped into him as she reached to frame his face, then she stretched up and pressed her lips to his, and blatantly, with flagrant demand, invited his conquest.

A conquest impossible to resist.

That was how Deaglan saw her. The taste of her was intoxicating, the feel of her beneath his hands a lure he found utterly irresistible. Kissing her—being kissed by her, the give and take, the inevitable dueling of their tongues—filled his mind, set his desire alight, and actively stoked his passions.

He couldn't get enough of her; novice though she was, her willful enthusiasm was nectar to his baser needs. She was no bored matron, no courtesan; she was a lady of independent mind and will who had decided on this—who wanted him to show her all he knew and was making her wishes blatantly obvious in every possible way.

At one point, she nipped his lower lip and made him growl. Her fractured breathing as he responded by trailing kisses down the delicate column of her throat was music to his ears.

He was in no hurry, and for a wonder, neither was she, content, it seemed, to follow where he led at whatever pace he chose to set.

He chose slow. He chose intense. From experience, he knew it was possible to achieve both simultaneously. Not easy, but worth every tithe of the effort, and with her, he knew she would repay that effort tenfold.

Keeping her trapped in the moment, weaving a cage of sensation for her wits, he peeled her clothes from her, baring her inch by delectable inch. Worshipping each curve and hollow revealed with his fingertips, with his lips, with his tongue. Tasting her, inhaling the perfume that rose from her heating skin, gorging himself on the bounty she offered—missing nothing, claiming all, devouring.

By the time the laces of her stays unraveled beneath his expert fingers, he'd waltzed them to the side of the bed. He drew the lightly boned garment from her and let it fall to the floor, leaving her body screened only by her fine silk chemise and drawers and even finer silk stockings. Those he left for now.

Silk of that quality was a useful erotic aid. He let the fabric shift and slide between her even-smoother skin and his rougher hands, a tantalizing, teasing tactile caress that built expectation, ratcheting her nerves—and his—tighter. Tauter.

Plumping one of her pert breasts in his hand, he bent his head and pressed heated, open-mouthed kisses over the firm mound, then, through the silk, licked the tip, bringing a soft moan purling from her throat. His lips curved in wicked expectation, then he closed them over the dampened fabric, over the tight bud of her nipple, and sucked lightly.

Her fingers spasmed on his head. He suckled harder, then licked and laved, before turning his attention to her other breast and repeating the exercise until she was panting, eager and wanton and tense as a bowstring, his for the taking.

Then her breasts swelled as she drew in a massive breath. And she steadied, drew her hands from his hair, and reached for his cravat.

He was so surprised that she remained capable of independent thought and action that he let her unravel the simple knot, then she fell on the buttons of his waistcoat and, seconds later, his shirt. The press of her hands on his chest, screened only by the layer of fine linen, jolted him into action of his own. Into more definitely scripting what should come next. He shrugged out of his coat and let it fall, eliciting a purring sound of approval. His waistcoat went the same way, then she slipped the last button on his shirt free and hauled the halves wide, revealing his chest to her hot, hungry gaze.

He felt her survey like a wash of flame, seized the second to drink in the raw need, the flagrant desire etched in her face, then he caught her arms and pulled her to him and crushed her lips beneath his.

And felt her palms connect with his bare skin.

Pru had never felt compulsion like this. If this was desire, if this was passion, she now understood why ladies lost their heads in pursuit of such glory. Not that she'd attained the glory yet—no, that was still to come, and she was even more committed than she had been an hour earlier to sampling and savoring every single sensation all the way to that end.

She wanted it all, and she wanted it now. Yet if the maelstrom of their kiss was any indication, he had his own agenda, and novice that she was in this sphere, she couldn't judge whether she wanted to push ahead faster or not.

She couldn't decide whether she wanted to usurp the reins or, instead, trust in his skills...

No question—not really; she gave up all resistance and, instead, devoted herself to following his lead and feasting her senses and mind to the full on each and every highlight along the path down which he steered them with unhurried, almost languid confidence.

Freed by her own decision of all need to direct, she let her senses bloom fully, let them and all they absorbed dominate her mind and sweep her ever deeper into a sensual sea.

One he navigated with experienced insight. Her breasts ached—a sweet ache he knew how to assuage. Her skin was alive as it had never been before, nerves awake to each and every touch, every caress, every shift in pressure, every wash of heat elicited by his knowing hands and fingers. Need stalked her nerves, desire burned in her veins, and passion grew to a pounding tumult in her heart.

She was breathless, hungry in a hollow, yearning way she'd never felt before, and more than ready for whatever came next when he tumbled her onto the bed. She landed on her back, and he dropped down beside her, propping on shoulder and hip as he leaned over her and slowly, languorously, and very thoroughly kissed her, sending her wits waltzing again.

Then he broke the kiss and shifted back, swung around, and sat on the edge of the mattress.

She raised heavy lids to watch him, realizing from his movements and the dull thuds that reached her that he was dispensing with his shoes and stripping off his stockings. He'd already tossed aside his shirt, and the lamplight played lovingly over the sleekly powerful muscles of his shoulders and back. He reminded her forcefully of a fine Thoroughbred—built for performance.

Her lips curved at the thought, then he rose, glanced her way, then caught her gaze and held it as his hands went to his waist, and his fingers dealt with the buttons there. Then he dropped his trousers and stepped free of them—and although she had to wrench her gaze from his, she couldn't not look.

She felt her smile fade and her eyes widen as she took in the reality of what she'd earlier felt. The long, lean lines of his hips, flanks, and thighs only made the prominent jut of his erection, its thickness and wide engorged head, all the more notable. Noticeable, too.

An "oh" formed in her mind, but then he crawled back onto the bed, interrupting her view.

"You're not supposed to think," he reminded her, amusement threading through his voice.

On the words, he settled on his knees at her feet and, leaning forward, ran a hand up her leg, over the silk of her stocking, to the garter above her knee. Then he ran his warm, hard hand down again, all the way to her toes. She'd stepped out of her slippers along with her evening gown; aside from the stockings, her feet were bare. His hand cupped the arch of her foot; she registered it as a curiously possessive gesture.

He sent his hand, warm and slow, over her foot, over her ankle, tracing, languid yet sure, upward again.

She blinked and realized that, far from thinking, she'd even stopped breathing as she watched him prop on one braced arm and lean over her, following the glide of his hand over her knee and up her thigh to her garter—and just above.

Then he bent his head and set his lips to the bare skin above the lacy garter.

She sucked in a breath. Her lids fell as the brush of his lips over her sensitive skin impinged on her mind. Then she felt his fingertips hook into the garter, and slowly—achingly slowly—he drew garter and stocking down and followed the path revealed with his lips, brushing, caressing, learning.

By the time he'd bared her other leg in the same, slow, thorough fashion, she was panting, restless and shifting, eager and needy; that hunger for what she couldn't name had expanded and now commanded her wits, her will, her entire awareness.

She reached for him, fingertips sinking into heavy muscle as he raised his head, and she arched up and pressed her lips to his and poured all she felt—all she wanted—into the kiss.

Show me, show me, show me.

She hadn't thought she'd said the pleading words aloud, but in a gasping gap between scorching kisses, he growled, "Soon."

Soon couldn't come quickly enough.

She gave up using words and, instead, communicated her impatience, her flaring need and wanton demands, via her hands, her lips, and her tongue, then she realized she could use her body to caress his—most effectively.

In the heated haze of the ensuing engagement—with him directing and her whipping them both on—he stripped her drawers from her, wedged one hard thigh between hers, then, lazy and yet intent, he stroked the inside of her thighs until she was well-nigh mindless, and at last, he touched her where she longed to be touched. He found her entrance, parted folds already slick, circled and caressed, then finally sank one long finger deep into her body.

Her senses sparked and bucked and reared—she caught a glimpse of glory before her world steadied again. Only to find her awareness dominated by the feel of his finger sliding, probing, then withdrawing and returning to a rhythm she recognized as a prelude of that yet to come.

Instead of relaxing her in any way whatever, the knowledge only spurred her impatience, only stoked the heated lustful pressure that was pushing her on and gave it teeth.

Beneath him, against him, she writhed and invited—nay, demanded and commanded—until, on a muffled curse, he drew his hand from between her thighs and wrestled her from her chemise.

At the first instant of body-to-body contact, naked skin to naked skin, she lost her breath entirely, and her head spun. It continued spinning as his hands roved her body, claiming, possessing, ardently stoking her passions and his to fresh heights.

Yet despite the whirlpool of sensations he created and set whirling so powerfully, trapping them both, he remained always there, her anchor in this particular storm. With his lips on hers still voracious, his hands gripping her curves possessively, he drew her beneath him and sent expectation—hers and his—soaring.

Then he rolled, taking her with him, lifting her to straddle him as he settled on his back.

When, surprised, she blinked her eyes open and stared at him, he arched one maddening black eyebrow. "You're an expert rider, or so I've been told."

Through the heat surging within her, fed by the flames his hands, constantly stroking over her skin, provoked, she managed—she had no idea how—to raise a challenging eyebrow back. He'd set her over his thighs. Boldly, she reached for his erection, wrapped the fingers of one hand about the hard, hot length—and paused to savor the dichotomy of such satin-soft skin stretched over burning iron.

Her gaze was drawn to the prize she held, the broad head, the thickly veined shaft. She would have liked to spend more time admiring it appropriately—and putting into practice some of the whispers she'd heard—but the pounding in her blood all but shouted: *Later*.

Surrendering to that drumbeat in her veins, she shifted forward—just as he reached between her thighs and touched her. Her senses flared, expanding, and she realized that, behind his languid sophistication, he was as tense as she, his nerves as taut as hers.

His need every bit as urgent as hers.

He helped her guide the broad head of his erection to her entrance; the instant she sank just a little way down, his hands shifted to close about her hips.

When she met his eyes, she could see fire burning hotly in the emerald depths.

"At your pleasure," he murmured, and while there was both challenge and understanding in the gravel of his voice, nothing could dim the heat of the passion in his eyes.

She caught her breath and slid down a little farther, only to find her senses turning inward, focusing on the utterly indescribable sensation of the intrusion of his body into hers, of the easing of her inner muscles and the slickness of her sheath as she edged lower. Then she sucked in a breath and sank lower still.

Sensing the resistance of her maidenhead, she caught her lower lip between her teeth, gathered herself, and pressed down—all the way.

The expected yet sudden rupture sent pain the equivalent of a sharp pinch lancing through her—all but gone in the time it took her to register it. In the next instant, her senses were swamped, overcome, overwhelmed by the feel of him buried inside her, the tensing grip of his fingers about her hips, the flaring tension in the body between her thighs, the tightening of already rock-hard muscles beneath her hands.

Deaglan damned near lost his mind in the instant she engulfed him completely. Her sheath all but scalded him, and in instinctive reaction to the inevitable pain, her until-now untried inner muscles had clamped around him. *Tight* around him. That his eyes didn't cross was a wonder.

Before he could even think to move—or to urge her to do so—she shifted. Experimentally. Enough to force him to battle a powerful urge to

thrust up into her. He'd decided—he didn't have the wits to wonder why
—that it was important she take the lead at this point, so he gritted his
teeth, held onto his libido with both hands, and waited.

Luckily, as he'd remarked, she was, indeed, an excellent rider. She
needed no instruction in how to rise up, then sink down. In less than a
minute, she'd set a pace that was demanding enough—consuming enough
—to capture his entire awareness. Given his experience, that was no
minor feat.

Her legs and thighs were supple and strong, her body lithe and limber.
Backlit by the lamplight, like a goddess spun from moonbeams and
crowned with gold, she rode him, increasingly unrestrained, with joy and
abandon etched in her face as she tipped her head up and gave herself
wholly to the moment.

To him.

He didn't have wits available to wonder if she realized that, if she
even thought in such ways. Yet through the mounting pleasure, through
the escalating rhythm and the pounding beat, through the rising tension
that unrelentingly gripped them both, he—expert that he was—noticed
that occasionally her lids would rise enough for her to study him, and
then she would shift and clench those powerful inner muscles of hers and
take delight in the wave of pleasure that swept across his features.

She was open, direct, and honest in her passion, wild and true to her
own nature, and instinctively sharing.

She was...eye-opening to him, he who had bedded more women than
he could count over the past two decades.

He'd joined her in her ride long since, thrusting up to meet her down-
ward plunge, heightening the pleasure for them both and driving her
ever on.

Their gazes met and held, then pleasure broke over them and the
connection shattered, only to catch again, hold again, a minute later.

Her body moved relentlessly, tirelessly, between his hands, her
plunging rhythm a compulsive beat, one that echoed in his loins, in
his heart.

One that called to him as inescapably as she had from the first.

He sensed her nearing the inevitable peak. Selecting the route that, to
his mind, was most certain to deliver the experience he wanted her to
have for her first time, he half rose, shifting her on him as he leaned
forward and took one tightly budded nipple into his mouth and suckled
hard.

Her head fell back, and she gasped, then a soft keening cry spilled from her lips as she shattered in his arms.

Pru had thought she'd known, but she hadn't—the explosion of sensation as her tension spiked and, like an overtightened spring, shattered and flew apart was so intense it blinded her as it rolled through her mind in a brilliant white wave of scintillating pleasure.

For a moment, she hung in that golden place, outside reality, and drank in the glory.

Small wonder it was addictive.

Even as her senses and wits slowly returned her to physical awareness, she felt Deaglan's arms around her, then he rolled, and she found herself on her back beneath him.

She blinked up at his face, shadowed now; the lamp was burning lower and lower. Yet the fires in his eyes still burned, if anything even hotter, more intense, than before.

Then he shifted, and she realized he hadn't yet gained his release.

Her body was humming, awash with pleasure, yet very ready to take him on—to see this engagement through to the end. She let her swollen lips curve, slid her hands—slowly—up his chest to slide her fingers into his hair and grip. Her gaze locked with his, she moistened her lips, then stretched up to touch them to his, murmuring at the very last second, "Your turn, my lord earl."

He huffed out a laugh against her lips, but it was a sound laden with tension. Then he angled his head and claimed her mouth anew—and let the fire in him free.

He rode her then, in a fast, forceful, driving rhythm that, somewhat to her surprise, caught her up, and then she was racing with him. The crinkly black hair that adorned his chest abraded her nipples, and the rhythmic movement of him over and around her and so powerfully inside her strung her nerves tight until her senses screamed for release.

Riding hard, pushing harder still, they strove for the pinnacle she'd earlier reached.

They raced on, desire a whip that drove them both, passion a raging compulsion in their veins.

The thud of their hearts was deafening, their need all-consuming.

In a wild, breathless, gasping rush, they crested the peak and raced on —straight on into another, even more potent explosion of the senses that ripped her awareness from this world.

Ecstasy blazed through her, far, far brighter and more intense than before. The glory returned, deeper, more profound, and wrapped about her.

Pleasure rolled through her, a wave even greater, even more powerful than before; effortlessly, it swamped her and dragged her under. Through the golden haze, she felt Deaglan stiffen in her arms, registered his muffled groan, then, as if every steely muscle had turned to jelly, he slumped upon her. Instinctively, she tightened her arms about him and held him as, together, they drifted in the peace of that golden oblivion.

A smile on her lips, she felt satisfaction coursing beneath the pleasure. She'd wanted to know, to experience it all, and she'd got her wish. Lids too weighty to lift, she stroked his back in gratitude, in simple thanks, then surrendered to the tug and slid into exhausted slumber.

Deaglan finally caught his breath, finally marshaled enough strength to disengage and lift from her. He slumped beside her; with his face half buried in the pillow, he opened one eye and looked at her.

She slept on, oblivious of the puzzle she'd become.

He breathed in more deeply and tried to find his mental feet. Tried to work out what had happened—what had made this time, of so very many times, so intrinsically different.

Admittedly, it had been over eighteen months since he'd bedded any woman, but he couldn't make himself believe that abstinence explained... her. Her and him, and what had just occurred.

He let his gaze rove her face, his attention lingering on those luscious lips. Lips he wanted to possess, even now.

He frowned and tried to gather his wits, but they remained unresponsive, interested only in dwelling on all that had transpired over the past half hour.

With the warmth of her within arm's reach, he wasn't up to the challenge of finding a logical answer to the question she and the events of the night posed, yet the weight of his extensive experience wouldn't let him shrug the encounter aside.

It had been...special.

Extraordinary and compelling—even addictive—and that to him, who had long grown jaded with the activity.

He would have to work out why bedding her had so snared him and decide what, if anything, that meant. For him and for her.

Luckily, given she'd been a virgin—and judging by her reactions, no man had ever even touched her before—she would have nothing against which to measure their...more intense, more senses-stealing, more elementally gripping intimacy.

An intimacy that had felt infinitely more intimate than any he'd experienced before.

He would have to work out the reason why, but he wasn't going to do so tonight.

Accepting that, he closed his eyes and let sleep take him.

He slid from the warmth of her arms and left her sleeping.

He paused for a moment to study her face, then turned and silently collected his clothes. He laid them on the end of the bed; his gaze rested on her features while he dressed. He pulled up his trousers, buttoned the flap, then shrugged on his shirt, leaving it open. Coat, waistcoat, and cravat he bundled beneath his arm, then bent and picked up his shoes and discarded stockings.

Dawn had yet to break; it was too early for any staff to be about. No one would see him walking to his apartment at the far end of the house. Luckily, Felix, Maude, and Cicely had rooms in the central, family wing; he wouldn't pass their doors on the way.

Still, he lingered, studying the woman who had come alive in his arms, who had writhed beneath him, openly wanton, unrestrained in her passion. Softened by sleep, her delicate features gave no hint of the vibrancy, the sheer verve and delight in life that dwelled inside her. Her fearlessness, her fervor, her energy, and her unabashed enthusiasm were so very different to any woman he'd encountered before.

Her passion was a roaring blaze compared to the small fires he'd known.

In that, she matched him far more closely than any other woman ever had.

He stood for long minutes looking down at her as the realization sank in that, despite her willfulness, her strong-mindedness, her independent thinking—despite even her obstinacy—she was the only lady he'd ever wanted to spend not just nights with, but days.

Even days without number.

How long he stood staring at her—at what he was beginning to recognize as his fate—he didn't know, but eventually, he turned, padded across the room, and slipped silently out of the door.

CHAPTER 8

$\mathcal{D}$eaglan took his time over breakfast, waiting to see if Pru would appear. After such an energetic night, most ladies of his acquaintance would sleep late, often not emerging until the early afternoon.

He seriously doubted Pru would follow her more sophisticated sisters' path, yet if she'd woken and rethought her direction, she might opt for a tray in her room in order to avoid him, at least for a time.

He wouldn't have wagered either way, yet when, just a few minutes past her customary time, he heard her footsteps approaching and registered the swift, swinging pace, he couldn't own to any real surprise.

She breezed into the parlor, a bright, sunny smile on her lips. She beamed at him and Felix. "Good morning."

Deaglan nodded an appreciative welcome—which she acknowledged with an even brighter, near-incandescent smile.

Felix blinked, then stared.

Pru busied herself at the sideboard, then came to the table. Deaglan rose and held her chair for her, then returned to his own.

Her smile still in place—she seemed unable to stop smiling, which had him battling a smug, too-revealing grin—she informed Felix, "I summarized my findings last night, and I can't wait to do the rest of the assessments, especially as we're now moving into the even more high-quality horses."

"Ah." Felix nodded, as if accepting that as the reason for her brightness. But as she looked down and buttered her toast, he slid an alarmed glance at Deaglan.

Having expected the look, Deaglan met it with a cool authority that stated very clearly that whatever was going on was not Felix's concern.

While Felix didn't look convinced, he desisted.

For several minutes, the three of them sipped and ate in peace.

Deaglan waited with unfeigned patience. He'd slept for another hour in his own bed and woken refreshed—and with an altogether unexpected understanding clear in his head. He'd been a touch rattled at first; he'd poked at the inescapable conclusion, trying to dislodge it or see a way around it. Finally, he'd realized his heart wasn't in it—that the only reason he was resisting was because he hadn't seen it coming.

He'd had no idea such a situation might blindside him, as it had.

Luckily, it was transparently obvious that his nemesis—she sent by Fate to bring him to bended knee—had enjoyed her leap into intimacy with him and was planning no hasty departure.

He'd already given some thought to his necessary campaign. He knew women well enough to appreciate that leading Pru to think that changing her mind about her desired end to their liaison was her idea rather than his would be his best route to success. To achieving the end result he now wanted.

Such a path would require a subtle hand; he would need to lay the prospect before her without in any way pleading his cause.

Begging for her hand would cede all power to her, and he was constitutionally incapable of going down that road.

Of course, if she dug in her heels, he would fight for what he wanted —her hand in his for all time. But there were ways of fighting for a lady that didn't involve weapons or words, and he knew them all.

After cleaning her plate and finishing her toast, she picked up her teacup, sipped, and met his eyes. "Will you be about to assist in the stable today?"

A straightforward question with another underneath; she knew how she felt about the past night, but she couldn't be certain about his reaction —about his willingness to continue their liaison.

He smiled and let her read his answer in his eyes. "I wouldn't miss it." He let a heartbeat pass, then added for their audience, "As you say, the quality of the horses yet to come is greater than those you've already examined. I'm keen to see how you rate them."

She set down her cup, her smile more confident. "In that case, shall we make a start?"

He rose and drew out her chair.

Felix rose, too, and followed them out. "I'll come and watch for a while, then do a round of the kennels."

Pru bestowed a smile on Felix, but it wasn't the same smile—the one with a personal, private warmth—with which she'd gifted Deaglan. Content—more so than he'd felt for quite a while—he held the side door open and followed her into the side court.

He might have limited time in which to change her mind, but when it came to turning a lady's head, he had all the experience in the world.

The following day was Sunday. Pru had spent most of Saturday in pleasant company doing pleasant things. More, while working with the horses side by side with Deaglan, she'd discovered that her senses, while still leaping and reacting to the inevitable touches and brushes, no longer built her inner tension to distracting heights; instead, those touches warmed her with an anticipation all the more comforting in that she'd had every expectation of said anticipation being admirably satisfied come the night.

As indeed, it had been. After the rest of the household had retired, Deaglan had come to her room—to her arms, to her bed, to her body.

The confirmation of the previous night's rapture had been nothing short of delicious; he'd made it so.

She'd woken that morning to find him gone again, but she'd joined him and the rest of the family about the breakfast table, after which they'd attended Sunday service in the castle chapel, along with about half the staff and several local families who drove in to join the small congregation.

She'd forgotten that most of Ireland remained Catholic; the Fitzgeralds, however, were staunchly Church of England, as were most of the higher-ranking families. The social exchanges after the conclusion of the service had given her an abbreviated view into the local Anglican community.

Now, however, after changing their church clothes for riding attire, she and Deaglan were heading for the stable; he'd suggested using the hour before luncheon to take two of the horses she wanted to trial out for a short ride.

As she walked beside Deaglan, she was conscious of a spring in her step, an eagerness to engage with her day beyond anything she normally felt.

Clearly, instigating a liaison with him had been a wise and sensible move; she was learning things about herself she would never otherwise have known.

Deaglan eyed Pru sidelong and fought to hide a self-satisfied smile. To his eyes, she'd become increasingly easy to read, he suspected because, due to their intimacy, between them, she'd dropped her shields. Throughout yesterday and all through the night, he'd played to her expectations—to her script—allowing her as much leeway as he could to lead, as much freedom as he could convince his own naturally dominant nature to allow her.

Somewhat to his surprise, his nature had, more or less, fallen into line; all in a good cause was, apparently, a sufficient reason to play by her rules —for now.

The relaxed and buoyant mood she was transparently enjoying as a result was a step in the direction he wished her to take.

Letting her ride out with him, ostensibly to test two horses, was another element in his campaign. The more joy and pleasure she found in his company, the easier his task would be.

They'd crossed the side court and were nearing the stable arch when the rattle of carriage wheels approaching along the drive reached them. Deaglan swallowed a sigh and halted.

Pru halted, too, and met his eyes. "Do you have any idea who that might be?"

He shook his head. "But it will, most likely, be someone after me—or at least someone for whose arrival I should be present."

She smiled easily and touched his arm. "Let's go and look—it might not take long."

Unspeakably glad that she hadn't suggested going riding alone, with him to follow if he could—a plan he would have had to veto, forcefully if necessary—he nodded, and they set off to circle the castle to reach the front door.

They'd just gained the porch when a heavy, rather ancient traveling carriage came swaying around the last bend in the drive.

Deaglan took in the sight and groaned—feelingly.

Pru glanced at him. "Who is it?"

"Aunt Esmerelda—my mother's older sister. She drops in every now and then—always out of the blue. She, Maude, and Patrick are old friends, but while Patrick and Maude are, as you've discovered, undemanding, Esmerelda is a meddling busybody." And given the present situation vis-à-vis him and Pru, a visit from Esmerelda might well transform into his worst nightmare.

The carriage rocked to a halt at the base of the steps. Henry the footman had already been dispatched by Bligh to open the carriage door, which Henry did with all due aplomb.

Deaglan watched his aunt—who in his mind was rapidly attaining the status of a harbinger of doom—descend from the carriage.

Beside him, Pru sucked in a breath. "Your aunt is Lady Connaught?"

He glanced at Pru. "Yes." Another level of horror loomed. "Do you know her?"

"Not personally." Pru's tone had lost all hint of the relaxed and buoyant. "But we have met. Her ladyship moves in the same rather rarefied circles as my mother and aunts."

He inferred that fact presaged the obvious danger. "She usually only stays for a few days—a week at most. We'll just have to be careful."

He touched her back, a signal for her to follow, then went down the steps to greet his aunt—who had already spotted them and was blatantly staring.

Just as Pru had recognized Esmerelda on sight, Esmerelda had recognized her.

"Deaglan, my boy!" Bluff and hearty, Esmerelda was slightly deaf, so tended to boom. She finally dragged her gaze from Pru and smiled up at him. "You look to be in excellent health."

"As do you, Aunt." Deaglan bent to dutifully buss Esmerelda's lined cheek. "I trust the crossing was calm?"

Esmerelda waved. "Calm enough." Her gaze returned to Pru as Pru halted at the bottom of the steps, a few feet away. Esmerelda opened her mouth.

Smoothly, Deaglan stated, "Allow me to present Miss Prudence Cynster, with whom I understand you're already acquainted. Miss Cynster is here to look over the pater's horses with a view to a possible breeding arrangement between Glengarah and the Cynster Stables."

A smile as urbanely polished as Deaglan's on her lips, Pru curtsied, then stepped forward and took the hand Esmerelda held out. "It's a plea-sure to see you again, ma'am."

"A pleasure to see you, too, Miss Cynster. Have you been here long?"

"Not quite a week, ma'am. Lord Glengarah's collection is extensive, and our assessments of quality take time."

"I see." Esmerelda turned her sharp hazel gaze on Deaglan. "So! Finally taken the plunge, have you?"

Deaglan froze. How much had the old besom already deduced?

Esmerelda waved a nonchalant hand. "I always knew you harbored hopes of setting up the stable as you have the kennels. Your father was ridiculously shortsighted in opposing your ideas. I'm glad to see you haven't given up on them."

Deaglan shared a glance with Pru and breathed again. He offered Esmerelda his arm. "Indeed. But do come inside, Aunt. Maude will be happy to see you, and Patrick as well. Cicely, Maude's niece by marriage, is here, too, keeping Maude company."

"Is she, by God! Hmm." Esmerelda gripped his arm and, leaning heavily upon it, climbed the steps.

Pru fell in on Esmerelda's other side.

Deaglan saw Esmerelda shoot Pru a look every bit as assessing as any Pru had directed at his horses. "So, miss. What does assessing the quality of horses entail?"

Pru explained in simple terms while they escorted Esmerelda into the drawing room. As he settled his aunt in an armchair by the fire, Deaglan reflected that there would be no more comfortable evenings in the library; Esmerelda was a stickler for proper form.

Hurrying footsteps heralded Maude and Cicely. Maude greeted her sister-in-law with affection, which was clearly returned, then introduced Cicely, who demurely bobbed and uttered the usual phrases.

Even though less than an hour remained until lunchtime, tea was called for to revive Esmerelda; Deaglan often thought older ladies' liking for tea at any hour was more to give them some ostensible purpose while they sat and gossiped.

Certainly, that was Maude and Esmerelda's intention. Although they shared a bored glance, neither Pru nor Deaglan was unwise enough to attempt to slip away.

Then Felix arrived, having no doubt been advised by Bligh of her ladyship's arrival.

As Felix was something of a favorite of Esmerelda's, that eased the attention on Deaglan somewhat. He sat quietly and watched and listened. As he'd expected, it wasn't long before Esmerelda turned her eagle eyes back on Pru.

"I have to own, Miss Cynster, that I'm not as surprised as I might have been to see you here, without one of your brothers or relatives for company. I understand you spent some months last year jauntering about Scotland in similar unattended fashion. I gathered from your grandmother that that trip concerned horses as well."

Deaglan looked at Pru. That was more than she'd revealed thus far; would she say more?

But Pru was made of sterner stuff. She merely smiled and replied, "I'm often required to travel far afield to assess the horses we consider for our program."

"Well." Esmerelda set her cup on her saucer. "Given your age and that you have so determinedly turned your back on the marriage mart, I suppose that at least keeps you busy."

Deaglan managed not to react, not to reveal his interest in any way, but he was starting to wonder at whom Esmerelda was directing her comments—at Pru or at him.

Esmerelda continued, "That said, few spinsters in the ton, however old, could get away with active involvement in, of all things, horse breeding. Then again"—Esmerelda made a moue and shrugged—"you are a Cynster, after all. I suppose it's to be expected."

Naturally enough, Pru ventured nothing in response.

That, of course, was by no means the end of his outrageous relative's interrogation of their principal guest. Pru's presence was far too interesting for Esmerelda to let it pass unremarked; as she continued to hold forth about the ton and members of Pru's family, Deaglan was almost thankful that, for once, it wasn't him in his aunt's sights.

Unfortunately, that was Pru, the lady he wished to persuade to be his countess; he didn't want her put off the idea because of Esmerelda.

But his unknowing intended coped quite well, deflecting Esmerelda's too-pointed questions with ease, answering only those she considered safe, and doing so with a completeness that ate up the time.

A shrewd tactic; Deaglan committed it to memory, even as he listened to the comments Esmerelda drew from Pru on topics he hadn't thought to address.

For quite the first time in his life, he had to wonder if Esmerelda's arrival might be to his advantage. She would be overjoyed at the notion of him taking Pru as his countess. Who knew? In this instance, Esmerelda might even be of help.

Pru was exceedingly well versed in dealing with the likes of Lady Connaught, but given what she presently had at stake, she took care to keep her guard high.

A part of that was keeping her gaze from Deaglan; their earlier shared glances had been mistakes—errors of judgment—but as far as Pru could detect, her ladyship hadn't noticed. Certainly, she'd given no sign of suspecting the existence of any close connection between Pru and Deaglan—the connection they both wished to keep secret.

Despite Lady Connaught's inquisition—nothing out of the ordinary compared to what Pru regularly faced from the likes of Lady Osbaldestone and other grandes dames of the ton—Pru held her own, and when the luncheon gong sounded and they all rose and, in a loose group, headed for the dining room, she fell in behind her ladyship and, under cover of Maude and Lady Connaught's ongoing discussion, managed to safely share a wryly amused smile with Deaglan.

Deaglan sat his aunt on his left and installed Pru in her customary place on his right. As the meal progressed, he noted Pru's awareness remained fixed in large part on his aunt; it was a watchful stance that, at least to him, signaled that she was ready to deflect and defend.

He considered her absorption and decided that, all in all, given the situation between him and her, her being distracted by Esmerelda was no bad thing—not if it meant that Pru had less of her mind free to see through and armor herself against him.

After luncheon, Pru and Deaglan finally managed to get away on their ride. Pru chose two of the stallions for which she'd already completed her ring-based assessments.

When, as they waited for the grooms to fetch and saddle the horses, Deaglan asked how riding a particular horse informed her evaluation, she explained, "I don't need to ride most horses to complete a full assessment, but particularly with stallions, I can gauge their strength and most especially their temperament much more effectively when on their backs. It's a final confirmation that I prefer to do. In part, it protects us, the Cynsters, from introducing a stallion that might not have the right temperament for breeding useful horses for training on the track, but conversely, it also protects the owner—you, in this instance—as well. If I've ridden a stal-lion and had no hint of underlying temperament difficulties, then there's no impediment to the horse being a breeder and commanding a high fee at stud."

Deaglan held her gaze for several seconds, then asked, "Are you sure you don't want to ride all the stallions here?"

She laughed. "No—no need. From working with them in the ring, I can tell which horses are canny enough to hide a nasty temper. Those are the ones I need to ride, and all in all, the riding caveat, as it were, applies to only a few of your stallions thus far."

"Good to know."

The grooms led out the horses—the first, a strong black she would swear was a near-descendant of the Darley Arabian, and the other, a powerfully built, muddy-brown stallion she was certain was a direct descendant of D'Arcy's White Turk. She'd asked for her saddle to be put on the black. Deaglan wanted to ride out to a small school that was part of the estate and examine the building. Once there, he would switch the saddles, and she would ride the brown stallion back.

After lifting her to her saddle—creating a moment when, with his hands firm about her waist, she looked into his eyes and saw heat spark and smiled in secretive delight—he swung up to the back of the brown and gathered his reins. "Ready?"

She nodded and followed him out of the stable yard.

They turned northward. As soon as they were free of the cobbles, Deaglan urged the brown to a canter, and she drew alongside. The black moved fluidly beneath her, responding smoothly and, if anything, eagerly to her directions.

They were soon crossing the fields. With the wind of their passing ruffling her curls, she tipped up her face and breathed in, and a corner of her heart started to sing. How she loved this—riding a powerful horse over lush green, with good company by her side, and sunshine a pale wash about them. The air was fresh and clear, with the breeze carrying a tinge of moisture and the faint tang that reminded her the sea wasn't that far away.

Normally while doing an assessment far from home, she would have worked through at least Sunday afternoon to finish the task sooner, but here, now, she was content to do nothing more than verify the tempera-ments of the two stallions and otherwise enjoy the day.

She slanted a glance at Deaglan. His attention was focused ahead; she smiled to herself and faced forward, too.

Truth be told, she had no intention of rushing to reach the end of what, by anyone's gauge, was a major undertaking; assessing fifty-two horses at once was an eye-opening feat. As she'd told Deaglan, she was not in the habit of making her final decisions on assessments hastily, without due consideration and study; in that, she'd spoken the unvarnished truth, as witnessed by her present occupation. She wouldn't judge a horse as worthy of her program's time without being convinced beyond question of that horse's quality.

And now, of course, there was also the fact that she was enjoying their liaison far too much to bring it to an unnecessarily early end.

She was, therefore, happy to simply look about her and enjoy the day. Smiling to herself, she urged the black to a slightly faster pace as Deaglan led the way on.

Deaglan held to a canter; as they climbed the gentle rise of the fields, he caught Pru's eye and nodded to the escarpment rising sharply a little way ahead. "That's Kings Mountain."

She looked, then nodded back.

A little later, when they reached a grassy plateau of sorts, he slowed the brown and, when Pru came alongside, pointed to the steely glimmer of water to the southeast. "That's Glencar Lough."

She raised a hand to shade her eyes. "The river that runs along your southern boundary—does it come from the lough?"

"Yes. That's the Drumcliff River." He paused then added, "There's a waterfall toward the eastern end of the lake that's quite pretty. If you have time later, perhaps we can ride over one day."

"Hmm." She lowered her hand. "Does the estate have fields bordering the lake?"

"A few. We use them as summer meadows for the cattle."

He touched his heels to the brown's sides, and they rode on.

This excursion was part of his campaign to plant the notion of becoming his countess in her mind. The more he considered the prospect and the more time they spent together, the more convinced he grew that, strange though in some ways it seemed, she was, indeed, the lady he needed by his side.

He'd wanted to start to show her his lands—the enterprise that commanded most of his time. The estate and its demands formed and always would form a large part of the reality of his life, and that would extend to the life of his wife. Looking forward, their lives would not be the oft-envisioned pampered social life of wealthy aristocrats, but an active life engaged with managing farms, kennels, and stable, and guiding and protecting his people.

Until now, he hadn't spent much time thinking about a wife for the simple reason that he'd imagined no lady of the right breeding to become an earl's spouse would find such an existence attractive. He was only thirty-four; he'd assumed he could wait five or more years, then offer for some well-bred lady and sacrifice her and himself on the altar of duty. Now that he'd encountered Pru, he was no longer thinking in terms of sacrifice; having her as his wife would involve none—not on his part and, he was increasingly hopeful, not on hers, either.

Given your age and that you have so determinedly turned your back on the marriage mart. Esmerelda's description of Pru had made him realize just how different—how thoroughly unconventional—she was.

Even more than her age and despite any marital disinclination, given her interest in pursuing an active life, he suspected—hoped—that she would find what the earldom of Glengarah had to offer enticing.

Eventually, they reached the small stone cottage he'd declared should be made into a schoolhouse. It sat on a rocky shelf of land, with flattened and cleared areas before the south-facing door and to the building's west, while to the east and to the rear, a stand of trees gave some protection from the icy winds that occasionally swooped down the side of the ridge to the north.

He dismounted and tied the brown's reins to the ring set in the old cottage's corner post, then walked to where Pru had halted and, for once, waited. He smiled at her, reached up, and lifted her down.

He didn't immediately release her, and she didn't make any attempt to step away. Instead, she looked up at him, searched his eyes, then smiled. "Thank you for suggesting I come with you. To my English eyes, your fields are quite astonishingly green, and the land seems...unusually peaceful." She glanced at the fields below the school. "Restful. It's quiet —quieter than I'm used to when in the country."

He released her and turned to look at the fields, too. "I never spent all that much time in the English countryside. This is relatively normal for here."

Together, they strolled toward the school's door.

"Of course," he went on, "it's Sunday. Although the Anglican fami-lies come to the chapel at the castle, the majority of the farming families are Catholic. They walk or drive down to the church in Rathcormack, about two miles away. Some even go to Drumcliff or Sligo for the day."

"What about the minister—Reverend Kilpatrick? Is he part of your household?"

Deaglan shook his head. "Given there aren't that many Anglicans in this district, he rotates between three large houses. We have formal services only every third week."

"Ah. I see."

They'd reached the door—freshly painted and rehung. Deaglan turned the knob, unsurprised to find it unlocked. He pushed the door wide, noting that it swung easily and noiselessly, stepped over the threshold, looked around, then walked deeper into the single room, allowing Pru to follow him inside.

Three windows, all now fully glazed, had been set into the walls, one in the center of each of the east, south, and west walls, permitting decent light to penetrate what had previously been gloom. A large blackboard was affixed to the north wall, and a single row of double desks—ten places in all—ran down the middle of the room, facing the blackboard. Another desk and a chair for the teacher sat in one corner, facing the row of desks, and shelves ran below the west window, hosting books, chalks, slates, and other teaching impedimenta.

"I decided to make this into a school for my farmers' children last autumn. The cottage had lain empty for some years, and it's within easy walking distance—a child's walking distance—of five farmhouses." He met Pru's eyes. "I'm trying to convince the estate families that it's not a bad thing to send their children to school." He grimaced lightly. "In that, I've met with only partial success, even though all the families have more than enough children to be certain that enough of them will remain to tend the farm."

"Have you managed to hire a good teacher?"

"I believe so—he's from Drumcliff originally and won a scholarship to schools in Dublin and eventually taught at a grammar school there, but he was always looking for a way to come home. Reverend Kilpatrick suggested him, and his references were sound. He's accepted as a local by those on the estate, which has certainly eased his way."

"I see." She looked about with obvious interest. "So what are we doing here today?"

"O'Donnell, the teacher, reported that there was a leak in one corner of the roof. Not a large one, but as he said, it'll only get worse." Deaglan glanced at the corners at the rear of the cottage.

"Here." Her head tipped back, Pru pointed at the spot where the hip and rafters met in the southeast corner behind the door. "You can just see the wetness where the timbers meet."

Deaglan joined her. Standing beside her, he stared, then humphed. "It's a new roof—I'll need to send the workmen back. O'Donnell was right—that's only going to get worse, and the timbers will rot. That was the main reason we had to replace the roof in the first place."

He waved her to the door, but she paused and looked back at the row of desks. "This seems very neat and orderly. How many children attend?"

"So far, only six, but it's a start."

"You have seats for ten and space for at least another row of desks." She glanced at him. "Are there more children who might come?"

He grimaced resignedly. "The six we have are all younger children—meaning third, fourth, or more. The older boys and the oldest girl are usually kept on the farm to help their parents."

She nodded understandingly. "I've heard that's often the way, especially when there isn't a surfeit of farm laborers willing to work for food and board."

He grunted. "This is Ireland post-famine—there's no such surfeit."

"So"—she turned to the door—"you provide the school and teacher, and I assume the books and all such materials."

He nodded and followed her outside. "If you have any suggestions about how to persuade the parents to send more children, I'd be happy to hear them."

She started toward the horses. "I haven't had any personal experience, but I have several relatives who run schools on their estates, and I've heard Mary—she's the Marchioness of Raventhorne—mention that she's found supplying food a sound strategy."

"Food?" He fell in beside her.

"Yes—for the children's lunches. What they call dinner."

He raised his brows. "I wonder..."

She glanced at him. "Is your cook a local?"

"Yes."

"Why not lay the question before her and see what she thinks? You have six pupils and a teacher, and all they'd need is a slice of pie, bread and cheese, and apples, or something similar. Perhaps a groom could ferry up a basket every morning. Mary found that even on their estates—

which are in Wiltshire and relatively prosperous—that not having to feed their children dinner on school days was a definite inducement to parents to send their children to school."

He nodded decisively. "We'll try that." He met her eyes. "If it worked in Wiltshire, it should certainly work here." Where the memory of hunger was recent and acute.

While he switched the saddles on the horses, she looked around. "What happened to the people who lived here?"

"They left for America with others of their clan. During the famine, many ships sailed from Sligo. All those who went hoped to make a new start in fresh fields." He set down his saddle and lifted hers from the black's back. "Sadly, no one here has heard from them again."

"They died?"

"No one knows, but many who sailed away at that time didn't make it to the other side." He cinched the girth on her saddle, now on the brown stallion.

She stared out over the fields. "I know little about the famine, only that it occurred. How did those who remained here—on your lands—fare?"

He hoisted his saddle onto the black. "Better than most. We were—relatively speaking—among the lucky ones. Around here, the effects of the famine were patchy, and our farmers and field workers didn't rely on potatoes, either as a crop or to feed themselves. Our land isn't particularly suited to potatoes or even other crops, so we run animals, mostly, and we buy in whatever extra feed and supplies we need. The famine still had an impact, but it was far worse in many other areas." He cinched the saddle girth, then met her eyes. "Ready?"

She nodded.

Leaving the black still tied to the ring, Deaglan met her by the side of the brown and lifted her up to her saddle. The big horse shifted, reacting to the different balance of the side saddle, but Pru immediately settled the stallion. Satisfied, Deaglan returned to the black, freed the reins, and mounted. The black also skittered, then accepted Deaglan's greater weight and calmed.

Deaglan met Pru's eyes. "Is that what you mean by temperament?"

"Yes and no." She gathered her reins. "That much is normal. But if he kept twitching and sidling and his cantankerousness continued to grow, that would indicate a potential problem."

"But so far, these two are clear."

She nodded and tapped her heel to the brown's flank, and they set off down the gentle slope toward the castle, the battlements of which were just visible in the distance.

The descent necessitated walking for some way. Thinking of her earlier question, Deaglan volunteered, "One of the reasons Glengarah fared better than many other similar places was that the estate already had other established income streams aside from crop farming."

She shot him a glance. "You mean the kennels?"

He nodded. "And the cattle and even the sheep. When the blight struck, we weren't totally dependent on getting out a crop, and we could and did divert income from our other, unaffected enterprises to prop up those farmers who could no longer produce anything of worth."

"That was your doing, wasn't it? The diversion of funds?" When, surprised, he met her eyes, she grinned. "Felix said you'd set up the kennels—that you were in charge there."

He grunted. "I'd set up the kennels about five years before the famine started. The business was doing well and, thankfully, had reached the point where it didn't need me to be physically present to direct it. I had good people in place, and they knew what I wanted done. Even though I wasn't here to oversee it, they continued to pass money from the sales of the dogs to the estate families in need."

With the black walking behind the brown, Pru allowed herself a smug smile, knowing Deaglan couldn't see it; him being behind the diversion of funds had been a guess, and now she'd learned just a little bit more about what drove him.

About what motives were pushing him to set up a breeding establishment based on his late father's horses.

Felix had revealed that the onset of the famine and the prospect of hardship for the estate's families was what had driven Deaglan to confront his father, to fight for what he believed should be—even to the point of accepting banishment from the land, people, dogs, and horses he was transparently devoted to.

Reviewing all she'd learned thus far, it seemed abundantly clear that, from a relatively early age, he'd taken responsibility for the estate—meaning the land and all on and associated with it—squarely onto his shoulders.

That was a characteristic she applauded and one she would remember; it was such an intrinsic part of him, it would unquestionably influence him in their upcoming negotiations.

Her gaze swept the fields before them, falling in verdant shades of green all the way to the ribbon of the river. Memory tickled, and she shifted in the saddle to glance back at Deaglan. "While traveling from Dublin, I noticed a lot of run-down cottages. Many crumbling stone fences and...well, a general air of decay." She faced forward and gestured expansively to the area before them. "But here, there's none of that. No signs of that level of hardship."

She didn't ask, and for a few paces, the silence from behind was absolute. Then, it seemed reluctantly, he admitted, "There were such signs here when I came back. While I'd been away, my father had neglected even the most basic repairs. I made it a priority to set things right."

She nodded. "Everyone in my family would do the same. We've been large landowners for too long not to understand that our prosperity is entwined with that of the people who work our estates." After a moment, she added, "It seems strange your father wasn't of similar mind."

He huffed. After several seconds, he said, "I always put it down to him not being born here, as Felix and I were. He—the pater—never felt any innate connection to the place."

She recalled what Maude had earlier told her. Puzzled, she threw a frown Deaglan's way. "Didn't he at least think of Glengarah as his ancestral home?"

"Curiously, no, perhaps because he wasn't in the direct line for the title. He was third and quite distant—a cousin of the man who was expected to inherit from an uncle. Papa was born in Dublin and spent his life until his thirties on the east coast. It's a kinder, softer environment. Other than visiting in the way of relatives, he'd had nothing to do with Glengarah. Then an unexpected illness and an equally unexpected accident landed him with the title. He was thirty and a bachelor, living a life of ease—and the next day he was an earl with a large estate on the wild west coast, with responsibilities he never truly understood." He paused, then went on. "As you might expect in such circumstances, his marriage to my mother was arranged, and she proved a godsend, for she understood how to run a large estate. While she was alive, all went reasonably well—from what I've heard, she never allowed Papa's lack of real interest to get in the way of the estate being well run. And he hadn't yet developed his obsession with horses—that came after Mama died."

She tipped her head. "That explains your father's lack of understanding, I suppose."

"Perhaps." His voice hardened. "But it doesn't excuse his refusal to step up and do the right thing by the estate and the people dependent on it."

There was nothing she could to say to that; he was right, and clearly, he knew it.

As if signaling an end to the discussion, Deaglan urged the black up to pace beside the brown, then shifted into a canter. "There's a stretch just ahead where we can gallop."

He didn't ask if she wished to; that would have been a silly question.

They reached a long stretch of even ground, and after a single glance at each other, slapped their heels to the horses' flanks and loosened the reins. They rode neck and neck as the horses' hooves pounded, and they raced over the green.

Even carrying Deaglan's greater weight, the black was fast, but the brown was stayer material and, with a longer stride, kept pace with an ease that had Pru inwardly marveling. Inwardly gloating. What a find he was!

As the trees marking the end of the field loomed, Deaglan straightened in the saddle and eased the black back to a canter. Pru followed his lead; once she'd slowed the brown to pace alongside, Deaglan glanced at her face. Her fair skin was flushed with exhilaration, and her eyes sparkled with unaffected joy. The sight made him smile broadly.

She noticed and beamed back. "That was wonderful! I wish I could ride like that every single day." She looked down and stroked the brown's neck.

You could if you married me. Deaglan didn't allow the words to escape; he wasn't that much of a fool.

As they cantered on in companionable accord, he reviewed the progress of his campaign. Her questions—her genuine interest in the estate in general and the school in particular—he saw as encouraging; he'd deliberately told her more—revealed more than he would have had it been anyone but her asking—despite knowing she was seeking to understand why he wanted a breeding agreement, why he'd thought of approaching the Cynsters now.

What he sought to gain.

Still, if his revelations nudged her into thinking along the lines he wished...

He slowed to a walk, then drew breath and said, "I should confess that it wasn't me who wrote to the Cynsters—to you as head of the Cynster Stables' breeding program." He turned his head and met her eyes, which were widening in surprise. "It was Felix. He wrote in my name. I should explain that, once I returned, as you've now seen, there were a great many things that needed to be dealt with on the estate. Prior to leaving, I'd largely been running the stable for years—under my father's aegis, maybe, but I oversaw all the day-to-day matters, and in that, Felix had always been my right hand, there as much as in the kennels. When I left, I knew Felix would step in and keep both kennels and stable functioning, but Felix had never been in any position to ensure the correct decisions were made regarding the wider estate—I was the only one who could push my father into doing what was needed there."

Fixing his gaze on the glimpses of the castle visible through the screening trees, he drew in a deeper breath and went on, "When I returned and saw all the damage my father's neglect had caused, compounded by the impact of the famine, I felt compelled—honor-bound, if you like—to put everything on the estate right, have everything functioning again as it should, before I allowed myself to take up the reins of the stable again.

"I'd always intended to resume control and establish some sort of breeding enterprise, but I insisted on putting that off until I'd seen all right elsewhere..." He paused, then forced himself to speak the words. "To be perfectly frank, I wasn't entirely sure I wouldn't grow as obsessed with breeding from the collection as my father had become assembling it."

She humphed dismissively. "You won't. You don't have that sort of character."

He wanted to ask how she knew, but the words were...too much what he wanted to hear. Remembering what he'd intended to tell her, he went on, "I'd discussed my hopes with Felix, and he shared them. Knowing that the estate's problems were almost fully rectified, he decided to help by writing to you—testing the waters, as it were."

She smiled. "When did he tell you?" Amusement laced the words.

"A few minutes before you came rattling up the drive. Remember, the post carrying your reply was delayed."

She nodded. "I remember."

"So taking up the reins of the stable was to be my ultimate reward for getting all else on the estate fixed and functioning again. Your arrival simply brought the event forward a few weeks."

Pru glanced at him. Today was obviously a time for sharing...she suspected it was now her turn. "The reason I responded with such alacrity to Felix's invitation—in your name—was because, as Lady Connaught mentioned, I've been hying hither and yon across the British Isles, searching for just such horses as those in your father's collection—horses displaying strong characteristics from the foundation bloodlines. Not that I knew that of your horses then, but there was enough in Felix's letter to raise my hopes, and as you doubtless realized, once I laid eyes on the horses, I knew I'd found what I'd been searching for. That's why I've remained to do full assessments in order to come to some agreement to use your horses in our breeding program."

She met his eyes and read the obvious question in the emerald green. Her lips quirked, and she faced forward. "To understand why I was searching for such horses, you need to comprehend what the end goal of our breeding program is. I'm known throughout the Thoroughbred world as being extremely picky about what horses I allow into our program. The reason for that is simple—we already have excellent, high-quality bloodstock, so any horse I bring in has to offer something more.

"You would also need to know that the ranking of racing stables is a direct reflection of the racing abilities of the Thoroughbreds coming into those stables—the ranking is based on races won. Some stables just buy in horses, but others, like us, run a supporting breeding program. So the ranking of the Cynster Stables—which means the racing stable—is dependent on the breeding program producing exceptional racers. Currently, the Cynster Stables—now run by my brothers, rather than my father—are vying for top spot in the racing stable rankings, with at least four other stables, all also with breeding programs, nipping at our heels. For the last ten years of my father's reign, the Cynster Stables held the top spot by a significant margin."

She cut him a glance. "I suspect you can understand how my brothers feel."

His brows rose. "Under pressure to perform at least as well as your father?"

"Indeed. Which means I have to find horses that will improve already excellent bloodstock—not something easily done. The only way I could think of to achieve that was to find and introduce horses that carry exceptionally strong characteristics of the original foundation lines."

When he remained silent, Pru looked at him. And found him regarding her quizzically. She arched her brows in question.

"You're being remarkably open as to why you need our horses."

She met his eyes levelly. "It seems the time for candor and trust."

Deaglan held her gaze; whether she'd intended it or not, she'd hooked him with those words, yet straightforwardness and openness sat easily on her. He tipped his head in agreement and acceptance.

He faced forward, hesitated, then said, "One more question about your breeding strategy—all the current Thoroughbreds hail from the foundation bloodlines, albeit many generations past. Why go back, as it were?"

"Because the original traits we so valued have become watered down." She widened her eyes at him. "Don't you find the same with your dogs...oh, no. They're pure-bred, so you wouldn't see the same thing happen with them. Thoroughbreds are anything but pure—they are very much cross-breeds, and that leads to weakening of the critical traits the further down the generations you go. With Thoroughbreds, we need to go back and reintroduce the strongest possible carriers of the desired characteristics every now and then—and none of us have, not for decades."

She'd now told him everything he needed to know to comprehend what underpinned her desire for a breeding agreement.

He appreciated that—appreciated also that, with them sharing a bed and their bodies, too, hiding the reasons behind their business needs and wants wasn't, perhaps, an honorable or wise tack. They trusted each other in one sphere; she'd now shown him she trusted him in another—one that was vitally important to her.

If he wanted her as his wife, he had to trust her. Completely, implicitly.

Almost everything he'd revealed to her had been about the past.

"As I said, the estate is now performing reasonably well."

Her head came around; her gaze, curious and intent, fixed on his face.

He smiled wryly. "That said, I'll be happier once a deal is struck and the stable is at least paying its way. Although the estate is now running in the black, there's too little leeway and next to no buffer if another disaster like the blight strikes." He met her blue eyes. "Until I sign an agreement that will see the stable make an equitable return to the estate, I won't—can't—rest easy."

She held his gaze for a long moment, then inclined her head. "Thank you for telling me that. Now we both know where the other stands."

They did, indeed, and he had to admit that having lowered those screens with her—and having her do the same with him—left him feeling far more confident.

"Aside from all else," she said in a pensive tone, "making the stable pay its way will free up capital to support improvements on the estate—like the bridge and the school."

"Exactly." It seemed they understood each other well. He looked ahead. "We can canter for the rest of the way—if you're up to it."

She made a rude sound, and the brown pushed into a ground-eating stride.

He smiled and set the black to keep pace.

CHAPTER 9

*T*hat evening, while in Lady Connaught's sight, Pru religiously monitored her behavior throughout the gathering in the drawing room and didn't relax her vigilance over the dinner table.

Despite affecting an air of disinterest regarding her and Deaglan and pretending to be distracted with other happenings, Lady Connaught surreptitiously watched them with an eagle eye.

Deaglan, Pru noted, was just as careful as she in keeping his guard high and rigidly controlling his interactions with her.

They settled at the dinner table to what Pru suspected was intended as a welcome dinner for her ladyship; certainly, judging by the silverware, there were to be more courses than the usual five.

Jay had been invited to join the company to balance the table, but the result did not seem to be to Lady Connaught's liking. As dictated by precedence, Deaglan had escorted his aunt to the table, and Felix had therefore given Pru his arm, leaving Jay to escort Cicely, which he did with easy grace and considerable Irish charm, neither of which appeared to endear him to her ladyship.

She humphed, the sound one of transparent disapproval, as Jay, having seated Cicely next to Patrick, who tonight occupied the foot of the table, drew out the last chair—the one beside her ladyship.

Pru couldn't decide what about the perfectly personable steward Lady Connaught objected to, but given her age and her standing within the ton,

it was possible her ladyship regarded Jay O'Shaughnessy as a social infe-
rior, no matter that he was Deaglan's distant cousin.

Thankfully for them all, on that subject, Lady Connaught elected to
hold her tongue.

However, despite the failure of her earlier inquisition, she appeared
addicted to the practice and took aim at Pru. "Tell me, my dear, how are
your dear brothers? Any hint either of them is likely to settle down
anytime soon?"

Pru lowered her soup spoon. "Nicholas and Toby are younger than I,
and these days, both are heavily involved in running the racing stable. I
doubt either of them have spared any thought at all for marriage."

"Dear me—so very industrious, the lot of you." Her ladyship waved
her spoon, luckily empty, at Pru. "I have to wonder what Sebastian—the
current duke's father—would have thought on seeing so many of his
descendants and near-relatives devoting so much of their time to such
activities. As I recall, he was the epitome of the well-heeled, well-bred
nobleman, quite a high-stickler as they used to say—no doubt he'd be
spinning in his grave."

Pru sternly quelled the impulse to share an amused glance with
Deaglan. From all she'd ever heard, her great-uncle Sebastian had
managed the far-flung estates of the dukedom of St. Ives in exemplary
fashion. He might have been a pillar of the ton, yet that hadn't precluded
him from keeping a very firm grip on a broad range of financial and business affairs. If anything, it could be said to have been his lead that had
resulted in what her ladyship termed the current generation's industry.

"Ah, well." Once the soup plates were removed, Lady Connaught
swung her gaze to Felix. "Felix, dear boy, will you be coming to Dublin
later this month?"

"Ah." Felix cast a faintly panicked glance at Deaglan. "I'm…ah, not
sure I can manage the time away, not just at the moment."

"Indeed?" Lady Connaught widened her eyes at him. "But now
Deaglan is here and refusing to budge, surely you can take the time to
look about you a trifle. Attend some balls and parties. Deaglan had his
years in London—at least I can't accuse him of being a hermit and
knowing nothing of our world. But you! You need to get out and cast
your eyes about you."

"Yes, Aunt." Felix grasped the distraction of the fish course being
presented to turn aside and busy himself with something else.

Lady Connaught leaned forward and, across Jay, addressed Cicely.

"Cicely, my dear girl, when do you plan to rejoin society? I assume your mama will be looking to see you in the next few weeks."

Pru had long since realized that Cicely was at Glengarah hunting Felix. Yet being intelligent and with her feet firmly planted on the ground, she'd kept her pursuit subtle, careful, and quiet, and in Pru's estimation, was inching ever closer to her goal.

While addressing the trout amandine on her plate, Pru watched as Cicely, not at all discomfited, smiled sweetly and replied, "I have no plans to return to Dublin just yet. You'll recall that Mama has my sisters in hand this year. Judging from their letters, they've been in a whirl simply getting ready for the Season."

"Ah, yes." Her ladyship absentmindedly tapped her fork on her plate. "Alice and Corrine, isn't it?"

"Yes." From there, Cicely plunged into a recitation of the latest news her sisters and mother had imparted, which succeeded in diverting her ladyship into a long exchange of social trivia, which drew in Maude as well.

Under cover of the general distraction, Pru and Deaglan exchanged several amused and entertained glances. At one point, Deaglan leaned closer and murmured, "Remind me to thank Cicely—she's saved us all."

Pru grinned.

Finally, Lady Connaught turned her attention to the foot of the table. "What-ho, Patrick? Colonel Smythe-Wallace sends his regards. Says he might come this way in June and look you up."

"How's the old blighter doing?" Patrick asked.

Her ladyship's reply and Patrick's reminiscing carried them through to the end of the meal.

With Cicely, Pru followed Maude and Lady Connaught from the room, leaving the men to their whiskey. Despite Pru's reservations over what the next minutes might bring, once settled in the drawing room, Lady Connaught contented herself with chatting on innocuous subjects, even after the men joined them.

Only when the tea was being dispensed did Pru realize that Jay hadn't reappeared in the drawing room. She could understand why; throughout her inquisitions over the dining table, her ladyship had utterly ignored him, even though he'd been seated beside her—a put-down if ever there was one.

When Pru approached the tea tray to return her empty cup and saucer, Lady Connaught turned to her. "So you'll be here for some time yet—

assessing the horses my late brother-in-law became such a bore about. Are they really worth so much of your time?"

Pru inclined her head. "It seems the late earl had a very good eye for horseflesh."

Lady Connaught humphed. "I suppose each of us must have something we're good at, heh?"

Deeming that required no answer, Pru kept mum, but she noted that her ladyship's eyes had strayed to Deaglan.

But her ladyship only asked after the dogs, and Pru seized the opportunity to move to a safer distance.

Not long afterward, Maude rose, and Lady Connaught pushed to her feet. "Indeed—I'm ready for my bed."

The four ladies exchanged goodnights with the three remaining men, then turned toward the door.

As at the rear of the foursome, Pru started in that direction, Deaglan fell in, pacing slowly beside her. He angled his head toward her; to any observer, they could well have been discussing their plans for tomorrow.

Instead, Deaglan murmured, "Subtlety is not Esmerelda's strong suit, which leads me to hope that we've managed to convince her that your sole interest here lies in the horses."

Pru softly returned, "I'm not so sure, but we can only hope. If she guesses"—she raised her eyes to his—"that there's anything more, given her connection to my aunts especially, that might prove...difficult." She let her gaze and her lips soften and had to force her hand to remain at her waist and not rise to touch his cheek. "That said, I've always thrived on taking difficult fences."

He laughed and halted. And with a nod and a promise in his eyes, let her continue in the other ladies' wake.

Pru was smiling softly as she caught up with the others at the foot of the stairs. As Lady Connaught glanced around, Pru wiped the dreamily expectant expression from her face; despite her confident words to Deaglan, she didn't need to invite trouble.

Her ladyship's sharp gaze fell on her face and lingered for a second, then the old lady humphed, swung around, and started up the stairs.

With all due demureness, Pru followed. In commencing her liaison with Deaglan, she hadn't expected anyone of Lady Connaught's ilk to appear, yet even had she known...having experienced what she already had, explored as she already had, she couldn't imagine holding back from falling into bed with the wickedly wild Earl of Glengarah.

When Deaglan, Felix, and Patrick eventually retired, Deaglan retreated to his apartment to wait for the house to fall silent before he made his way to Pru's bedroom—to her arms and her bed.

His aunt's arrival made discretion imperative.

In the past, somewhat to his surprise, Esmerelda hadn't made all that much fuss regarding his hedonistic life in London. She'd tried once or twice to haul him into the haut ton, to the balls and parties at which noblemen like him were supposed to seek their brides, but when he'd resisted, she'd accepted with a shrug and reasonably ready grace. Given her views were very much those of her generation, he suspected she'd decided he was sowing his wild oats and had left him to it.

Now, however, he was five years older and the earl rather than the heir, and he'd continued to resist her efforts to winkle him out of Glengarah and into society.

He had to wonder what had brought her there. The London Season had started, yet here she was, supposedly calling to spend time with Maude and Patrick. A high degree of suspicion as to Esmerelda's motives was surely justified.

In his sitting room, he paced before the hearth and reviewed the dangers consequent on Esmerelda's presence. The room she used lay in the same wing; he should wait long enough for her to fall asleep.

His thoughts turned to Pru, to their final exchange in the drawing room. Clearly, she wasn't contemplating any retreat to safety, either. He wondered what her ready declaration said of her current thinking, her current feeling regarding him and their liaison.

Had she reached the point of wondering if it might continue—of not wanting it to end?

He couldn't convince himself that she had; they'd spent only two nights together thus far. Not even he could hope to sway a woman—any woman—in such a short time, and Pru Cynster was very definitely not just any woman. She was obstinate and strong-willed, and beneath that he'd detected a…not wariness but guardedness. And he hadn't yet learned why she had—as his aunt had confirmed—turned her back on marriage.

Yet judging by her words and actions, she was enjoying their liaison and wished it to continue regardless of Esmerelda's arrival—indeed, in the teeth of any potential danger; that was at least a step in the right direction.

A sound in the corridor reached him. He halted, tilting his head the better to hear...

The stumping clump of his aunt's footsteps approached his door, then she rapped imperiously upon it.

Deaglan debated not answering, but she would only barge in.

His jaw tightening, he crossed to the door and opened it. "Aunt. What is it?"

She narrowed her eyes on his. "As if you don't know."

Waving him back, she stumped in. Leaving him to close the door, she made her way to one of the pair of armchairs angled before the hearth and sat down.

Accepting that there would be no escape, Deaglan closed the door and followed; he elected to sit, elegantly asprawl, in the armchair opposite.

When Esmerelda said nothing, just regarded him consideringly, he languidly arched one eyebrow.

Her lips primmed, then she lifted her chin. "I'm here to ask what your intentions are regarding Miss Cynster."

Honestly surprised—even shocked—he allowed both brows to rise high.

When he didn't rush into speech, Esmerelda snorted. "I'm not blind—and I would have to be to miss what's going on under this roof. Yes, Maude might have given no sign, but she's not blind, either. Nor is Patrick, and even Felix is not such a nodcock." Esmerelda paused, then went on, "Not sure about Cicely. Plays her cards close to her chest, but she's a downy one, regardless—she's sure to have seen it."

Having disabused him of any belief in the efficacy of their discretion to date, Esmerelda refocused on him. "So, my good sir, as Prudence's father isn't here—and for that you should thank your lucky stars, incidentally—and neither is yours, also a blessing, it falls to me to point out that your answer will affect both families, and that in a fairly dramatic fashion. A Fitzgerald seducing a Cynster? That would certainly set some vicious cats prowling, wanting your blood." Her sharp eyes bored into his. "So, my lord, what have you to say?"

Deaglan regarded her every bit as consideringly as she had him. He could see no way out, no way of not answering or sliding around the issue —not with Esmerelda.

I might do worse than to have her on my side.

"Firstly," he said, "if there was any seducing involved, it was very much a mutual endeavor."

Esmerelda's eyes widened. "Really?"

"Trust me—the current situation did not come about by straightforward choice, not on my part or hers. The...attraction was simply too great to resist—and we did, both of us, try to resist. However, be that as it may, your supposition is correct. Miss Cynster and I are engaged in a liaison." He held up a hand to stay the protest he saw leap to Esmerelda's lips. "That being said, there is, at present, a discrepancy in how she and I view the path ahead of us."

He paused, and impatience built in Esmerelda's expression while he rapidly canvassed his options. Given what she'd already known and what he'd just told her, his only viable way forward was to confess to the rest. Holding her gaze, he evenly stated, "My preferred future is to front an altar with Pru's hand in mine. She, however, currently believes we're engaged in a liaison of limited duration, one that will end when she leaves Glengarah. At the outset, she made it plain that was what she wanted— she effectively made it a condition, one to which I agreed. At the time"— he shrugged—"I assumed that was what I, too, wanted."

"But you've changed your mind. Huh." Esmerelda regarded him as if she hadn't seen him clearly before, then she sat back, her expression suggesting that she was digesting the information, juggling it into some picture in her mind. Eventually, she said, "She's very well-grounded in the ton—she grew up within it, of course. So she knows ton ways, knows the dangers, so to speak—I suppose that explains why she insisted on such a condition. She wanted to tie your hands just in case you decided that having a Cynster to wife would be an excellent idea."

"So I assumed. And of course, she's doubly correct in thinking that, were I so inclined, me using our liaison to force her to the altar would be considered by most in the ton to be an exceedingly advantageous move. Not only would such a marriage be socially acceptable, but in light of the Glengarah horses, her knowledge of Thoroughbreds, and her experience in managing the Cynster breeding program, such an alliance would be virtually priceless."

Esmerelda snorted. "All very well, but you don't want to wake up one fine morning to find yourself tied to the bed and your wife standing over you with a gelding knife in her hand."

Deaglan couldn't hold back a horrified exhalation.

Esmerelda waved. "Yes, that's an exaggeration, but the concept is sound. You can't force her into marriage. I warn you that, beneath those gold curls and sunny disposition, there's a Cynster temper lurking. Don't doubt it. But to return to the matter at hand…hmm." Esmerelda glanced at him. "She was a virgin, wasn't she?"

Deaglan held her gaze and reacted not at all.

"I'll take that as a yes, which, you'll be interested to know, fits with all I've heard of her. According to her grandmother and great-aunt, Prudence has been supremely uninterested in every male, eligible or otherwise, ever presented to her. Her mother has quite given up, which, apparently, has been Pru's goal."

Deaglan hesitated to ask, but he needed to know. "Do you have any idea why she's turned her back on marriage? It seems an entrenched attitude—do you know of any specific reason for it?"

Esmerelda pursed her lips and appeared to wrack her extensive memory, yet after a full minute, shook her head. "I never heard that there was any incident—any love of her life who married someone else or anything of that ilk."

"So you know of no reason from her past that would have set her so determinedly against marriage?"

"Believe me, my boy, if I did, I'd tell you." Esmerelda met his gaze. "I take it you're intending to change her mind?"

He nodded. "But clearly, it's going to take time. And if the reason for her aversion to marriage doesn't lie in her past… It's like fencing in fog. I can't see what to take aim at."

Esmerelda huffed. "Whatever it is, you need to figure it out, because one thing I can tell you is that it would be exceedingly unwise to allow her to leave here without your ring on her finger. If she slips through your grasp while here, I wouldn't want to wager on your chances of drawing her back—she'll immerse herself in her blessed breeding program, which I gather is what she's wont to do, and not even you will be able to winkle her out."

Luckily, I still have five horses up my sleeve.

"So you'd better get persuading, my boy." With that final pronouncement, Esmerelda pushed to her feet.

Deaglan rose. "As I said, it's early days yet, but I believe I've made some progress."

"Good—keep at it." Esmerelda looked struck, then chuckled. "Given your method of persuading, what a thing to have to say!"

She clomped to the door and waited for Deaglan to reach around her and open it. When he gripped the knob, she halted him with a raised finger. "One thing. If your efforts at persuasion don't succeed, you might organize for me to discover the pair of you in some compromising situation. Not that I'm suggesting I would follow through and apply the customary pressure, but the prospect alone should be enough to get even Prudence Cynster to sit down and properly consider your offer—which, after all, is no shabby thing."

"I pray," Deaglan drily replied, gripping the knob harder and turning it, "that it won't come to that."

"Hmm...you and me both." Esmerelda clumped into the corridor, then paused to wave up its length. "You'd better get persuading, then." As she started toward her room, Deaglan heard her mutter, "Lord knows, if any man is expert in the many ways of snaring and redirecting a lady's mind when there's a bedroom in the offing, it's you."

He couldn't resist muttering in reply, "Thank you for your confidence."

He shut the door, then stood and stared at the panels while his aunt's footsteps faded.

While he'd been correct in assuming he would have Esmerelda's backing over marrying Pru, he was no longer so sanguine as to whether his aunt would prove a help or a hindrance.

Still and all, she'd answered a few questions, thus clarifying his current predicament.

He had to make greater strides in convincing Pru to at least consider the prospect of marrying him—before his aunt lost patience and took matters into her own hands.

If she did...

"Heaven help us all." His face setting, he reached for the doorknob, opened the door, and headed for Pru's room.

CHAPTER 10

*D*espite the pressure applied by his aunt, Deaglan wasn't one to rush his fences, especially when his quarry hadn't yet realized she was being pursued; he was in no hurry to break cover and risk spooking her.

On Wednesday morning, he sat at the breakfast table with his next major gambit clear in his mind and waited, calmly, for Pru to appear.

Galvanized by his aunt's prodding, he'd spent the past three nights and the days between paying attention—and not just to Pru's preferences in the bedroom, which were proving significantly more adventurous than those of the average well-bred lady; he could meet and fully satisfy such desires easily enough. But he'd concluded that, in order to make her view the position of his countess as not just meeting her every need but, indeed, offering far more—thus transforming the position into one she actively wanted to claim—he needed to learn all he could about what in life was important to her.

He needed to work out what, then deliver it.

Sometime on Monday, he'd been struck by an epiphany regarding what had set her against marriage; he'd finally realized that as the answer didn't lie in her past, and he couldn't see how it might be in her present, then it had to reside in her future. That there was something about how she saw marriage affecting her life that she was determined not to accept.

The thought had given him pause. Could the problem be children? If she didn't wish for children... He was an earl, and even though Felix was there as his heir, hale and whole, once married, they would be expected to produce more Fitzgeralds.

For a moment, he'd been thrown—not just by the prospect of such a situation but even more by the startling realization that, despite always assuming he would have children, if foregoing them was the price he had to pay to keep Pru in his life, he would pay it without hesitation.

Then common sense had reared its head, and he'd remembered that she was the eldest of four siblings, that she ranked among the older children in a large, extended family. Having children and babies about probably barely registered, and in this age, few women allowed being with child to overly restrict their lives.

Unfortunately, there were no children at the castle with whom to test his theory, but yesterday, he'd arranged for the pair of them to ride out on the pretext of allowing her to trial another two horses and to call in at the school along the way, to check on the workmen fixing the roof.

At that time, the children had been at their desks, and when Deaglan had summoned O'Donnell, the teacher, to talk to the workmen with him, Pru had readily volunteered to oversee the children—all six of them—and had held them captive with tales of England and growing up in and around the Cynster Stables on Newmarket Heath.

Deaglan, O'Donnell, and the three workmen had been captivated as well.

He'd been relieved her problem wasn't to do with children; if he'd been extra-attentive last night, she hadn't complained.

During Monday and Tuesday, by dint of a comment here, an apparently idle query there, he'd managed to learn that she valued many of the same traits he did—such as honesty, loyalty, and commitment. Along with place, home, and family; indeed, their views on all the important subjects in life seemed aligned.

And while he hadn't dared ask outright what had given rise to her stance against marriage, courtesy of the lazy, apparently aimless questions he'd been posing in the moments of aftermath, when he'd taken care to ensure she was floating on a pleasured cloud, he was starting to get an inkling of what the answer might be.

This morning, he'd decided to risk his hand. If his gamble paid off, it would definitely be worth it. If it didn't, he would have squandered his most valuable bargaining chip going forward.

He'd weighed the rewards and had discovered that, to him, winning her to wife now loomed as fundamentally more important than sealing the best deal with the Cynster Stables. Quite the realization, that had been.

He heard her footsteps approaching, and unbidden, his gaze went to the doorway. He was ready with a smile when she breezed in, transparently happy and looking forward to spending the day with him and his horses.

She bade him and Felix a cheery "Good morning" and headed for the sideboard.

He waited until she'd settled to a plate of kippers and eggs, then lowered his coffee mug and said, "You've only got three horses left to test in the ring."

She nodded and swallowed. "I'm hoping to write up my notes this afternoon—after that, I'll know which of the horses I still need to ride to finalize my assessments." She paused, then her eyes sought his, and more slowly, she said, "It seems I'll be finished with the assessment stage by tomorrow afternoon. After that, we can commence negotiations."

The lack of enthusiasm in her voice over the impending end to her reason for being there—and being able to share her bed with him—was music to his ears. He managed not to grin, but instead, held her gaze and said, "Actually, once you've finished your assessments in the ring, there's something else I want to show you. Something that I suspect will push back negotiations for a few days."

The interest that lit her face was all he could have hoped for. "Oh?" She considered the food on her plate. "In that case, I'd better finish this and get out to the stable and plunge into those last three assessments."

Pru attacked her breakfast with renewed enthusiasm. She'd floated down the stairs in the mood of pleasant expectation to which she'd grown accustomed to being in thrall over the past days; it was remarkable how spending a glorious night in the arms of a talented lover set one up for the day.

And there was no question but that Deaglan Fitzgerald deserved the title of "wicked." And "talented." He'd introduced her to passion on a grand scale, to desire that burned inferno-bright, and to positions she hadn't dreamt were possible. As for his attentions... It was hardly any wonder that she was perennially smiling.

But then the prospect of commencing negotiations—the prelude to her leaving Glengarah, bringing an end to their liaison—had cast a shadow over her happiness. Luckily, a temporary one; trust Deaglan to have thought of some way of prolonging their affair.

While it would need to end at some point, she wasn't ready for it to end just yet.

Felix engaged Deaglan in a discussion about the kennels, then Felix excused himself and left to deal with getting several dogs ready to be collected by their new owners.

As soon as she'd cleared her plate and drained her teacup, Deaglan rose and drew out her chair for her, and they left for the stable.

Side by side, they walked toward the stable yard. Looking around, Pru couldn't comprehend how her nighttime interactions with Deaglan, the closeness she could feel growing and burgeoning between them, made everything around her—the entire scope of her senses—somehow seem so much more intense.

Her entire world seemed more colorful, more intriguing, more actively engaging.

As if my life itself is more vibrant.

She and Deaglan made straight for the exercise ring and knuckled down to complete the last three assessments. As these horses—two stallions and a mare—ranked as the most superior in the entire stable, she couldn't hurry her process along; she had to be absolutely certain of these horses, had to have given them every chance to display any weakness, before she could declare herself fully satisfied that their true quality lived up to their visual appearance.

Consequently, it was close to lunchtime when Deaglan led the third horse back to his stall.

By the time he returned, Pru had jotted down her notes; as she looked up, the luncheon gong rang.

Deaglan smiled at the impatience she didn't try to hide, reached out and drew her against him, and stole a quick, surprisingly sweet, if also a little heady kiss.

"Come on." He released her and caught her hand. "The faster we eat, the sooner I can show you something I hope will make your day."

She heaved a sigh. "You really do know how to string a lady along."

He laughed and tugged her on.

True to his word, as soon as they rose from the luncheon table, Deaglan steered her outside again—across the side court and into the stable.

She glanced at his face, at the slight smile curving his lips. "It's here —this thing you want to show me?"

He nodded. "It is. Follow me."

She wasn't about to do anything else. Intrigued, she paced by his side down the stable's aisles—along the first, into the second, and around into the third. Finally, they turned the corner into the fourth aisle and, eventually, drew level with the last stalls—those of the three horses she'd worked with that morning.

Deaglan halted and swung to face her. "Now—close your eyes."

She looked at him, then did.

"Don't move."

She sensed him stepping away from her, she thought toward the wall that marked the end of the aisle. An odd grinding noise reached her ears, then a faint breeze brushed past her face.

Then Deaglan returned and took one of her hands. "Here. Take my arm." He stepped to her side and looped her arm with his, placing her hand on his sleeve. "Now," he said, his voice carrying a hint of amused excitement, "walk with me."

He started forward, and obediently, she walked with him, matching her pace to his as he led her...forward. But how could that be? She'd been facing the wall—hadn't she?

Then he turned her to the left, and they walked on perhaps ten paces. She had no idea where they were.

"Stop here." He halted, and she stopped. "Face right." She pivoted with him, then he lifted her hand and unwound her arm, but kept her hand in his. "Now," he breathed, his voice a whisper of alluring invitation, "open your eyes."

She did. Then she blinked and looked again.

They stood facing six stalls. Five were occupied, containing five horses she hadn't seen before...

All five horses had put their heads over the stall doors and were looking at her—at them—with interest.

She stared—and stared, literally unable to believe what she was seeing. "These..."

Her wits were whirling too quickly for speech. On a strangled gasp, she stepped forward, raising the hand Deaglan wasn't holding to gently stroke the velvet nose of the most magnificent stallion she'd ever seen.

The horse was real—he lipped her fingers as if searching for a carrot.

"Oh." The sound shivered from her lips. She still couldn't find words.

Then she looked to right and left, and the magnitude of what Deaglan was showing her crashed through her.

"Oh. My. Lord." She looked at him. "These horses are superb. How on earth...?"

His smile turned wry. "These are the jewels of my father's collection. He considered them the pinnacle of what he'd hoped to collect—to assemble in one place. After he had all five, he stopped buying new horses."

"He was right—there is absolutely no chance of improving on these." She went up on her toes and looked along the stalls, left, then right. "Three stallions and two mares. A Darley Arabian, a Byerley Turk, and a Godolphin Barb—all the strongest representatives of those lines that I have ever set eyes on."

He nodded. "And the mares?"

She shook her head. "I have no words. Even without closer examination, I would say without fear of contradiction that they are the best examples of the foundation mares in existence."

Her mind was not just functioning again but racing. So many questions were flooding in; she voiced the most important. "Why?" She met his eyes and wondered if he would answer.

His lips quirked again, but his gaze remained steady. "I was holding them back—the ultimate bargaining chips. I hadn't thought how, exactly, I would use them, but at that time, I didn't know you." His gaze grew weightier, more intense. "Now that I do, I decided to show you—to put all my cards on the table, as it were."

She kept her eyes on his and drew in a slow breath, then let it out on the words, "You've decided to trust me with this. You're trusting me to give you the deal you want."

"No—I'm trusting you to give me the deal Glengarah needs, because you understand why we need it."

She let his words sink in—into her brain, into her heart—even as she read that simple truth in his eyes. Between them, things had changed, and trust—trust of this magnitude—was, indeed, now there. She trusted him implicitly; he'd just demonstrated how much he trusted her.

She looked again at the horses. These were his future—his estate's, his people's, his. He'd handed her the reins of the negotiations, put her on the box seat, but...he'd also taught her that, between them, the greatest joys came from sharing. "These horses are your trump cards, and by showing them to me, making me aware of their existence, you've made it impossible for me, as head of the breeding program of the Cynster Stables, to walk away without securing a licensing deal that includes these horses."

She turned her head and met his eyes. "We cannot afford to have any other stable do a deal with you."

He smiled reassuringly and lightly squeezed her hand. "Just as well, then, that I have no interest in making an arrangement with anyone but you."

She read that truth in his eyes, too, and the emotion that welled and surged through her was nearly strong enough to make her sway. She glanced around. The stalls faced onto a grassed area, open to the sky and bordered by four plain, angled walls. She looked to her left, at the door through which he'd brought her—presumably a concealed door set in the wall at the end of the fourth aisle. "I'm not even sure where we are."

He chuckled. "My father was rather more than reclusive—when it came to his collection, he was paranoidly secretive. The stable was originally just the first aisle, then he added the second, third, and fourth as he found and purchased more horses. But he drew up the design of the stable before he added the second aisle—this aisle was built at the same time as the second aisle. Later, when the third and fourth aisles were built, they completed the design—a design created to securely house the gems of his collection away from all eyes bar those he permitted to see them."

She frowned, trying to make sense of the design, then pointed to the wall bordering the grassed area to the immediate right of the row of stalls. "So that's the rear wall of the stalls in the second aisle?"

"No—it's the rear wall of the stalls to the left of the first aisle. The stables are constructed like a pentagonal spiral. Each side—each aisle—is shorter than the one before, and the angle of the corners, as you've probably noticed, is larger than the usual ninety degrees. While the first aisle has stalls on either side, with the carriage horses accommodated in the stalls on the right as you walk down, the second, third, and fourth aisles have stalls only on the left, with the area on the right devoted to grassed courtyards limited by the outbuildings and the exercise ring. The fifth aisle, the one we're now in, has, as you can see, stalls only on the right, and they look onto the courtyard formed by the backs of the stalls in the first"—he pointed to the wall she'd indicated, then progressed around the four blank walls—"second, third, and fourth aisles."

She could finally see the design in her mind. "That's...ingenious. I would never have known these stalls and horses were here—there's nothing that makes one think there might be more stalls after the end of the fourth aisle."

Deaglan nodded. "That was the pater's intention—to hide these horses away from the world."

"He truly was a collector's collector."

"Indeed."

She drew in a breath, then swung around to face the horses again. After a moment of drinking in their magnificence, she slanted a glance at Deaglan. "I take it I should assess them?"

He smiled and waved her on. "Please. I need to know their true value as much as you do."

She hadn't brought her notes with her, so he sent a groom running to fetch paper and pencil. Then she went into each stall and completed a thorough visual survey—her heart in her mouth over finding some flaw, but no. She saw nothing to undermine her initial view—which meant these five horses were as much her future as his.

It took her four hours working in the ring before she allowed herself to accept her assessment of the first three horses—the two mares and the Byerley Turk stallion—as solid and unchallengeable. Essentially, beyond question.

"Enough for today." Deaglan shut the stall door on the bay stallion; he hadn't previously seen signs of weariness in Pru, but the excitement combined with four uninterrupted hours on her feet in the ring, working three strong horses, had taken its toll, and she was drooping.

She hesitated, clearly tempted by the last two stallions, but then nodded. "You're right. I wouldn't do them justice if I pushed on."

He hadn't been concerned about that.

He walked her back through the door into the end of the fourth aisle. While he closed and locked the door, she examined the mechanism. "Definitely ingenious" was her verdict.

They walked side by side through the stable and on across the side court. Deaglan glanced at her face as she raised it to the last of the day's sunshine—saw the expression of sheer joy and delight that still cloaked her features, felt a corresponding tug in the center of his chest, and concluded that his gamble had paid off.

Looking ahead, she sighed, then said, "Just so you know, I understand why you held back those five horses. Had I been in your shoes, I would have done the same."

He smiled. "Good to know." And it was; something in him settled a little more confidently into contentment.

They reached the side door, and he opened it, but instead of walking through, she halted and swung to face him. She met his eyes, her gaze open and direct. "Thank you for showing me your father's gems—they truly are the jewels of the Glengarah collection." She paused, then drew breath and said, "Were those five horses the only horses in the collection, they would nevertheless be enough to guarantee an alliance with the Cynster Stables."

It isn't just the Cynster Stables I want an alliance with.

He bit back the words and, holding her gaze, inclined his head. "Thank you for being so open."

That brought a swift grin to her lips, then, her eyes brightening anew, she swept around and entered the house.

Smiling as well, Deaglan followed.

Pru led the way along the corridor toward the front hall and, with every swinging stride, gloried in the sense of simple happiness—she could find no other word for it—that was welling and swelling inside her, making her steps light, her heart light, her emotions buoyant.

She felt like dancing giddily—like some silly girl—and all because Deaglan had trusted her enough to show her his five most fabulous horses.

It wasn't the horses themselves that had set her heart filling, then overflowing, but the gesture, one she knew in her bones had been made possible by the closeness that had grown between them, fueled by their intimacy.

She hadn't previously realized that such a straightforwardly physical act, one of giving and receiving pleasure, could reach so deeply and affect so much more. Yet for him and her, it had—it did.

As they reached the front hall, she met his eyes and let her smile reflect all she felt.

She hadn't known that the link between them that was, day by day, night by night, growing ever stronger could be the source of such unalloyed happiness.

That it could become something so precious—something she didn't want to lose.

∽

The following morning, Pru completed her assessment of the final two stallions in the Glengarah collection.

After luncheon, as she, Deaglan, and Felix made for the library to finally begin discussing a breeding arrangement and Felix asked how she'd fared that morning, she admitted, "I was glad that I had an entire session to examine those two stallions alone. Of all the horses I've ever assessed, they rank as the two that, being the most perfect, therefore necessitated the greatest and most lengthy scrutiny."

"But they passed?" Felix asked.

"With flying colors." She glanced at Deaglan. "As your brother can attest, I became quite crotchety when I couldn't find the slightest fault with either of them."

Deaglan grinned and, setting the library door swinging, waved her in.

They made themselves comfortable in the armchairs before the hearth.

"So," Deaglan said, his gaze on Pru, "horse breeding being rather different from breeding dogs, where do we start?"

"It's customary to begin by outlining what each side would expect to see in the deal." Pru met his eyes, then glanced at Felix. "In this case"— she returned her gaze to Deaglan—"the Cynster Stables would want an exclusive license to breed from the Glengarah horses. Exclusivity is going to be very important to us."

Sober now, Deaglan inclined his head. "I can understand that, but in return, there would have to be some degree of reciprocity with breeding stock, and of course, the breeding fees would need to be commensurate with exclusivity."

Pru signaled her agreement with a dip of her head. "Regarding fees— which is, generally, the simplest matter to decide—we've found it easiest for both sides to use as a base figure the average cost of upkeep per horse per annum." She looked at Felix. "Do you know what that figure is?"

Felix blinked, then glanced at Deaglan. "Ah…no. We've never had reason to work that out."

Pru nodded. "So that's one thing you'll need to do before we can get down to specifying the details of our agreement." She met Deaglan's eyes. "This is the purpose of an initial discussion—to highlight those matters we need to clarify before we can commence detailed negotiations."

He looked at Felix. "We should be able to extract those figures from the stable accounts."

"And," Pru continued, "while you're doing that, I'll need to go through the acquisitions ledger. I need to learn from whom your father bought each horse and confirm the entries in the General Stud Book. That will provide provenance of the bloodlines of each horse and will clear them for entry into the Cynster breeding program."

Felix frowned. "You still need to do that even after your assessment?"

"With horses such as those here," Pru explained, "confirming the GSB listing is a mere formality—my assessment counts for more. Unless a horse passes my assessment, we don't bother checking its registered bloodlines."

"So"—Deaglan straightened his legs—"we all have preparatory work to do before we can settle into actual negotiations." He caught Felix's eye. "Are the stable accounts and ledgers still in the stable office?"

Felix replied with a resigned air, "Still where Papa insisted on keeping them."

"In that case"—Deaglan pushed up from the armchair—"I suggest we go and hunt them out."

Pru and Felix rose, too, and the three of them made for the door.

On reaching it, Felix, frowning, said, "I assume Papa kept an acquisitions ledger—he remained secretive, increasingly so, over where he'd got the horses, right up until he died." Felix looked at Deaglan. "I can't remember seeing such a ledger."

Deaglan thought, then shook his head. "I can't recall seeing such a thing, either, but if it exists, it'll be in the stable office." He opened the door and waved Pru through. "Let's go and see."

The three of them were crossing the front hall when Jay emerged from the corridor leading to the side door.

He took in their purposeful strides and halted. "Whither away?"

"The stable office," Felix said. "Miss Cynster needs to see the acquisition details for the horses in the collection."

Deaglan paused to ask Jay, "Do you have any of the stable accounts or ledgers in the estate office?"

Slowly, Jay shook his head. "No. They're all in the stable office."

"Good." With a nod of dismissal for Jay, Deaglan waved Pru and Felix on down the corridor and fell in behind them.

❦

They found the stable accounts in the stable office, which proved to be a good-sized room built at the end of a corridor leading away from the aisles hosting the horse stalls. What they failed to find, despite searching high and low, was any acquisitions ledger.

Instead, they discovered that the purchase of each horse had been entered in the stable accounts, just like any other expense. Luckily, sufficient details of each purchase had been noted.

Pru sighed. "I suspect the fastest way forward will be for me to comb through these"—she waved at the pile of stable accounts, one large ledger for each year—"and extract the relevant information." She looked faintly exasperated. "Essentially, I'll be creating the acquisitions ledger your late father didn't bother with."

Deaglan grunted. "That's all of a piece with his refusal to even consider using the horses in any commercial enterprise. He probably knew he should have kept an acquisitions ledger, but reasoned that if he didn't, the horses would never be exploited in any way."

"In that," Pru said, "he reckoned without you two and me." She paused, head tilting in thought, then went on, "In fact, now I think of it, given that I will be the one assembling the ledger, and I've already done an exhaustive assessment of each of the horses the ledger will list, then in light of how important the Glengarah acquisitions ledger will be to you and the Cynsters and the deal we'll strike, and even more, to the value of the resulting foals, I rather think I'll get Dillon Caxton—he's the current Keeper of the Stud Book of the Jockey Club and Mama's cousin—to verify the contents of our new ledger." She paused again, eyes narrowing, then nodded decisively. "Yes, indeed. That's what we should do."

Deaglan exchanged an intrigued glance with Felix and saw no reason to argue.

Pru was regarding the account ledgers. "But if I'm poring through these, how will you two go about getting your figures for the average cost of upkeep?"

"I've been thinking about that." Deaglan sank his hands into his trouser pockets. "Rather than go line by line through the account ledgers, I can't see any reason why we can't simply use the expenses entered for the upkeep of the stable in the estate records. Say for the past eighteen months—since the pater died and during which time no horses were added. If we combine those amounts, adjust to the average for twelve months, then divide by fifty-seven horses, that should give us the figure we want—shouldn't it?"

Pru looked hopeful and didn't argue.

Felix slowly nodded. "I think it should be sixty-four horses, to include the carriage horses, but otherwise, I can't see why that wouldn't work."

"Good." With that agreed, Deaglan started collecting the account ledgers.

Between them, they ferried the ledgers for the past fifteen years into the castle and, at Pru's suggestion, upstairs to her bedroom.

She crossed to the round table before the window. "Put them here."

Straightening from setting down the pile he'd carried, Deaglan looked at her. "Are you sure you want to work up here?"

"Yes—it's quieter, and the others are much less likely to interrupt me." She eyed the stack of ledgers. "I'll need peace if I'm to get through all these in any reasonable time."

Deaglan accepted that with a grimace and caught Felix's eye. "In that case, we'll leave you to it and get on with assembling our figures. We'll be in the library if you need us."

Pru nodded, and they left her opening the unused ledger they'd brought from the stable office—soon to be the official Glengarah Stable Acquisitions Ledger.

Smiling, Deaglan shut the door behind him and, with Felix, headed for the stairs.

~

Late that night, when the rest of the house lay slumbering, Deaglan opened the door to Pru's room to find her in her nightgown and robe, poring over the ledgers by lamplight.

He smiled at the sight and closed the door.

She looked up at him and smiled, her curls lovingly gilded by the soft light. She waved at the ledgers. "Sadly, at my current rate of progress, it'll be days before I locate the entries for all fifty-seven horses."

His smile deepened; that news didn't dismay him in the least. He shrugged out of his coat and draped it over the back of a chair, then, unbuttoning his waistcoat, walked toward her. "Is there something you'd rather be doing?"

She laughed softly and set aside her pen. "As it happens…"

He reached for her hand, and she allowed him to draw her to her feet as she breathlessly concluded, "I rather think there is."

He drew her to him, into his arms, then bent and brushed a light—teasing—kiss across the lips she eagerly offered. "Actually," he murmured, "I thought that this"—with a tip of his head he indicated the pile of ledgers on the table—"was a distinctly novel way of seducing a lady."

Her answering laugh was low and sultry. "In that, you wouldn't be wrong." She wriggled her arms up and draped them about his neck. From close quarters, she met his eyes, moistened her lower lip, and said, "But seduction is all about the journey, isn't it? And you know how impatient I get to reach the end."

He did, indeed; that was a trait he used to advantage—both his and hers.

"So." Her lips skated along his jaw, then rose to flirt at the corner of his lips. "I suggest we move on, and you show me your true colors."

He would have laughed, but her lips shifted and pressed to his in flagrant demand, then she reinforced her command with passionate fervor.

With an incandescent ardency impossible to resist.

He didn't want to—no longer had reason to—hold back; he let the reins fall, gripped her head between his hands, and gave her what she wanted.

Heat, desire so intense it cindered all restraint, and passion so powerful, so elemental and profound, it seemed dredged from their souls.

The bed was there, and soon, they writhed upon it, tempting, inciting, worshipping, and ravishing.

Until they were far beyond control.

Until a power beyond them both whipped them on and rode them.

Into blinding ecstasy.

Into a shattering of the senses that left them scoured, hollowed out, only to be filled anew, made anew, as pure emotion rushed in and sated them.

And left them floating on a blissful sea.

Together and at peace.

CHAPTER 11

$\mathcal{P}$ru woke beside Deaglan in the dark of the night. She lay still, her eyes half closed, and waited for sleep to claim her again.

She was warm and relaxed; he was lying on his stomach with one arm slung over her, and his large, lean body put out so much heat it was impossible to imagine ever being cold again. Not if he was there.

Vaguely, she wondered what time it was. The glow of satiation still flowed through her veins, so she suspected dawn was still hours away.

A flicker of light at the edge of her vision had her raising her lids and focusing.

At first, she couldn't make sense of what she was seeing—a constantly shifting dappling of light on the wall opposite the windows.

Then she realized what it had to be, sat up, thrust back the covers, slid from under Deaglan's arm, and rushed to the windows.

He rumbled, "What is it?"

Pru stood rooted before the window and stared at the flames leaping above one end of the stable. "Fire! The stable's alight."

"What?" Deaglan was out of the bed and by her side in an instant. Then he swore and lunged for his clothes.

Pru didn't waste time talking. She rushed to the armoire, hauled out a skirt, and started scrambling into it.

His shirt hanging open, Deaglan stamped into his shoes, then raced for the door.

Seconds later, still buttoning her bodice, Pru hurried after him.

~

Pru caught up with Deaglan in the deepest part of the stable. Like her, he'd gone straight for the five most valuable horses, leaving the other horses—valuable though they also were—to the many grooms and stablemen who had already been rushing out of the castle and pouring from the barracks that formed part of the stable complex.

From what Pru had registered in her mad dash around the aisles— ignoring the cacophony of neighs, thumps, and thuds from the stalls, the rushing clatter of hooves as horses were led out, and the distant, sinister whoosh of flames broken by the occasional crack and crackle that was rising over the baying of the hounds, and dodging grooms, stablemen, and frightened horses—the fire seemed to be somewhere along the corridor that led away from the corner where the first aisle met the second. She hadn't noticed what lay along that corridor— she'd walked it earlier when they'd gone to the estate office which lay at the far end—but she knew there were no horse stalls along there.

The smoke had been thickest in the first aisle, and the grooms getting the horses out of the stalls on both sides of that aisle had been having a time of it getting halters on their already-spooked charges. The situation in the second and third aisles hadn't been as bad, while the horses in the fourth and in this hidden section had only just started to get the scent of smoke.

Deaglan had already got halters on three of the horses—the two mares and one of the stallions.

Pru snatched the halter for the Byerley Turk stallion from its peg, released the latch on his stall door, and crooning comfortingly, slipped in, and after a few seconds spent convincing the huge beast that he needed to behave, she got the halter on and led him slowly out.

Deaglan walked the last stallion from his stall. He glanced briefly at her. "I told the men to work progressively from the first aisle. Can you handle two?"

She nodded. "Give me the mares. I suggest we take these out as a group—the mares in front with me, you following with the stallions."

Tersely, Deaglan nodded. They sorted out the reins, and he held the stallions back so she could walk the mares forward. "Go through the concealed door and out onto the grassed area facing the fourth-aisle stalls, to the far side, then turn left. There's a gate between the buildings that should by now be open. It leads into a paddock that should be safe. Someone will have put up tether lines by now."

Pru nodded and led the mares out. The smoke was starting to thicken. Luckily, she'd thought to stuff a silk scarf in her pocket; she'd wrap it around her face once they'd got these horses safely away.

She was impressed to find the gate to the long paddock propped open and the tether lines already in place at the far end of the grassy slope. Clearly, the Glengarah stable had a fire drill in place—a very big point in its favor. As she led the mares down the lines, she noted a watchful older stableman with a shotgun over his arm standing guard at the lines' far end and glimpsed another armed guard at the rear of the paddock.

Once she'd settled the mares at the end of one row, as far from the stable as possible, Deaglan brought up the stallions, who had, unsurprisingly, proved more of a handful but, eventually, had followed the mares they knew. Pru helped him tether the skittish beasts, then stopped to tie her scarf in place.

Seeing her doing so, Deaglan hunted and pulled a kerchief from his pocket and knotted it about his head, covering his nose and mouth. Then he looked at her. "Ready?"

He didn't try to tell her to stay there in safety and look after the horses. For that, she could have kissed him.

She nodded and hurried to keep pace with him as he strode, half ran, back into the stable complex.

They plunged into an escalating melee; as the smoke thickened, the horses became harder to control, and something approaching chaos threatened. Given how valuable the horses were, no one wanted to unnecessarily allow them to run unchecked.

Pru lost sight of Deaglan as she stepped in to quieten horses she'd recently worked with. Many responded to her authority, as they had in the ring mere days before. She worked alongside the Glengarah stablemen, and also George and Horricks, to walk the more nervous of the horses out to the tether lines set up in the two paddocks that had been designated as safe zones.

Both, she noted, had guards in position, and sand buckets had been placed along the boundary closest to the stable complex.

The late earl might not have kept an acquisitions ledger, but he'd clearly paid all due attention to the safety of the horses he'd collected.

She worked up the fourth aisle, through the third, and into the second. By then, most of the horses were out, and only a few difficult stallions remained. She helped halter those, then handed them over to the stablemen.

Peering up the now-empty second aisle to where increasingly thick smoke blocked her view, she asked one of the older men, "Where's the fire located? Do you know?"

"Not precisely, ma'am, but it's somewhere down by the office." He nodded toward the opening to the corridor. "There was a wall of flames down there before, but I think they've nearly put it out."

She nodded her thanks and slowly walked toward the junction between the first and second aisles.

A breeze had sprung up and was blowing the smoke back toward the fire's source.

Deaglan loomed out of the thinning smoke still wafting in the first aisle; he saw her walking toward him and halted where the aisles met.

Pru felt tiredness drag at her as she continued toward him; now the panic was past, and it seemed the danger was contained, the urgency that had kept her moving was fading.

Deaglan took in her state as she approached. He hadn't known she'd followed him into the stable until she'd appeared in the hidden aisle; his first instinct had been to send her fleeing right out again, but then she was haltering the stallion, and there'd been no time to argue—and she was one of the most competent there when it came to managing panicky horses.

He'd left her working from that end of the stables—farthest from the fire—and gone to help the men struggling with the heavy carriage horses and the riding horses in the first aisle. Thor had been difficult; the big brute had refused to allow anyone but Deaglan close.

Unexpectedly, Pru's presence had also helped calm the men. As he'd headed away from her, he'd noted the way the men had glanced at her; the sight of her there—that he'd allowed her to be there—had been interpreted as meaning that the situation wasn't as dire as they'd feared.

Thankfully, that had proved to be the case.

She halted beside him, her gaze on the smoke still billowing around the far end of the corridor. "Did you lose any horses?"

"No. All are safe."

"Unharmed?"

He nodded. "For which I'll happily thank every saint."

A ghost of a smile touched her lips, then she sobered. "Do you know how bad it is?"

"I've only heard—I haven't yet seen." He glanced around. Felix had worked alongside him for a time, then Deaglan had sent him to see to the dogs; as the smoke had been blowing toward the kennels, they'd been howling like banshees.

Somewhat to his surprise, he'd later seen Cicely, wrapped in a coat, dispensing fresh water to the men as they'd staggered into the safe paddocks to get their breaths back.

He returned his gaze to Pru. He and she were smoke-stained and liberally sprinkled with flecks of gray ash. "Apparently, the fire started near the end of the corridor. Luckily, the draft from the open courtyards blows down the corridor, so the flames were pushed in the other direction— away from the stalls. Instead, the fire ran into the estate office. They've been fighting it mostly from outside. There won't be much if anything left."

She glanced at him, her gaze sharper. "Lucky, then, that all the ledgers that matter are up in my bedroom."

He met her gaze and felt an icy chill grip his gut. If they'd lost those ledgers, lost the acquisition details they contained, his father's vaunted collection would have been well-nigh worthless.

A large, burly figure lumbered out of the smoke. Waving a hand before his face, Rory Mack, the head stableman, staggered to a halt and bent over, wheezing.

Deaglan waited.

Eventually, Rory straightened, nodded his way, and croaked, "It's out."

Deaglan looked down the corridor, but the far end was still wreathed in gray smoke. "Any notion of what caused it?"

Rory's breathing had eased; he dragged in a deeper breath and looked back down the corridor. "Best I can make out is that a lighted lantern— must have been turned low or one of the watchmen would have seen the glow—was left on the ground not far from the office. No idea why, and none of the lads I've spoken with so far knows anything about it."

"But our lanterns have guards," Deaglan pointed out.

Rory nodded. "Aye, but seems this lantern was knocked over, and oil ran out over the burning wick and spilled across the floor. We've been using the alcove along there to stack extra bales of hay—remember? Near as we can figure, that's what went up, and then the framing timbers and rafters caught. We're damned lucky the breeze was blowing the other way." Rory suddenly realized Pru was there. He bobbed his shaggy head. "Excuse the language, miss."

Pru smiled wearily and waved the transgression aside.

Deaglan frowned. "I can accept a lantern forgotten on the floor—just. But why would it tip? They're designed to be hard to knock over."

Rory huffed. "I said the same, and one of the older men said he'd seen it before. Rats fighting. They're big enough to send a lantern flying."

Deaglan snorted. "It might be shutting the door after the horses—or in this case, the rats—have bolted, but we need more cats. We don't seem to have as many around as we used to."

"Aye." Rory nodded. "We've lost several recently—just old age—but haven't got more kittens in on account of they tease the dogs."

"The dogs will have to learn to put up with the cats," Deaglan grimly stated.

"I'll get onto it," Rory promised.

Deaglan had been eyeing the end of the corridor; the smoke had now thinned enough for him to see the smoldering timbers at the far end and catch glimpses of the night sky where the roof had fallen in. He started walking. "Let's take a look at the damage."

Rory grunted and led the way.

Deaglan glanced back to see Pru following. "You don't have to come."

She shrugged and kept walking, albeit trailing him. "I'd like to see."

Deaglan faced forward.

They came to the area blackened by the flames.

Rory stopped and, when Deaglan halted alongside, pointed farther down what had once been the end of the corridor and was now a burnt wreck. "See—there's the lantern."

Moonlight was pouring in through the gap in the roof, combining with the residual smoke to cloak the scene in a ghostly haze. Deaglan made out a lump of twisted metal lying amid ashes and charred debris that had fallen from above.

Rory's finger traced a line to their right. "And we think that darker trail there is the track of the burning oil, spilling out and heading for the alcove. Once the flames reached the straw...well, it would've gone up quick." Rory glanced at Deaglan. "Lucky you raised the alarm when you did. We might have lost the tack room or worse if we hadn't got to it so quickly."

Deaglan saw no reason to reveal that it hadn't been he who had first spotted the flames.

Pru came to stand just behind Deaglan and placed a hand on the back of his jacket—whether to comfort him or herself, she didn't know. She'd been in the office just hours before, and now, it was a smoldering ruin. The door and all inside the office had been reduced to ash; the brick walls, crumbling here and there, were largely intact, but the beams of the roof had burned and crashed down. Even where the three of them stood, six or so yards from the office door, there was no longer any roof; looking up, she saw stars twinkling far above, framed by the spectral black fingers of charred rafters.

"Luckily," Rory said, then amended, "if one can use that word, the storeroom here"—he waved to the left—"was less than half full. We lost a little feed, but nothing much else to speak of. No tack, no harness. Not even our supply of shoes."

Deaglan grunted. "We got off lightly." He turned his head and met Pru's eyes. "Very lightly, all in all."

She nodded slightly. With respect to the stable account ledgers, they'd narrowly escaped a horrendous situation. Her mind refused to contemplate what losing the ledgers that would normally have been in the office would have meant—and not just for the Glengarah estate. "All because of a couple of rats," she murmured.

Deaglan reached back, caught her hand in one of his, and squeezed reassuringly.

Hurrying footsteps approached, and Deaglan released her fingers as they turned to see Jay striding up.

He was as soot-streaked as they. "I've been down in the paddocks—all seems settled there now." He looked past them at the gutted office. "Good Lord. Is everything gone?"

Deaglan felt his jaw tighten, reminded again of how much they'd nearly lost. "Everything that was in there."

He turned to Rory. "Those beams will have to come down so they don't drag on the rest of the roof. Once everything's cooled, we'll clear all we can, then I'd like you to get your brother up to take a look." Rory's brother was a master carpenter and lived in Drumcliff. "We'll need to decide what we want to rebuild and replace. I'm thinking we might change a few things."

Such as having an office in the stable at all.

"Aye." Rory nodded. "I'll get him to come up once we've cleared."

Deaglan turned away and noticed that Pru was rubbing her arms. But Jay was there, so he merely cupped her elbow and started walking back along the corridor.

Jay fell in on his other side. "We'll need to decide what to do with the horses."

"I'm going to go out to the paddocks now." Deaglan glanced back, catching Rory's eye and signaling for the head stableman to follow them.

Pru looped her arm in his, and the four of them walked on.

When they reached the end of the first aisle, Deaglan halted, waved the other two men to go ahead, then turned to Pru. He lifted her hand and brushed a kiss across the back of her knuckles. "Thank you—if it wasn't for you and your quick thinking, this would have been much worse."

She huffed. "As matters stand, I have nearly as much riding on your horses as you do."

He smiled. "Nevertheless." He glanced after Rory and Jay. "You should go in."

She turned her hand, hooked her fingers in his, and drew his hand down between them. "I'm too twitchy to sleep, and I could do with some fresh air to clear my lungs."

So she walked with him out to the paddocks, where he moved among the men, thanking them for their efforts and listening to their reports on the horses.

Pru, meanwhile, lent her aid in calming those horses that were still skittish.

Deaglan noted the respect with which all the men now viewed her; previously, only a handful had seen her in action with the horses, but after tonight, all knew she possessed what many termed "the touch," the ability to commune with and soothe even the most panicky beast. Most considered that a God-given talent.

And of course, she'd completely upended their views of high-born ladies by rushing out of the castle and straight into the smoke-filled stable as she had.

They moved on to the second paddock, and after checking on the horses and speaking with the men there, leaving Pru soothing the five most precious beasts, Deaglan retreated to one corner of the paddock with Rory and Jay. It didn't take long to decide that their best option was to leave the horses where they were; the night was mild enough, and the air in the paddocks was more or less smoke-free. Trying to rehouse already-unsettled horses into stalls that smelled of smoke would be a fool's errand, and they all knew it.

"I'll put on extra guards—triple those we already have." Rory glanced at the blackness of the fields all around. "Just in case it wasn't an accident and some bugger got the idea that setting a small fire would get the horses out into the open fields where a few might not be missed straightaway."

Deaglan grunted an assent. Horse stealing was almost a tradition— one of the reasons for the hidden stalls. He, too, glanced around. "We may have to keep them out until the day after tomorrow. We'll need to muck out all the stalls and get in fresh hay."

Rory bobbed his head. "I'll draw up a roster for the men so we'll have plenty who can stand guard tomorrow night, too."

"Do." Deaglan watched Pru approach. "Is there anything else we need to decide now?"

There wasn't. Rory lumbered off to speak to the men.

Pru joined Deaglan and Jay, and the three of them made their way around the stable and into the side court.

Ahead of them, groups of grooms and stable lads were stumbling back to their beds. "We've left plenty of men on guard overnight," Deaglan told Pru. "This lot will take over in the morning."

She nodded, somewhat relieved to know that he was taking no chances.

Looking toward the side door, she saw Felix escorting Cicely inside and smiled to herself. Cicely was proving to have a remarkably strong will, something Pru appreciated in any woman.

The three of them were the last to approach the side door. They were still some way from it when Jay halted. "I'll leave you here."

Pru remembered that he lived in the gatehouse with his mother. She was so tired she had to battle an urge to lean against Deaglan.

Jay nodded respectfully to her. "I hope, Miss Cynster, that you managed to get everything you needed from the stable ledgers." He grimaced and glanced at Deaglan. "I always said that the ledgers should be kept in the estate office, but of course, your father would never listen."

Deaglan grunted. "As we all know, he was set in his ways. Luckily for us—for Miss Cynster hasn't finished extracting all the details from the ledgers that we'll need to negotiate our deal—we'd brought the account ledgers for the past fifteen years up to the house."

For a moment, Jay was silent, then in heartfelt tones, said, "Thank Mary and Joseph and all the saints."

"Indeed." Deaglan met Pru's eyes, then nodded to Jay. "Goodnight."

Jay echoed the word, raised a hand in salute, and headed toward the front of the house.

Deaglan sighed and, taking Pru's hand, with a tired smile for her, walked on to the side door.

Inside, they found Maude, Esmerelda, Cicely, Bligh, Mrs. Bligh, and Pru's older maid all waiting to hear their report.

"Felix didn't know much," Esmerelda informed Deaglan.

He stifled a sigh, and judging it to be his fastest route to getting upstairs to Pru's bed, he rapidly outlined the damage to the stable office, stated that other than the things in that room, they'd lost little, that the horses were safe and secure, and that he believed the cause had been a regrettable accident that was unlikely to be repeated.

Sufficiently reassured, everyone consented to return to their beds.

Deaglan and Pru were the last up the stairs. When they stepped into the gallery, there was no one about to see Deaglan accompany her to her room.

He opened the door, and she walked in.

He made to follow, but halted on the threshold.

Pru realized he'd stopped. She glanced back, saw him hesitating, half in and half out of the room, and arched her brows. "What?"

He wrinkled his nose. "I reek of smoke."

She laughed softly, retraced her steps, caught his hand, and tugged him on. "We're a good match, then."

Deaglan let all resistance fall from him and allowed her to tow him all the way to her bed, thinking, as he felt her fingers locked with his, gently tugging, that truer words had rarely been spoken—they were a good match.

More, they made an excellent team.

CHAPTER 12

*I*n the middle of the following morning, Deaglan, with Pru by his side, made a quick tour of the stable complex. The taint of smoke still hung in the air, but daylight confirmed that much of the complex was undamaged and unmarred, and the stablemen were busy with brooms and mops, clearing up the detritus of the evacuation. After surveying their efforts, Deaglan confirmed with Rory that the horses should be left outside until at least that evening, freed to amble about the nearer paddocks and breathe the fresher air under the watchful eyes of several of the older men, while the younger hands refreshed the stalls and the estate handymen barricaded off the damaged section at the end of the corridor.

Finally, after examining the wreck of the office, Deaglan gave orders that the area should be left undisturbed until the next day, to allow the bricks to cool and the timbers to finish smoldering.

"Ask Callum to come up tomorrow," Deaglan told Rory. "No sense in getting him up today."

"Aye—that's my thinking, too."

Leaving Rory lumbering off to oversee the refurbishing of the stalls, Deaglan and Pru headed back to the castle. In the front hall, they passed Jay and Bligh discussing how many barrels of beer needed to be ordered to replenish the cellar.

Deaglan nudged Pru on. "The library. It should be blessedly deserted at this hour."

That proved to be the case. After ushering Pru inside, Deaglan shut the door, then faced her. "The stable accounts. After nearly losing them last night and realizing just how valuable they are in terms of the estate's future, I've decided I had best keep them under lock and key. Will you need them for much longer?"

She widened her eyes at him. "I've only just started. I have to scan the entries on each page to pick out the purchases relating to horses. Your father didn't make them stand out in any way—they appear in exactly the same way as a bale of hay."

Deaglan cursed beneath his breath and ran the fingers of both hands through his hair. "Even if he wasn't intending to exploit the horses for profit, the pater could at least have kept a proper record of when and from whom he got each horse." He paused, then looked at her. "Are the entries giving you enough to go on to verify the bloodlines?"

"So far, yes. I only need the name of from whom he bought the horse, the date of purchase, the name of the horse, and a general description of the beast. Once I have those noted for all fifty-seven horses, I'll sit down with the General Stud Book"—she glanced at the shelves lining the walls —"I'm sure there'll be an appropriate edition somewhere here—"

"There are any number of editions on the shelves over there." Deaglan nodded toward the right of the fireplace.

She glanced that way. "Good. Although it might take a little time, hopefully, I'll be able to match each of the Glengarah horses to their entry in the studbook, which will confirm who their progenitors are, which is the critical information we need to underpin breeding value." She looked back, met his eyes, and with a faint smile for his exasperation, observed, "At least your father did write down the necessary details of each purchase. As matters stand, he's given us enough to go on with."

He sighed. "Only because you're willing to spend hours extracting the information from the stable accounts and creating the acquisitions ledger my father should have had from the first."

"Oh, the ledger I create will be better than that—a definite advance on the average acquisitions ledger, given I'll get Dillon Caxton to verify it. That will put the provenance of your horses—and their potential offspring —beyond question going forward."

He studied her. "I don't know that I fully comprehend the implications of that, but I do most sincerely thank you."

Her smile was both delighted and self-deprecatory. "I have to admit that I enjoy doing that sort of work—matching horses, their descriptions, their breeding and bloodlines."

He found himself smiling back; her sunniness was infectious. "When do you think you'll be ready to talk further regarding our negotiations?"

She primmed her lips in thought, then replied, "I would rather get the purchasing information for all fifty-seven horses noted down—out of the account ledgers—and make a start on formalizing the bloodlines, at least of the most valuable twenty or so horses. That will give us a solid base from which to estimate the breeding value of the collection as a whole." She met his eyes, and this time, her smile held a challenging edge. "That, of course, will dictate how high I'm willing to go regarding stud fees and how far in terms of breeding exchanges and the sharing of offspring."

She paused, then added, "But to answer your question, another two days should suffice. With luck, I'll be finished with the stable accounts by tonight or tomorrow morning at the latest."

He tipped his head in acceptance, meeting her smile with one of his own. "In that case…" He reached for her, drew her to him, bent his head, and kissed her.

She softened in his arms, pressing closer, and came up on her toes to kiss him back.

With the same directness, the same blatant passion he lavished on her.

And the magic rose and took them, surrounded and embraced them. It was utterly unlike anything he'd experienced before, this instant connection that was powerful enough to stop the world in its tracks and become, for them, everything.

All.

He savored it—as did she—then reluctantly, he drew back.

He raised his head and looked into her face. Her lids rose, and he found himself falling into the bright blue of her eyes. He had to wonder if she knew how unusual, how precious, the intangible yet potent link between them was.

The thought that she might not—that she might never see what, increasingly, he did—rattled him. Unsettled him. He hid the disturbing sensation behind an easy smile as he released her, but caught one of her hands in one of his. "Perhaps you'd better leave me to manage the estate while you return to scouring the ledgers."

Her eyes laughed at him, and her lips curved. "I suspect you're right."

He stepped back, and she moved past him to the door, and he followed.

There, she paused and faced him. "I need to concentrate and get this done. Don't look for me at the luncheon table—I'll have a tray brought up." Her expression grew serious. "And as I agree with you about the ledgers, I'm going back to them right now, and if I leave the room, I'll have one of my people come up and keep watch over them. There's no sense in taking any chances at all—not until we've extracted all the information we need. Once we have"—she lightly shrugged—"they become just another set of old accounts."

He nodded. "Thank you." He squeezed her fingers, then eased his hold and allowed her to draw them free. Reaching past her, he opened the door. "Until dinnertime, then."

"Indeed. Until then." With a last smile for him, she walked out and turned for the front hall.

Hearing footsteps farther down the corridor come to a halt, Deaglan leaned into the corridor and looked that way.

Jay had stopped a yard short of the estate office door; he looked inquiringly back at Deaglan. "Do you need me for anything this morning?"

Deaglan thought, then shook his head. "How are the repairs to the bridge coming along?"

"Joe says they're almost done. He'll want you to come and inspect the work when it's finished."

Deaglan nodded. "When all's complete." With a tip of his head to Jay, Deaglan shut the library door and headed for his desk. He slumped into the chair behind it and stared unseeing over the desktop littered with correspondence, notes, and reports.

Eyes narrowing, he calculated, evaluated, and pondered which front he should—could—advance on next in his campaign to convince his nemesis that remaining forever at Glengarah was what, in her heart, she wished to do.

In the small hours of the following morning, Pru, lying slumped, boneless and warm, beside Deaglan in her bed, jerked awake.

Her mind racing, her body tensing—she had no idea why—she lay unmoving and reached with her senses.

What had jarred her awake?

Why was she—her instincts—reacting as if danger threatened?

Then she heard a small creak, followed by the unmistakable sound of a stealthy footstep.

Abruptly, she sat up, catching the covers to her bare breasts. The room was wreathed in shadows; no moon shone through the clouds.

A figure—a denser, defined darkness—stood midway between the half-open door and the window.

Woken by her movement, beside her, Deaglan stirred.

"Who the devil are you?" The challenging words rang out before she'd thought.

The intruder startled and glanced her way, just as Deaglan reared up and swung around to look.

The intruder balked, then spun and bolted through the door.

Deaglan swore, flung back the covers, swore again when he was forced to free his legs and feet from the tangled sheets, then leapt from the bed and charged in pursuit.

His eyes were well-adjusted; despite the lack of light, he could see well enough in a house he'd known since birth. Three paces along the corridor leading to the main stairs, he skidded to a halt, scanning ahead.

There was no one in the corridor; even with the delay of the sheets, the intruder couldn't have reached the gallery and plunged down the main stairs, out of sight.

Grimly, Deaglan strode for the door in the corridor's paneling that concealed the entrance to the servants' stair. The instant he touched the panel, it swung free.

Cursing anew, he opened the door and walked onto the wooden landing. He halted and listened, but whoever it had been was long gone. He debated rousing the household and instituting a search, but if the man had known where the servants' stair was...

His face setting, Deaglan returned to the corridor, closed the stair door, and stalked back to Pru's room.

She was still sitting up in the bed, eyes huge in the poor light. "He was after the ledgers."

Deaglan grunted. He shut the door, walked to the bed, and fell on his back beside her. "He got away down the servants' stair. I didn't realize which way he'd gone until he'd effectively vanished."

After a second, he reached down and hauled the jumbled covers over him. "He didn't expect me to be here."

"No." She slid down in the bed; her hand reached for his, and their fingers twined. In a smaller voice, she murmured, "I wonder what would have happened if you hadn't been."

So did he, but he pushed the unhelpful thought aside. He wouldn't be able to exact suitable vengeance for scaring her until he caught the man... "Did you see enough to be sure it was a man? Could it have been a woman?"

When she didn't reply, he glanced at her face.

She'd closed her eyes, and a faint frown tangled her brows as she plainly thought back. "No. From the way he moved, it was definitely a man. A woman doesn't stride like that."

He nodded. "I thought it was a man as well." After a moment, he said, "He came here to steal the ledgers."

She hesitated, then ventured, "I'm starting to wonder if the fire was no accident, and the ledgers were what it was actually about. Burning the ledgers—destroying them. But why?"

The confusion in her voice echoed his own, then a chill touched his spine. He considered the prospect for several long seconds. Could it be? "If someone didn't want any deal between Glengarah and the Cynster Stables to go ahead, then destroying the ledgers—and with them the provenance of the horses—would be, at this moment in time, the surest way to do that."

He felt her turn her head to stare at him. "But that wouldn't just ruin any deal with the Cynster Stables—it would wipe out any chance of doing a deal with any stable. Destroying the horses' provenance would make them next to valueless... Well, they'd still be fabulous horses, but with very much reduced breeding value. That would harm the estate."

"Primarily, and I know of no one who would benefit from harming the estate." He glanced at her and met her eyes. "But you mentioned that there are several stables in competition with the Cynsters. Could one of them have sufficient incentive to simply not care about rendering the Glengarah collection worthless if, in so doing, they prevented the Cynsters from using the Glengarah horses to leap far in advance of the other stable?"

She stared into his eyes for several seconds, then wrinkled her nose and looked away. After a moment, she murmured, "Sadly, that's not beyond the realm of possibility."

He freed his fingers from hers, lifted his arm, looped it about her, and drew her against him. She snuggled close, and he pressed a kiss to her curls, then softly said, "Our intruder knew the location of the door to the servants' stair, something I can't imagine anyone other than those currently living under this roof would know, so we'll need to consider each and every possibility, no matter how apparently far-fetched."

"Ah" was all she said.

"But in the morning." He settled deeper into the mattress and felt her gradually relax against him. "For now...let's sleep."

For a wonder, they did.

After breakfast, during which, with Pru's consent, Deaglan told Felix of the attempt to steal the ledgers, Pru walked with Deaglan to the stable. Jay was waiting for Deaglan at the stable entrance. While Deaglan went with his steward to talk to Rory and Rory's brother, Callum, who'd come to start work on the repairs, Pru ambled down the aisles, confirming that the horses had recovered from the excitement of the fire; if anything, she felt they'd all benefited from their time roaming in the paddocks.

Satisfied, she made her way down the corridor to where Deaglan stood with Jay, Rory, and a man who was plainly Rory's brother; the four were still engaged in a discussion of their options.

As she neared, Deaglan swung to look at her. "Do you know of any other stable with an office located within the stable?"

She halted beside him, thought, then shook her head. "No. None." She met his eyes. "They might have a place for receiving goods, but no office as such."

He nodded and looked at Jay and Rory. "We don't need an office. As Callum says that we'd be best replacing the roof and using the outer walls as they are to support it, then let's use the space for something else."

They settled on transforming the space that used to be the office into a storage bay, something Callum informed them would take the least time to make good.

With that decided, Deaglan left Jay, Rory, and Callum to organize the work. Pru walked beside him up the first aisle toward the stable entrance.

As they stepped into the spring sunshine, Deaglan sighed and looked ahead—at the castle on the other side of the court. "In some strange way, getting rid of the stable office feels like dropping the last lead weight from my father's day from my shoulders."

Pru glanced at him; his expression was impassive, his face as unreadable as it usually was, yet his tone held undercurrents she couldn't mistake. She murmured, "I understand that, quite aside from his stance over the stable, your father was a major obstacle to your drive to improve conditions on the estate, yet when you speak of him...I hear regret. You regret having been at loggerheads with him."

The glance he cast her was sharp; she made no move to meet it.

Then he halted, and she stopped by his side. He swung to look at the hills to the north, then turned his head and met her eyes. "I do regret it. We were alike in many ways—in our love of horses, among other things—yet he had a...I suppose you'd call it a weakness. One I didn't have. He needed direction—something that gave him a goal to work toward. While Mama was alive, that wasn't an issue—he had her as his lodestar, his guiding light. After Mama died, his search for some path to take led to his obsession with horses on the one hand and his utter disregard for everything else on the other."

"So you weren't always at loggerheads."

"No. Not at all." He looked at the hills again, then sighed. "We were close for a long time, even after Mama passed. It was only about five years before his death—a few years before I left—that his persistent neglect of the estate became something I could no longer pretend not to see."

He paused, but she could see there was more, that he was revisiting and re-evaluating.

Eventually, he went on, "He wasn't grounded in the estate as I was— as I am. As Felix is. Papa never had roots sunk in this soil, and that showed. Anything he felt for the estate was superficial, shallow, while our connection with it runs bone deep."

After several seconds, he met her eyes again, with a faintly lopsided, self-deprecating smile. "My fall from his grace was a long, drawn-out process, one that wore on us both. And while you're right in that I regretted his actions, regretted that he died with no peace between us, I'd expected that, and despite all, I couldn't do other than I did. I never regretted doing all I could to improve the lives of the people of Glengarah."

Pru held his gaze. "Nor should you." Then she allowed her lips to quirk upward. "But it sounds as if you were equally stubborn, equally adamantly set on your course."

He arched a superior brow. "I prefer to think of it as committed and determined."

She laughed, then they both turned as Lady Connaught came barreling surprisingly quickly toward them.

"There you are!" Her ladyship halted and looked up at Deaglan. "I hope this business with the fire hasn't damaged your prospects with the horses."

Deaglan cut a glance at Pru. "No, Aunt. Pru and I are currently working to assemble the necessary information to advance to formal negotiations on an agreement."

"Good." Lady Connaught switched her gaze to Pru and nodded decisively. "Excellent!"

After a second of intense scrutiny, her ladyship turned back to Deaglan. "Now, tell me, dear boy, aside from the horses, what are your plans for the estate? I know you— —you'll have various irons just waiting to be shoved into the fire. So what are they, heh?"

To Pru's amusement—and not inconsiderable surprise—her ladyship proved adept at winkling a great deal of information from Deaglan, a man not given to sharing easily. His aunt seemed to consider any hesitation on his part as an invitation to prod and pull and tease every detail of whatever was in his head from him. And as she was shrewd and sharp-witted, there was little she missed.

It was quite entertaining and also informative. Pru hadn't known that the estate encompassed fishing rights on Glencar Lough and along the Drumcliff River that led from the lough to the sea, or that the fish drawn from the river and lake were both a staple on the tables of the estate families and also sold in Drumcliff and Sligo, providing another source of income to the estate. Likewise with the hunting rights on the wild land above the escarpment of which Kings Mountain was a part.

And Lady Connaught had been right; Deaglan had plans for it all.

Watching the pair of them, one verbally prodding, the other defending and deflecting, Pru rather thought that while Deaglan had most likely come by his strength, both physical and mental, from his father, judging by the similarities between him and his maternal aunt, he'd almost certainly inherited his mental acuity—his sharpness and shrewdness— from his mother's side.

The combination was formidable—something she would have to bear in mind when they started formal negotiations.

Naturally enough, his aunt's inquisition made Deaglan itch to be elsewhere. When Rory came looking for him and halted a few yards away, hovering, Deaglan seized the chance to wave at the head stableman and claim, "I have to deal with this, Aunt."

Lady Connaught looked at Rory, then humphed. "Very well." She waved Deaglan and Pru off and turned back toward the castle. "I'll speak with you later."

"Not if I can help it," Deaglan muttered beneath his breath, and he saw Pru's lips twitch as she turned with him to face Rory.

Rory's question was quickly dealt with, then, glancing over his shoulder in the direction his aunt had gone, Deaglan waved toward the kennels. "I should check with the kennel master—I've been neglecting him and the dogs of late. Come, and you can take a look at the latest litters while I speak with him."

The dogs comprised another strand of the net he was hoping to weave to hold Pru to Glengarah. Not trap but actively encourage her to remain.

The kennel master found them just inside the entrance and walked with them to the large whelping stalls that presently housed two litters of golden beagles and one of the smaller red-and-white spaniels.

Pru was obviously entranced by the small bundles of fur that tumbled over their own outsize paws in an effort to reach her and lick her fingers and snuffle under her hems until she laughed and crouched down.

He could have told her that the boisterous puppies would take that as an invitation to play, but held his tongue and, instead, watched, along with the kennel master, Sheppard, as she was bombarded from every side. As she clearly didn't mind in the least, he left her to the puppies and gave his attention to Sheppard, who took the opportunity to bend his ear about a young red-and-white dog he wanted to buy in.

After listening to a paean on the dog's qualities, Deaglan gave his permission for Sheppard to approach the owner, a landowner outside Drumcliff, with an offer.

Sheppard was pleased. "I'm fairly sure I can get the lad for a good price. Shields from Lord Whistler's kennels bred him and told me about the beast—the nodcock in Drumcliff insisted on buying three from the same litter, and now, he's got his hands full. Shields all but begged me to see if I could persuade the man to part with the best dog. He'll not know which is the best, of course. Shields would love to get the beast back, but they're full up over there, and the nodcock is apparently the sort who will never admit he made a mistake in buying the three—not to Shields, anyway."

Pru had gone from one litter to the next, leaving happily exhausted puppies and grateful dams in her wake. With the last of the litters tiring, she rose and glanced at Deaglan. When she saw him watching her, she arched a brow. "Have you finished?"

He nodded. "Ready to leave?"

She glanced down at the twin bundles of golden pelt currently curled by her feet. "I think they're asleep." She edged back a step. Instantly, both pups raised their heads and stared up at her.

Sheppard chuckled. "I think they've adopted you."

Having hoped for just such an occurrence, Deaglan leaned on the stall wall. "You could take them with you—a present from Glengarah."

Her face said she was tempted. "Perhaps," she temporized. But she bent and patted both glossy heads before sliding out of the stall door—all without taking her eyes from the pups, who sleepily stumbled in her wake. After latching the door, she leaned on it and looked down at the wrinkly faces. "They are a very distinctive color."

"Aye," Sheppard said, pride in his voice. "There are other goldish breeds, but it's only Kerry beagles have such a bright gold to their coat."

Deaglan—along with a knowing Sheppard—watched the battle Pru had to wage to turn away from the pups.

When she finally managed it, Deaglan waved her toward the kennel entrance. "We'd better get back to our respective tasks."

She nodded and fell in beside him. They strolled into the sunshine and headed for the castle's side door, only to see Felix emerge, spot them, and come walking purposefully toward them.

Taking in his brother's expression, Deaglan put out a hand and touched Pru's arm; she glanced at him and halted with him, roughly in the middle of the large court, well away from any other ears.

Felix joined them. "I, ah…" Felix's gaze swept the area. "Rory looked in to say that Callum thought the repairs would take until mid-next week to complete. Apparently, he'll have to cart timbers for the replacement rafters up from Sligo." Felix brought his gaze back to Deaglan.

Deaglan nodded. When Felix simply looked at him, he huffed impatiently. "You can speak before Pru. What else?"

Felix raised a hand and, briefly, pinched the bridge of his nose. "This might sound a touch far-fetched, but I was wondering if the burning of the stable office, where the stable account ledgers should have been, and the attempt to steal them last night might have anything to do with the Cynsters' interest in the Glengarah horses."

Deaglan shared a glance with Pru. "We'd wondered the same thing."

"Oh, good." Relief washed over Felix's face, and he looked inquiringly at Pru. "So do you have any idea how others—not your family— might have learned that you were coming to evaluate our horses with a view to a possible deal?"

Pru blinked. "That's an excellent point." She plainly thought, but then shook her head. "I can't think how anyone beyond my immediate family and our staff could have known. I can assure you no one would have spoken of it, not to anyone. As you can imagine, everyone associated with the Cynster Stables understands how critical it is to keep visits such as this secret."

Felix frowned. "But for our theory to hold water, someone else must have heard that you're here, at the very least."

Deaglan grimaced and caught Pru's eye. "You rode into Sligo—what was it, ten days ago? You're quite distinctive—especially given you were riding Macbride—and am I right in guessing that many associated with Thoroughbred breeders would recognize you on sight?"

She wrinkled her nose. "I've been hobnobbing on racetracks and with breeders since I could walk."

He nodded. "And there are several trainers of Thoroughbreds in the area around Sligo, and all visitors pass through the town. It's possible— even likely—that someone saw you with Felix, recognized you both, and leapt to the obvious conclusion."

"And," Felix said, "there's been plenty of time since for the news to have been passed on, and even for someone to have come over from England, if they were so inclined."

Pru sighed. "All of that is entirely possible—horse trainers are inveterate gossips." She paused, then frowned. "But if we assume that it was someone sent by another breeding stable to ensure no deal was struck between Glengarah and the Cynster Stables, and we further assume that they somehow learned from the locals that all the stable ledgers were kept in the stable office and, subsequently, set the stable office alight, how did they learn that the ledgers we need weren't consumed in the fire?"

She looked at Deaglan, then at Felix.

Felix grimaced. "That's not that hard to explain. Most of our stable hands drink at the local pub in Rathcormack. Anyone wanting to know what's going on here would just have to sit in the inglenook and listen, and last night, all the talk would have been about the fire. We didn't tell anyone to keep news about the ledgers a secret, and several of the men saw us carry the ledgers out and to the castle on Thursday. On top of that, many of the maids walk out with the grooms and stablemen, and the maids chatter all the time about everything."

Pru pulled a face.

"But," Deaglan said, "how did our intruder of this morning know the ledgers were in Pru's room? Or even where her room was?"

Pru thought, then said, "Well, there are the maids, of course. And we don't know how long he'd been in the house. He might have searched downstairs first, found nothing, and decided my room was the next most likely place. If he'd talked to someone from the house, he might have learned which room was mine, or even just known which was the guest wing and quietly checked every room until he reached mine. Risky, but I didn't hear him until he was halfway across the room, and then only because a board creaked."

She paused, then went on, "And he would have been expecting a single acquisitions ledger, not an entire pile. That's why, when I surprised him, he didn't just lunge for the table, swipe up the ledger, and run—he couldn't, because there were so many of them."

Deaglan nodded. "Then he realized you weren't alone and fled empty-handed."

As he had earlier over the breakfast table, Felix tried valiantly to appear oblivious of the implications of that statement.

Deaglan shook his head. "That still doesn't explain how he knew of the servants' stair."

Felix shrugged. "Just luck? Or perhaps he'd chatted up one of the maids?"

Deaglan frowned. "That's possible, but I'm not sure it's probable."

Pru caught his eye. "Do you know if Bligh found any sign of a break-in?"

To Felix, Deaglan explained, "I asked Bligh to check this morning." To Pru, he said, "Apparently, one of the windows in the laundry room is permanently left ajar to air the room of the steam from the coppers. This morning, the laundry maid found the window swung wide, which it has to be tugged from outside to achieve, and she was most incensed to discover dirt on her bench, so it seems likely our villain gained entry that way. Bligh reported that, henceforth, he will be locking the laundry door every night. It's a thick old door with a heavy lock, so whoever it is won't be able to use that route again."

Felix looked pointedly at Deaglan. "I think we should set guards around the house and the stable—and possibly the kennels as well."

His expression hardening, Deaglan slowly nodded. "No need to tell anyone else about the intruder—the fire is excuse enough."

Felix glanced at Pru. "What about the ledgers?"

"I haven't yet finished with them," Pru replied, "but we decided it was best if Deaglan kept them locked away while they're not actually in my hands."

Deaglan met Felix's eyes. "I've put them in the library safe, so only you or I can get them out."

Felix nodded. After a second during which they all plainly reviewed their safeguards, Felix said, "As far as I can see, that's really all we can do."

"Not quite." Pru glanced at Deaglan. "We should proceed with our preparations and the negotiations at a greater pace—as fast as we reasonably can."

Deaglan read her eyes, then, swallowing his reluctance, nodded. "Because once the deal is done, there'll be no reason to continue trying to scupper it."

"Exactly," Pru said. "I doubt any likely culprit—assuming they are another breeder or the agent of one—would seek to harm the horses themselves. After all, the stable fire was neatly set to burn the office and not run toward the stalls."

"Hmm. Regardless," Deaglan said, "I'll post guards until we're confident that whoever is behind these attempts has given up and gone away."

The three of them exchanged glances; it seemed they'd reached an accord.

Deaglan waved, and they set off for the side door.

He wasn't thrilled with the notion of rushing to conclude a deal; he wanted as much time as he could get to change Pru's mind before he mentioned the word "marriage."

Still, he told himself, if the worst came to be and they completed the deal and she insisted on leaving, he would find some way to prolong their liaison, even if that meant following her back to England.

They entered the castle. As they walked along the corridor to the front hall, Pru said, "It's only just after ten o'clock." She glanced over her shoulder and met his eyes. "I suggest we take possession of the library, fetch out the ledgers, and while I continue to ferret out the acquisitions, you two can work on tallying your figures for calculating the average cost of upkeep for the horses."

Felix cast a trepidatious glance at Deaglan, who understood exactly what his brother feared. Neither he nor Felix were particularly good at arithmetic. As earl, Deaglan managed, but only just, and only because he'd been specifically taught how to perform every single calculation he needed in order to maintain oversight of the estate.

Tallying figures to work out the average cost of upkeep per annum for their horses was something outside his ken.

But he balked at confessing that to Pru; he and Felix would have to manage.

As they crossed the front hall, making for the corridor leading to the library, Deaglan glanced up and saw Esmerelda standing at the gallery balustrade, watching them.

Even over the distance, he felt the weight of her pointed, distinctly meaningful gaze.

It was almost threatening.

Facing forward, he didn't try to pretend that his aunt wouldn't do something rash—if, in her mind, he pushed her to it.

Her message had been clear enough: He had to convince Pru to marry him soon, or else Esmerelda would step in—with potentially disastrous results.

Pru settled in a straight-backed chair at the library table that Deaglan and Felix had dragged to sit beside one of the long windows. The table all but groaned under the weight of the ledgers, which the brothers had retrieved from the safe and stacked before her.

Deaglan and Felix subsequently retreated to the armchairs before the fireplace, leaving her to get on with her listing of acquisitions while they collated the figures they would need to tally for the average cost of upkeep.

Already well and truly sick of scanning the entries made in the late earl's florid hand, Pru concentrated on not missing any entry describing the purchase of a horse—as distinct from purchases of harness, carriages, feed of all types, horseshoes, and the like. She'd elected to start with the earliest ledger—from fifteen years ago—and judging from the notes she'd made on each horse, once she'd succeeded in picking up the entries for the oldest horses in the stable, she'd worked steadily forward, going through the ledgers for each successive year.

She reached a stretch seven years ago during which the earl had acquired a string of horses, allowing her to fill in the details for a large number of horses in a relatively short time.

Every now and then, she checked her emerging list of acquisitions against her notes, then continued on. She was determined to complete the task—to uncover the purchasing details for all fifty-seven horses—today, so she could move on to the more interesting activity of matching the acquisitions with the information in the studbook, thus confirming the bloodlines she was convinced each horse possessed.

Finally, she had only the details for three more horses to find.

Then two.

One.

"Hallelujah!" She quickly scribbled down the relevant information—for one of the mares stalled in the secret aisle—then sat back and, triumphantly, surveyed her notes and the list. "My fifty-seven-piece jigsaw is complete."

That was what it felt like.

"Congratulations." From his armchair, Deaglan smiled at her.

She picked up the ledger she'd entered the acquisitions in and waved it at him. "You, my lord, now have a proper acquisitions ledger."

"Thank God for that!" Felix looked at Deaglan. "Do we still need to store the stable accounts in the safe?"

Across the room, Deaglan met Pru's eyes. "Until we've sealed our deal, let's take no chances." He arched a brow at her. "Have you finished with them?"

She nodded and pushed the last account ledger away. "I hope so—I pray I need never look at them again!"

Deaglan laughed. "Perhaps we'd better leave them out for now, until you're completely certain you need nothing more from them."

Pru huffed, but nodded. She pushed back her chair and rose. "There's still an hour before luncheon. I'm going to start matching the acquisitions with the entries in the studbook."

Deaglan smiled and waved at the shelves behind him, to the right of the fireplace.

Pru crossed the room and started scanning the spines; given she knew what she was looking for, picking out the relevant editions of the General Stud Book didn't take long. She drew out the three heavy tomes she expected to need—the 1836, 1840, and 1844 editions; cradling the books in her arms, she headed back to the table. "I take it the estate has a subscription with Weatherbys—you have all the editions going back to 1828.”

Deaglan nodded vaguely; he and Felix had returned to their tallying.

As she settled with the oldest edition open before her, Pru wondered what was taking them so long. Then again, she didn't know how the costs for the stable were entered into the estate records the brothers were so closely perusing.

Their subdued voices were a rumble in the background as she flicked through the pages of the studbook, hunting for the entries for each horse listed in the new Glengarah acquisitions ledger.

Twenty minutes later, there was a tap on the door. It opened to reveal Cicely. She saw them, smiled, and came in. “There you are. I wondered where you'd all disappeared to.” She shut the door and walked farther in.

Deaglan and Felix came to their feet.

Felix waved at the estate records—another set of ledgers—that he and Deaglan had spread around themselves. “We're trying to get everything in order so we can start the negotiations.”

“Oh.” Cicely dragged her gaze from Felix and looked at Pru, then Deaglan. “Can I help?”

She glanced again at Pru.

Pru looked down at her listing and, with something like wonder, pronounced, “I've already found ten of the horses in the studbook, so I'm progressing quite quickly.” Faster than she'd expected, in fact. “And I'm not sure how anyone else can help—it's really a one-person job.” She looked across the room at Deaglan. “How are you and Felix faring? You must have your figures sorted out by now.”

The looks she received in reply were decidedly sheepish. “Actually,” Deaglan said, “we're not quite sure we've tallied things correctly. Accounts really aren't our forte.”

Cicely brightened. “I'm good with accounts and figures—I've been trained to manage a household, after all.” She walked toward the armchairs. “Perhaps I can help?”

Deaglan cravenly held out the list he'd been working on. “Please do.”

Cicely took the list; studying it, she sat in the chair beside Felix's.

Deaglan and Felix resumed their seats.

Amused, Pru watched from the corner of her eye as Cicely questioned the brothers as to what they'd thought they were doing, then took charge.

With greater confidence that Deaglan would soon have the correct figure on which to base their fee structure, Pru returned her attention to her new acquisitions ledger and the editions of the General Stud Book.

The farther down the list of horses she progressed, the more her heart soared. Every entry she located in the studbook confirmed her assessment of bloodline and value—there was absolutely no doubt that the Glengarah collection was a find beyond price.

Indeed, it was the find of the century; the other major breeders would turn green when they heard of it.

They'd turn bilious when they learned that the Cynsters had secured an exclusive license to breed from what was, collectively, the highest quality bloodstock in the British Isles—very likely in the world.

Joyous excitement bubbled and fizzed in her veins.

Then a tap on the door heralded the arrival of Jay. With a polite nod to them all, he walked in, transparently surprised by their industry. He surveyed the scene, taking in the estate ledgers piled around Deaglan and the stable accounts stacked before Pru. "Can I help with anything?"

Deaglan shook his head. "Cicely is proving a wonder at tallying the figures we need. We're nearly finished." He looked at Jay. "Did you want me?"

"I came to let you know that the work on the bridge is finished and ask whether you wanted to ride out this afternoon and inspect Joe and his men's handiwork."

Deaglan glanced at Pru, then looked again at Jay. "I'm sure Joe and the men have worked wonders. I'll take a look in the coming days. Meanwhile, you might check on the ford. If the water coming down the stream was powerful enough to weaken the bridge, chances are the ford will be in bad shape."

Jay nodded. "I'll ride out this afternoon and take a look. If it's been badly scoured, we might need more stone to shore it up."

Deaglan nodded.

Jay looked around once more, then tipped them all a salute and left.

Pru returned to the exciting business of confirming her fondest hopes, while Deaglan and Felix gave their attention to Cicely and attempted to follow her calculations.

CHAPTER 13

*T*hey broke for luncheon, being careful to return the stable accounts to the library safe before quitting the room.

Thanks to Cicely, Deaglan was now confident that he had the correct figure for the average cost of upkeep per horse per annum to advance when they finally commenced negotiations.

As they settled about the luncheon table, he fixed his gaze on Pru. "How much longer do you think you'll need to finish checking the horses in the studbook?"

He'd noticed she'd been smiling virtually non-stop. Her expression didn't dim as she replied, "I'm more than halfway through the list, so it should only take an hour or so more. And there have been no problem horses so far—meaning horses without an entry in the book. That's heartening. I suspect your father truly knew what he was about—no matter their looks, he didn't buy horses that didn't have that level of breeding provenance."

Once they'd served themselves from the platters placed before them and everyone was either eating or, in Esmerelda and Maude's case, chatting, Deaglan asked, "Are you far enough along to take a break?"

She glanced up, and her face cleared. "Actually, there are two stallions I still need to ride."

He nodded. "We could take them for a gallop—you can ride one on the way out and the other back to the castle."

She beamed. "That will be perfect—I need to try them in a gallop."

Deaglan glanced at Felix. "Are you interested in joining us?"

Felix considered, then reluctantly shook his head. "We've another red-and-white bitch close to her time. I told Sheppard I'd help keep an eye on her. He's trialing some of the beagles, so he and his lads will be out for the afternoon."

"Deaglan, dear boy," Esmerelda boomed from farther down the table. "I received a letter from Lady Harrington this morning. Your godmother, if you recall. She wanted to know when you expected to be back in Dublin."

"Not for some time, Aunt," Deaglan repressively replied.

Naturally, Esmerelda saw that as an invitation to wax eloquent on the attractions of the social season in Dublin. Deaglan kept his head down and his attention on his plate; from the corner of his eye, he saw that Pru was losing her battle to hide her grin as his irrepressible aunt continued to fire her cannon at the impregnable wall of his indifference.

By the end of the meal, even Esmerelda had to concede defeat. She sighed gustily. "Very well. I suppose I'll write and tell Millie Harrington that you're still fixed here for the nonce."

"Thank you," Deaglan said. "And please convey my regards as well, and that I will let her know if I expect to be in Dublin."

Esmerelda brightened at that.

Wishing to escape while he could, Deaglan arched a brow at Pru. When she set her napkin on the table, he rose and drew out her chair.

Farther down the table, Jay rose, too. He caught Deaglan's eye. "If you need me, I'll be finishing up in the estate office, then I'll head down to the ford."

Deaglan nodded and, with Pru, turned to the door. Leaving the others still chatting about the table, they walked into the front hall.

Pru halted and looked at Deaglan. "I need to change into my riding habit."

She was wearing a pale-lemon morning gown, which made her golden curls glow even more brightly. Deaglan nodded. "I'll wait here." He didn't know which horses she wished to trial, so there was no point going to the stable ahead of her.

She flashed him a smile, whisked around, and hurried up the stairs. He watched her go, smiling at her transparent eagerness.

Deaglan looked around as Felix came up. Jay had already vanished down the corridor to the estate office.

Felix halted, a slight frown on his face. "About that order for beagles from the North Leitrim pack, I was thinking..."

By the time Pru descended the stairs, her figure snugly encased in her blue velvet habit, the train looped over her arm, and her jauntily feathered hat perched on her curls, Deaglan and Felix had decided to hold off fulfilling the North Leitrim pack's order for five Kerry beagles until they had at least one more healthy litter in hand.

The three of them walked to the side door and out into the side court. They started across the cobbled expanse and had just reached the point where Felix, bound for the kennels, would part from Deaglan and Pru when the patter of running footsteps behind them brought all three to a halt.

They swung around and saw Cicely wrestling a large shawl over her shoulders as she hurried to catch up with them.

She flashed them all a smile, then halted with her gaze resting on Felix. "Aunt Maude suggested that, while keeping an eye on things in the kennels, you might show me the dogs. I haven't had a chance to see them yet."

Pru saw uncertainty flash behind Felix's eyes.

"Ah..." His gaze fixed on Cicely, Felix managed, "I'll have to stay reasonably close to the bitch we're watching."

"But," Deaglan said, and Pru noticed that he, too, was looking between his brother and Cicely, "you won't need to be inside her box. She'll most likely be sleeping for much of the time. You can easily amble about and introduce Cicely to the beagles and the other setters."

Felix's hesitation held for a second more, then evaporated, and he nodded. "Yes. All right." He waved Cicely toward the kennels and fell in beside her. As they walked away, Pru heard Felix ask, "Will you be frightened if the beagles jump up?"

Pru smiled, met Deaglan's eyes, and arched her eyebrows.

Deaglan shrugged. "Who knows?" He turned toward the stables. "But it seems we're finally free to go. Shall we?"

She laughed and strode on. "Let's shall."

Five minutes later, they led out the two stallions she wished to trial, both blacks but, at least to her eyes, quite distinct. One, named Kahmani, was a descendant of Alcock's Arabian, while the other, Hector, was of the lesser-known Leedes Arabian line. Kahmani presently carried Pru's saddle, and Deaglan's saddle was on Hector.

She led Kahmani to the mounting block. Deaglan held the horse's head while she climbed into the saddle, then he swiftly mounted. They both settled and gathered their reins and, after sharing a satisfied glance, as one, they nudged the stallions into a walk, out of the stable yard and into the side court.

Jay was striding down the cobbles toward the stable. He tipped them a salute. "On my way to the ford." Then he slowed and looked at Deaglan. "By any chance, will you be going anywhere near Mrs. Comey's?"

Deaglan glanced at Pru. "We hadn't decided on any specific direction —we could go that way." He refocused on Jay. "Why?"

"It's just that the ford's in the other direction, and I wanted to let Mrs. Comey know that Jem Thatcher will call by on Thursday about repairing her roof—he's busy until then."

Deaglan nodded. "I'll stop by and tell her." With a dip of his head to Jay, Deaglan wheeled Hector to the north.

With a gracious nod to the steward, Pru set Kahmani to follow Hector, leaving Jay walking on toward the stable.

Deaglan glanced back as they trotted beneath the arch in the old castle wall. After confirming she was close, he shifted smoothly into a canter.

As Pru came up beside him, she let her senses free to register the bunch and flow of the muscles of the horse beneath her. His gait was flawless, powerful and easy. She let her gaze slide over the horse alongside, watching the play of muscles and tendons beneath the glossy hide. Then she raised her eyes to Deaglan's face and found him watching her, a smile on his lips.

When he arched his brows in question, she looked ahead. "Is there somewhere along our path we can go to a controlled gallop, and then to a flat-out run—the latter at least for a hundred or so yards?"

From the corner of her eye, she saw him nod.

"We can take the track that runs along the water meadows, parallel to the river. There's a safe stretch for galloping nearly half a mile long."

"Perfect."

Briefly, he glanced her way. "We can ride out that way, then climb up to Mrs. Comey's cottage—it's in the shadow of the escarpment. Then we can switch horses and ride back to the castle by the same route, so you'll be able to assess both horses over the same ground, albeit in the opposite direction."

She nodded eagerly. "That will do very well."

They rode on, then when she saw the run opening up before them, Deaglan shot her a glance. "Come on!"

At his command, Hector surged.

Kahmani was only a heartbeat behind.

They thundered down the track, hoofbeats pounding in a resounding thud; Pru held Kahmani in so that Hector was galloping a half-length ahead, giving her a clear view of Hector's stride—poetry in motion.

Then she raised her voice and called, "Let him go!"

Deaglan loosened the reins fully and gave the huge black his head, and Hector lengthened his stride even more.

They flew across the beaten ground as Pru freed Kahmani from all restraint, and the equally powerful stallion with his lighter load steadily gained on the more heavily burdened Hector.

They were racing neck and neck when the end of the straight section loomed ahead, and in wordless concert, they eased the horses back, first to a gentler gallop, then a canter, and finally, as they rounded the next curve, to a trot.

Pru glanced at Deaglan, met his eyes, and smiled—a huge, beaming, satisfied smile. "That was...fabulous!"

He grinned. "Makes your blood sing, doesn't it?"

She nodded. "Moments like that are one of the rewards of going to the bother of keeping horses such as these." Leaning forward, she patted Kahmani's glossy neck. "You, my lad, are a wonder." The horse contemptuously flicked his head, and she laughed. "And yes, you already knew that."

Still grinning, Deaglan waved at a narrower path that snaked down the rising slope to join the track just ahead. "Mrs. Comey's cottage is up that way. It's single file from here on."

Pru nodded and held Kahmani back, then set the horse to follow Hector as they toiled slowly up the rise toward the cooler shadows cast by the line of mountains that, as she understood it, formed the rear boundary of the estate.

They passed small fields planted with this and that, but most of the land was given over to grazing sheep or cattle. The farmhouses she saw nestled among the paddocks appeared well-tended, neat and in good repair.

The narrow track grew even narrower and led them even higher, and views of the river valley below opened up behind them. Pru drew Kahmani to a halt and swiveled in her saddle to look west, south, and east. Deaglan drew rein and waited. After letting her eyes drink in the sights—the sparkle of sun on rippling water of at least three shades of blue, the many hues of green represented in the patchwork of fields, and the dappled browns and much darker greens of mountain and skirting forest, she turned her head and met Deaglan's eyes. "The sea to the west, mountains to the south far enough away to protect without shading, and the lake—lough—to the east, with the river running east to west along your land... Many would say this is a piece of paradise."

He drew his gaze from hers and looked down on his lands, then he dipped his head. "It could be. It should be." He paused, then more quietly added, "That's my dream."

Pru felt the reality of that—the simple truth of the sentiment— resonate inside her.

Then Deaglan shook his reins, and Hector walked on, and she set Kahmani to follow.

She finally saw a small cottage a little way ahead. The track widened, and she urged Kahmani up beside Hector. "Who is Mrs. Comey? Does she live alone up here?" The last farmhouse had been more than ten minutes down the track.

"She's my old nurse—mine and Felix's. She married Comey late, after we'd left the nursery, and came to live with him out here. When he died—that must have been about six years ago—we offered her a place back at the castle, but she decided she'd rather remain here." Deaglan met Pru's eyes. "I think she'd grown used to the peace and quiet—Lord knows, she didn't get much of that during her years as our nurse."

Pru chuckled. "I imagine not." She saw the door of the cottage open and a tall, sturdy-looking, rather heavy-boned woman clad in a neat homespun gown with her gray hair up in a white cap step onto the stoop to watch their approach. "Still," Pru murmured, "she must get lonely. There's no one close enough to just have a chat."

"Oh, she does get lonely—that's why we're here." Deaglan threw her an amused look. "And why Jem Thatcher will be here on Thursday. Mrs. Comey is forever finding little things that need fixing—and she much prefers to have either me or Felix arrange if not actually do the repairs. Me coming up to deliver the message will make her day."

That certainly seemed to be the case, if the woman's wide smile as they halted the horses was any guide. Deaglan swung to the ground, tied Hector's reins to the hitching post at the edge of the small yard, then came around to lift Pru down.

Despite the nights she spent in his arms, she still found that moment of weightlessness breath-stealing. At least it was no longer comprehensively senses-stealing.

After Deaglan had secured Kahmani's reins to the hitching post, he briefly met her gaze, then, with a fond smile softening his face, led the way to the door. "Good afternoon, Meg. How are you faring?"

"Mercy me, it's a fine day an' all, and I'm as well as can be, your lordship." Mrs. Comey bobbed an abbreviated curtsy. "But what brings you out this way, my lord?"

Mrs. Comey tipped to the side, and her bright gaze latched onto Pru as she crossed the yard in Deaglan's wake.

Deaglan turned to include Pru. "Allow me to present Meg Comey, my nurse of long ago." To Mrs. Comey, he said, "This is Miss Cynster. She's here to examine our horses."

"Is she, indeed?" Mrs. Comey's eyes had grown wide. She bobbed another curtsy. "Welcome, miss." Mrs. Comey's gaze cut to Deaglan's face, a hint of knowing in her eyes. "I hope you're finding your stay here pleasant?"

Pru reined in a too-wide grin and inclined her head. "I am, thank you." She doubted Deaglan and Felix had successfully fooled Mrs. Comey over much; there was a sharp shrewdness in her eyes that belied her otherwise unremarkable and comfortable appearance.

"Jay's been on to Jem Thatcher about your roof," Deaglan said. "As Miss Cynster and I were riding out this way, Jay asked me to let you know that Jem will call by on Thursday to take a look."

Mrs. Comey nodded. "Good. I don't want the rain seeping in—not that it's got that bad yet, but mark my words, it will."

"No doubt. But Jem will put all right."

"Aye, he will—and I thank ye both for coming up out of your way to let me know." Mrs. Comey brightened. "You must let me repay you with a draft of my cider, and I've just pulled a seed cake out of the oven."

"Seed cake?" Deaglan paused, clearly tempted.

"Aye—your favorite." Mrs. Comey waved to the bench along the front wall of the cottage. "Sit you down in the sunshine, and I'll fetch you mugs and slices of cake."

Grinning, Pru complied. As Deaglan sank down beside her, she bumped his shoulder with hers. "I take it you like seed cake."

He shrugged. "As she said, my favorite—and her seed cake is a work of art."

When the cake arrived, accompanied by mugs of tart, refreshing cider, Pru had to admit his assessment wasn't wrong. The cake had just the right texture—not too heavy, not too light—and the taste was delicious.

When she said so, Mrs. Comey, standing in the doorway, watching them eat and drink, beamed.

After a moment, Mrs. Comey said, "You'll be pleased to hear, your lordship, that the wretched pine marten hasn't been back."

Sober as a judge, Deaglan nodded. "That is, indeed, welcome news."

Pru looked from his face to Mrs. Comey's. "A pine marten? What's that?"

Both were happy to tell her, building a picture of a wild, ferocious animal.

"Cross between a fox and a cat, it's like," Mrs. Comey said, "with the bad-tempered habits of both."

Deaglan nodded. "Multiplied several times over."

"But it's the smell that's the worst, you see. Got into my shed and decided to nest in a corner, and it was all I could do to hold my nose and step inside the door!"

Deaglan caught Pru's eye. "I evicted it several weeks ago, but they're wily beasts—I wouldn't put it past that one to bide its time, then come back and make itself comfortable again, just to spite me."

Pru laughed, but Mrs. Comey nodded. "Aye—they're like that."

Deaglan had polished off two slices of cake. He drained his mug and handed plate and mug back to Mrs. Comey with thanks. "We need to get on." He glanced at Pru. "I'll change over the saddles."

Lipping cake crumbs from her fingers, she nodded. For one second, his eyes fastened on her lips, then he straightened, turned on his heel, and walked across to the horses.

Mrs. Comey watched him unsaddle Pru's horse, then his, a puzzled expression on her homey face. "Why's he doing that?"

"I'm trialing both horses," Pru explained. "I need to get a feel for how each horse moves beneath me when I'm on their back, and also through watching as Deaglan rides and gallops the other alongside."

Mrs. Comey transferred her inquisitive gaze to Pru. "Trialing. Like they do with the dogs?"

Pru smiled. "Not in the same way, but it's the same idea—done for the same reason. To get a clear idea of the quality of the animal in relation to what you want the animal to do—which, in the case of Thoroughbred horses, is to race."

"So you're looking over the Glengarah horses with a view to racing them?"

Pru decided that as Mrs. Comey was such an isolated soul, there was no harm in answering. "With a view to breeding race horses from them."

"Ah." Mrs. Comey nodded. "I heard tell that was always the master's"—she tipped her head at Deaglan—"greatest wish. To set up breeding with all those horses his pa collected."

Deaglan had finished saddling both horses.

"Yes." Pru rose and handed her plate and mug to Mrs. Comey. "Thank you for the lovely afternoon tea. That was, indeed, the best seed cake I've ever had the pleasure of eating."

Mrs. Comey blushed and bobbed. "Thank you, miss. It's been a pleasure to meet you an' all."

Deaglan led the horses closer. With a last smile for Mrs. Comey, Pru went forward—and held her breath as Deaglan closed his hands about her waist and lifted her to her saddle, now on Hector.

He met her eyes for an instant—in which he plainly, and smugly, read the effect his touch still had on her—then he released her and turned to farewell Mrs. Comey.

Then he swung up to Kahmani's back, took a few seconds to let the horse settle under his greater weight, then nodded at Pru. "Do you want to lead the way down?"

She smiled. "All right." With a last wave to Mrs. Comey, she turned Hector and set him onto the track.

The descent was as slow as the ascent had been, if not slower; neither of them were willing to risk the horses' legs.

Pru admired the glimpses of the valley as they plodded lower, passing the farmhouses and the fields until finally they reached the wider track that ran parallel to the river, although at some distance—a meadow's distance—up from the bank.

Relaxing, they shared a smiling glance and set off at an easy canter, looking forward to rounding the next bend and galloping again.

Deaglan was congratulating himself on having shown Pru another facet of his life—both past and present—when the sound of a shot cracked the valley's peace, and the ground between the two horses' front hooves exploded.

He and Pru reacted instantly—instinctively controlling the panicked horses as they tried to rear—but as Pru's wide eyes met his, he saw his own shock reflected in the blue. Realized... "Go!" he barked.

She didn't hesitate but sent Hector flying around the corner and onto the straight stretch beyond.

He held Kahmani on Hector's heels as they rode hell for leather for the safety of the castle—getting out of range of whoever had shot at them as fast as they could.

They didn't ease their pace until they were clattering up to the archway in the castle wall.

They drew rein in the stable yard, safe and unharmed, yet their hearts were racing as never before.

Deaglan swung to the ground, crossed to Hector's side, and lifted Pru down. Screened by the two large horses, she flung herself against him and clung tight; he crushed her to him and felt her trembling.

He was shaken, too, even if he wasn't quivering.

Then Pru hauled in a huge breath and stepped back, yet she kept a tight grip on his sleeves. She glanced in the direction from which they'd come. "What...?"

His jaw was clenched hard; he managed to growl, "Rifle shot."

"But who?" She looked into his face. "We were in clear country—they had to have been able to see us."

Beyond grim, his gaze now on the distant hills, he nodded. "I know. But the shot could have come from some distance—even from the top of the escarpment."

She stared at him. "You think they meant to..."

After a moment, he said, "I don't know what they intended by doing so, but yes, I think whoever made that shot lined it up deliberately." Finally, he met her gaze. "They had us in their sights."

She blinked, then murmured, "Us or the horses."

He grunted an assent.

Two grooms had arrived and were waiting to take the horses. Deaglan told them to return the horses to their stalls and rub them down and feed and water them, then he closed his hand tightly around one of Pru's, and together, they headed for the castle.

They'd only just left the stable yard and started across the side court when the rattle of carriage wheels reached them. They halted and watched as Esmerelda, in the castle's gig, passed beneath the arch in the outer wall.

She drove up and halted the gig beside them—giving Deaglan and Pru a clear view of the rifle propped against the seat beside her. He stiffened at the sight and felt Pru do the same.

Alerted by the rattle of the wheels on the cobbles, two grooms came running. While one solicitously helped Esmerelda down, Deaglan, his face an unrevealing mask, released Pru's hand, reached into the gig, and picked up the rifle. He sniffed the barrel; the gun had been recently fired.

Catching Esmerelda's eye, he arched a brow. "Taking potshots, Aunt?"

Esmerelda made a rude sound. "I'll have you know my eye is as good as ever." She waved toward the rear of the gig. "I got a couple of hares for the pot, but there's not much else about. Poor sport." She ordered one of the grooms to take the hares to the kitchen, then turned to Deaglan and nodded at the rifle he still held. "You can put that back in the gun room for me. I need to get upstairs."

She was about to turn away when their wooden expressions registered; she paused and regarded them for a second, then frowned. "You're both looking a trifle wild-eyed. I assure you I didn't hit anything else—just a rock or two. I'm not so old as all that."

With that declaration, uttered in the tones of one slightly miffed, she turned and stumped off toward the side door.

With Pru, Deaglan stood and watched her go. The grooms removed the gig, leading the horse toward the stable.

Esmerelda reached the side door. When it closed behind her, Pru murmured, "She wouldn't, would she?"

"Shoot at us to scare us, thinking it a good way to fling us into each other's arms?" Deaglan let his words hang in the air, then glanced at the rifle. "Let's see if there's any other gun out."

Pru nodded, and they walked briskly toward the side door. He noted that Pru cast several watchful glances to either side; so did he. Neither of them was likely to forget that moment on the track—the heart-pounding shock of it—anytime soon.

They entered the castle, and he led her to the gun room, tucked under the main stairs, the door concealed in the paneling opposite the library.

Deaglan set the rifle on the central table for cleaning and, with his gaze, followed Pru as she circled the room, scanning the racks set along the walls.

Eventually, she halted and, resting her hand in the single blank space, looked at him. "It seems that's the only gun out."

He stared at her hand—at the empty slot—and heard himself say, "Esmerelda's a crack shot. If she'd been aiming for either of us—or the horses—she wouldn't have missed."

Pru sighed and folded her arms. "So it's possible it was her—and she intended to miss—because she's a meddler." She tipped her head, her gaze growing distant as she thought. "Regardless of whether she suspects our liaison or not, it might have been her way of administering a swift kick to us both."

"As much as it pains me to admit it, I can't rule that out. One of her favorite and frequently uttered sayings is that life is too short." He saw no benefit in revealing that Esmerelda had seen through their façades from the first; as Pru had correctly stated, whether they were engaged in a liaison or not wouldn't have mattered to Esmerelda, to her reasoning.

After several moments of silent pondering, Pru met his eyes, her own gaze direct. "Do you think it was her?"

He held her gaze, thought, then grimaced. "I honestly don't know. I can't even guess."

$\sim$

That evening, when, at the end of the meal, the ladies rose to repair to the drawing room, Pru turned to Deaglan as he drew back her chair and whispered, "I need to speak with you, preferably now."

Deaglan met her gaze, then looked at Maude and Esmerelda, already with their heads together, and Cicely, trailing behind them, then murmured, "Hang back, slip away, and go to the library—I'll meet you there."

Pru nodded and went, initially walking briskly, as if to catch up with the others. She slowed as she neared them, drawing level with Cicely as they crossed the front hall. When Maude and Esmerelda walked into the drawing room, Pru stopped Cicely with a hand on her arm.

The younger girl looked at her inquiringly, and Pru said, "Please tell Maude and Esmerelda that I'm a trifle indisposed." At Cicely's look of concern, she assured her, "Nothing serious, but I believe I'll retire early. I'll see everyone in the morning."

Cicely nodded. "I'll make your excuses. Sleep well."

Pru smiled weakly and made for the stairs. She started up them, but halted on the landing and turned back. Cicely was gone, and the drawing room door was shut. Pru ran lightly down the stairs and into the corridor leading to the library.

Once inside, she fell to pacing before the hearth.

Two minutes later, the door opened, and Deaglan walked in. He closed the door, regarded her for a moment, then turned the key in the lock. "I assume we don't want to be interrupted."

She nodded. "No, indeed."

He strolled toward her. "So what did you want to talk about?" He waved her to an armchair, then moved past her to the sideboard and the decanter of whiskey that stood on the tray there.

Too restless to sink gracefully into the chair, she perched on the chair's arm. "I've been thinking about that shot."

She watched Deaglan absentmindedly pour whiskey into two glasses. Then he realized what he'd done and turned to arch a brow at her. She nodded. "Yes, I'll join you."

What she wanted to say was serious enough to warrant a stiff drink.

"And?" he prompted, turning back to the sideboard and setting down the decanter.

She sighed. "And I believe we should consider the possibility that the shot—even if intended purely to scare us—wasn't fired by your aunt, which, once I calmed down, seemed altogether too far-fetched, even for her, but by someone else entirely."

Frowning now, he came to hand her one glass, then, cradling the other, sank in an elegant sprawl into his usual armchair. "Who—and to what end?"

"As to their identity, I can't say, but as for why, then anyone who wanted to prevent a breeding agreement between Glengarah and the Cynster Stables might have considered scaring me off an excellent move."

His frown deepened. She watched as he raised his glass—

Time slowed.

She felt her eyes widen as the implication of what she was seeing registered...

She lunged at Deaglan, flinging out a hand. *"No! Don't drink that!"*

He froze.

And then she was there, setting her own glass on the side table beside his chair and easing his glass from his fingers.

Staring at her, he let the glass go. "What is it?"

She straightened, holding up the glass to the lamplight, then she shifted to the side, letting the light from the flames merrily leaping in the hearth reach the glass, too. Then she pointed at the base of the crystal tumbler. "See? There."

He sat up, focusing on the bottom of the glass. Gently, she swirled the liquid and heard his breath catch.

Slowly, he pushed to his feet. He took the glass from her, turning it and examining the colorless crystals detectable only by the swirling distortions of light they created as they dissolved into the whiskey.

Deaglan swore beneath his breath. He met Pru's eyes, then stepped around her and strode for the French doors. He opened one door, strode to the balustrade, and flung the tainted whiskey onto the bushes below.

For a moment, he stood and stared into the night, then, jaw clenching, swung around and returned to the library, to the sideboard and the jug of water that stood on the tray. He sloshed water into the glass and noticed his hand wasn't entirely steady. "Any idea what that was?"

He glanced at her. She'd remained standing and had wrapped her arms about herself as if she was cold. But she'd picked up her glass of whiskey. He reached for it. "Give me that."

"No. It's fine." As if to demonstrate, before he could stop her, she raised the glass and took a sip. His gut knotted, but she was plainly unaffected and unconcerned—about that, at any rate. "There's nothing wrong with my drink," she went on, "or with the whiskey in the decanter. And I've checked the other glasses. The crystals..." She halted and drew in a breath, then continued, "The poison was in your glass. Only in your glass —the one you always use. I've seen you do it countless times just in the short period I've been here at Glengarah—you always take the glass in the front left corner of the tray for yourself."

He held her gaze for a long moment, then he turned and walked outside and tossed the water out of the poisoned glass. His head was spinning; he could barely think. He returned inside, this time shutting and locking the French doors.

She watched him as if she couldn't take her eyes off him.

He hesitated, then walked to the sideboard, set aside the tainted glass, chose another, and poured himself a good two fingers of whiskey.

He checked, but saw no swirling trails. He sipped, swallowed, and felt the whiskey burn its way down his throat. The warmth softened the edges of the lump of ice that had formed in his chest. Fleetingly, he closed his eyes. What if he'd mixed up the glasses and given her the one with the poison, and he hadn't seen...

He stopped breathing, then forced his eyes open, forced his lungs to expand, and with effort, thrust the thought aside. He'd taken his usual glass, and thank all the heavens, she'd been there, with him, to see and save him.

Slowly, he turned and walked to where she waited, standing beside his chair. He set his glass on the side table and reached for her, then sat and drew her onto his lap.

Still cradling her glass in one hand, she curled against him, burrowing her free hand around him and squeezing tight.

He dropped a feeling kiss on her golden curls, then freed one hand and reached for his glass. After sipping the whiskey as she did the same, he said, "If someone truly wanted to kill me, this was a ham-handed effort. Normally, I would look down into the glass as I poured. I would almost certainly have seen the crystals then. But just now, you were talking, and I was listening to you as I poured, then I turned and looked at you, and I didn't really look back at the glasses. No one could have predicted that." He paused, then rested his cheek on her curly head. "We don't even know if the crystals were poison and not, for instance, salt. I think this was meant to scare me."

"And me." She lifted her head and met his eyes. "This might have been another attempt to scupper our prospective deal—by demonstrating, salt or poison, their ability to reach into Glengarah Castle and kill you, thus frightening you and me as well."

That she cared enough to see herself being swayed by a threat against him—dissuaded from seizing something she'd spent years searching for and that she'd admitted was critically important to her... He knew how to read that confession; he held her gaze and ruthlessly suppressed his elation—so incongruous at that moment.

Pru studied his face—the hard, unyielding planes that gave so very little away—then frowned and looked down. She took another sip of whiskey and felt his hand lightly stroking her side—soothing, reassuring —felt the heat of his chest against her shoulder, the comforting hard warmth of his thighs beneath hers; gradually, her thoughts settled and cleared. After a moment, she said, "I'm always being told that I'm too impulsive—that I leap to conclusions too readily. I have to wonder if I'm doing that now."

"How so?"

She met his eyes. "What if the incidents today—the shooting and the poison—were actually attempts on your life? What if they're not connected in any way with the stable fire or the attempt to steal the ledgers?"

He looked puzzled. "Why on my life? Who do you imagine would be behind such attacks?"

She frowned, then conceded, "It can't be Felix. He is next in line, isn't he?"

Deaglan nodded. "But as you say, it won't be—can't be—him. That's simply not possible. Felix and I are close—close enough that I know he would never betray me."

She lightly grimaced. "Even I can see that. So it's not Felix...but you have to admit that to outsiders, those who've never seen you and Felix together, which is most of the world, were you to die in suspicious circumstances, then Felix would be the obvious suspect." She straightened as something else struck her. "And indeed, if Cicely hadn't decided at the last moment to go with Felix to the kennels, Felix would have been alone for most of the afternoon—if you had been shot and killed, he wouldn't have had anyone to vouch for him."

Warming to her theme, she waved toward the sideboard. "And who better than Felix to know in which glass to place the poison, and normally, if I hadn't asked to speak with you now, the most likely scenario for the next time you used that glass would have been when Felix—and possibly only Felix—was in the room with you."

A wave of icy sensation swept her, and she shuddered. "You might have died in Felix's arms, and he would have been the prime suspect."

Deaglan drew her back to rest against his chest. "You're scaring me."

She doggedly replied, "I'm trying to convince you "

He frowned. "It's not Felix "

"No, but if you die and Felix is convicted of your murder, he can't inherit, so who inherits then?"

He couldn't hold back a disbelieving snort. "It can't be him, either. If Felix and I are both gone, the estate goes to our cousin, Freddy Fitzgerald." He tipped his head and looked into her face. "You might have heard of him."

She blinked. "Freddy Fitzgera... *The* Freddy Fitzgerald who prances around ballrooms in brightly colored coats and struts like a peacock in Hyde Park every clement afternoon during the Season?" She looked at him in amazement. "That Freddy Fitzgerald? He's your cousin?"

He had to grin. "Sadly for all concerned, yes. And as it seems you know something of him, you won't be surprised to hear that Freddy's greatest fear is of having to shoulder any sort of responsibility. He's all but allergic to it. His worst nightmare would be to inherit Glengarah or even a smaller estate. I suggested settling one on him once, and he went into a panic—I had to swear I wouldn't do it before he calmed down. And on top of that, he detests the weather in Ireland—he invariably comes down with a cold or a chill whenever he's obliged to visit." He paused, then went on, this time seeking to convince her, "Freddy is entirely content living a life of ease in London, essentially as Glengarah's pensioner. From his point of view, he has far more to lose through my death than he stands to gain—indeed, he wouldn't see me dying as gaining him anything at all."

She studied his face, then sighed. "Well, the prospect had to be explored." She slumped back against him.

He tightened his arms around her and pressed a kiss to her forehead. "Thank you for thinking of it." After a moment, he went on, "I don't think anyone is seriously trying to kill me. I have no enemies that I know of. So I think your earlier suggestion has merit—that all the recent incidents are the work of someone trying to scare us both off from forging a breeding agreement between the Glengarah and Cynster Stables."

Pru humphed. Her brain was too tired to continue to pursue such thoughts; she felt drained after the shocks of the past hours.

But he was still there, and she was sitting on his lap, and he had locked the door.

And...

She sat up, set her now-empty glass on the side table, then shifted to face him, framed his face between her palms, and drew his lips to hers.

She kissed him slowly, taking her time to savor and explore, to let her need for reassurance well and spill through the caress, to tempt him and herself to lay the shocks of the day to rest in the most passionate, intimate way.

Deaglan was only too ready to follow her lead, to seize the moment and claim her mouth. Her curves.

Her.

Passion answered their combined call, rose, and roared through them.

Within seconds, they grew desperate to assuage their mutual, bone-deep need of affirmation, of confirmation that they were alive, there, together still, able to glory in the wonder that together, between them, they could create.

The result was fast, furious—blindingly intense. Every touch, every gasp, every moan.

She hauled her skirts from between them. He fumbled and freed the flap of his trousers, then lost his breath as she found him and held him tight.

He caught her hips and lifted her, and she guided the engorged head of his erection through the slit in her drawers, then sank down and took him deep.

For a finite second, they froze, caught—snared—on the brink of passion's precipice.

Then they let the reins fall.

Her hands locked about his face, she rose, then sank down. He gripped her hips, fingers digging in as he urged her to a faster pace.

On.

On.

With deliberation and utter devotion to each other's need, they let desire flare and flame and take them, let passion drive them up, racing through the flames and on to the very pinnacle of ecstasy.

The bright moment trapped them, surrounded and captured them, then shattered all around them in scintillating brilliance.

The glory held, then faded, and she slumped in his arms.

He closed them about her, hearing their breathing ragged and raw, their hearts pounding in their ears as the soft silence of his library wrapped about and cradled them.

He dipped his head and whispered in her ear, "Nothing has changed. Nothing about this."

Pru raised a hand and blindly traced his cheek. "You're right," she murmured and knew she'd lied.

Later that night, while, screened by wispy clouds, the moon rode the sky, Pru lay beside a sleeping Deaglan and listened to the steady rhythm of his breathing. He was sleeping the sleep of the deeply sated, and she should be, too.

Only she couldn't stop thinking…

Of him.

Of the revelation—the epiphany—that had struck during their earlier, frenetically frantic coupling in the library.

As revelations went, it qualified as earthshaking, at least for her.

She hadn't had any inkling that recent events—all the little things she'd learned about him, the insights she'd gained about what drove him

—were steadily chipping away at the bedrock of the decision that had, for the past decade, informed her approach to life.

She'd had no notion that the foundation of that decision had eroded and weakened to the extent that the sudden realization that on the track back to the castle, or later in the library, she'd come within a whisker of having him ripped from her life forever would shatter her guiding principle into a thousand shards.

Leaving her mentally falling.

Flailing and floundering.

Now, she'd landed and, finally, steadied.

But the landscape of desires, of wants and inner needs, she now found within herself was entirely different from the forces that had driven her when she'd arrived at Glengarah.

Looking back over her time there, she had to admit that, once again, as her mother and brothers so often warned her, she should have looked before she'd leapt. Given what she now knew—of herself as well as Deaglan—she wished she hadn't made her "no marriage" declaration.

She really was too impulsive for her own good—not in commencing a liaison with Deaglan but in putting such restrictions on its evolution.

That said…she couldn't, even now, even knowing all she did, be sure that marriage to the wicked Earl of Glengarah would suit her, yet she was very certain she needed to explore the possibility.

The wonder of it was that his horses didn't even register in her assessment—which, as this was about her, said a great deal.

She stared up at the shadowed canopy, and the feelings that the events of the day had sent coursing through her rose again—as if to remind her that they were there, in her veins now, and weren't about to fade. A certain stripe of possessive anger—of fury at whomever had targeted him and sought to take him from her. A primitive emotion, perhaps, yet too strong, too violent and powerful, to deny.

She tried to point out to that less-than-rational side of herself that he wasn't hers yet, but her heart, it appeared, had already made its choice.

In trying to not admit that…who was she attempting to deceive?

Her grandmother and her great-aunts had taught her better than that.

They'd also taught her a great many other things—such as the signs to watch for in the man who might be hers.

She thought back over his behavior. She could hardly accuse him of not mentioning marriage when it had been she who had refused to allow the word to be uttered. Yet from quite early in their acquaintance, he'd been protective, instinctively so in a way she recognized; she'd seen just that same tight-lipped protectiveness in enough Cynster marriages to know it for what it was—and understanding what emotion drove it, to feel hope.

He would, she was sure, be protective in a general sense toward any lady, yet she was far more than "any lady" to him.

That, she decided, was promising.

So what do I want to do?

She let go of all resistance and allowed her mind to follow that track.

Do I want to rescript our arrangement to allow us to explore the possibility of marriage?

The answer came loud and clear.

Turning her head on the pillow, she looked at Deaglan, at what she could see of his face as he lay slumped on his stomach alongside her.

She let her gaze rove the features she could see—the unruly black hair, the muscled arm and shoulders exposed above the covers—and let herself accept what she now knew to be her truth: He was the man—the one man among all men—from whom she didn't want to walk away.

CHAPTER 14

he next morning, Pru, Deaglan, Felix, and Cicely were rising from the breakfast table when Bligh sailed in and announced, "My lord, a groom just brought word that a gentleman is riding up the drive on a black horse that, the groom informs me, is distinctly notable."

"Thank you, Bligh." Deaglan looked at Pru.

She blinked, then understanding dawned. She stared, faintly stunned, at Deaglan. "I suspect it's one of my family." *Good lord—who have they sent?*

She hurried from the room, aware of the others following close behind.

She halted on the porch and looked down the drive; Deaglan halted beside her, his hand on her back a reassuring touch.

The rider had yet to appear around the last bend. Nearer to hand, Jay was just passing, mounted on a showy nag Pru dismissed after a bare glance; it was not one of the collection.

Jay saluted the small band gathered on the porch. "Off for my usual monthly meetings in Sligo."

Deaglan nodded.

Pru focused on the bend in the drive.

Seconds later, the rider rounded the curve at a slow canter, and Pru's gaze locked on him.

Toby!

He encountered Jay and slowed to ask some question, and Jay turned and pointed to the group on the porch. Toby looked, then tipped his head to Jay, tapped his heels lightly to his horse Midnight's sides, and came on.

Pru viewed his approach with undisguised irritation. "It's Toby, my younger brother," she informed Deaglan and the others in a tone that boded ill for her sibling.

Through narrowing eyes, she watched Toby draw Midnight to a halt at the bottom of the steps; even at that distance, she could see the open curiosity in his face as his gaze played over the castle and the three people at her back.

She swept down the steps as he dismounted with the fluid grace that screamed of his horsemanship, that he'd been riding before he could walk.

He'd barely got both boots on the cobbles before she bailed him up.

"What are you doing here?" Hands on her hips, she glared at him. "I do not need a babysitter."

As usual, nothing threw Toby off his assured stride. With Midnight's reins in one hand, he regarded her with his customary amused tolerance and an easygoing smile. "Good morning to you, too, sister."

Before she could step back, he swooped and kissed her cheek—and whispered, "Not your usual style."

As he straightened and regarded her quizzically, she realized he was right; normally, no matter the provocation, she would never upbraid her siblings before others not of the family.

Does that mean I now view Deaglan, Felix, and Cicely as family?

She rather thought it did. But for whatever reason Toby had come, he was there now, and she needed to make the best of it.

She met his gaze, but before she could think of what her next question should be, Toby's gaze lifted to a point beyond her right shoulder. She glanced around and saw that Deaglan had followed her and had rounded Midnight to halt just behind her.

She swallowed a sigh.

Toby didn't wait for any formal introduction. Deploying a genial and confident smile, he nodded to Deaglan and offered his hand. "Glengarah, I presume? Toby Cynster."

Deaglan glanced fleetingly Pru's way and grasped Toby's hand. "Welcome to Glengarah Castle, Mr. Cynster."

Toby's grin was immediate and, as usual, infectious. "Toby, please."

Deaglan released Toby's hand and, his features easing, nodded. "Deaglan."

Toby swung his gaze to Pru. "We received your letter, which made it clear this deal would be an important one for the Cynster Stables. No one even thought to question your abilities regarding negotiating and closing the right deal for us, but everyone agreed"—he glanced at Deaglan—"that if the stakes proved to be as high as your letter suggested they would be, then you should have some Cynster support."

Pru blinked; she could hardly argue that, and now the first spike of her temperamental reaction was fading, she was beginning to see benefits in having Toby there.

Toby's grin turned wry. "Naturally, your news pricked Papa's curiosity, and he started quietly asking around, and the more he heard... Well"—he slid his hands into his breeches pockets and smiled widely at Pru—"it was me—on the grounds I work most closely with you in the breeding program—or Papa himself. Mama, Nicholas, and I, and even Meg, thought you'd prefer me."

Horror seeped into Pru's expression at the thought of her father arriving out of the blue at this juncture. Toby saw it, and his smile grew broader.

With all righteous anger deflating, she met his eyes and nodded with open gratitude. "Thank you for coming. Far, *far* better you than Papa." She almost shuddered.

Toby chuckled, but his eyes, she noted, grew watchful and alert—faintly suspicious—as he shifted his gaze to Deaglan, who, she discovered, was eyeing Toby measuringly in return.

She looked from one to the other as several seconds passed in what she recognized as a typical wordless male assessment...

Her temper sparked anew, and she stepped between them. Facing Toby, she jabbed a finger into the center of his chest—hard. Having succeeded in capturing his attention, she wagged the same finger in his face. "Don't start imagining anything."

Toby blinked his eyes wide. "Me?" He nearly glanced at Deaglan, but stopped himself and, all innocence, asked, "What would I imagine?"

Eyes narrowing to shards, she slapped his arm. "Stop it."

Toby's features eased into a relaxed smile.

Pru humphed and gave up; Toby was next to impossible to manage and also acutely observant. He would see what he would see, and there was little she could do about that.

A footman had already retrieved the bag and saddlebags that had been strapped to Toby's saddle. Now a groom came to take Midnight; Toby handed over the reins, and as the horse was led away, Pru glanced at Deaglan, who tipped his head to her, then waved Toby up the steps. "Come and meet the company."

With Deaglan on one side and Toby—the exasperating yet unfailingly supportive sibling with whom she spent the most time—on the other, Pru climbed to the porch and waited while Deaglan performed the introductions, then handed Toby into Bligh's care to be shown to a room.

"We'll be in the library when you come down." Deaglan nodded to the corridor off which the library lay.

Toby saluted and started to turn away.

As Pru had expected, he cast a last glance her way. She met it and nodded. "Go and get cleaned up, then we'll take you to see horses that will eclipse the horses of your dreams."

Toby's brows rose, then he replied, "I'll be down in a few minutes."

Pru watched him go, shook her head, then drew in a breath and, with Deaglan, headed for the library.

Toby Cynster was as good as his word. Ten minutes later, he opened the library door and walked in, his expression stating he was eager to see the Glengarah collection for himself.

Pru rose, and Deaglan came to his feet, and without more ado, they made for the stable.

Deaglan noticed that as they crossed the side court, Toby looked around, taking in all he could see. His gaze focused on the kennels, from which the occasional woof emanated.

"Dogs?" Toby glanced at Deaglan.

Deaglan nodded, his gaze drawn to the two beasts now barreling toward them. Molly and Sam; he'd neglected the pair recently, too caught up with the horses and Pru. "You're about to meet two."

Toby swung around a second before Sam and Molly reached them. The dogs cavorted, greeting Deaglan and wanting to sniff and engage with the two visitors, especially Toby, who laughed and crouched to be at their level, ruffling their ears and examining their faces.

A good fifteen minutes went in answering Toby's questions; Deaglan didn't miss the glance exchanged between brother and sister—an acknowledgment that if Deaglan already ran a dog-breeding operation and had for years, establishing a horse-breeding enterprise wouldn't be beyond him.

Eventually, Deaglan ordered Sam and Molly back to the kennels, where, during the day, the pair largely roamed free.

Toby watched the dogs go. "Very handsome breeds. They'd do well in England, too."

Deaglan waved toward the stable, and they walked on.

As they entered the first aisle, Pru sternly told her sibling, "You can't stop and examine every horse. Just glance over them and remember—the quality improves the farther into the stable we go."

Toby met her gaze, then nodded. "All right. Fifty-two horses, wasn't it?"

"Actually," Deaglan said, "it's fifty-seven." He didn't add anything further, and Pru shot him a smile.

For Deaglan, Toby's reactions to the Glengarah horses were even more satisfying than his sister's guarded first reactions had been. Toby's jaw literally dropped. At one point, his eyes looked ready to fall from his head.

By the time they reached the hidden aisle and the last five horses, he'd run out of adjectives and even expletives.

Pru was clearly pleased with her brother's response. "'Magnificent' just doesn't seem emphatic enough, does it?"

His eyes glued to the three stallions in the last three stalls, Toby dazedly shook his head. After a moment, he said, "Even with your report as a warning, even reading between the lines doesn't prepare one for this." He waved at the horses. "This much."

Thinking to drive home the point, Deaglan glanced at Pru. "Why don't we show your brother the paces of one of the stallions? Choose which one you think will most impress in the area of the Cynster Stables' greatest interest."

As he'd expected, Pru nodded eagerly and turned to survey the horses, while Toby looked like a child at Christmastime.

"This one." Pru indicated Rosingay, the horse she'd labeled as the strongest representative of the Godolphin Barb line, a powerful stallion with a deep chest and a hint of russet in his dark hide. "But for Toby, let's ride him in the ring rather than just pace him on a leading rein."

Deaglan nodded. These five horses were the least ridden of all in the collection, but he had exercised all three stallions over the past eighteen months. After bridling the horse, he led him out of the stall.

In the second aisle, opposite the barn housing the exercise ring, Deaglan handed Rosingay to a groom to saddle and joined Pru and Toby, who had paused to examine several of the horses in the stalls in that aisle more closely.

Five minutes later, the groom returned with Deaglan's saddle on Rosingay. Deaglan took the reins and led the horse to the exercise ring, with Pru and an openly excited Toby trailing behind.

The three of them entered the ring, and Toby swung the gate shut.

Deaglan led Rosingay to the ring's center and was about to mount up when Pru laid a staying hand on his arm.

"No—let me ride him." She met Deaglan's eyes, her own alight. "I know the order of paces we use."

Deaglan saw the eagerness and effervescent excitement in her eyes; he knew what it was like to show off a discovery to a sibling. "You just want to show off your find."

She made a rude noise and nudged him away from the stirrups as Toby, standing back with his hands in his pockets and watching, remarked, "She just wants to show off all around."

Deaglan gave ground, but held on to the bridle as he pointed out, "That's my saddle. Don't you want to change to yours?"

She waved a dismissive hand, hiked up her skirts, slipped her half-boot into the stirrup, and swung up to the saddle.

Rosingay shifted a little, but then her hands were on the reins, and he calmed.

Although her half-boots were loose in the stirrups, Pru nodded at Deaglan. "Let him go."

He did. He stepped back, then, with Toby, retreated to stand with his back to the fence and watch as Pru slowly walked Rosingay around the ring.

Then she shifted into a gentle canter.

Standing beside Deaglan, Toby narrowed his eyes and drew in a long, slow breath as if waiting for something...

Something that didn't happen. "Damn," Toby murmured, "he really is superb."

Pru circled past them, then, as she rounded the ring, fluidly urged the horse into a longer stride.

Rosingay screamed.

The powerful horse reared, then bucked—dislodging a shocked Pru from his back.

She flew through the air and landed on her back on the ground.

Horrified, Deaglan rushed straight for her.

Toby did, too, but then diverted to catch the reins of the huge horse, who was stamping and shaking his head as if confused.

Deaglan fell on his knees beside Pru. His heart felt like a lump of ice being crushed in a vise.

He stared into Pru's face. Her eyes were closed; she wasn't moving.

Deaglan's savoir faire deserted him. Anguish took hold. "Pru?" He closed his hands gently about her shoulders; he could barely steady his voice enough to plead, "Pru, darling! Please, sweetheart, open your eyes."

Darling? Sweetheart?

If Pru had needed any prod to drag in a breath and open her eyes, those words provided it. She blinked, then stared into Deaglan's face—glimpsed his horror, his distress, the overwhelming fear etched on his chiseled features. Then intense relief swept across his face and wiped his initial reactions away.

She lifted a hand, and he engulfed it in one of his and gripped hard.

"I'm just winded," she managed to wheeze.

With his help, she struggled up to sit, leaning against him. Then, frowning, she looked around and located the stallion, standing close to the center of the ring. Toby had calmed the horse, and now both horse and Toby were regarding her anxiously.

She frowned more definitely. "What happened?" She glanced at Deaglan. "Why did he scream?"

Toby snorted. "You tell us." After a moment, he went on, "You'd gone from a walk to a gentle canter without any problem. Then you gave him the office to lengthen his stride, and he did. But he only took one pace, then he screamed."

Pru nodded. "As if he was in pain." She continued to frown as the moment replayed in her mind. "I can't understand it. There was nothing —I felt no jerk or change in his gait. He just went straight into reaction without anything to prompt it."

Toby stared at her, then more softly said, "All I saw happen was that you came down into the saddle..."

He turned to the horse. Crooning to the beast, who now appeared calm and perfectly well-behaved, Toby swiftly undid the girth strap and carefully lifted the saddle from the stallion's back.

Toby turned the saddle over and examined the underside, then, his features locking into a grim mask, he carried the saddle to Deaglan and

Pru. Toby halted before them and pointed—to a large silver needle embedded point out in the thick cushion under the saddle's rear, just to one side of center. "See? It's been deliberately pushed into the cushion at a spot that would only get pushed down when at a faster pace. When Pru moved into a fast canter, she came down harder and at a slightly different angle and drove the needle into the horse's back, just off the spine—effectively delivering an intense shot of pain."

Deaglan reached out and touched a fingertip to the needle's point, then showed them the smear it left on his skin. "That's blood."

Toby nodded. "A diabolical act." He glanced at Rosingay. "Luckily, the stallion seems otherwise unaffected." He looked back at Pru, then returned his gaze to Deaglan. "Normally, I'd be asking who was trying to harm my sister, except it wasn't her saddle."

Deaglan held Toby's gaze.

"It was yours," Toby continued. "You were supposed to be the one involved, and your weight coming down on the saddle would have driven the needle much deeper. In fact..." Still holding the saddle, Toby paused, then went on, "Chances are you would have been thrown immediately you'd sat—before you'd settled and properly taken up the reins. So you would have been thrown in the stable yard—on the cobbles. And you would have fallen a lot harder than Pru."

His gaze steady, direct, and unwavering, Toby focused on Deaglan. "So who is trying to kill you?"

Deaglan felt Pru's anxious look and turned his head to meet it. He studied her eyes, with ease reading all she was thinking, yet wasn't saying.

He was aware of Toby watching their wordless exchange, his attention shifting between them, then Toby ventured, "This isn't the first attempt, is it?"

Deaglan looked back at the man he hoped would one day be his brother-in-law. "No."

Toby studied him for an instant, then straightened. "I think I need to hear this."

Deaglan nodded curtly. "But after Pru has been seen by Dr. Reilly."

He turned to her and was met with a frown.

"I was only winded," Pru protested. "I'll be fine in a few minutes."

Deaglan's jaw set. "Regardless, you need to be checked over. Who knows what else you jarred loose?"

"All of me is where it should be," she insisted, only to realize that Deaglan wasn't listening.

He rolled to his feet, dusted off his hands, and with his face set in his aloofly arrogant earl's mask, bent, scooped her off the ground, and hoisted her up, settling her against his chest.

Toby—the traitor—grinned and strode for the gate. He swung it open and stood back—still grinning—as Deaglan carried her out.

"Bring that." Deaglan tipped his head at the saddle Toby was still carting under one arm.

Pru tried to argue, insisting she had taken no real hurt, yet one part of her was secretly thrilled by Deaglan's adamantine insistence and rather curious to see where it might lead.

Deaglan paused to send two older stablemen to see to Rosingay, then strode on.

Although she was tallish, she was generally described as willowy; she wasn't that heavy, so she wasn't surprised when Deaglan managed her weight with ease, carrying her across the side court and into the castle as if she was no real burden.

She expected him to set her on her feet in the front hall, but no.

Alerted by Deaglan and Toby's ringing footsteps, Bligh arrived and was instantly solicitous.

She tried once more to assert that she had suffered no injury, but she might as well have been speaking in tongues; all three men ignored her.

Deaglan instructed Bligh to send a fast rider to fetch the doctor, who, apparently, lived not far away.

Pru managed to catch Deaglan's eye and glared. "I really don't need a doctor."

The muscles in his jaw tensed. "Humor me. For my peace of mind, if not your brother's and that of everyone else here, allow Reilly to examine you and pronounce that all is well."

She stared into Deaglan's eyes. At the edge of her vision, she was aware of Toby's intrigued expression; her brother was nowhere near blind and was more than quick-witted enough to correctly interpret the overbearing protectiveness Deaglan was exhibiting—essentially over nothing.

Toby would also correctly interpret what she was about to do, but she couldn't stand against Deaglan's need—the need she could see in his eyes. Beneath his rigid façade, he was shaken—very likely more than she was.

She sighed mightily and capitulated. "Very well. Do your worst and summon your Dr. Reilly."

Deaglan humphed and started up the stairs, taking them two at a time. Toby set the saddle on a side table and followed, but was now some way back.

As they crossed the gallery, Deaglan muttered, "Having Dr. Reilly see you isn't supposed to be a punishment."

She squinted up at him. "Do you always send for Reilly when you get thrown?"

"That's not the point. And Lord knows, I would rather it had been me." He forged on, looking ahead rather than at her. "That, I could have swallowed—absorbed. But you?"

Abruptly, he looked down and met her eyes; his own were fierce. "That, I can't accept. That, I *won't* accept."

They'd reached her room; Toby came running and opened the door, and Deaglan carried her through.

As he laid her gently on the bed, Pru reflected that "darling" and "sweetheart" and the fire behind his last words were, all in all, distinctly promising vis-à-vis her revised tack.

Then a patter of footsteps heralded Maude and Cicely, who descended on Pru, shooed Deaglan and Toby from the room, then fussed over her, all but forcibly stripping her of her day dress and tucking her into bed.

So determinedly insistent were they, she gave up all resistance and surrendered to being taken care of by everyone—even the little doctor when he arrived—even though, as she well knew, there was absolutely no need.

Having been thrust into the corridor and left, along with Toby, to stare at the closed door of Pru's room, Deaglan turned, caught his hopefully soon-to-be brother-in-law's eyes, and stated, "I need a drink."

Toby nodded. "I could do with one myself."

They strode back to the front hall, and Deaglan led the way to the library.

Going in, he made straight for the sideboard and the decanter and glasses left on the tray there.

Toby followed him in and closed the door, then paused, taking in the room. Then he came forward with a huffed laugh. "This is so much like home."

Deaglan had picked out two glasses from the second row on the tray and was carefully examining them. "So Pru said." Satisfied that both glasses were free of any crystals, he set them down, poured whiskey into both, then picked a glass up and checked it again before handing it to Toby.

With a puzzled look, Toby accepted the glass. "Is that some strange Irish custom?" He nodded at Deaglan's glass as he subjected that to a last check, too.

Deaglan took a sip from his glass, then met Toby's eyes. "No. That's because Pru spotted what we believe to have been poison in my glass last evening, just before I drank."

Toby blinked. Slowly. "Ah."

"Indeed." Deaglan waved him to the armchairs. Once they'd sunk into the chairs' comfort and Toby had taken a cautious sip of his own drink, Deaglan took a healthy swallow of his whiskey and said, "Why don't I fill you in on our recent strange events?"

Toby gestured for him to continue. "Please do."

Deaglan paused, deciding where to start, then commenced with the stable fire, followed by the attempt to steal the ledgers, him and Pru being shot at while riding, and the poison in the glass.

By the time he fell silent, Toby's normally relaxed expression had grown tight. "And now we have a needle in your saddle cushion."

Deaglan studied the younger man. He estimated Toby was in his mid-twenties, yet he seemed a great deal more mature than, for example, Felix. There was a steadiness about Toby that was all but instantly apparent, a type of resolute internal strength—possibly similar to his sister's strength of will. Regardless, that steady, clear-eyed temperament made Deaglan feel a great deal more comfortable over divulging all to Toby; it was almost a relief being able to relate the whole confusing business to another male, one he sensed he could trust.

He'd already realized that Pru trusted Toby, which was just as well, given that relating the incidents of the stable fire and the attempt to steal the ledgers had, of necessity, implied that Deaglan was sharing Pru's bed. Not that he'd made a point of it, but he'd noticed the hardening in Toby's hazel gaze and knew Toby hadn't failed to catch that point.

But he made no mention of it, either, apparently accepting the matter as a fait accompli. Either that or respecting his sister's wishes and accepting that she knew what she was doing in taking Deaglan as her lover.

Deaglan wished he knew what she was thinking. The shock of seeing her fall, of finding her lying motionless with her eyes closed, had—quite literally—sent him to his knees. As for that "darling" and "sweetheart," let alone what had tumbled from his lips later...he'd never felt so emotionally stripped bare, and on multiple fronts, in his life.

Footsteps in the corridor were followed by a rap on the door. At Deaglan's "Come," Dr. Reilly entered.

After shutting the door behind him, Reilly accepted Deaglan's offer of a drop of whiskey and settled in another of the armchairs.

Deaglan handed the doctor a glass, then resumed his seat. "How is she?"

"I'm pleased to be able to report that Miss Cynster sustained no serious injury."

"No concussion?" Deaglan asked.

Reilly savored a sip of the whiskey, then shook his head. "No. Nothing of that nature. Just a few bruises, and no doubt, she must have been badly shaken, but from what I understand of the circumstances, she fell well, as it were."

Toby huffed. "As children of Demon Cynster, one of the first things we're taught is how to fall—and we all do it often enough that the knack becomes second nature."

Deaglan saw Reilly's lips twitch. "So I was given to understand by your sister. At some length."

Toby grinned. "That, I don't doubt."

Reilly sipped, then sobered. "Sadly, falling well aside, Miss Cynster seems disinclined to follow my prescription of bed rest for the next few days. She was quite adamant about that, in fact. The best I could wring from her was her consent to rest if she felt she needed to, but that was the extent of her concession."

Toby nodded. "Again, that's no surprise." His gaze flicked to Deaglan. "Frankly, I'm amazed you've been allowed to examine her at all."

Toby's eyes remained trained on Deaglan's face, allowing him to read Toby's interpretation of the reason for his sister's unusual compliance, along with Toby's approval of Deaglan using his influence to ensure the doctor saw her.

Reilly finished his whiskey and set down the glass with a sigh. "Be that as it may, I have done what I could and insisted that she remain in her room, quiet in a chair if not in bed, for the rest of the day. She may come down to dinner only if she's steady on her feet and suffering no lasting megrims at all. Lady Connaught and Mrs. O'Connor saw fit to strongly support me in that, so I'm hopeful our reluctant patient will abide by my directions at least that far."

"Thank you, Reilly." Deaglan rose, and the doctor got to his feet. "We'll endeavor to see that she does."

Trailed by Toby, Deaglan saw the doctor out to his gig, then returned to the front hall. He halted at the base of the stairs and glanced at Toby, who had halted alongside, his gaze directed upward.

Then Toby glanced Deaglan's way. "I suggest that, if we want Pru to remain anything like quiet for the rest of the day, we'll need to provide sufficient distraction."

Deaglan nodded and led the way back to Pru's room.

CHAPTER 15

*A*fter convincing Maude and Esmerelda that Deaglan and Toby wouldn't allow their difficult patient to stir a foot from the chair by the window in which she was ensconced, and consequently, it was safe to leave them in charge—a declaration that had Pru unhelpfully rolling her eyes—Deaglan finally shut the door on Pru's would-be nursemaids. Then he and Toby drew up straight-backed chairs and sat facing Pru, and the three of them revisited the recent incidents from the stable fire to the needle in the saddle, this time exploring Pru's and Deaglan's thoughts on who might be responsible for the spate of attacks.

Toby pursed his lips, then offered, "While I appreciate your reasoning that it could be someone who wishes to ensure no deal is done, how, exactly, they might have pulled things off is less easy to see." He looked at Deaglan. "For instance, take this latest incident with your saddle. I assume the tack room isn't locked?"

Deaglan shook his head.

"So," Toby went on, "the deed—which was certainly no accident— could have been done by anyone familiar with saddles and horses."

Deaglan pulled a face. "After the fire, I placed guards around the stable for several nights, but I've since stood them down—there seemed little point, and they all have daytime duties."

"So if someone approached at night, under cover of darkness…" Pru studied Deaglan. "Anyone at all could have slipped in and placed that needle."

"Not quite anyone." Toby looked at Deaglan. "How would they have known which saddle was yours?"

After several moments of silent consideration, Deaglan met Pru's eyes. "Earlier, we canvassed the possibility that, while the motive to scupper the deal might come from beyond Glengarah's borders, whoever it is has managed to find an...agent, if you will—someone inside the estate who either agreed to do our distant villain's bidding for suitable recompense or was someone our villain could bend to his will."

Toby slowly nodded. "Someone here to carry out the required actions —that fits. Indeed, it fits better than anything else. And if I'm recalling correctly, the timing for such a scenario—the time between Pru visiting Sligo and the stable fire—holds water as well."

Deaglan sat back. "Once they learned Pru was here, they had time to find someone local they could pressure into doing their dirty work."

Pru might be stuck in the chair until evening—virtually the whole blasted day—yet she wasn't of a mind to simply sit back and let matters unfold, let some nameless, faceless person continue to try to kill Deaglan.

She focused on Toby—he who was known within the family as someone one could turn to in any fix. "So what should we do? Reinstate the guards, only this time around the castle?"

Toby met her eyes, then shook his head. "A place of this size can't be effectively protected by patrolling guards—it's too easy for someone to avoid them."

"So what, then?" she asked.

Toby held her gaze, then looked at Deaglan. "As far as I can see, at this point, all we can do is to protect you, yourself, as best we can. That, of course, won't be easy to do if, as might well be the case considering the crystals in your whiskey glass, the agent in question is one of the indoor staff."

Deaglan shook his head. "I've known virtually everyone here from birth—mine or theirs. The notion that one of the staff is working hand in glove with someone from outside, someone with no connection to the estate, is...very difficult to swallow."

"Be that as it may," Pru said with some severity, "someone here is a real threat to you, and I can't see how we can protect you from them making another attempt, especially an attempt like shooting from a distance."

"We can do what we can to make it harder," Toby said, "until we strike our deal. That seems to be the crux of it—the Cynsters and Glengarah forging a breeding agreement."

"Indeed." Pru nodded. "That's a highly pertinent point. Once the deal is done, there'll be no motivation for any further attacks." She paused, then conceded, "We've been discussing these latest incidents as if our villain is out to murder you, but in reality—even with the needle in the saddle—every incident could merely have been intended to scare you off."

"Or to injure and so distract and delay. Or simply to make me feel that doing a deal with the Cynsters wasn't worth the risk." Deaglan paused, then met Toby's eyes. "I'm still having difficulty accepting that there are other breeding stables out there who, having got wind of a possible deal about to be forged between the Glengarah and Cynster stables, would stoop to this level of underhanded behavior."

Toby held his gaze for a moment, then looked at Pru. "How much have you told him?"

Pru sighed and met Deaglan's gaze. "As I recently explained, this is not just the usual breeding deal. A comprehensive exclusive agreement between the Cynster Stables and Glengarah has the potential to elevate the Cynster racing stables to the very top of the Thoroughbred tree. What I didn't spell out is the potential for quite massive future earnings such a deal will create, not just for the Cynster Stables but for Glengarah as well."

She paused, her gaze locked with Deaglan's, then went on, "Your father created a remarkable and immensely valuable resource, but refused to capitalize on it. You are intent on exploiting that resource. What you have to accept is that the quality of what you're working with—your father's collection—necessarily catapults Glengarah into the same league as the Cynsters. By virtue of your father's obsessive collecting, you are now playing on the same turf as us—as all the major breeding stables. We all need to refresh our bloodlines, and to that, you hold the key—and the potential riches involved, and for others, the corresponding losses, will be enormous."

Silence reigned as Deaglan allowed her words to sink in.

Then Toby said, "All that is to say that, yes, indeed, there are competitors out there with incentive enough to do what's been done here to date, and in a case such as this, with stakes as high as this, I wouldn't put it past some of them to stoop to murder."

~

He sat in deep shadows in a corner of the taproom. Although a mug of weak ale stood before him, he didn't dare risk taking a sip and shifting his eyes from the man seated opposite.

No one else was near enough to overhear them; the other patrons recognized a predator when they saw one and were avoiding even glancing at Finn and his two thugs, who overflowed chairs positioned between Finn and the rest of the tavern.

"I realize," Finn said, "that you hadn't foreseen the necessity of steps such as those you're now being forced to undertake." With a far-too-understanding, shark-like smile, he continued, "But in your case, that's the way the dice have fallen." A brow quirked. "Or should I say, the way the nags have run?"

The smile returned, an unsettling sight—even in the poor light, he could tell the gesture didn't reach Finn's eyes; over the two years he'd been meeting with Finn, he'd never seen the pale, icy depths warm.

"As we've discussed before," Finn continued, his tone positively dripping reasonableness, "if the Cynsters strike a deal with your employer, I cannot imagine that the earl won't take up the reins of the stable in the same manner as before he left Glengarah."

How on earth Dougal Finn came by such knowledge, he didn't know, but the bastard always had his finger on the pulse of every little thread in the vast web of his empire.

Finn went on, "You've been lucky—*we've* been lucky—that his lordship hasn't turned his attention to the stable before this. He's not his father, with his head in the clouds. He's a landowner of a very different stripe." Finn paused, then more quietly added, "A reality you'll have to find some way to...nullify."

"I've been trying." The words burst from him, their helpless tone one he hated to hear spilling from his lips. "I did as you suggested and tried to bury the evidence. But that didn't work, and now, it's out of my reach. So I tried to scare them off—him and her both—but so far, she's still there."

Finn's fleeting smile was sharp as any knife. "And now, I understand, her brother's come to join her. Sounds like they're getting ready to sign that deal."

"They're not there yet—they haven't even begun negotiations." He didn't think they had. "What I've been doing has slowed them down, at least."

Finn heaved a dramatic sigh. "Slowing down, while helpful, isn't a long-term solution. As I've explained before, you need to make certain you can continue to run your little arrangement into the future—at the very least until you've paid off your debt. How are you going to pay what you owe me without that source of funds?" Finn shook his head in mock sadness. "No. Simply delaying the inevitable by a few weeks isn't acceptable. While I'm heartened to hear you've been attempting to rid yourself of the threat, my only advice is: Try harder."

From across the table, Finn's gaze bored into him. "The long and the short of it is, my friend, that you either remove the threat his lordship poses—and I don't give a toss how you do it—or else I'll have to take steps to cut my losses."

An ominous silence closed about him, smothering, seeming to cut off his air.

His gaze dead level, Finn leaned closer. "Do you understand?"

He forced his head to nod. Swallowed. "I've tried again today—a trap of sorts. He might be gone by the time I get back. At the very least, he'll be injured and out of commission for some time. The deal with the Cynsters might not go ahead."

"Might not." Finn slowly—almost regretfully—shook his head. "Might not, my friend, isn't going to be good enough."

He swallowed again. "I know. But it'll give me time to arrange something more...permanent."

Finn's expression brightened, and he nodded. "Now, you're talking sense."

Over luncheon—a cold collation taken in Pru's room—she, Deaglan, and Toby were joined by Felix and Cicely.

Earlier, Cicely had broken the news of the needle in the saddle and Pru's resulting fall to Felix. He'd been shocked; more, as an ardent horse lover, he'd been utterly horrified not just over the danger Pru had unknowingly faced but at the unthinking, potential damage to such a valuable horse. Felix had dutifully gone to the stable and checked on the stallion and was able to report—to everyone's relief—that Rosingay seemed none the worse for the morning's shock.

As, all rather sober—quieter than they usually were, mulling over the situation and hoping to stumble on some glimmer of understanding as to what it all meant and who was behind it—they addressed their plates, Pru became aware that Toby was eyeing her in an assessing manner.

Finally, as Cicely rang for footmen to fetch the platters and plates away, Toby looked at Deaglan. "Given that Pru is chair-bound, depending on where things stand, perhaps we might start preliminary negotiations?"

Deaglan looked ready to leap on what Pru felt certain was intended as a distraction; before he could speak, she summoned a weak smile and said, "Actually...I have to admit I'm not really feeling up to it."

That, of course, put paid to the idea. Pru met Toby's eyes; only he would guess she was lying. The others were all instantly solicitous, but before they could decide that she needed to be left all alone to rest, she broke in to suggest, "Perhaps, Toby, instead, you might take a more comprehensive look through the stable. I'd value your opinion, especially on the horses in the fourth and fifth aisles. Oh, and also Deaglan's mount, Thor. He's in the first aisle on the left."

Toby was instantly diverted, as she'd known he would be. He got to his feet, ready to leave.

Pru looked at Felix and smiled. "You might want to go with Toby and keep him in line. He's liable to get overexcited."

Toby made a rude sound, but couldn't deny it.

Felix readily offered his escort.

By that time, Pru had transferred her gaze to Cicely.

The other girl was biting her lip, clearly wondering how to insert herself into the proposed excursion.

Pru again caught Felix's eye. "And after all her hard work tallying the stable expenses, perhaps Cicely would like to accompany you, too?"

Cicely nodded eagerly. "I would like to see how all the costs come about."

Toby glanced at Pru, then smiled and offered Cicely his arm. "No reason the three of us can't explore the stable together. We can leave our elders to their afternoon naps."

Pru arched her brows in grande-dame fashion, Felix and Cicely laughed, Toby grinned, and Deaglan waved the three of them off with a superciliously arrogant air.

Pru chuckled as the trio departed, meeting two footmen in the doorway. She and Deaglan watched as the footmen cleared the plates away, then Deaglan closed the door on the world, leaving the two of them in blessed peace and privacy.

Returning to sit in the chair next to Pru's armchair, Deaglan met her gaze. "Cicely is interested in Felix."

"Indeed. And Felix is interested in Cicely, although he's still at the stage of figuring that out."

"And Toby?"

"Comes from a long line of matchmakers. I predict he'll do all he can to goad Felix into not just realizing the nature of his interest but acting on it, too."

Amused, Deaglan shook his head.

A tap fell on the door.

"Yes?" Pru called.

Toby stuck his head around the door. "I just had a word with Bligh. Given we have no real idea what's going on here, he and I thought it best to leave a footman on duty in the corridor." Toby tipped his head toward the stairs. "He's a few doors down—in sight but not hearing—with orders not to allow anyone to approach this door, not without first gaining your or Pru's permission."

Deaglan nodded. "Thank you."

Toby saluted, drew back, and closed the door.

Pru stared at the door, then said, "I take it that means not even your aunt will be able to interrupt us unexpectedly."

"It sounds that way. Your brother is climbing in my estimation hour by hour."

She laughed, then turned thoughtful. "Actually, his suggestion of an afternoon nap has a certain appeal."

Deaglan studied her features. Despite the shock of the morning, she didn't appear the least bit tired or weak—not at all fragile.

As if to prove that point, she tossed back the shawl Cicely had draped over her knees and pushed to her feet.

Deaglan rapidly came to his, ready to catch her if she swayed—

She turned in to his arms and kissed him. With intent. Her hands rose to frame his face and draw him and his senses in.

Without hesitation, he answered her call, kissing her back, matching her increasing ardor as, by mutual accord, they let their reins fall and raced headlong into passion's beckoning conflagration.

She was leaning against him, her body molded to his, when she pulled back from the fiery exchange to pantingly whisper, "I believe we should expect my legs to give way—might I suggest we repair to the bed?"

He chuckled deep and low, then murmured back, "Your merest wish is my command."

He felt her lips curve against his, then he bent and swept her into his arms and carried her to her desired couch.

He laid her on the coverlet, then came down beside her; propping on one arm, he studied her face. "Are you truly recovered enough?"

She reached for his head and drew his face closer; she ran her lips over the edge of one earlobe, then whispered, "I wasn't damaged that much in the first place."

When she kissed him again, desire on her lips and heady passion on her tongue, he took her at her word and took her on. Met her challenge.

He was more than ready to do so on every count.

With open devotion, he worshipped her, with hands and fingers, lips and tongue, tracing the curves he gradually—step by slow step—exposed. There was no need to rush; they could linger and savor, admire and claim every inch along the road to completion.

When she lay bare on the satin coverlet, he was still fully dressed; noting that, she almost managed a frown and reached for him, but he drew away, out of her reach. After settling on his knees by her feet, he drew her second silk stocking free, tossed it aside, then, meeting her eyes, his own heavy lidded, he looked into the bright cerulean blue and, circling her ankle with his fingers, raised her bare foot, trailed the fingertips of his other hand over the underside of her arch, then, still holding her gaze, raised her foot higher and traced the same path with his lips.

She shuddered, and the rushed tempo of her breathing escalated further.

Her eyes remained locked on him as he continued his slow exploration, running his fingertips over the curves of calf, knee, and eventually thigh, at each stage following the same path with his lips, lingering in the sensitive hollows and letting the warmth of his breath on her skin excite her senses even further.

She was restless and needy, tense and waiting by the time his ministrations reached the tops of her legs, then he spread her thighs wide and dipped his head to pay homage to the delectable flesh that beckoned—passion slick, scalding hot, flushed, swollen, and inviting.

He licked, laved—heard her breathing fracture. Thought to teasingly murmur, "With a footman on guard, you'll have to be quiet. We wouldn't want him rushing in to find out why you'd screamed."

Pru managed to gasp, "I own myself surprised that you haven't educated your footmen on the desirability of not hearing certain things."

He paused in his ministrations to murmur, "They haven't needed to know before. I've never entertained a lady here—only you."

That revelation sent an unexpected rush of relief entwined with smug pleasure coursing through her. *Oh.* Then his tongue probed, and her world shook, and she caught a purling moan before it spilled past her lips. Instead, she forced herself to gasp, "I can be quiet."

If I try really hard.

He tested her resolve—almost to the breaking point. When he sent her spiraling over passion's edge and she fractured in a sunburst of glory, she had to press the back of her hand against her lips to mute her pleasured scream.

Deaglan watched passion take her, wring her out, and sate her. He would never get tired of that sight, not if he lived for a hundred more years.

Ignoring his own state, taking his pleasure in hers, when she slumped, utterly boneless, on the covers, he grinned—entirely pleased with himself —then swung around and stretched out beside her.

He raised a hand and idly played with her golden curls, then let his hand drift gently, soothingly, over the sleek, desire-dewed curves of her body. He adored being able to do that—to simply admire her form, her limbs, the subtle curve of lean muscle sheathed in satin-soft skin.

Too soon, she stirred, then he felt her gaze trace his face. He didn't meet her eyes; he was fairly certain hunger and need still burned in his.

But then she shifted; rolling toward him, she came up on one elbow, looked into his face, then smiled.

And turned her attention and her fingers to undoing the buttons of his waistcoat and shirt. "My turn."

He studied her face and quietly marveled at the lighthearted expectation of pleasure investing her features. "You don't have to."

She raised her gaze to his face, and this time, he met her eyes. She briefly studied all he let her see, then a slow, sultry smile curved her lips. "If you think I'm going to pass up the opportunity to have my wicked way with you in daylight *and* assured safety, you'll need to think again."

He laughed, but then she had his shirt unbuttoned and spread her hands across his chest—and the hunger and need he'd until then held back roared to the fore.

He reined in his instincts—enough, at least, to let her lead. To allow her to script the play as she diligently divested him of his clothes, then used her mouth on him in flagrant mimicry of all he'd done to her.

Except, this time, he called a halt before she could push him over the edge. He wasn't surprised that she didn't fight his directive but, instead, rose up, swung her leg over his hips, and straddled him.

On a long, slow exhalation, she sank down and took him in, pressed low and took him deep into the lush, scalding pleasure of her body, then tightened about him, holding him there, on the cusp of sensual insanity.

He stared at her in wonder—at all he could see in the deliberate, open devotion lighting her face—and with something approaching awe, murmured, "You're insatiable."

Her lids rose enough for her to pin him with her blue gaze, then one fine brown eyebrow arched. "And you're not?"

On the word, she rose up, and his lips curved as his lids fell and she settled to ride him.

With unrestrained passion and exuberant desire—with a devotion to the moment and to him that wrapped about his soul.

For her, he would always hunger and yearn.

Of her, he would never have enough.

With her, he could sate himself fully and yet remain addicted.

Addicted to her, forevermore.

Because she was the one, the right woman for him.

That single conclusion burned bright in his mind as completion took her, then him.

Late that night, with darkness shrouding the bed, Deaglan lay, utterly sated, beside the woman he now accepted held the keys to his future—all of them, in quite literally every way.

They lay side by side, on their backs, staring upward. He knew she hadn't yet surrendered to sleep but, like him, lay relaxed and, at least in her case, drifting in that hazy space to be found only in passion's aftermath.

He hadn't forgotten his Uncle Patrick's words: *Cynsters only marry for love.*

At the time, he'd dismissed the insight as irrelevant, assuming that marriage—and therefore love—would play no role in any deal forged between them. Now, after the events of the day, the horror of seeing her thrown, land, and lie unmoving, and the sheer weight of the emotion that had brought him to his knees and nearly undone him, nearly unmanned him, made ignoring that emotion and all that had evolved and developed between them impossible.

If love was what it took to secure her as his wife, he could offer her even that.

He felt an increasing pressure to speak, to raise the prospect of a marriage between them, but couldn't find the words to broach the subject, not in the face of her initial, clear and unequivocal, stipulation.

The last thing he wanted was to spook her in any way—to make her draw back from him. Especially not now Toby had arrived, someone to whom she might delegate the final forging of a deal should she decide she wished to leave Glengarah.

He needed to find some conversational avenue to lead into a discussion of marriage.

After several moments, keeping his tone easy, his voice low, he ventured, "You seem to have enjoyed your time here. Do you have any thoughts of spending more time in Ireland after our deal is finalized?"

He didn't turn his head but, instead, continued to stare at the canopy.

Pru stirred, then fell still again as the prospect of returning here rolled through her mind—so tempting, so alluring. Deep in her heart, she acknowledged what she'd known for days—that she felt at home here even more than she did on the downs at Newmarket. There was something about this country—its relative wildness—that spoke to her soul.

And then, there was him. And his horses and his castle and his people...

I want to stay.

That small voice inside her rang clearly. She'd never been sure who that voice spoke for, but suspected it was her inner self. Her true self, the one shielded inside her outer armor.

Yet staying there, with him, hadn't been part of the agreement she herself had insisted on.

And realistically, she could stay only if they wed, and he wasn't speaking of that, so...

Was he asking if she would consider spending time at Glengarah, helping to set up the breeding program they would soon formulate?

That had to be what he meant; the thought left her feeling oddly hollow.

She cleared her throat. "I assume you mean spending time here helping you set up the breeding program. I daresay that might be possible." She forced herself to lightly shrug. "We'll have to see how matters pan out."

Deaglan's heart sank. Her tone had been not exactly dismissive but almost disinterested. Certainly not interested, not eager at all. But more, the fact she'd interpreted his question in a business sense rather than personally cut even deeper.

Aren't we personal enough?

It was all he could do to respond with a noncommittal grunt.

Her response sent his mind whirling into darker clouds of the sort he hadn't encountered since his father had banished him. Her failure to embrace his tentative invitation to explore a future there with him felt every bit as bad.

He loved her, of that he no longer harbored any doubt. But did she love him? Regardless of his stance, his feelings, whatever he might say, could she ever come to consider marrying him?

Reviewing every second of their time together, he could find no answer. He honestly couldn't tell—had absolutely no clue—whether she cared for him in that way or not. Now she'd fully explained how incredibly important the deal between Glengarah and the Cynsters was to her and her family, every hint of caring he'd thought he'd seen in her could merely have been an outcome of her need to secure that deal.

He lay beside her and wracked his brains and sensed her slide into slumber.

Still, he continued thinking, wrestling with emotions and impulses with which he had no experience—he, who was considered one of the greatest lovers in the ton. What a joke!

None of his past gave him any useful insights for the here and now.

His life was different, and so was he.

Gradually, the churn of his thoughts calmed, leaving one decision standing unshaken and unwavering, shining and true.

He wasn't going to give up.

That was simply not in his nature, not over things that truly mattered to him.

He'd held to his dreams with the horses and now stood on the cusp of seeing those dreams realized.

He would hold fast to the dream of having her as his wife.

But just as he had with the horses, he would play a waiting game. In pursuing her, he would wait until the negotiations between them were completed. Over and done, the deal signed and sealed.

They both needed the agreement, and asking for her hand—even signaling clearly that he intended to do so—might be interpreted as a ploy to throw her off balance and gain advantage... No. He didn't want the business alliance with the Cynsters to intrude upon, much less become intertwined with, their personal relationship.

Admittedly, separating the two wouldn't be easy; they were who they were, and it was the mutual need for an agreement that had brought them together. But once the deal was done, putting it to one side and speaking strictly on a personal level would be possible; until the deal was done... he couldn't see how they could manage that.

And that evening, they'd agreed to begin formal discussions on the morrow.

An end to the process was in sight.

Once their deal was struck, he vowed he would bend the knee to Fate and simply ask her to be his wife—placing his heart and his future in her hands—regardless of how much a part of him rebelled at the thought of being so very vulnerable.

If that was the price he had to pay to have Prudence Cynster as his wife, so be it.

CHAPTER 16

*A*fter breakfast the next morning, Pru, together with Deaglan, Felix, and Toby, entered the library to commence formal negotiations.

Not only was she feeling unsettled over what Deaglan might be thinking regarding future business visits, but she was also no longer sure that sending Toby to look over the stables had been a wise idea; he now had stars in his eyes and, over the breakfast table, had waxed lyrical about several of the horses.

In the full hearing of Deaglan and Felix!

Admittedly, she'd had weeks to grow accustomed to the quality of the Glengarah horses, whereas Toby had had only twenty-four hours to absorb their impact.

She, Deaglan, and Felix claimed their now-customary chairs while Toby made for the armchair opposite hers.

As soon as they'd settled—Pru with her sheaf of notes and Deaglan with a handful of sheets presumably listing the stable's costs—Deaglan caught her eye and dipped his head in invitation. "Ladies first."

She arched her brows; this was obviously not Deaglan's first negotiation. At the edge of her vision, she saw Toby roll his eyes. Deaglan noted it and grinned unrepentantly at her brother.

Men! As Mama frequently states, they're all boys at heart.

Regardless, she'd been prepared for the ploy and crisply stated, "The most critical elements we, the Cynster Stables, would want included in any breeding agreement we would consider undertaking with Glengarah are, first and foremost, exclusivity, meaning exclusive access to all Glengarah breeding stock. Secondly"—she ticked the points off on her fingers—"we would expect to establish a roster of selected Glengarah mares to be sent to the Cynster stable at Newmarket to be covered by Cynster stallions, and vice versa"—another digit—"and finally, that the breeding fees for each horse exchanged are to be agreed upon on an individual basis." That made four points in all. She looked up to see that Deaglan had sobered and fought back a smile; there were benefits to going first and being able to set the agenda.

When she arched her brows, inviting his response, he stirred, then said, "To your first point, we would need to have a limit placed on the period of exclusivity—say five years—with, of course, an exclusion for any and all in-stable matings of Glengarah mares and stallions. We would also require an agreed written arrangement for sharing the offspring of all matings within the program—perhaps on some form of alternating dispositions working from highest to lowest fee as determined each breeding season." He paused, his gaze on Pru's face, then went on, "And as part of any deal, we would expect to receive ongoing advice from the Cynster Stables for our own breeding program, one run separately but parallel to the breeding that will fall under the Cynster-Glengarah agreement—a program wholly based on Glengarah bloodstock."

Pru met Toby's eyes. They'd seen the Glengarah horses; they knew that the most spectacular breeding successes were likely to come from Deaglan's proposed Glengarah-only program. However, that was very much a long-term wager given that none of the Glengarah horses had established racing pedigrees, while the Glengarah-Cynster breedings using proven racers would yield more immediately valuable offspring.

She'd known from the first that any Glengarah breeding outside the proposed agreement would prove a sticking point in getting her father's and Nicholas's support. Toby's, too, but judging from his expression, although he didn't like even the thought of such a competitor, having seen the Glengarah bloodstock, it was a pill he was willing to swallow.

Looking at Deaglan, she stated, "With those aims as our goals, I believe we'll be able to come to an agreement." She glanced at her notes, not that she had anything written there she needed to read; all her experience, her knowledge, was in her head. "First, regarding exclusivity, would you consider..."

They settled to haggle.

She and Deaglan went back and forth and eventually agreed on an initial ten-year period of exclusivity, excluding in-stable breeding, with the provision that, if both sides were satisfied at the end of the term, the agreement could be extended in three-year increments, or if changes needed to be made, to renegotiate in good faith prior to any other stable being allowed access to Glengarah bloodstock.

That, Pru felt, was the best deal they could hope to get—viewed from either side.

"Right, then." Deaglan leaned forward, his forearms on his thighs. "I accept your second and third points—the establishing of rosters to exchange horses between Glengarah and Newmarket. Those rosters will need to be drawn up and finalized every year—shall we say by November first? That will allow sufficient time to arrange and effect safe transportation between the two stables."

Pru nodded. "We'll need to review the results of each year's foaling plus the quality of the colts and fillies produced the previous year before drawing up the rosters for each breeding season."

Deaglan watched Pru and Toby exchange glances, then Pru said, "Such reviews can't really commence until July, preferably August, so finalizing rosters by November first seems eminently sensible."

She paused, then went on, "That brings us to the division of offspring."

Deaglan felt very much on his mettle as they embarked on a discussion of the sharing arrangements for the prospective Cynster-Glengarah and Glengarah-Cynster matings. This was Pru's area of consummate expertise; even Toby bowed to her knowledge without hesitation. And Pru wasn't inclined to sell the Cynster name, experience, and expertise short; he hadn't expected her to.

The bargain she tried to drive was a hard one—a difficult one for him to swallow.

However, although he'd shown her the five horses he'd intended using as bargaining chips, he'd retained one rather large chip with which he hoped to soften her stance. To tempt her into giving him and Glengarah more.

He waited until they'd pushed back and forth and had, apparently, reached a standstill—still too far from his ideal for him to accept—before, after sitting silently in his chair for nearly a full minute, he captured her gaze and said, "What if Glengarah offered to include within this agreement a limited number of Glengarah-Glengarah matings—say three per year?"

He had to give her credit; she blinked and stared at him, but didn't otherwise react. Then she looked at Toby.

Her brother didn't have her control; he was obviously ready to leap on the chance.

She immediately looked back at Deaglan and said, "Five per year. And we would have to agree on the mating pairs."

He was careful not to let his smile show. "Four, and that's my upper limit. And all such breedings will occur here."

She hesitated for an instant, then nodded. "Agreed."

He inwardly rejoiced. Getting ongoing advice was one thing; seeing that advice in action would be even more valuable. Learning from the Cynsters, having inside access to their accumulated knowledge, would ensure he didn't waste time with crosses that were unlikely to result in high-quality foals.

"So"—he leaned forward again—"to return to the proposed splits of the offspring."

Pru met his eyes, and although he saw in the blue of hers that she'd recognized his ploy in unexpectedly introducing a greatly desired prize into the agreement, she was now willing to back away a little from her hard line over sharing the offspring to secure the expanded deal.

They eventually reached an accord, with twenty percent of the Cynster-Glengarah offspring accruing to Glengarah, plus thirty percent of the Glengarah-Cynster offspring and fifty percent of the Glengarah-Glengarah offspring. That last figure had been hard fought, but the fifty percent of Glengarah-Glengarah offspring that would travel across the Irish Sea to Newmarket had been his concession, and he wasn't about to weaken and give the Cynsters more.

Once the splits were decided and accepted, working out an agreed method for determining which offspring accrued to whom went quickly and relatively smoothly.

And when it came to the provision of Cynster advice, as Toby cynically remarked, even if the Cynster Stables stood to get only two of the four foals from the included Glengarah-Glengarah matings, having secured their interest with that offer, they would be proffering advice on all Glengarah matings even if Deaglan didn't want it.

Even though he realized both Toby and Pru—who had agreed—were entirely serious, Deaglan had to smile.

Pru considered the structure of the deal as it was taking shape in her mind and nodded. "Very well. With all those points decided and out of the way, that leaves us with the fees to settle." Although normally straightforward, in this case, setting breeding fees might easily become the trickiest part of a deal that had already proved tricky enough. She studied Deaglan, well aware that she needed to pitch the Cynster offer at a level that would lock in all the details they'd agreed on to that point—an offer so attractive that Deaglan wouldn't even consider talking to any other stable, let alone invite a competing offer from one of the Cynsters' competitors.

She thought that, between them, they'd engineered a well-balanced and fair deal thus far. The fees were the final hurdle, and while she believed that both sides were well-disposed to sealing the deal, she would have to hit the right note with her offer—an offer that was entirely hers to make.

The weight of familial responsibility was palpable.

"There are," she said, meeting Deaglan's eyes, "several alternative fee structures used in arrangements such as this." Briefly, she outlined them; all were complex, to the extent that she saw both Deaglan's and Felix's eyes glaze over.

She glanced at Toby; she doubted he'd yet realized that the Fitzgerald brothers had an aversion to complicated calculations. She hoped Toby had the nous to hide his surprise at the offer she planned to make and to keep his mouth shut about it, too.

She switched her gaze to Deaglan—who, predictably, was now faintly frowning—drew breath, and said, "However, in this case, I'm inclined to offer a single flat fee, specific to each horse, to run for the first five years of the agreement, the fee applied to each horse to be reassessed at that point and determined for the following three years, then revised again for the last two years of our arrangement."

Now came the part about which she hoped Toby would hide his astonishment. "I'm going to propose that we determine the fee for each horse based on a multiple of the Glengarah stable average yearly cost of upkeep per horse, with the multiple for each specific horse determined by its quality as evidenced by my notes and its verified bloodlines. And with the multiple for each horse to be adjusted at five and eight years, as just mentioned. Of course, these fees apply only to the matings with offspring going to the Cynsters. The matings with offspring going to Glengarah will attract no breeding fees either way." She tried not to rush the rest, to make it sound like a normal offer. "The fees I would suggest as appropriate would have multiples falling between one and a half and four."

To Toby's credit, he managed to keep silent, although she could feel his shocked gaze boring into her.

Deaglan didn't notice, too busy staring at her himself, an enigmatic expression on his face. Eventually, he drew breath and, without shifting his eyes from hers, said, "You really want access to our horses."

She inclined her head. "I also want exclusivity. Without it, we can't do a deal—or at least, not this sort of deal, where we all stand to gain so much. I've therefore elected to make our offer sufficiently attractive that you should not have any second thoughts whatsoever about accepting."

She thought she saw his lips twitch, but then he stilled them.

Deaglan's grasp of arithmetic was more than sufficient to comprehend the largesse she was offering—on top of all the other benefits established in the preceding discussion. That said, he knew what he would have offered had he been in her shoes and what he would give to secure such a deal. He held her gaze and stated, "Make the multiplier range one and a half to five, and you have a deal."

Toby shifted, then stilled. When Deaglan glanced his way, Toby said, "Having the top multiplier at four was a generous"—he glanced at Pru —"*very* generous offer."

Deaglan followed Toby's gaze to Pru.

She met his eyes and waved at her brother. "You see?"

He held her gaze and nodded. "I do. But we'll only get one chance at this—to craft a deal such as this particular one." He paused, then more softly asked, "So…how much do you want to breed from the Glengarah collection?"

She stared back at him for a very long moment, then slowly inclined her head. "A top multiplier of five. It appears, my lord, that we have a deal."

Unable to sit still, Deaglan straightened in the chair and only just stopped himself from crowing.

Pru struggled to hide her satisfaction, but couldn't entirely suppress her smile. No matter how one measured it, the deal was a good one all around. She drew in a huge breath and exhaled, feeling a great deal of the intangible weight slough from her shoulders. "Excellent. Now all that remains is to agree on the figure for the average cost of upkeep per horse per annum to be entered as our base amount." She arched her brows at Deaglan. "What was the figure you two and Cicely came up with?"

Evenly, Deaglan replied, "One hundred and seven pounds."

"What?" Pru nearly tumbled from her chair.

Toby was struck speechless; slack-jawed, he simply stared. Then he shook his head and looked at Pru. "That can't be right."

Gathering her scattered wits, Pru returned Toby's stare. "Could there possibly be that much difference in costs between here and England?"

Now looking troubled, Toby shook his head. "I don't know, but Kentland's never remarked on it, and he knows our costs."

Puzzled, Deaglan looked from brother to sister. "What's the Cynster Stables' figure?" He looked at Toby. "Do you know?"

"Of course." But rather than state an amount, Toby looked at Pru.

Deaglan did the same and saw that she was staring at the floor, a frown knitting her brows. Then she glanced up at Toby, then at Deaglan. "We're straying into what is generally held to be sensitive information among Thoroughbred stables. In the interests of our future association, we will share our figure, but given we suspect that someone in the employ of a competitor might be among the household staff, can you summon a footman—one you trust—and position him in the corridor where he won't be able to overhear us in here but can keep all others away from the door?"

He held her gaze for a second, then rose, tugged the bellpull, and walked to the door. "We should have thought of that earlier."

"Indeed," Pru replied. "But better late than never."

Behind him, he heard Toby say, "I'll check the terrace."

By the time Deaglan returned, leaving a footman on guard in the corridor, Toby had given the all clear for the terrace. Deaglan resumed his seat and nodded at Pru. "All secrets are safe."

She inclined her head, hesitated for an instant—long enough to underscore that this was not information she readily shared—then quietly stated, "Within our breeding program, our current costs per horse run to fifty-eight pounds per annum."

Deaglan blinked.

"And," Toby added, "Papa and Mama being as they are, our costs are, if anything, on the extravagant side."

"But...but..." Felix stared at Toby. "That's just over half what our costs are." Felix switched his gaze to Deaglan. "And we're certainly not extravagant!"

Deaglan frowned. "We must have calculated it wrongly."

"Or," Pru said, "perhaps there's some major difference in the way your stable—being a collector's stable and not one organized on commercial lines—is run."

Deaglan shook his head. "I have no idea. This is the only stable I've ever been involved with."

Frowning slightly, Pru suggested, "Let's call in Cicely and ask her to bring her notes. We need to work out what's going on here and not just in order to finalize our deal."

Deaglan agreed. He went to the door and dispatched the footman to fetch Cicely.

When Deaglan returned to his chair, Toby asked, "While we're waiting for Cicely, why don't you tell us how you came up with that figure? Was it from invoices or payments or...?"

"We worked off the estate accounts," Deaglan replied, "because your sister needed the stable accounts to extract the information for the acquisition of the horses."

"I had to create an acquisitions ledger," Pru put in. "The late earl hadn't bothered with one."

"Huh," Toby said, then looked again at Deaglan. "So you worked off the estate records and not the actual stable accounts."

Deaglan nodded. "Perhaps there's some discrepancy between the two. There shouldn't be, but..."

"Indeed," Pru said.

A tap fell on the door, and Cicely looked in, then came in, shut the door, and with a sheaf of papers in her hand, came to join them.

The men all rose, and Felix gestured Cicely to the sofa across from Pru. Cicely sat, and Felix sat beside her.

As Toby and Deaglan resumed their seats, Pru said to Cicely, "We need to check your calculations. How did you work out the figure for the cost per horse per annum?"

Cicely blithely replied, "We worked from the stable charges in the estate accounts. There are three sub-accounts, each of which has an entry every month—one sub-account is for feed and all other consumables, another is for wages, and the third is for repairs to the building, new harnesses, extra saddles, and such like. We tallied the three sub-accounts for each month, then added all the months and divided the result to get the average for a month, then divided again by sixty-four—that's the fifty-seven horses in the collection plus seven carriage horses—to get the average per horse per month, then multiplied by twelve to get the average per horse per annum."

Pru nodded. "That should have worked."

"From how many months all told did you draw amounts?" Toby asked.

"We worked from the estate records for the years of '49 and '50, plus the first two months of this year, so twenty-six months in total." Cicely paused, then added, "That period includes the last eight months of the late earl's life, while Deaglan was still away."

Cicely looked from Pru's frown to Toby's. "I triple-checked the totals. Everything adds up."

Slowly, Pru nodded. She looked at the papers in Cicely's lap. "Do you have the monthly figures for the three sub-accounts? The figures you tallied to get the amount spent by the stable for each month?" When Cicely nodded and started shuffling through the papers, Pru said, "Tell us the three sub-account figures for a given month—any month will do."

Cicely pulled out a sheet, studied it, then read, "For the month of February last year, the charges for the stables were—for wages, thirty-eight pounds, for buildings and other goods, another thirty-eight pounds, and for feed, a sum of four hundred and ninety-four pounds. That's a total of five hundred and seventy pounds for the sixty-four horses for that month."

Pru met Toby's eyes, then looked at Deaglan. "It's your charges for feed that are astonishingly high. The other charges are comparable to ours, and our breeding stable is of similar size—we have sixty-seven horses in total. But our charges for feed per month would be closer to two hundred pounds, not nearly five hundred."

They all looked at each other, transparently mystified.

After a moment, Pru said, "It might be instructive to examine the ledgers more closely—not just those for the past two years but those for earlier years as well. I know there's been a famine here since '45, but I wouldn't have thought that would have affected feed for horses, at least not to such an enormous and continuing extent."

"It didn't," Deaglan somewhat grimly said. "I wouldn't have expected our costs to be massively higher than yours, even over the hunger years. A little higher, perhaps, given we buy in virtually all of our grain, but not more than double your costs." He pushed to his feet. "The estate ledgers we used are in the estate office. I'll fetch them."

"But"—Cicely held out a hand to stay him—"the estate accounts show only the charges for each sub-account." Cicely looked at Pru. "If

I'm following your thinking correctly, you want to check if there's an unusually high cost for a particular thing—like hay."

Pru nodded. "Yes. Exactly that."

"In that case"—Cicely looked at Deaglan—"it's the stable accounts we need to study."

Deaglan looked at Pru and arched a brow.

Correctly interpreting the question in his eyes, she shook her head. "When I worked through the stable ledgers, I looked only at the entries for the horses. I didn't pay the slightest attention to the day-to-day expenses, but those ledgers should show what, exactly, is sending your feed costs so high, and whether something changed and when that occurred."

Deaglan looked at Felix. "The stable ledgers are in the safe here."

Felix nodded and rose. "I'll fetch them." He headed for the far end of the room.

Cicely rose, too, and went to help.

As puzzled as any of them, Toby leaned forward, his forearms on his thighs, and as Deaglan sank into his chair, asked, "While they're fetching the ledgers, can you confirm the time line of the stable for me and Pru? For instance, how long ago did your father start the collection?"

Deaglan stated, "He'd always been interested in horses, but started actively working on the collection as such in '35."

Toby nodded. "So about fifteen years ago."

"He made it a personal challenge," Deaglan continued, "to collect the strongest examples of the foundation bloodlines, not to show or breed from but purely for the gratification of knowing he owned them. At first, he bought and sold animals, but from about ten or so years ago, he stopped selling and only added to the collection, until about two years ago, a little before his death, when he bought his last mare and decided the collection was complete."

Felix returned, a pile of ledgers in his arms. Cicely followed, bringing more.

"Papa," Felix said, joining the conversation, "would travel the length and breadth of Ireland, and into Scotland and England as well, in pursuit of particular horses."

"As you've seen," Deaglan said, "he was highly selective in the horses he bought."

Pru nodded. "All right. That gives us some notion of how long the stable has been functioning as a 'collector's stable.' I would expect costs per horse to have remained fairly steady over, say, the past ten years."

Felix had stacked the ledgers on the low table before the sofa. "We've brought the stable account ledgers for the past eight years."

"That should do." Pru looked at Deaglan, Felix, and Cicely. "Why don't each of you take the account ledger for one year and flick through, looking at the expenses noted for the various feedstuffs for, let's say, March, June, and October. Let's see if they add up to nearly five hundred pounds each month."

Deaglan rose from his chair and joined the other two on the long sofa. They sorted through the ledgers. Deaglan took the ledger for '47—four years ago—while Felix took the one for '46, and Cicely pulled out the ledger for '45.

The three sat and dutifully leafed through the pages.

Pru exchanged a glance with Toby, and they reined in their impatience and waited.

Somewhat to Pru's relief, Cicely was seated between the brothers, and they were showing her the entries they found, checking their addition with her; Pru had greater confidence in Cicely's arithmetical skills than those of Deaglan or Felix.

With Cicely's help, Deaglan finished scanning through his ledger first. He shut it, stood, and returned it to the pile. Meeting Pru's eyes, he moved to reclaim his previous seat. "All three months were the same or close enough. Somewhere in the high four hundreds."

She nodded. Cicely finished checking Felix's sums, and Felix, too, shut the ledger he'd scrutinized. "The costs in '46 look the same—all three months were close enough to five hundred pounds as makes no odds."

Finally able to turn her full attention to the ledger she'd selected, the one from '45, Cicely frowned. "That's odd. These entries are in a hand I don't recognize."

Felix leaned across to look. "That's Jay's father's hand. He was the previous steward."

"He died in mid-'45," Deaglan said, "and Jay, who had been trained to the position, stepped into his father's shoes."

"Ah. I see." Cicely continued to flick through the pages. "In June, the hand changes to Jay's—which is the same hand as in the later ledgers." But her frown only deepened as she scanned the entries for the three nominated months. Eventually, Cicely raised her head and looked at Pru, then at Deaglan. "The feed costs in March, June, and October of 1845 ran to about one hundred and eighty pounds per month." Cicely glanced at Toby. "More in line with the Cynster Stables' figures."

Deaglan felt as if his head was spinning. He shifted, then stilled and asked, "So when did the costs go up? And why?"

Felix stared at Deaglan, then reached for the ledger he'd just set down. "Let me check January '46."

He opened the ledger and turned to the right page. Cicely leaned across, and together, they scanned and added up the entries.

Cicely reported, "The charges for feed in January '46 were at the lower level. About one hundred and ninety pounds in that month."

"Try February," Deaglan said.

Several minutes later, Cicely said, "February's feed costs were still low—one hundred and seventy-six pounds that month."

Deaglan concluded, "So March '46—which Felix has already checked —is the month the feed costs increased."

"Let me recheck." Cicely took the ledger onto her lap and rapidly scanned. Then she nodded. "Yes. The costs for feed leap in March '46, virtually from the beginning of the month. They go from one hundred and seventy-six in February to about four hundred and twenty in March."

Deaglan watched as Cicely continued to flick through the ledger, pausing to scan and mentally add. She looked up and said, "The feed costs for April are about four hundred and eighty pounds."

"We've already checked June and October," Felix said, "so it looks as if the costs went up at the beginning of March '46 and have stayed high ever since."

Deaglan looked at Pru.

Her expression serious, she caught Cicely's eyes. "Go back to February '46 and compare the various feed costs with those noted for April, two months later."

Cicely nodded and did so.

After several minutes had ticked by, she looked up and said, "It's everything." She focused on Pru. "Every bill is roughly double and a bit more."

Toby looked from Felix to Deaglan. "Did something happen in February '46 that would account for a sudden escalation in feed costs, a rise in prices that, subsequently, remained high?"

Feeling very much as if he was on the brink of discovering something he wasn't going to like, Deaglan slowly shook his head. "The famine started in '45. By February '46, it was hitting hard. Times were bad, that's true enough, but around here, we had sufficient—certainly for the horses. Feed for them was mostly bought in, so wasn't under such threat—it was food for people that was in short supply. It was people who went hungry, although those on Glengarah lands fared better than most."

"Only because," Felix muttered, "before you left, you'd pushed them into small-lot farming and keeping animals for themselves. But yes, you're right—the people here escaped the worst and got by. Only a few of our families left."

Then Felix's face cleared, and he looked at Deaglan. "But there *was* something that happened here in February '46—something major."

Deaglan frowned. "You mean me falling out with Papa—"

"Over the stable," Felix said.

Deaglan inclined his head. "Indeed." To Toby, he explained, "I left Glengarah and didn't return until eighteen months ago—after my father died."

Toby nodded, then looked at Pru, a faint lift to his brows.

Pru read his look and turned to Deaglan. "If we could ask—what were the specifics of your disagreement with your father? Given the timing, that might be relevant."

Deaglan frowned. "I can't see how, but it's no secret. I was trying to get my father to allow the collection to be used as the basis for a breeding program. The estate needed the income, if nothing else to balance the drain on the finances from the upkeep of the stable. But he wouldn't have it. The stable was his creation, and he wanted it to remain just the way it was—simply for his personal gratification. I stalked out, and he bellowed after me never to darken Glengarah's doors again. So I didn't. Not until he was cold."

"So you were familiar with the overall costs of the stable back then?" Pru questioned. "When the feed costs were lower?"

Deaglan shook his head. "Papa kept everything to do with the stable close—he never encouraged me to poke my nose even into the estate accounts. I was schooled in the structure of the estate, but never made privy to the specifics. So I never knew what the stable was actually costing, but obviously, as the stable costs came out of the estate coffers, the stable had to be a drain, as it contributed nothing back."

Puzzled, Toby asked, "So who oversaw the stable back then?"

Deaglan's lips thinned. "Theoretically, Papa, but he found accounts as boring—and as challenging—as Felix and I do. In reality, I was more actively involved in the day-to-day decisions than Papa or Felix, but more in a general sense. I left all the ordering of feed and so on to the head stableman, Rory Mack. He's been in charge of the stable for close to ten years. I'd never looked at the stable accounts"—Deaglan tipped his head toward Pru—"not until Pru needed them."

Toby frowned. "So what happened after you left? Who kept an eye, general or otherwise, on the stable then?"

Felix waved a hand. "Me. But I was even less involved in the details than Deaglan, and as you've seen, I'm hopeless with figures. Papa was the same. He would walk the aisles, looking at the horses and choosing one to ride—he rode a different one every day. With Deaglan no longer about, I kept a closer eye on the horses themselves, making sure they were exercised and properly cared for. And as we always had, I left all the ordering to Rory. Like Deaglan, I'd never looked at the stable accounts until the past few days."

Deaglan looked at Toby. "Papa died eighteen months ago, and I returned then. But the rest of the estate had suffered due to my father's neglect for too many years. I made a decision to leave the stable as it was —it had always rolled along with minimal oversight—and devote my time and energies to rectifying all the problems Papa had allowed to accumulate and fester, before I allowed myself the indulgence of picking up the stable's reins again. It was always my intention to commercialize the stable, as I'd previously done with the kennels, and they were not under any threat or stress. There were no problems there."

He paused, then, his face hardening, added, "I was determined not to become the sort of landowner Papa had been—one who ignores his responsibilities in favor of admiring his horses."

Toby glanced at Felix, then looked back at Deaglan. "So until the past few days, neither of you had examined the stable costs."

Deaglan grimaced. "Not in detail. When I returned and finally had access to the estate records and could study the accounts, I discovered that the drain on our funds due to the stable was significantly more than I'd thought, but given the number of horses we have..." He shrugged. "I assumed the costs were a reflection of that."

He looked at Pru. "We've never worked out our costs on a per-horse basis before. I thought the figure we came up with was high, but I assumed that was just how things were."

Pru held his gaze and evenly stated, "The way this appears to be playing out is that someone—someone here at Glengarah—leapt on a chance created when you left the estate and were no longer here, closely involved in the stables on a day-to-day basis, regardless of whether you looked at the stable accounts or not. It was someone who knew that, with you gone, they could get away with inflating the feed costs."

She watched Deaglan and Felix exchange a long look.

Pru waited, but it was Toby who stated the inescapable conclusion. "For the past five years, ever since March '46, someone has been using the feed costs of the stable to bleed the estate." Toby straightened in his chair and met Deaglan's gaze levelly. "It's either your head stableman, your steward, or both."

That neither Deaglan nor Felix could bring themselves to believe it of either man was written all over their faces.

"Both Rory and Jay," Deaglan finally said, "were born here. They grew up alongside Felix and me and have served the family for most of their lives. Their families have served ours for at least two generations before them."

Felix started shaking his head. "No. It has to be someone or something else." He looked at Pru. "You've met Jay and Rory. They have good lives here—what reason would they have to steal from the estate?"

Toby said, "They might have a reason you know nothing about—a debt, a personal need. You can't be certain there isn't something there, something they've kept hidden, especially from you two."

Pru shifted, drawing everyone's attention. She looked at Deaglan and Felix. "How are the orders for feed handled?"

After a second, Deaglan replied, "As far as I know, Rory decides what's needed and tells Jay, who places the orders with the suppliers."

"Who sees the invoices?" Toby asked.

Deaglan glanced at Felix. "I don't think Rory does." Deaglan looked back at Toby. "Jay places the orders, and the invoices, I assume, would come to the estate office. Jay then pays the invoices and"—he nodded at the stable ledgers—"as we've seen, enters each purchase in the stable accounts and later makes the monthly entries in the estate records." He frowned. "But Jay orders what Rory instructs him to buy, and presumably when those orders are delivered, they match what Rory's expecting."

Deaglan looked at Pru. "I can't see how, if the orders and deliveries are double or more what's needed, the grooms and other stablemen wouldn't notice. If a swindle like that existed, surely they would all have to be a part of it?"

Pru grimaced. "And that's very hard to imagine."

The five of them fell silent, juggling the facts, trying to assemble what they'd discovered into a believable picture.

A sharp rap fell on the door.

Somewhat distractedly, Deaglan called, "Come."

They all looked across the room and saw Jay walk in.

He hesitated, plainly taken aback to find all of them gathered there. Pru saw his gaze fall to the stable accounts, piled on the low table, then Jay looked at Deaglan. "If I could speak with you privately...?"

Pru caught Deaglan's eyes and, with her own, did her best to convey a warning that Jay might be a villain—that until they knew otherwise, they should exercise caution in dealing with him.

Deaglan held her gaze for a second, then looked at Jay and waved with his usual easy grace. "Whatever you have to say, you can speak before us all."

Jay was obviously reluctant, but walked closer. He halted at the end of the low table and, his expression now one of poorly concealed concern, said, "While I was in Sligo yesterday, meeting with our suppliers as usual, I heard a rumor that Rory Mack had been seen drinking with some thugs in the Blackbird Tavern, of all places."

Deaglan shot a glance at Toby and Pru. "It's a seedy hedge tavern on the edge of the town."

Jay nodded and continued, "That didn't seem like our Rory at all, so a little while ago, I went to find him and ask what it was about—if he was in trouble or..." Jay gestured vaguely, the worry in his face deepening. "He should have been finished with the morning's chores, but I couldn't find him in the tack room or anywhere in the stable. I asked around, but the other men haven't seen him since this morning, when he gave them their day's tasks."

Deaglan, Felix, Cicely, Toby, and Pru were all exchanging meaningful glances, something Pru saw Jay note.

She returned her attention to the steward as Deaglan did the same.

His features growing grim, Jay went on, "At first, I just thought he must be somewhere about, but then I noticed marks on the floor outside the tack room—scuff marks and such—signs of a struggle. A desperate struggle. When I looked closer, there were what looked like drag marks leading to the side entrance." Jay paused, then added, "And there's blood on the floor, too."

Deaglan rose to his feet; Toby and Felix did, too. "You think Rory's been seized by these thugs?"

Jay met Deaglan's eyes. "That's what I fear. It can't have been too long ago—the blood was only just turning sticky. I thought you'd want to mount a search."

Deaglan nodded curtly and looked at the others—at Toby, Cicely, Felix, and lastly Pru. "Regardless of what trouble Rory's got himself mixed up in, he's one of ours. We'll haul him out of it." Deaglan glanced at the ledgers. "We can sort everything else out later."

No one argued. Now as anxious as Jay, Deaglan waved the steward ahead, and they followed him out of the room.

CHAPTER 17

*N*ot wanting to miss anything, Pru left Cicely to break the news to the rest of the household and went with the men to the stable.

Once inside, with Deaglan, Toby, and Felix, she followed Jay down the corridor and around to the tack room, where they examined the evidence of violence Jay had found.

As Jay had intimated, it appeared there had been a scuffle of some sort, resulting in several drops of blood spattered on the dusty boards, then two roughly parallel drag marks led toward a side gate that gave onto a presently empty paddock.

All rather grim, they returned to the first aisle. Deaglan dispatched Jay and several grooms to gather all the stable hands and any other men they could find. Felix strode off to the kennels to summon all available hands from there.

With just the three of them left waiting, Toby looked at Pru, then at Deaglan. "It seems likely that your head stableman, this Rory, is the one behind the excess feed costs—or at least played a part in the scheme. Could his thuggish friends be the ones behind the attacks on you?"

Deaglan frowned. "I can't see why they would come after me."

"Because," Toby insisted, "you were the threat. Not to belittle Felix, but it's almost certainly widely known that he isn't likely to scrutinize the stable accounts—he hasn't for the past five years, and this scheme started under his watch, so to speak. Whoever they are, they never saw Felix as a danger. But then you came back, and it's likely every bit as widely known —certainly to Rory—that your ambition has always been to set up a proper breeding operation. And *that* means you would, at some point, focus on the costs of the stable—and as we've seen, that's exposed their scheme. You looking closely at the stable operation is the one thing those behind the scheme don't want, and you inviting Pru to stay signaled you were about to do just that. To them, removing you and replacing you with Felix would allow their lucrative little scheme to continue, potentially indefinitely. Essentially, the profits of Glengarah—all the rest of the estate —would be going into their pockets."

Deaglan grunted, then grimaced. "When you put it like that...yes, I suppose it is possible that whoever snatched Rory was behind the other incidents."

Men started arriving, then Felix returned, bringing a group of kennelmen.

As more men gathered, Pru realized she couldn't participate in any search dressed as she was. She tugged Deaglan's sleeve and, when he looked at her, leaned close to say, "I'm going to get changed. Don't you dare leave without me."

He met her eyes, then nodded.

She released him and hurried out of the stable and across to the castle.

She rushed straight up to her room, stripped off her day dress, and snatched up her riding habit. She'd donned her blouse and wrestled her way into the voluminous skirt and was tying it at her waist when a light rap fell on the door, then it opened, and Toby looked in.

Pru met his eyes, and he arched his brows at her.

She knew what he was asking and nodded. "I agree. It certainly seems like Rory was involved, but we shouldn't forget that Jay might well have been Rory's partner in crime."

"It occurred to me," Toby said, "that we've only Jay's word about seeing Rory with some thugs in that tavern. And the scene in the stable could have been staged. There might be no thugs. Instead, Rory could be out there somewhere with a rifle, waiting for another chance to take a shot—a better shot—at Deaglan."

The words—the picture they painted—sent ice spiraling through Pru, chilling her from the inside out. Grimly, she reached for her jacket. "I'll follow Deaglan. Perhaps you should follow Jay."

Toby nodded and saluted her. "I'm going to get my pistol. I'll see you in the stable yard."

Pru finished buttoning her jacket, then had to sit to unlace her half-boots and haul on her riding boots. Finally correctly shod, she ignored her riding hat, picked up her gloves and quirt, and rushed out and down the stairs.

In the front hall, she passed Cicely, who stopped and called, "I wish I was going with you."

"Just as well you aren't—we need someone to keep an eye on things here..." Pru paused and swung to face Cicely. "The stable accounts—we left them out. Can you put them back in the safe?"

Cicely nodded and changed direction for the library. "And I'll try to keep Esmerelda from stumping out to join you."

"Please!" Pru fled.

She reached the stable yard as men, all mounted, started to stream out, scattering to every compass point. She rushed on and found Deaglan near the stable entrance, Thor's reins in one hand; he was giving orders to several of the older men regarding searching the various buildings scattered about the castle.

Jay was there, too, mounted on a powerful bay.

Toby trotted out, astride Hector and leading Kahmani, who had Pru's saddle on his back. Toby flashed her a grin. "They said you'd ridden him before."

Pru threw him a kiss and hurried to take Kahmani's reins.

Deaglan appeared by her side and lifted her up to the saddle. As she settled her boot in the stirrup, he met her eyes. "I've sent the men out searching in pairs. Given the time since someone last saw Rory and now, and that the blood was only just thickening, whoever seized him can't have got far. Especially not if they're carting Rory, unconscious, with them—he's no lightweight."

Pru nodded her understanding.

Deaglan looked at Toby and went on, "Because the castle is more or less in the center of the estate, I've had to send men in every direction. There are a lot of places these thugs might have dragged Rory to—luckily, most of the men searching know the area well. It's possible Rory and his captors haven't left the estate, but even if they've managed to cross our boundary, they can't have gone much farther yet."

Toby nodded. "So there's a chance your searchers will catch up with them. What then?"

"I've given orders that one of the pair is to race back here and report while the other follows at a distance. We don't want to lose them, but I also want no confrontation without the numbers being on our side."

Toby nodded. "Good decision."

Deaglan glanced at Pru. "I've kept the Sligo Road for you and Toby to cover. If you ride reasonably hard, you'll come up with anyone before they reach the town's outskirts. There are searchers already out in the fields to either side of the road—if you need any help, they're searching on a line several hundred yards to either side."

Pru studied his face, then nodded and gathered her reins. "What about you?"

He grimaced. "Of necessity, I've drawn the short straw. Felix and one of the grooms have ridden out to check the tracks up into the hills directly north of here. I'll ride out to the northwest, checking the fields and cottages as I go, but there's not much out that way, and it's the shortest distance before the hills rise, and after that, there's no way on. Once I can see the end of the highest field, I'll ride back. That way, I'll be here if and when any of the others sight Rory and return to report."

Pru nodded.

Deaglan rounded Thor and mounted.

Pru looked at the last of their group. "And Jay?"

Jay backed his horse, preparing to wheel for the yard's exit. "I'm heading directly west. It's a longish ride to the boundary, with only a few cottages along the route. If I find anything, I'll send someone from the cottages."

Deaglan had settled in his saddle. He gathered Thor's reins. "Right, then—let's get searching."

He tapped his heels to Thor's sides, and the huge horse surged.

Jay fell in alongside Deaglan. Pru exchanged a look with Toby as, side by side, they followed the pair under the stable arch.

Once out of the yard, Deaglan wheeled hard right and headed off along a broad climbing track while Jay cantered off on a narrow run between fields. Pru and Toby dutifully rounded the house and, as one, urged their horses into a gallop down the drive and onto the road to Sligo.

Pru gave thanks it was Toby with her; they thought so much alike, she rarely needed to explain. The instant they reached the solid surface of the road, they set a thundering pace, riding hard for the next five and more minutes. Then Pru slowed and looked around.

Toby stood in his stirrups and did the same. "There!" He pointed off to the right. "There's two of them, just ahead of that stunted tree."

Pru looked, then swung Kahmani's head toward the tree.

They soon came up with the pair of Deaglan's men delegated to search in that direction. Pru glibly explained that while she and Toby had seen nothing of Rory, they had to return to the castle, and asked the pair, once they'd completed their search, to return via the road, just in case.

She seriously doubted that any thugs intent on kidnapping Rory—and why kidnap him anyway?—would have happily set off on the open road to Sligo. If they'd taken the road at all, it would have been in the other direction—into less populated areas. Regardless, at this point, it wasn't Rory's safety that was uppermost in her mind.

The stablemen, having seen her with Deaglan over the past weeks, readily agreed, and Pru and Toby peeled away and struck out, apparently for the castle, but once they were out of sight of the stablemen, Pru swung Kahmani northward on a heading she estimated would land her on Deaglan's trail.

Both she and Toby possessed excellent directional sense; when they neared the route Jay had taken, she glanced at Toby, caught his eye, and tipped her head to the west. "He'll be somewhere that way."

Toby met her eyes, then his jaw set, and he shook his head. "No. And there's no point arguing—I'm not leaving you."

She glared at him. When that had no effect, she snapped, "Toby! We need to know if Jay's a part of the scheme!"

Utterly unmoved, Toby shrugged. "Consider this. If anything happened to you, first, Deaglan would have my hide. Then Papa would rip into me, followed by Nicholas, and lastly, Mama. No, actually, the last —and most fearsome, because no one ever sees it in her—would be Meg." His face set. "So just shut up and ride."

She gritted her teeth, but she knew that look. She faced forward and urged Kahmani to an even faster pace.

Deaglan rode back into the stable yard, having seen no one unexpected and nothing suspicious at all. He'd spoken with two of his farm workers, but neither had spotted anyone or anything moving about the fields that morning.

Satisfied that whoever had taken Rory hadn't gone that way, Deaglan had ridden hard to get back in case anyone else had had better luck, but there was no one waiting impatiently for him.

He dismounted before the stable entrance and led Thor inside.

The stable was strangely quiet; the older men he'd sent to search the castle outbuildings and grounds hadn't yet returned, and he'd dispatched everyone else on the wider search.

He opened Thor's stall and unsaddled the stallion, then, with nothing better to do, started brushing him down.

All the while, he strained his ears, hoping to hear hoofbeats riding in —someone, anyone, coming with news.

He'd known Rory all his life. He'd have taken an oath Rory was as honest as the day was long. Rory had been the one he'd trusted to keep the stable running as it should when he'd left five years ago—Rory's the hands into which he'd entrusted the well-being of the horses of the Glengarah collection.

Rory had simply been there, a part of Deaglan's life. He wracked his brain, yet couldn't recall anything—not one little change in behavior or odd comment to which he hadn't paid due attention—that might have alerted him to something having changed in the man he'd known and unquestioningly trusted for so long.

He hoped it was all some horrible mistake—or if not, if Rory was behind the infernal scheme, that there would be some reason, some excuse Deaglan could comprehend and accept so that between them, he and Rory could make things right.

Rory had been a friend for so long...the looming betrayal cut like a knife.

Deaglan was latching Thor's stall door when he heard hoofbeats nearing. Not racing but riding purposefully in.

He walked out into the stable yard as Jay swung under the arch. Deaglan stopped and watched as Jay slowed, then halted the horse. "Anything?"

From the tight set of Jay's features, he already knew the answer.

Jay shook his head and dismounted. "Nothing out that way." He tied the horse's reins to one of the hitching posts, then met Deaglan's eyes. "But I thought of something."

When Deaglan arched his brows, Jay hurried on, "A place where the thugs might have hidden Rory if they'd done away with him. He's that big, that heavy, they wouldn't have wanted to drag him far."

Deaglan frowned. "That's true enough, but where..." Then he realized. "The old cellar." He spun on his heel and strode into the stable.

Jay hurried after him. "Exactly. Those drag marks led us toward the gate, but they didn't go that far. What if the thugs realized they couldn't drag Rory far enough away, so they hefted him up and carried him around to the cellar?"

Deaglan slowed. "How would they know where the cellar was?"

Drawing level with him, Jay shrugged. "If they'd been watching the place from a distance, say with a spyglass—and they must have been, to pop in and find Rory without anyone seeing them—they most likely would have seen one of the stable lads open the trapdoor and go down. We still store extra lanterns and things like that down there."

Although decades ago, the stable cellar had been declared too damp to store feed or even leather, metal and wood survived well enough.

Deaglan lengthened his stride. They reached the tack room and turned away from the spot where they suspected Rory had been struck down, walking on and around into the short corridor that ran down the far side of the tack room. On the opposite side of the corridor lay a storeroom that backed onto the exercise ring. The last yards of the corridor were floored with stone, and that end was open to the elements. Beyond lay one of the large paddocks they'd used on the night of the fire.

The trapdoor giving access to the cellar stairs was set in the last section of the wooden floor. Deaglan halted and looked down at the door. The wooden surface was suspiciously dust-free. He glanced at the boards they'd just crossed, confirming the entire area looked freshly swept. Not that he could deduce much from that; as in any stable, grooms were wielding brooms for much of their day.

He bent and gripped the ring set into the trapdoor's surface and hauled the door up.

As soon as it started to lift, Jay reached down and helped him swing it back. They stood and looked down at the inky blackness into which a fixed wooden stair descended.

"I'll fetch lanterns." Jay hurried back up the corridor. There were lanterns and tinder on a shelf a little way back.

Deaglan crouched at the lip of the hole and listened. After hearing nothing, he lowered his head and called, "Rory?"

His voice echoed away into the cellar, bouncing off the stone walls and ceilings, before fading away to silence. Deaglan strained his ears, but heard nothing in response.

As Jay returned, lighted lanterns in hand, and the beams played onto the stair, Deaglan saw another drop of still-gleaming blood and a reddish-brown smear on one of the treads.

Am I going to find Rory alive or dead?

His face setting, he reached for the lantern Jay held out. "You were right. He's down there."

Jay didn't reply but watched as Deaglan turned and, taking the lantern with him, went quickly down the stairs.

Once on the ground, he played the lantern beam over the immediate area. He wasn't surprised not to see Rory. The cellar was extensive; from the bottom of the stairs, two long corridors stretched away into the darkness—one to the left, the other to the right—each with chambers giving off to either side.

Jay joined him and added his lantern beam to Deaglan's before saying, "If they had the sense to bring him down here, dead or alive, they wouldn't have dumped him close to the stairs."

Deaglan grunted in agreement. "You go left—I'll go right. Call if you find him."

Jay nodded, and they parted.

Deaglan made his way deeper into the right wing of the cellar, playing the beam of his lantern before him in an effort to avoid the numerous obstacles that littered the beaten-earth floor.

As he reached each archway that gave access to a side chamber, he paused and carefully scanned the chamber's floor, but found no body or even signs of disturbance; no one had gone into those areas for months, if not years.

He'd just realized that the floor of the corridor also showed no hint that anyone had passed that way in a decade when, from a long way behind him, he heard Jay call, "I've found him! They've beaten him, but he's alive."

"Thank God." Deaglan turned and made his way back toward the stairs.

From the lip of the open hole at the top of the cellar steps, Pru and Toby heard Deaglan returning and shared a wide-eyed look.

They'd arrived at the spot in time to hear Deaglan send Jay one way while he went in the other. Toby had risked hanging his head down into the cellar, then had pulled back and murmured that the cellar appeared to be one long area, with the stairs dropping into the middle of a corridor that extended to either side, with rooms giving off on either side of each arm of the corridor.

Pru had leaned close and whispered in Toby's ear, "So unless Jay turns and follows Deaglan—which we'll be able to see from here—Jay won't be any threat to Deaglan."

Toby had nodded. He'd glanced around, then left her, only to return minutes later with two lanterns, already lit, but completely shielded. He'd handed her one and kept the other.

They'd remained crouched about the hole in the floor and waited to see what transpired. They had no reason to think Jay was in league with Rory and a party to the scheme, yet if he was...

Pru suspected they would shortly find out. She hadn't liked having Deaglan acting as a lure, essentially as bait, but that was the way matters had played out; she had to trust that, if Jay was a villain, she and Toby could reach Deaglan in time to spoil whatever ploy Jay had planned.

But now Deaglan was heading toward Jay.

Pru and Toby stared down into the cellar and saw Deaglan stride across the bottom of the stairs and, with his lantern beam playing ahead of him, plunge on in the direction Jay had gone.

Pru looked at Toby, then leapt to her feet, hiked up her skirts, and clinging to the lantern with the same hand as her heavy skirts, crept silently down the stairs as fast as she could.

She reached the ground, peered to the left, and saw Deaglan's back as a shadowy silhouette against a distant splash of lantern light. He was striding openly, and the sound of his footsteps echoing off the stone walls and ceiling provided excellent cover for her and Toby. With her skirts in one hand and the fully shielded lantern in the other, she started after Deaglan, knowing Toby, descending cautiously behind her, would follow.

She hurried as much as she dared, praying she wouldn't stumble or kick something. Archways to right and left gave access to spaces drenched in darkness. The corridor led straight on; Deaglan strode confidently toward the distant glow, which was steadily growing stronger.

Then a hand closed over her shoulder, and she jerked to a halt, gritting her teeth to hold back a squeal.

Toby ghosted past her, moving quickly and silently to place himself before her.

She bit her lip, holding back all the violent, sisterly protests her mind supplied, and quickly followed.

Toby drew ahead, his body effectively screening Deaglan's from her sight.

Then Toby paused and shifted to the side, allowing her to see past—into the chamber at the corridor's end.

A thick stone arch marked the entrance to the chamber. Deaglan had passed beneath it, but Toby had drawn into the shadowy space to one side of the arch.

Pru made for the corresponding space on the arch's opposite side, slipping into the denser shadows. From their concealing depths, she peered out, into the chamber, as Deaglan, who had slowed, paused several paces beyond the archway, not that far ahead of them.

He was staring at Rory, who sat slumped, apparently senseless, against the back wall. Cuts and deep bruises marked the large head stableman's face, and blood matted the hair on one side of his head and ran in a thick line down his cheek.

Jay was crouched by Rory's feet, his lantern trained on the fallen man; the reflection of light off the back wall was the glow they'd been seeing.

Deaglan started forward again. "He's alive?"

Jay replied, "Alive enough."

Then Jay swiveled around, swinging the lantern up and training the beam directly onto Deaglan's face—into his eyes.

Jay straightened, raised a pistol, and leveled it at Deaglan—who had instinctively turned his head aside and lifted a hand to shield his eyes.

Jay fired.

Pru's heart stopped.

She couldn't move—she couldn't even scream.

A ringing clatter, a near-deafening cacophony of clanging metal, jarred her.

The glare had caught her eyes, too, but as the beam of light swung away and she blinked and her sight returned, she saw Jay scowling at something to her left.

After a second, he bent and set down the pistol. "You couldn't make this easy, could you?"

The clanging continued.

And Jay pulled out a second pistol. "Just as well I came prepared."

Pru shifted into the archway and stared at where Jay was looking, at the scene his lantern was now illuminating—and saw Deaglan very much alive.

He'd flung himself aside at the last second; Jay's bullet had clipped his right shoulder. Unfortunately, he'd landed in a stack of discarded metal pails and was grimly flailing to free himself, battling to regain his feet.

Jay wasn't about to let him do that. He stalked closer.

Pru started to step forward, only to have Toby cut her off and thrust her back as he moved quickly and silently into the chamber, his footfalls masked by Jay's.

Jay halted, and Pru froze. So did Toby. Terror clawed her spine. She watched Jay calmly set down his lantern, then straighten, raise his gun, and calmly check it, and ice clamped about her heart. The gun was one of the new revolvers; she didn't know how many chambers he had loaded.

She couldn't risk taking another step, not with both Deaglan and Toby at risk.

What can I do?

She'd never felt so devastatingly helpless in her life.

"You had a good life in London." Jay refocused on Deaglan, still thrashing among the pails. "Why couldn't you stay away?"

"What sort of bastard are you?" Deaglan spat. "Rory was your friend as much as he was mine. How could you kill him?"

"Oh, he isn't dead," Jay replied, and the smile in his voice was plain as he went on, "Haven't you worked it out yet? Rory is slated to hang for your murder."

With that, Jay straightened his arm, taking careful aim at Deaglan.

"Oh no you don't!"

The words burst from Pru's lips.

Jay jerked the barrel up and swung toward her.

She ducked behind the side of the arch as a thunderous retort rocked the chamber, and bricks shattered inches from her face.

Immediately, she heard a furious roar. She peeked out in time to see Deaglan launch himself out of the pails and onto Jay's back.

The pair crashed to the ground and rolled. Deaglan was hampered by his injured shoulder, and Jay was almost the same size. They wrestled, rolling back and forth across the earthen floor.

Pru remembered her lantern; she flicked open the shields and put the lantern on the ground inside the archway. Then she hurried closer to the fighting men, frantically searching the ground. The gun was no longer in Jay's hand, but she couldn't see where it had landed.

Like her, Toby opened his lantern and set it down, then circled the fighting men; he had his pistol in his hand, but with the way Deaglan and Jay were rolling around, getting off a shot was impossible.

Toby called, "The revolver?"

"No idea," Pru called back.

His face contorted into a mask of malicious fury, Jay hauled back one fist and sent it flying toward Deaglan's face. Deaglan turned his head at the last second, and the punch glanced off his skull.

Thuds and grunts filled the air.

Pru swore beneath her breath. She'd had enough.

She looked around, hoping to find something useful. Her gaze landed on an old broomstick propped against the wall near the archway. She rushed across and grabbed it; she wrapped both hands around one end and hefted it, then ignoring Toby, still tracking the wrestling pair with his pistol and meanwhile swearing at her to keep back, she skirted the heaving mass of male muscle until she reached their feet.

She waited until they were both on their sides, with their hands locked around each other's throats, then she swung the broomstick high, filled her lungs, and screamed, *"Stop!"*

The sharp command froze both men—just for a second.

A second was all she needed. She brought the stick whizzing down and broke the end over Jay's head.

His head was hard; he was stunned, but nothing more.

Toby swore, set down his pistol, and lunged and caught Jay by the collar, then hauled him up and away from Deaglan.

Deaglan followed, scrambling to his feet, his gaze, distinctly feral, locked on his distant cousin's face. "Allow me," he grated. Then he hauled back his fist and plowed it into Jay's face.

Jay's jaw cracked.

Deaglan felt a spurt of satisfaction—enough to compensate for the pain in his knuckles and the throbbing in his shoulder. He staggered and watched as Jay slumped in Toby's hold.

Toby peered around into Jay's now-unconscious face, then nodded. "Good job."

Toby opened his hand and let Jay fall unceremoniously to the floor. *"There* it is." Toby bent and picked up Jay's second gun, which had been hidden beneath their bodies.

Deaglan drew in a tight breath, straightened fully, and swayed. Then a force of nature hit him—all soft curves and searching, grasping hands.

"Thank God—thank God!" She seized his face and kissed him as if, through the kiss, she could hold him to her.

He swept his arms around her and crushed her to him as blessed relief poured through him.

As the wave crested and broke, memory struck, and fear, raw and visceral, surged anew. He shifted his hands to her upper arms, gripped, broke the kiss—and held her back enough to glare at her. "Don't you ever do such a foolish thing again! Drawing the attention of a murderer with a loaded gun in his hand!"

All heat and passion, she instantly fired back, "I wouldn't have had to if you'd taken care not to be alone with that murderer! The one with a loaded gun in his hand!"

"I didn't know he had a gun!"

"That's beside the point!" She waved her arms in the air. "He was one of the two we suspected, and yet you happily went down into a dark cellar alone with him."

Accusation burned in her eyes. She jabbed a finger into his chest. "You tried to tuck me safely away by sending me down the Sligo Road with Toby, but it was always you our villain had in his sights. You —not me!"

He stared at her, at the tears pooling in her eyes—which she furiously tried to blink away—and could find no answer, couldn't get his tongue to form any words.

She swallowed and, in a softer, almost-sobbing tone, said, "You nearly died. What would I have done if you had?"

What he saw in her brilliantly blue eyes rocked him to his soul.

Then her gaze shifted to his shoulder, and she all but wailed, "And he shot you!"

He caught her hand before she could touch the wound. "It's just a flesh wound."

"But it's still bleeding!"

"Not a lot."

Toby had viewed the beginning of the exchange with a cynically amused eye, then had turned away and left them to it. After collecting his pistol and checking that Jay was still entirely unresponsive—and noting that his brother-in-law-to-be, a status of which he no longer had any doubt, packed a punch to be wary of—Toby crossed to crouch beside the still-unconscious Rory.

He checked the pulse at the base of the man's throat and was reassured by the steady thump.

As he drew his fingers away, Rory groggily stirred. He mumbled incoherently, then, with his eyes still closed, grumbled, "What the devil's that racket?"

Toby didn't bother hiding his grin. "Just two lovebirds fighting. It's about to end, now reality's sinking in."

Almost on the words, Pru seized Deaglan's lapels and looked into his face. "I don't want to fight with you. I only want you safe and well."

Deaglan closed his hands over hers, holding them against his chest. "I don't want to fight with you, either. I need you too much."

She studied his eyes, then slid one hand free and raised it to his face, cradling one cheek as she held his gaze. "And I need you— alive. Thank heaven you are."

She stretched up on her toes, and he met her halfway. The kiss was the sweetest he'd ever known, sending the remnants of their panic and fear dissipating like smoke on a vibrant, vigorous breeze.

Eventually, he drew back and rested his forehead against hers. "Thank you for coming—for rescuing me."

She sniffed. "You might have rescued yourself, but I couldn't risk it— you must see that."

He raised his head and smiled into her blue, blue eyes. "I'll never see that, but I accept that's how you see things—see me—and with that, I don't wish to argue."

"Good—you'll never win." She stretched up and touched her lips to his again, then drew back and, twining the fingers of one hand with his, turned to where Rory lay slumped.

Hand in hand, they walked to join Toby where he crouched beside Rory, who had, it seemed, regained his wits.

Deaglan halted with Pru by his side. Was Rory innocent, or had he, too, been a part of the betrayal, only to be betrayed in turn by Jay?

"Rory?" When Rory squinted blearily upward, Deaglan asked, "What happened?"

Rory frowned. "I don't rightly know. Last I remember, I was walking out of the tack room, heading for the storeroom…" He lifted a hand to his head and gingerly touched the wound.

"Leave it." Toby reached out and drew Rory's fingers away. "We'll need to get that cleaned and tended."

Rory's frown had darkened. "Someone hit me over the head. Hard.

Don't remember much more after that, not until I woke up down here. Then I heard a shot and..." Rory shifted and peered around Deaglan and Pru at Jay, still slumped senseless on the floor. "I heard Jay say as I was going to hang for your murder. I opened my eyes then and saw him point his gun at you, and... I must have blacked out again."

Deaglan nodded. "You have no notion who hit you?"

Rory shook his head. "My hearing's not the best, as you know. Didn't hear anyone creeping up."

Distant sounds from above ground had been drifting to them over the last minutes. Now, they heard someone shout, "The trapdoor to the old cellar's open!"

They heard the thump of many feet rushing overhead, then Felix called down, "Deaglan? Are you down there?"

"Yes!" Deaglan replied. "Wait there—we'll join you in a moment."

Toby looked at Deaglan and Pru. "You two go up and send a handful of men down. I'll keep an eye on our patient and would-be murderer until then." He glanced assessingly at Jay. "He's not going to wake up for a little while yet—he'll need to be hauled up the stairs."

Rory had also been looking at Jay; he shook his big head. "He was going to kill you. I would never have thought it—wouldn't have believed it if I hadn't seen and heard it with my own eyes and ears."

Deaglan felt much the same. The relief of having Pru safe, of having all the people who mattered still alive, had dulled the sting of Jay's betrayal. It would take time for that cut to heal, for the deadening sensation inside to fade, but...

Deaglan nodded to Toby and, without looking again at his erstwhile steward and distant cousin, escorted Pru back to the cellar stair.

CHAPTER 18

*O*n emerging from the cellar, Deaglan gave orders that Jay was to be hauled up, tied up, and confined in the tack room, the door of which had a heavy, if rarely used, lock. He also arranged for Rory to be helped to the castle so the staff there could properly tend his injuries. After that, leaving Felix to oversee that all was done, Deaglan surrendered to Pru's insistence and allowed her to chivvy him into the castle.

Ten minutes later, stripped to the waist, he was sitting on the end of his bed and fighting not to hiss and, instead, meekly accept Pru's ministrations as she bathed his wound.

She was fussing—something he had a constitutional aversion to—albeit in a determined, resolute, and stubborn way that was entirely her own, and in light of what he could still see in her face, the lingering traces of the emotion driving her, he kept his lips shut and outwardly stoically endured, while inside, he allowed himself to dwell on what the emotion gripping her meant—for him, for them both.

On their way across the front hall, they'd diverted to the drawing room, and with Pru flanking him, he'd stuck his head around the door to report to Maude, Esmerelda, Cicely, and Patrick that matters had come to a head, and while they'd found Rory alive, albeit roughed up, they'd discovered it was Jay who had been behind all the recent incidents. Predictably, all four had been shocked, and Maude, Esmerelda, and Patrick had turned grave. From the distance of the doorway, with his injured shoulder angled out of their sight, he'd reassured them that, although he was somewhat the worse for wear—something they could plainly see—all he required was a change of clothes, then he would come down and assuage their curiosity, and meanwhile, Pru, Felix, Toby, and indeed, everyone else were unharmed and well.

If his aunts and uncle had seen anything odd in Pru accompanying him upstairs, they'd made no comment.

Finally, she wound a gauze bandage over his shoulder and around his upper arm, covering the gouge Jay's bullet had made; she fiddled, then tied the gauze off and patted the knot. "There. That will do for now."

He caught her about the waist, drew her between his spread knees, and kissed her soundly.

"Thank you," he said when at last they drew apart.

With her hands resting lightly on his shoulders, her eyes searched his. Etched in the summer blue were so many feelings—emotions, reactions, impulses.

Needs, wants, desires.

There was so much he wanted to say—so much she needed to hear—but...

He felt his lips quirk and, his eyes on hers, softly said, "Sadly, this is not yet over."

She held his gaze, her own open and direct, then sighed and tipped her head in acquiescence. "We need to go downstairs and work out exactly what happened."

He moved her back, rose, and headed for his armoire. "That, I fear, is part of being an earl—one always needs to be there."

While he found and donned fresh breeches and shirt and another jacket, and combed his hair, she gathered the cloths and bowl she'd used to clean his wound and set them on the dresser.

Downstairs, they found the rest of the company in the library, partaking of sandwiches, ale, cider, and tea, and realized they'd missed luncheon.

Once Deaglan and Pru had helped themselves and settled in their usual chairs, balancing their plates and with glasses of ale or cider at their elbows, Felix and Toby led what became, essentially, a reinterpretation of recent events now that they knew Jay had been the driving force behind them.

Maude put her finger on one of the still-missing pieces of the puzzle. "I cannot conceive of why Jay would act in such a way. He had a secure place with us here, and to my knowledge, neither he nor his mother, Moira, have ever dropped any hint that he was dissatisfied with his lot."

After a moment of studying their puzzled faces, Toby said, "There's obviously something you don't know." He paused, then added, "Something not even his mother knows."

Deaglan set aside his empty plate and picked up his glass of ale. He took a sip and looked at Toby, then at Pru. "We need to speak with Rory."

Pru met his gaze. "We still can't be sure Rory wasn't working with Jay and this latest incident was a falling out between thieves, as it were."

Maude made a distressed sound. "Surely we haven't harbored two traitors in our midst?" She met Deaglan's eyes. "I've known Rory Mack as long as I've known you."

Deaglan dipped his head; he'd known Rory for even longer. "We need to get to the bottom of this, here and now." It was painful enough assimilating that Jay had been prepared to kill him, but if Rory had turned against them, too...they needed to know and quickly.

Deaglan drained his glass, set it down, and got to his feet.

Pru rose, too, as did Felix and Toby.

"If I might suggest," Toby said, "let me ask Rory about the supplies used in the stable. He knows we're working on a breeding agreement, so won't think it odd. You three all know him better than I do—watch and see if you think he's answering honestly or not."

Deaglan nodded; it was a sound suggestion.

They found Rory in the housekeeper's room, seated in a chintz-covered armchair and sipping tea from a mug while being stood over by Mrs. Bligh.

When Rory saw them and started to get to his feet, Mrs. Bligh clapped a hand on his shoulder and pushed him down. "Now is not the time for such things. I told you—you stay in that chair until I give you leave."

Rory sent a pleading look at Deaglan, who had to smile and say, "That's all right, Rory—this is Mrs. Bligh's domain."

Mrs. Bligh nodded. "Quite right."

The housekeeper—who had also known Rory from birth—had wound a thick bandage around Rory's head; seeing him raise a hand to the knot, she slapped his fingers away. "You leave that alone—no poking. If you must go and get yourself hit over the head, you have to bear the consequences."

Rory looked at them helplessly.

Mrs. Bligh bustled about setting a chair for Pru and another for

Deaglan. Toby helped by fetching straight-backed chairs for Felix and himself.

"Right, now." Mrs. Bligh bent a severe look on Rory. "I'll leave you to talk to his lordship, but I'll be back the instant they're finished with you, and I want to see that posset all drunk, do you hear?"

Rory bobbed his bandaged head. "Yes, Mrs. Bligh."

With a sound suspiciously like a humph, Mrs. Bligh whisked around the door and shut it behind her.

Pru smiled at Rory. "How are you feeling?"

Rory stared at the liquid in the mug he held. "Better now, but I'm not sure about this stuff."

"No getting out of it, I'm afraid," Felix said. "Not even Deaglan would dream of daring to countermand Mrs. Bligh."

Rory sighed and sipped, then looked at Deaglan. "So was it Jay lit the fire in the stable, too?"

Deaglan tipped his head. "So we think. But as you know, we're in discussions with Miss Cynster and her brother regarding setting up a breeding agreement involving our horses."

Rory's face lit up. "Aye—that'll be grand. We're all looking forward to hearing of it."

Deaglan could read nothing beyond eager anticipation in Rory's face. "As part of our discussions," Deaglan went on, "we've been reviewing our stable's costs, and Mr. Cynster has a few questions we hope you can help us with."

Rory switched his gaze to Toby. "Happy to help if I can, sir."

Toby smiled in his usual easygoing fashion. "It's really just the amounts of feed your stable goes through each month. Can you tell me how many bushels of oats you order to see you through a month?"

Rory promptly stated a figure and was just as quick with his responses when Toby asked about barley, hay, and lucerne.

After Rory had stated the last of the amounts, Toby looked at Deaglan, then returning his gaze to Rory, said, "Those are, indeed, the amounts we would expect for a stable of some sixty-plus horses. What's been puzzling all of us is why the orders put in to the suppliers are rather more than double those amounts."

When Rory blinked, clearly surprised, Toby picked up the stable account ledger he'd had Felix fetch from the library safe and had brought with them. Puzzled curiosity all over his homely face, Rory watched as

Toby opened the ledger, flicked through several pages, then turned the ledger and leaned forward to show him.

"See?" Toby pointed to an entry. "In March last year, the amount of oats ordered in was more than double what you say you use."

Rory frowned, then set aside his mug and reached for the ledger, and Toby let him draw it from his hands. Rory stared at the page, then flicked backward and forward. "Nay—this isn't right." He looked at Deaglan. "I'd know if that much was coming into the stable, month by month, and I can tell you it never has." He glanced down at the ledger again. "Why, to get through that amount, we'd need to run near to three times as many horses as we do. And as we don't…well, what would we do with all that extra feed?"

Rory raised his head and looked at them. Confusion and puzzlement and also an underlying confidence—a rock-solid certainty of what he knew—were evident in his expression.

"Just to be clear," Deaglan said, "you don't deal with the suppliers."

Rory shook his head. "I don't rightly know who our suppliers are, although I suppose I could guess—I always left that to Mr. O'Shaughnessy, and to Jay once his da was gone."

"And you never see the bills?" Pru asked.

"No, miss. They all go direct to the estate office—to Jay…" Rory's face took on an arrested look, then he shifted his gaze to Deaglan. "Is this all a part of what Jay was doing, then?"

Briefly, Deaglan caught Toby's eyes and fractionally inclined his head; he was satisfied Rory knew nothing about Jay's scheme. Looking back at Rory, slowly, Deaglan nodded. "We think so. But exactly how it all fits together, we're still not sure."

Rory looked thoughtful; he closed the ledger and handed it back to Toby, then shook his head. "It's just so hard to get my mind around this."

"Don't worry about that now—I'll let you know when we've sorted it out." Deaglan rose, and the others followed suit. Deaglan caught Rory's gaze. "That was a nasty knock Jay gave you—take it easy for a few days."

Rory had picked up his neglected mug. He waved it. "I'll be fine."

Pru, studying him, didn't bother correcting him; Rory wasn't the sort to readily relinquish his duties watching over the horses that, she realized, meant a great deal to him as well. Rory reminded her of the head stableman at the Cynster Stables…which set another hare running in her brain. "Rory, when you do return to the stable"—they all knew it wouldn't be long before he found his way back—"can you ask around the staff there whether anyone noticed Jay riding out unexpectedly—for instance, riding out at a time or in a direction they thought odd or wondered about?"

Rory bobbed his head. "Aye, miss, I'll ask, but I can tell you now that he often rode out westward. None of us could work out to where, and he never said, but wherever he went, it can't be more than a few miles away, because he was always back inside of an hour or so."

Pru smiled. "Thank you—that's exactly what I'd hoped to learn." The other three looked at her quizzically, but she merely smiled, and after reminding Rory to finish Mrs. Bligh's posset and not to overtax himself, she led the way from the room.

Despite pointed looks from Deaglan, Toby, and Felix, she refrained from saying more until they were back in the library. Maude and Esmerelda had decamped, but Cicely and Patrick were waiting to hear their news.

Pru waved at Felix to answer Cicely's and Patrick's questions, which he did.

Then Toby, slouched in the chair he'd claimed, said, "Cut line, Pru—what has your busy brain worked out now?"

She smiled broadly at Toby, then looked at Deaglan. "We know the amount of supplies that were ordered. Unless you wish to postulate that all the suppliers of feed—all of whom I suspect are established merchants in Sligo—are complicit in Jay's scheme, then I think we can be confident that whatever amounts were ordered were delivered."

"But," Felix said, "Rory would have known if those amounts were delivered here."

Pru nodded. "Rory and all of the stable staff. So that couldn't have happened, either."

"So," Toby said, "what did happen? We're not talking about a few bags but bales and sacks by the dozen."

"What I think happened," Pru said, "was that the delivery was split. That Jay had the main delivery made to whatever place he rode out to—westward from the stable, so a spot a delivery cart coming from Sligo would reach first. Then after unloading all the extra supplies there, he had the delivery men take the rest, the actual amount Rory had asked for, on to the stable."

She looked around at a circle of thoughtful faces.

Then Deaglan said, "There's no building in that direction that could be used for such a purpose. Two cottages on that general heading, but both are occupied and far too small to store that much extra feed, even for a day or so."

"Jay's been careful," Pru said. "He's worked everything out, so he would have put thought into that aspect, too." She met Deaglan's gaze. "I'm willing to wager that somewhere west of the stable is a building of some sort he's made into his warehouse."

Deaglan grunted. He leaned back and looked past her at the windows. "It's too late to ride out today." He met Pru's eyes. "But you're right— there must be something out that way. We'll ride out and search tomorrow morning." Then he glanced at the others. "But for now, why don't we try asking Jay what he did with all the feed and all the money he's bled from the estate?"

～

Deaglan walked into the tack room with Pru, Felix, Toby, and a surprisingly determined Cicely at his back.

With his wrists crossed and tied behind him, Jay had been lashed to a chair placed more or less in the middle of the good-sized room.

His face bore significantly more evidence of their fight than Deaglan's. Deaglan's final blow had left one side of Jay's jaw swollen and his lips cut. An earlier blow must have landed on Jay's left eye, which was swollen half shut, the skin around it already discolored.

Deaglan allowed his gaze to dwell on the man who, although they had never been close friends, he'd always considered inherently trustworthy, someone who, like him, had Glengarah's best interests at heart.

Glengarah—the estate, the land, the people—had been just as much Jay's home, just as much his inheritance, as Deaglan's.

Evidently, that hadn't been enough to win Jay's loyalty.

It seemed Jay had only ever harbored his own interests in what passed for his heart.

Deaglan glanced around, then crossed to pick up another chair from those lined up against the wall. Toby fetched one for Pru, and Felix one for Cicely.

Deaglan placed his chair squarely in front of Jay, with two yards between them, and sat, elegantly crossing his legs at the knee. Toby set Pru's chair behind Deaglan's and a little to his right, and once she'd sat, stood behind her. Felix and Cicely mirrored that placement on Deaglan's other side.

Leaving Jay facing a judge and jury of sorts.

"This scheme of yours," Deaglan said, "why did you start it?" That, of all the questions, was the one that puzzled him the most.

His lids low, partially screening his eyes, Jay studied him for several seconds, then straightened on the chair and raised his head. "Your father's negligence was to blame. He never really looked at even the estate accounts—just wrote out the drafts for whatever sum Papa requested." Jay paused, then, his tone harsher, said, "He was just asking to be taken advantage of." His lip curled. "And when my time came, I was happy to oblige."

Deaglan openly studied Jay. "Your father and my father were friends all their lives. While Papa and I did not see eye to eye on many points, he gave you a well-paid job, a home of your own, and a position of some standing, not just on the estate but in the wider community. Why risk all that?"

Jay tipped his head back and laughed hollowly. Then he shook his head and looked at Deaglan. "You really have no idea, do you? No notion of what it was like, knowing we shared the same blood in our veins—you, me, and Felix—watching the pair of you being lordlings, having well-nigh everything you could wish for just given to you, while I had to work every day to earn my keep. You treated me well—yes, I'll admit that—but I was never your equal. We were from the same stock, the same tree, yet I had to make do with what your father, and later you, allowed me to have—the crumbs from your table, as it were—while the spoils of the title and of the whole estate went to you."

Jay all but glowered at Deaglan, then at Felix. "So why not? I asked myself. Why not help myself to a nice steady income from the estate? Set up the equivalent of an allowance, like you used to get, like you pay Felix, Patrick, and Maude. I was family, too—a little more distant, perhaps, but connected nonetheless. And"—he shifted as if he would have gestured had his hands been free—"it was all there for the taking. Thousands of pounds a year. Your father never missed it. Even when you came back, you didn't notice." A sly smile curved Jay's lips. "In fact, you just worked harder to make the estate more profitable to balance the money I was siphoning off—the sums that the stable was apparently running through. I got quite a chuckle out of that—out of your resolve to improve the estate's returns before you gave your attention to the stable."

The curve of his lips deepened. "I did all I could to keep you focused on everything else."

When Jay fell silent, Deaglan asked, "What did you do with the extra supplies?"

He'd kept his tone even, unchallenging, yet he would have sworn he saw fear flash through Jay's eyes.

After several moments, Jay replied, "You don't need to know that."

Pru shifted, as did Toby and Felix. She looked at Deaglan; he felt her gaze and turned his head and met her eyes. When she arched her brows, he nodded, and she switched her attention to Jay. "We know you took delivery of the extra supplies at some place to the west. You might as well tell us where, because we are going to look, and we will find it."

For several seconds, Jay appeared to be considering revealing the location of his store, but then he shook his head and said nothing.

Pru narrowed her eyes on him. "I assume you sold the supplies you appropriated. To whom?"

And that, they all saw, was the point that caused Jay most anxiety; he compressed his lips and refused to even look at them anymore.

Pru asked two more probing questions, and Toby tried as well, but Jay kept his eyes averted and said not a word.

Finally, they rose, returned their chairs to the wall, and left Jay sitting, head hanging, with none of his earlier bravado visible at all.

As they walked back to the castle, Deaglan caught one of Pru's hands and gently squeezed. "Thank you for trying."

Walking on Pru's other side with his hands sunk in his pockets, Toby snorted and put words to what they were all thinking. "He's fallen in with someone he's too frightened to name."

With Pru and Maude, Deaglan spent the early hours of the evening at the estate's gatehouse, breaking the news of her son's perfidy to Moira O'Shaughnessy, Jay's mother, who lived at the gatehouse and kept it spick-and-span.

Mrs. O'Shaughnessy was devastated, yet the readiness with which she accepted the news led Maude and Pru to exchange a glance, then they set themselves to gently and sympathetically tease more from Jay's mother.

Deaglan tried to make himself as inconspicuous as possible and left the subtle interrogation to them.

In response to a question from Maude as to whether she'd had any suspicions of Jay's activities, Mrs. O'Shaughnessy dabbed at her eyes and revealed, "Oh, for a while now, I've suspected something was going on with him. When he was younger, he'd been good enough, reliable enough —very keen on learning how to be steward of the estate. His father and I never entertained any anxiety that he wasn't interested in eventually taking on the job. But when his father passed and Jay took over the stewardship... It wasn't long after that he changed."

"Changed in what way?" Pru prompted.

"Well, for a start, when he'd take his days off, he'd ride out bright and early and come home in the dead of night, reeking of whiskey and having to have me help him up the stairs. And while he was well away, he'd boast of how others now saw him as a great man." She frowned. "I never knew quite what he meant by that."

Deaglan suspected he could guess.

They learned more of how Jay had taken to avoiding his older sister, who was married and lived in the nearby village of Rathcormack, ignoring invitations to join what sounded like a happy little family and, instead, going out somewhere with unnamed friends on outings that invariably ended with him coming home well and truly soused.

"While he was drunk, he'd sometimes tell me his pockets were to let, but that it didn't matter." Mrs. O'Shaughnessy frowned. "I never understood that, either. I mean, one's pockets are to let, or they aren't. How can it not matter?"

They didn't attempt to offer an explanation. Instead, Maude took Moira under her wing and suggested transferring the harmless and also rather helpless woman up to the castle for the time being.

After exchanging a glance, Pru and Deaglan threw their support behind the move.

While he and Pru waited in the small but scrupulously clean sitting room for Maude and Moira to return downstairs after packing a small case for Moira, Deaglan murmured, "Whoever Jay has gone into business with might come calling, looking for him."

"Indeed."

They returned to the castle, and after Maude saw Moira settled with Mrs. Bligh, they repaired to the drawing room to report to the others, including Esmerelda and Patrick, who insisted on hearing all.

The action in the old cellar, related by Toby in colorful detail, was variously described as shocking, exciting, and—at least for Esmerelda—

Deaglan suspected it was revealing as well, even though Toby had skated over the specifics of Deaglan and Pru's heated exchange over Jay's senseless body.

Certainly, the pointedly goading look Esmerelda bent on Deaglan made her expectations clear.

Over dinner, they exhaustively discussed the possibilities of what they might discover when they rode westward in the morning and the various ways in which Jay might have sold the supplies he'd amassed.

"He must have had some sort of monthly arrangement," Toby mused. "He couldn't possibly have found a place out in the fields that would hold more than one month's worth of the supplies he diverted."

The conversation in the library grew desultory as it became increasingly clear that until they gathered further facts, they couldn't even guess which of their speculative scenarios might be even halfway correct.

Eventually, in part worn out by the excitements of the day, but also with a sense of being keen to see tomorrow dawn so they could find out more, the company retired relatively early.

Deaglan didn't bother heading for his bedroom. He hung back with Pru until they were the last up the stairs, then they loitered in the gallery until everyone else had closed their doors, before, hand in hand, ambling down the wing to her room at the end.

After following her inside, Deaglan shut the door on the world and felt the cares of the day fall from his shoulders.

Only to have more personal anxieties rise to the forefront of his mind.

He looked across the room at Pru as she stood before the dressing table, unhooking the pearl drops from her earlobes.

He and she were on the cusp of sealing the deal she'd come to Glengarah to forge. The purpose that had brought her there was all but achieved; under her stipulations regarding their liaison, soon, she would leave and ride away.

But they'd fallen in love—hadn't they?

What else was this feeling, this driving emotion—this compulsion?

After the events of the afternoon, he knew beyond question that love was what he felt for her, and given her actions, he had to believe that she loved him in return.

They might not, yet, have mentioned the word "marriage," hadn't yet addressed her aversion to the state, but surely love was enough—was an emotion strong enough—to overcome her resistance.

It's time.

He felt that in his bones. Time to risk his hand, to roll the dice and see how they fell.

If she denied him, denied their love?

His life would be a bleak shadow of what, with her, it could be, but if he didn't ask her—simply and directly—he would never know if such a glory was within his reach.

He focused on her and found that she'd turned away from the dressing table and started toward the bed, but she'd halted in the middle of the room, within the circle of soft lamplight, to look back at him.

There was a question in her eyes, one he read with ease.

He seized one last moment to study her, absorbing not simply the way the golden light gilded her features but, even more, taking in her strength, that fundamental impression he'd gained in the moment of first setting eyes on her—a strikingly feminine yet powerful determination to live a life of her own choosing.

He wanted her to choose him—him and Glengarah.

He walked toward her, halted before her, and took her hands in his.

Her lips curved fractionally, and she arched a brow in transparent invitation.

He looked into her eyes; all he could think to do was drop every shield he possessed and speak from his heart. "When I first laid eyes on you, I thought that…P. H. Cynster was taking a ludicrous risk in bringing such a delectable morsel as you, assuming you were his wife or his sister, to my home."

The curve of her lips deepened, and a smile broke through.

He tightened his fingers on hers. "Then I discovered who you were, and that you loved horses as much as I did, that you could ride as well as I, that you instinctively understood all that mattered to me, and that those same things mattered to you, in the same way. I learned that, contrary to my view of ladies of your station, I could trust you—completely and utterly and beyond question—and more, that you and I, together, without any real effort, could combine to create a formidable team, one capable of taking on any challenge and succeeding."

Lost in her eyes, he felt very much that he was pleading his cause and had to get it right. "I remember very well your stipulation regarding our liaison, that once our deal was done, our time together would end, and you would walk away. I don't know why you laid down such a rule— what prompted you to it—or indeed, why you're still unmarried, yet I

suspect that wanting your own life in charge of a horse-breeding establishment has more than a little to do with that."

Her eyes told him he was correct in his assumption, yet she made no
move to step back or draw her hands from his. Instead, her gaze direct
and serious, she waited—giving him the chance to say the words he
hoped she wanted to hear. He drew breath and went on, "I'm hoping—
praying—that love—our love, the love that's grown between us, that I can
see and sense in all we do, and I think you can, too—is strong enough,
powerful enough, to push you to rethink your decision." He lifted one of
her hands to his lips and pressed a light kiss to her fingertips before
adding, "To renegotiate and stay."

Before she could respond, he forged on, "It's obvious that I need a
wife, yet I haven't been looking or even thinking of who she might be.
What sort of lady she might be. I put that off, too. But now I look at you,
and I see everything I could possibly want in my wife and more. I see a
woman who will inform my dreams, who, with me, will shape my future
—the one woman above all others I want and need as my countess. So
change your mind, Pru darling, and stay—stay forever. And if you will,
marry me and be my countess."

Pru freed one hand, raised it, and pressed her fingertips lightly to his
lips. "Stop—because I have confessions of sorts to make, too." Held by
the warmth in his emerald eyes, she paused, marshaling her thoughts,
then said, "When I first laid eyes on you, I already knew your reputation,
and I could instantly see that it was well-deserved."

Was that a spark of smugness in his eyes?

She narrowed hers fractionally in warning and forged on, "And yes, I
felt the attraction and realized you did as well, and the notion of experi-
encing the delights of an arena that had hitherto proved out of my reach,
all within the bounds of a situation largely under my control, proved too
great a temptation to resist. But then I grew to know you—you and your
horses—and spent time with you elsewhere, in the castle and on the
estate. And I saw that you are so much more than simply the embodiment
of your reputation. You care—about people, about the estate in its widest
sense. You are driven by motives and desires I've been raised to not just
admire and respect but encourage and laud. At base, what drives you are
the same imperatives that drive me."

She paused, then went on, "We are who we are, and nowhere is that
more apparent than in how we treat those who are dependent on us.
Within our circle, that is what makes a man—or a woman. Not only could

I not find fault with any aspect of the challenge to which you've decided to devote your life, I discovered that I wished to do the same—to help meet that challenge by your side."

Relief slid through his features, and his fingers gripped hers more tightly.

She couldn't hold back her smile. "You wondered why I haven't married. The answer is simple—I was waiting for you. A man I can trust to see me as I am, rather than cast me in society's conventional mold, a mold in which I could never be comfortable."

His lips curved at that, but his gaze held understanding and glorious, burgeoning hope. But obedient to her warning look, he remained silent and let her go on.

"I come from a family that not only reveres marriage but marries only for love. Having never felt that emotion, not even a hint of it, I saw no benefit in pursuing that state. I fully expected never to marry—indeed, I'd closed my mind to the possibility of ever stumbling across love. But then I met you, came to know you, and over the last days, realizing that someone was trying to kill you... The thought of losing you, regardless of whether you returned my love or not, was like a knife to my heart.

"I knew, then, that love had caught me—that I wasn't immune." She turned her hands in his and gripped. "I knew, then, that you were and always would be my one and only love. Yet I still didn't fully understand what that meant." She drew in a breath, her gaze steady on his eyes. "Then Jay shot you, then he pointed a gun at your head and was about to end your life." She paused to let the spike of remembered tension fade, then more softly said, "After that moment, after the relief I felt when you survived, I cannot even pretend that I don't love you."

She held his gaze and said the words that, to her, represented the clearest statement of what lay in her heart. "You, Deaglan Fitzgerald, are the one man I do not want to walk away from."

"Don't." He raised her hands and, between their chests, pressed her palms together, closing his hands about hers. "Don't walk away—now or ever. Exercise your feminine right to change your mind and stay." He raised one hand and, his gaze holding hers, pressed a lingering, heated kiss to her fingers. "Accept me, become my countess, and stay here, with me, forever."

"I will," she said and meant it with every fiber of her being. "I do. I'll place my hand in yours willingly, with confidence and certainty."

One black brow arched provocatively. "I'll take willingness, confidence, and certainty and strive to add joy and delight as well."

She laughed.

He smiled into her eyes. "We'll argue, you know—that's certain, too."

"Oh, let's be honest—we'll fight and push and prod, especially over the horses."

"All that and more." Deaglan couldn't stop smiling. "We're far too much alike in so many ways—we both like to lead, to hold the reins."

"At least our shared life will never be boring."

"Indeed. It might not always be moonlight and roses, but against that, there'll always be—"

"Horses!" She laughed again, a sound that lifted his soul, that he vowed he would work to hear every day.

Holding her gaze, he waited until she'd calmed, then said, "We've been given an opportunity not everyone gets—a chance to embrace love and, through that, to find our greatest happiness. It's up to us to seize it, if we will. If we have the courage to follow our hearts. We're both definite and straightforward in our thoughts and deeds, so let's do this as we should—as best suits us. Miss Prudence Cynster, will you do me the honor of becoming my wife?"

Her smile transformed into one of heart-stopping radiance. Then she freed one of her hands and held it out to him. "I believe, my lord, that we have a deal."

He had to laugh, then he closed his hand about hers and used his hold to pull her into his arms.

Their bodies met and instinctively melded. There was joy in their kiss, an effervescent delight that sank into them and bubbled through their veins.

Passion was a siren's call at the edge of their awareness, luring them on.

Under knowing fingers, buttons slid free, clothes fell to the floor, and hands laced with hunger laid fire beneath their skins.

Why speaking their minds and admitting to love and agreeing to marry should make any difference, he didn't know, yet it did. It was as if they'd opened their souls to a different dimension in which every touch held promise in a universe made manifest by love, love acknowledged and accepted.

Caresses grew lengthy and languid; kisses supped and sipped and drew them in.

Skin pebbled and dewed as urgency flared, swelled, and burgeoned, its potency enhanced.

Desire sparked and flamed, a swirl of need that built and built, grew and grew, until its power became a vortex, trapping them, driving them, whipping them on.

Breathless, well-nigh mindless, they crested passion's heights, then the world fell away, and there was just them—together, bodies fused, hearts, minds, and souls as one—clinging as glory rained over them, surged through them, shattered and fragmented them, then forged them anew.

Into two, still, yet two who were no longer who they had been, but now, finally, were who they truly were. Who they were destined to be.

Later, when the scintillating glory had faded to a glow, he lifted from her and slumped on his back alongside her.

She murmured and turned to him, settling her head in the hollow below his shoulder and draping one arm across his chest.

More content than he'd ever been, he was drifting toward sleep when she murmured, "Just to be clear, I will always expect to work your horses and direct your breeding program."

He huffed out a laugh. "Just to be clear, I had assumed you would."

He felt her lips curve against his skin, then she pressed a kiss to his chest and relaxed fully against him.

He smiled, tightened the arm he'd slung about her, and together, they tumbled into sleep.

CHAPTER 19

*T*he next morning, Deaglan and Pru reached the breakfast table rather later than usual for them, and as if drawn by some attraction, not only Toby, Felix, and Cicely but also Maude, Esmerelda, and Patrick made their way to the parlor.

After glancing questioningly at Pru and receiving a smiling nod, Deaglan seized the unexpected opportunity to announce their engagement. Immediately, they were inundated with congratulations. Esmerelda beamed, Toby slapped Deaglan on the back and swooped to kiss Pru's cheek, and even Bligh, ferrying in more coffee, paused to convey the staff's best wishes with an almost-paternal delight.

Returning to his chair, still grinning, Toby caught Deaglan's eye. "You have no idea what you've let yourself in for."

Unperturbed, Deaglan arched a brow. "How so?"

"You haven't moved much within ton circles, have you?" Toby asked.

With a tip of his head, Deaglan conceded, "If by that you mean I've avoided the ballrooms and drawing rooms of London, you'd be correct."

"Exactly my point," Toby returned. "You haven't met the family yet. The female half will be eyeing you assessingly yet approvingly, while for the same reason, the male half will be eyeing you askance."

When Deaglan looked confused, Esmerelda, opposite, waved her fork. "Reformed rakes, the lot of them. It gives the ladies certain insights."

Deaglan glanced at Pru, horror in his face.

And she laughed, which made him smile.

A footman appeared in the doorway, signaling somewhat urgently to Bligh. As the butler departed, Patrick leaned forward and welcomed Pru to the family. "Good to have new blood, what? And Cynster blood is more appropriate than most."

The others laughed, then Bligh came hurrying in. "My lord. Ah…"

Deaglan took in Bligh's expression and instantly sobered; the butler's gaze had gone to Maude and Esmerelda. Deaglan knew that, whatever the news, his aunts were as unlikely to descend into hysterics as he was. "What is it, Bligh?"

Still, Bligh dithered, but Esmerelda frowned and commanded, "Spit it out, man. None of us here are wilting females."

Defeated, Bligh looked at Deaglan. "I've just been informed, my lord, that the stablemen who took Mr. O'Shaughnessy's breakfast tray to the tack room discovered Mr. Jay hanging from a beam, dead. Quite dead."

For a second, silence reigned, then cutlery clattered as they all—even Maude and Esmerelda—dropped their knives and forks on their plates and pushed to their feet.

Deaglan and Pru, closely followed by Toby, Felix, and Cicely, led the exodus out of the parlor, down the side corridor, and out and across the side court to the stable complex.

A crowd of stablemen clogged the space outside the tack room door. The throng parted as Deaglan approached. Her hand on the back of his coat, Pru followed him through the open doorway. When he paused just inside the room, she stepped to the right and, wide-eyed, took in the scene.

Jay's body had been cut down and laid on the wooden floor. Someone had flung a coat over his face, for which Pru was grateful.

Deaglan slowly advanced, circling to examine the body, and Toby and Felix joined him.

Cicely crossed the threshold, but immediately came to stand by Pru. Pru noticed the younger woman's face was chalky white.

For herself…she had to own to surprise. She wouldn't have thought Jay the sort to kill himself, no matter the charges against him. In talking to them yesterday, he'd seemed unrepentant, even cocky at times. Only when they'd touched on his accomplices had he grown fearful, and in that, his fear had been about those accomplices, not over facing a judge and jury.

While Felix remained standing by Jay's feet, Deaglan and Toby crouched beside the body; Pru heard them murmuring to each other, but couldn't make out what they said.

Then Deaglan rose and turned to Rory, who had been waiting at the side of the room. "How was he left last night?"

Rory looked at a pair of older men, waiting along the wall. "Horry?"

One of the men dipped his head to Deaglan. "Me and Sid here took him out to relieve himself about ten o'clock last night. Then we tied him up again good and proper"—he nodded at the chair, now lying on its side on the floor—"in the chair, just like he was before."

Toby rose and asked, "With his hands tied behind the chair's back and lashed to the chair?"

Both Horry and Sid nodded. "Aye," Sid said. "Might not have been comfortable, but that seemed the wisest choice."

"We weren't about to take any chances with him," Horry said. "Not after Rory told us how he used the stable to steal from the estate."

There was a dark muttering of agreement among the men inside the room and outside as well.

"And you locked the door after you?" Deaglan asked.

Both men nodded. "And we can be sure we did," Horry said, "because young Malcolm here"—he nodded to a young footman who was standing beside him and looked ready to faint—"brought the breakfast tray and had to call us over to unlock the door for him."

"Where was the key?" Toby asked.

"I'd kept it," Horry said. "We'd normally leave it on its hook by the stable entrance, but that seemed daft. Sid and me knew we'd be on duty in the second aisle first thing, so I kept it in me pocket. Safe."

Deaglan nodded. "Good thinking." He frowned down at the body, then looked up at the sawed-through end of the stout rope that had been tied about the thick central beam running across the roof; the end dangled a good four feet above Deaglan's head.

He looked at Rory, then at Horry. "Who cut him down?"

Horry nodded. "That would be us, my lord. Couldn't leave him swinging there."

Toby, Pru noticed, was also now staring up at the dangling rope. He stretched up and tried to touch the end, but it was over a foot beyond his reach.

Deaglan watched Toby, then asked Horry and Sid, "On what did you stand?"

"We didn't want to move the chair, so we brought in the stepladder."

Sid pointed to a tall ladder propped against the wall in the corner. "Horry grabbed his legs and supported his weight while I went up and sawed through the rope."

Deaglan eyed the ladder; so did Toby. Then Deaglan walked to the body's head, crouched, and straightened the cut end of the rope that, Pru surmised, was still fastened around Jay's neck.

That section of rope extended only just past the top of Jay's head.

Deaglan swiveled to face Sid. "How many steps up the ladder did you go to reach where you cut?"

"I had to go three steps up, my lord. Even then, it was a bit of a stretch."

Toby looked at Horry. "You held the body steady—you must have caught it as it fell."

Horry looked grim. "Aye, sir—that I did."

"Against your body, where did Mr. O'Shaughnessy's feet hang?"

Horry frowned. "Can't rightly say, sir, but I do know his knees were just above me shoulders. Bit of a juggle, it was, holding him steady and then letting him slide down—I caught him over my shoulder, like."

Toby looked at Deaglan, then walked to crouch on the other side of Jay's head. Deaglan raised the jacket tossed over Jay's face, and Toby reached beneath with both hands, clearly searching for something...

Pru realized what was wrong. She stared up at the dangling rope, then at the chair, then at Jay's inanimate form stretched on the floor. Creeping horror clutched at her.

"The body's cold," Toby reported. "He's been dead for hours, and there's a sizeable lump on the back of his head. It's swollen. That couldn't have happened hours after death."

Deaglan rose, walked the few feet to the chair, and righted it.

Suddenly, many there saw what didn't add up. Deaglan positioned the chair underneath the dangling rope and looked up at the sawn-off end. His expression grim, he stated, "Clearly, he didn't hang himself. The rope wasn't long enough to allow him to stand on the chair, then step off and kick the chair over."

Toby rose. "Agreed. This isn't a suicide—it's murder."

A collective gasp spread through the room, echoed by those congregated outside.

Sid and Horry had paled. "T'wasn't us, your lordship," Horry said. "But I had the key, and I swear it was with me the whole night. M'room's in the castle—no one could have crept in and got it, and I had it this morning, too."

Toby glanced at the lock on the door. "I wouldn't need a key to get through that." He walked to the door, bent, and examined the lock closely, concentrating on the outer side. "Aha—there are tiny telltale scratches." He looked at Deaglan. "Someone who knew how picked the lock."

Rory shuffled his feet. "That explains the rope, then." He nodded up at it. "I was wondering how it got in here—that's thicker than what he was tied up with, and we normally keep all the rope of that weight in the storeroom across the corridor."

Deaglan looked down at Jay and shook his head. "I believe we can conclude that whoever Jay was dealing with—whoever he was so frightened of he wouldn't speak of them to us—decided that the best way of preserving their own safety was to silence Jay, removing any chance of him bearing witness against them."

Deaglan sent a groom to summon the constable and the local magistrate —a neighboring landowner. Both constable and magistrate arrived at much the same time; Deaglan and Felix took them to the tack room and explained what had occurred.

Lord Jeffers, the magistrate, stroked his chin and agreed with Deaglan's interpretation. "I'll hold an inquest in a week's time. Doolan here can ask around in the meantime, but chances are we'll never have proof of exactly who the murderer was."

"Or," Deaglan added, "who ordered it done."

The others somberly agreed.

Lord Jeffers gave permission for the body to be given over to Mrs. O'Shaughnessy for burial. Maude was currently comforting the distraught woman; Lord Jeffers left Deaglan to convey his condolences.

After doing so—and greeting Reverend Phillips, whom Maude had summoned—Deaglan was glad to be able to leave all in Maude's and the minister's capable hands and retreat to the library.

Pru looked up as he entered, and the concern in her face—concern for him—eased the deadening sense of betrayal entwined with loss that seeing Jay's dead body and dealing with the repercussions of his murder had evoked.

"All done?" she asked.

He nodded.

Toby glanced at the clock. "We've hours yet to go until luncheon—time enough to ride out to the west and see what we stumble upon, don't you think?"

Deaglan readily agreed, as did Pru, Felix, and Cicely. They went out to the stable, and in the familiar chaos of Pru and Toby arguing over their mounts for the excursion and getting all the horses saddled and ready, Deaglan found peace and a hint of simple happiness returning.

He could look forward to many moments like this, with no cares beyond appreciating and enjoying his horses.

They mounted up and rode out, following the track Rory had mentioned—the same one Jay had taken the previous day—and the fresh air, carrying the softness of burgeoning spring, revived and refreshed them all.

Deaglan led, with Pru alongside him. They saw two cottages, both at some distance from the track. Quite aside from the compact size of the buildings, as Deaglan pointed out, both housed families; given the volume of feedstuffs Jay had successfully secreted, it was difficult to see even both cottages together being sufficient for his needs.

They rode on through fields primarily used for grazing interspersed with cultivated patches and finally reached the western boundary of the estate, denoted by a simple stone marker at the side of the track.

"Now what?" Felix let his horse, still frisky, circle the others.

Deaglan frowned. "Rory and several others said this was the way Jay rode, and no one seems to have seen him go in any other direction."

"Can you recall," Pru asked, "when we were searching for Rory and you assigned the directions for those riding out, whether you gave Jay this westerly track—or did he volunteer for it?"

Deaglan thought back, then Thor shifted beneath him. Steadying the horse, he met Pru's eyes. "He said he'd search this way before I'd given any orders."

"Right, then." Toby stood in his stirrups and peered ahead. "There's a largish roof I can see just over that next rise."

"That's one of Mr. Wilkes's barns," Felix said. "He's our neighbor—a bit of a recluse."

"There's someone working in that field over there." Pru pointed ahead to the left of the track.

"Let's see what they can tell us." Deaglan set Thor surging on, and the others followed.

When they drew level with the farmer, who was walking behind his plow, Deaglan hallooed, and the farmer slowed his horse, then walked over.

"Aye, my lord?"

"Beasley, isn't it?" Deaglan smiled easily. "Can you tell me what the barn there is used for?"

Beasley blinked slowly, then said, "Don't rightly know, my lord. You'd need to ask your Mr. O'Shaughnessy."

Deaglan hid his reaction. "Mr. O'Shaughnessy? Why's that?"

Beasley frowned in puzzled confusion. "Well, that barn's been rented to Glengarah for the past four, maybe five years. Only person I've ever seen heading to it was Mr. O'Shaughnessy, though, so I'd guess he'd know."

"Thank you." Deaglan fought to keep all grimness from his voice. If they'd needed any confirmation of the longstanding nature of Jay's perfidy, this surely was it. "As the estate is currently using the barn, I believe I'll take a look inside."

Beasley nodded. "Aye, my lord. If you didn't know about it, might be as well."

Everyone was in agreement, and with nods to Beasley, the others followed Deaglan on.

They dismounted outside the barn and tied the horses to bushes on one side of the cleared area before the closed double doors.

Felix reached the doors first. "They're locked." He held up the large padlock attached to a strong iron bolt, then looked up at the stout doors. "Even if the estate is renting the place, I suspect old man Wilkes won't appreciate us breaking in."

"No need for extreme measures." Toby nudged Felix aside, crouched, and attacked the padlock with what looked like two long, narrow pins.

"What are those?" Felix bent close to see.

"The latest in lock picks," Toby replied, his gaze on the padlock.

Deaglan met Pru's eyes and arched a disbelieving brow.

She lightly shrugged. "Cynsters are expected to have a range of skills, the males especially."

He shook his head, then Toby crowed, and the lock clicked open. Toby rose, removed the padlock, and slid the bolt free. He drew back one of the heavy doors while Felix opened the other.

Deaglan walked in, with Pru just behind him. Cicely and the other two followed.

Five paces in, they halted as a group and stared around at the utterly empty barn.

Then Pru walked toward one corner, crouched, and picked up something. She placed it in her palm, studied it, then said, "Oats."

Felix had wandered in another direction. He bent and peered. "There's barley here."

"Hay over here," Toby called.

Cicely came up to show Deaglan what she'd picked up. "Is this the grass they feed the horses?"

He looked and nodded. "Lucerne." He frowned. "Which, as Rory confirmed, we rarely if ever need to order in."

Toby came ambling back. "No reason Jay couldn't have ordered extra. Rory wouldn't have known, and your estate accounts show all feed consolidated to one entry."

Pru returned, joining the others who had gathered about Deaglan. "I think it's safe to assume that whatever Rory asked for would have been ordered in double quantities at least, and depending on demand from his clients, Jay ordered extra feed he knew he could sell on."

Deaglan looked at her. "So Jay doubled and more the feed orders from the month after I left Glengarah, stored the extra feed here"—he glanced around—"and at some point, his clients—or whomever he was working with—came and fetched the stuff. Meanwhile, if anyone thought to ask, Jay could say that the barn was being used by Glengarah as a temporary feed store, nothing more."

"So," Felix said, "he paid for the extra feed from the estate coffers and then pocketed the proceeds when he sold it on."

"The *inflated* proceeds," Toby pointed out. "By our figures, he was swindling up to three hundred pounds per month from the estate, plus whatever extra he got from selling the stuff at higher prices." He paused, calculating, then added, "He could easily have taken in five thousand pounds each year." Toby met Deaglan's gaze. "That's not an inconsiderable fortune."

Deaglan grimaced. "I wasn't here during the famine years, but even more recently, the value of feed on the black market...I assume it would be high. We have lots of pasture, so managed easily enough, but other regions didn't—other stables might well have been desperate at times and willing to pay well above the odds to secure a supply of feed."

"Huh." After a moment, Toby said, "Because Glengarah is a sizeable and long-standing purchaser, you—meaning Jay—would have been assured of supply and at favorable terms. In a localized sense, Jay might have been able to at least partially corner the market in, say, oats, guaranteeing a higher price for what he later sold."

Pru's expression was sternly disapproving. "It sounds as if he became the sort of middleman who squeezed his suppliers while overcharging those who purchased from him."

"And," Deaglan said, his tone hard, "Glengarah footed his bill." He shook his head. "The estate could have used the money he was bleeding from us to do so much for our people. Most made it through, but the hardship was real—that money would have made a difference."

Felix nodded. "It would have." After a moment, his expression uncomprehending, he said, "I know it's all true—all that we've learned about Jay—but I still can't see, can't understand, why he did it." Felix looked around at their faces as if hoping one of them had an answer. "He was as rooted in this soil as Deaglan and I are."

After a long moment, Toby offered, "Some plants suck the soil dry, while others nurture and sustain it."

Pru tipped her head in acknowledgment and added, "Actions like Jay's strike to the core of who and what we are—what we hope we are. It's dismaying and disheartening to discover among our ranks those willing to self-servingly exploit the tribulations of others."

Deaglan nodded. "That's it—the bit that makes this so hard to understand. Jay wanted for nothing. As steward, he was paid well and got the gatehouse to live in and had access to the kitchen gardens and so on. Despite what he said, and I read his supposed jealousy as nothing more than rationalization, in reality, it was greed—pure greed—that drove him."

Deaglan paused, then said, "But now he's dead." He glanced around. "And there's nothing here and no real way to work out who he was supplying and who, therefore, might have ordered him killed. For us, we've reached the end of the chapter." He met Pru's eyes. "It's time to close the book, lay it aside, and go on."

Pru smiled encouragingly, and when he held out his hand, she slipped hers into it.

With his free hand, Deaglan waved to the doors, and with the others at their backs, they walked out into the sunshine.

～

During luncheon, Patrick put his finger on what they were all feeling. "It's like we've had a death in the family, yet the one who died has turned out to be an imposter, and now, we don't know what to think—don't quite know how we should feel. We think we should feel bereaved, yet we don't. We feel betrayed and angry instead." He huffed. "It's confusing."

In that, he wasn't wrong, but hearing their conundrum put into words made moving forward a little easier.

After the meal, with Deaglan, Felix, and Toby, Pru settled in the library and focused on hammering out the final details of the breeding agreement they wished to put in place.

They recalculated the expenses, working from what Rory had actually ordered, and at Deaglan's suggestion, adopted the figure of forty-six pounds as the base cost of upkeep per horse per year; Pru and Toby agreed that was eminently reasonable.

With that settled, Pru sat at Deaglan's desk and wrote out the deal notes, listing all the specific points on which they'd agreed, all the details they wished incorporated into the final agreement.

Once Deaglan had read through Pru's effort and confirmed that everything they'd discussed was there, she took the note back and set about making a copy.

Somewhat puzzled, Deaglan asked, "What's that for?"

Toby replied, "She's going to make two copies, so we'll have three copies in all. The four of us, you two representing the Glengarah estate and the pair of us representing the Cynster Stables, sign all three copies. You then keep one, we keep another, and the third is sent to Montague and Son, our solicitor. They'll draw up the formal agreement, in two copies, and send them to you. You'll make sure all the points in the deal notes have been faithfully included, have your solicitor check it through, then sign both copies, send them back, then Papa will countersign both copies, we'll keep one, the other will be sent to you, and the deal will formally be in place."

Deaglan grunted and glanced at Pru. "Do we need to wait that long to get started?"

"No," she replied, without looking up from her transcribing. "We can start taking the first steps toward getting the breeding program in place immediately."

Deaglan looked at Felix, then at Toby, as the sensation of standing on the brink of finally accomplishing what he'd wanted and waited for so long to do welled, eradicating the bitter aftertaste of the morning.

Catching Toby's eye, he said, "I believe we should celebrate." He rose, crossed to the bellpull, and tugged it.

"The others should be here, too." Felix got to his feet. "I'll fetch them."

The door opened, and Deaglan turned. "Ah, Bligh."

After he'd ordered champagne brought up from the cellars and Bligh had departed, Pru set down her pen and caught Deaglan's eyes. "Come and check these over."

Deaglan joined her at the desk. Standing beside her as she sat in his chair, he scanned the three copies of the deal notes she'd made.

Bligh returned with champagne and glasses and, beaming, popped the cork and started pouring.

Deaglan reached the end of the deal notes, looked at Pru, smiled, and nodded. "Perfect."

She smiled back, then the other three ladies swept in, followed by Felix pushing Patrick's chair.

Deaglan straightened, and Pru rose, and leaving the deal notes on the desktop, ready to be signed, together, they went to join the others as a grinning Toby handed out glasses of the pale fizzy wine.

"Right, then." Toby raised his glass. "Here's to the alliance between the Cynsters and Glengarah." His gaze shifted to Deaglan and Pru, and his smile widened. "An alliance that will rest on far more than just horses."

Everyone laughed and drank—to Deaglan and Pru and to the horses.

Then the older ladies sat and inquired—with considerable shrewdness —as to how the new breeding arrangement would work. Would Pru need to return to Newmarket, now or in the years to come, or could all necessary be accomplished from here?

That was a question that led to several more. Although she would have to return to her home, and likely London, before their wedding—the finer points of which they'd yet to discuss—Pru seemed inclined to look favorably on her not having to travel back to England often, possibly at most once a year.

Esmerelda was waxing bright on the social scene in Dublin—Deaglan shared a sidelong glance with Pru and wondered how long it would be before his aunt realized that Pru would rather travel to Newmarket than plunge into any social whirl—when Bligh, who had retreated after the initial toast, returned.

When Deaglan looked Bligh's way, the butler said, "There's a… gentleman at the door, my lord, asking to speak with you."

Alerted by Bligh's hesitation in bestowing the status of gentleman, Deaglan asked, "Did he give a name?"

"A Mr. Cormack O'Grady, my lord."

"Ah. I see." Deaglan glanced at Pru and discovered that she and, indeed, all the others were looking at him in open question. He hesitated, then admitted, "I've never met the man, but I've heard his name. He's a rather…shady character who hovers on the fringe of aristocratic circles within the Irish Thoroughbred racing fraternity."

Felix nodded. "I've heard of him, too, but I've never crossed his path."

"I wonder"—Toby got to his feet as Deaglan rose—"whether this visit is in any way connected to the scheme Jay was a part of."

Pru and Felix stood as well. Felix said, "Courtesy of Constable Doolan, the news of Jay's death would have reached Sligo by midmorning—time enough for it to have spread through the taverns."

Deaglan nodded and turned toward the door. "Cormack O'Grady might have some answers we'd like to have."

And he might be the one who ordered Jay's murder, Pru thought as she determinedly strode in Deaglan's wake.

Tellingly, Bligh had not seen fit to invite O'Grady into the front hall.

Pru followed Deaglan onto the front porch. She paused just outside the door and stepped to the right, halting where she could see past Deaglan to the flashily dressed man who swung to face her betrothed.

Bligh had been correct in his estimation of O'Grady's social rank. He was a gentleman—just; there was something in his bearing, in his understated confidence, that came only from being born to that rank or higher. He was a large man, wide of shoulder and solid through the chest, and while his neckerchief and waistcoat were a touch on the gaudy side, the fabric wasn't cheap, and the cut wasn't poor.

O'Grady had been surveying all he could see from the porch; his expression as, after swinging around, he took in the four of them, then met Deaglan's eyes, was easygoing—affable, even—and there was a certain self-deprecating twinkle in his hazel eyes as he nodded deferentially to Deaglan. "Lord Glengarah."

Deaglan inclined his head. "Mr. O'Grady. I understand you wished to speak with me?" He didn't invite O'Grady inside, and he didn't offer his hand.

Nor did O'Grady. He eyed Deaglan for a second, then his smile deepened a fraction. "Aye, that I did. And I've a suspicion you know what's brought me to your door."

O'Grady's accent was thick, more Irish brogue than one normally heard from gentlemen or, indeed, businessmen. Pru wondered if it was cultivated to distract—like O'Grady's flashy clothes.

"Perhaps you should enlighten me" was Deaglan's flat reply.

O'Grady tipped his head, studying Deaglan as if wondering if he'd been wrong and Deaglan didn't know... After several seconds of open calculation, in a more careful tone, O'Grady said, "This morning in Sligo, I heard a whisper that your steward, O'Shaughnessy, had met with an accident—a fatal one." He paused, clearly waiting to see if Deaglan would confirm that. When Deaglan remained silent, O'Grady went on, "In a nutshell, I'm here to inquire whether you would like to continue the arrangement I had with O'Shaughnessy." O'Grady's lips twitched. "Stepping into your dead steward's shoes, as it were."

Deaglan swallowed his instinctive "no." O'Grady didn't strike him as anything remotely like an idiot; that was certainly not his reputation, either. Appearing at the scene of a murder within hours of its commission and asking a question that immediately identified him as the person who should be at the top of any suspect list didn't fit anything Deaglan knew of the man. So, instead, he tilted his head as if considering and asked, "What would be in it for Glengarah?"

"Essentially the same thing—the same arbitrage value—as O'Shaughnessy was pocketing."

"Just to be clear, O'Shaughnessy was buying extra feed through the estate accounts—and therefore paying the very lowest prices—and then...what? He handed the feed on to you, and you sold it at an inflated price?"

O'Grady nodded. "That's it. He showed me the invoices, and I paid him that amount, and I showed him my receipts, and we split the difference between his invoices and my receipts fifty-fifty. A nice little earner, it's been." O'Grady's gaze was shrewd as he studied Deaglan. "Were you inclined to continue the scheme, I'm willing to offer you the same split."

Despite all—his size, his knowing demeanor, his involvement in the scheme—Deaglan could detect not the slightest hint of threat from O'Grady. Still, the man might be a chameleon. "After considering your kind offer," Deaglan replied, "I fear I must decline."

Confirming Deaglan's assessment—after having had Deaglan confirm his—O'Grady accepted the refusal with a resigned shrug and an easy smile. "I rather thought you would, but it was worth my while to ask."

Curiosity prompted Deaglan to inquire, "How much was O'Shaughnessy making on the arbitrage—say on average per month?"

O'Grady replied without hesitation, "About three hundred pounds, give or take. A month, that is. Closer to four thousand over a year."

Added to the sum Jay had bled from the estate... *Eight thousand pounds a year?* Possibly more. Where the devil had all that money gone?

Deaglan had been watching O'Grady closely; the man looked to be thinking of making his farewells. "With respect to the accident that befell O'Shaughnessy, you wouldn't happen to know anything about that, would you?"

O'Grady's eyes and face hardened, but there was still no anger there. "If you're asking if I did it—whatever it was—or ordered it done, that's not my style. Ask around, and anyone will tell you. Dead men are of no use to me." He paused, studying Deaglan, then said, "For what it's worth, I'd heard—and I believe it to be true—that in recent times, O'Shaughnessy had become a client, so to speak, of Dougal Finn."

Deaglan couldn't stop his eyes from widening. "Even with the extra money, he was in debt?" That Jay had become a client of Finn's also explained where the money had gone; he'd gambled it away at the racetrack.

"I presume so." O'Grady shrugged his broad shoulders, "Wagering on the nags—it bites some men and poisons them, and then they can't leave it alone. And given Finn's rates are extortionate, being a client of his does tend to be a position of limited tenure, as it were. You either pay up or... something happens. It's well known Finn has a habit of ridding the world of clients who don't or won't or can't pay. I've heard he maintains that it provides effective inducement for others to remember to make their payments."

Deaglan grimaced. "I see."

O'Grady's faintly mocking smile returned. "I'm sure you do, now." He stepped back and executed a flourishing and surprisingly graceful bow to Pru. "Miss Cynster. A pleasure to be in the presence of racing royalty, as it were." O'Grady avoided Pru's incipient frown and directed a nod at Toby—"Mr. Cynster"—and another at Felix. "Mr. Fitzgerald." Then he looked back at Deaglan and saluted him. "Your lordship. I'll bid you good luck in your future endeavors."

Deaglan couldn't help returning O'Grady's incorrigible smile. "I wish I could return the sentiment."

"Ah, well. We each have our own row to hoe, don't we? Still, it's all about horses, isn't it?"

With that parting shot, O'Grady turned and quickly went down the steps. He crossed to where a groom was holding a powerful bay gelding, took the reins, mounted, and with a last general wave, rode off down the drive.

Deaglan felt Pru's hand slip into his.

"At least," she murmured, "we now know exactly what Jay's scheme was and, most likely, why and at whose behest he was hanged—that is, if we believe O'Grady."

He gripped her hand. "I think we can believe O'Grady—there was no reason for him to come here and tell us all he has, not if he wanted to avoid suspicion. As he said, giving me the chance of continuing with the scheme was, to him, worth the price of asking."

Deaglan turned with Pru toward the door. "If I'm interpreting correctly, Finn has taken his revenge, and as that involved murder, I suspect we won't hear any more from him."

In the front hall, Deaglan halted. Pru halted beside him. He waited for Toby and Felix to join them, met the other three's eyes, then said, "Given all O'Grady said, I think we can feel confident that we've reached the end of Jay's tale."

CHAPTER 20

They'd barely reclaimed their seats in the library—barely had a chance to remember that they hadn't yet signed the deal notes —when Bligh returned to report, "My lord, one of the grooms has come running to report that a carriage"—Bligh looked at Pru—"another good-looking one, is bowling up the drive. I'm informed the horses are prime-steppers as well."

Pru and Toby exchanged a horrified look. "It can't be," Pru breathed, then she was out of her chair and striding for the door with Toby on her heels and Deaglan and Felix close behind.

Bligh had whisked back into the front hall and taken up a stance by the front door; he saw Pru coming and opened it.

Pru stormed out onto the porch and halted. She watched as a carriage bowled in style around the last bend in the drive—and yes, it was another Cynster carriage, driven by John, her mother's coachman. The four black horses between the shafts were beauties; Pru knew because she'd bred all four in an experiment years ago.

John drew the horses to a halt at the base of the steps with stylish aplomb.

Pru started down, and the carriage door swung open, and her father stepped out.

"Papa!" Pru didn't try to hide her exasperation, but she couldn't help the instinctive warmth of her smile as she descended the last few steps.

Her father opened his arms, and she sailed into them, into the warmth of an embrace that had been an anchor throughout her life.

Then her father released her, closed his hands about her shoulders, and held her back from him. His blue gaze raked her face, then he humphed and eased his hold. "You're looking...strangely happy."

She beamed and declared, "That's because I am happy."

Toby had followed Pru down the steps and now shook hands and clapped shoulders with his sire and beneath his breath murmured, "You don't know how happy..."

Pru shot him a warning look, then brightening, turned to the open carriage door and met her mother's inquiring gaze. "And I'm doubly happy now you're both here."

At that, both her parents' brows rose. Her father shot her mother a glance. "Not quite the welcome we were expecting."

"I told him," her mother said, taking his proffered hand to climb down the carriage steps, "that you didn't need him to sort out this deal—that you were perfectly capable of handling it entirely by yourself, and now, you even had Toby at your back. But no, he kept staring at your report, and then nothing would do but for him to come all the way over here himself, just to see."

Pru grinned and embraced her diminutive mother. "We've already completed the deal notes, although we haven't yet signed them. We were just about to."

She realized her mother's eyes had fixed on the porch. She glanced at her father and saw that he was likewise transfixed. Both were staring at Deaglan, who now started, languidly graceful, down the steps.

Pru squeezed her mother's hand, ducked her head, and whispered, "Please keep a firm grip on Papa's reins and keep him in line."

Her mother cleared her throat and raised her chin. "I'll do my best, dear, but...you are the first of his daughters and his firstborn, you know."

Deaglan halted facing her father, which, as it happened, put him beside Pru. His lips curved in an easy, urbane smile, he inclined his head to her parents. "Sir. Ma'am. It's an honor, a pleasure, and a privilege to welcome you to Glengarah."

Her father nodded and gruffly replied, "Glengarah. Allow me to present my wife."

Deaglan took the hand her mother offered and bowed in precisely the correct degree. "Mrs. Cynster—it's truly a delight to have you here."

He straightened and met her father's eyes. "And you, sir. You arrive at a most opportune time."

"Is that so?" Her father's expression gave nothing away.

"Indeed." Deaglan glanced at Pru. "We were just about to sign the deal notes for our proposed breeding agreement. Perhaps you would care to cast your eyes over the horses of the Glengarah collection, then view the terms of the deal before we sign?"

In the circumstances, that was a generous and clever offer, one Pru suspected was designed to distract her parents.

But instead of accepting, her father looked at her.

She felt his gaze and met it.

After several seconds, her father returned his gaze to Deaglan and said, "No. You and Pru can sign the deal notes while her mother and I get settled. Then you can both take us to see these wonderful horses."

Pru's heart swelled. She beamed at her father, letting her pleasure at his openly declared faith in her judgment show.

Predictably, her father humphed and offered her mother his arm, which she took.

Deaglan was pleased on Pru's behalf; he accepted her father's edict with a gracious inclination of his head and waved the older couple up the steps. He flanked Pru as she climbed beside her mother, with Toby on her father's other side.

On the porch, Deaglan introduced Felix, then, once they'd entered the castle, found Maude, Esmerelda, Cicely, and Patrick eagerly waiting to greet their latest guests.

After making the introductions, Deaglan was encouraged by their combined elders to leave Maude, Patrick, and Esmerelda—who was acquainted with both older Cynsters—to see to Pru's parents. Deaglan duly retreated to the library with Pru, Toby, and Felix; Cicely joined them as well.

With Toby and Felix as witnesses, Deaglan and Pru signed the three copies of the deal notes.

Once Pru had carefully blotted the signatures, Deaglan sighed and smiled at her. "Done."

She beamed back. "Indeed."

He held her warm gaze for several seconds—basking in it—then sighed, rose, and settled his coat. "Now to broach the other agreement I need to make with your father."

Pru glanced around. "Actually, I would advise meeting Papa and Mama in here." She looked at Toby, Felix, and Cicely and arched her brows. "If you three could make yourselves scarce?"

Toby swung toward the door, with Felix and Cicely falling in at his heels. "Consider us gone," Toby called back. He opened the door, and the three departed, with Felix pulling the door shut behind him.

Deaglan looked at Pru. "Ready?"

She smiled. "Yes."

The confidence and certainty in that single syllable buoyed him. He crossed to the bellpull and, when Bligh appeared, advised him that he and Pru would await her parents there.

They didn't have long to wait. Less than five minutes later, Bligh opened the door and announced, "Mr. and Mrs. Cynster, my lord."

Deaglan rose, as did Pru. He waved her parents to the comfortable sofa; as they came forward, he saw them noting the amenities of the room, taking in the informal ambiance, and, as had happened with Pru and Toby, saw them relax, too.

Once they'd sat, he resumed his seat. Somewhat to his surprise, Pru elected to perch on the arm of his chair—a very clear signal that, unsurprisingly, had both her parents' brows rising.

In light of that, there seemed little point in attempting to introduce the subject gradually; as a group, these Cynsters, at least, seemed uncompromisingly direct.

He could handle direct. Locking his gaze with her father's, he said, "Quite aside from our mutually beneficial breeding agreement, I would like to ask for Pru's hand in marriage."

Her father's eyes narrowed to shards of steely blue. "Would you, now?" His tone, with its undercurrents of menacing aggression, didn't sound promising, but then he looked at Pru.

Quite what he saw in his daughter's face, Deaglan had no way of knowing, but it caused Demon Cynster—a rider renowned for never backing away from a fence—to ease back and change direction. He huffed, then noticed that he was also getting a highly pointed look from his wife. He appeared to read it, then huffed again and turned back to Deaglan.

"I can see that she's happy"—her father shot another glance at Pru, as if to confirm what he'd already deduced, then nodded—"and as with the breeding agreement, I trust her judgment."

That gained him beaming smiles from both ladies, and Pru leapt up and gave her father a fierce hug. Looking rather discomfited, he patted her shoulder.

Deaglan only just heard Pru's whispered, "Thank you, Papa. He's absolutely the right one for me."

Her father's eyes met Deaglan's. As Pru stepped back, her father grunted and somewhat disgruntledly said, "Well, as you've made up your mind, and all I want is for you to be happy and content, it seems I've precious little choice—and the man does have horses."

That made both Pru and her mother laugh, and Deaglan realized from whom she'd inherited that warm and gloriously uplifting sound.

"And yes," her father continued, "I most definitely want to see these vaunted animals, but first"—he fixed his gaze again on Deaglan as Pru returned to her perch beside him—"I would be failing in my duty if I didn't ask whether you and the estate are able to support your countess."

Deaglan inclined his head. Having anticipated the question, he had the answer ready—a condensed outline of the financial state of the earldom.

"So," he eventually concluded, "even without any income from the stable, the estate is solidly in the black." A thought struck him, and he added, "And indeed, without the drain from my late steward's self-serving scheme, we'll be something like four thousand pounds per annum better off."

Her parents pricked up their ears. "Self-serving scheme?" her father inquired.

Pru exchanged a glance with Deaglan and, at his nod, rapidly explained what had happened and what they had only an hour ago learned.

"So this scheme and its aftermath have now ended?" Pru's mother looked at Deaglan. When he nodded, she smiled—a smile very like her daughter's. "In that case, my advice is to put the matter entirely behind you. The pair of you stand on the cusp of starting a new life together, and that should now be your focus."

She glanced at Pru's father, then turned back to Pru and Deaglan. "I believe we're ready to see the Glengarah collection now."

Deaglan smiled, and they rose and made their way to the side door and out to the stable.

Pru was quietly thrilled when Deaglan, smiling understandingly, waved at her to take the lead in showing off the horses to her parents.

She was entranced to see her parents react to the sight of horse after horse as she had—with awe and wonder. In their cases, they had no reason to hide their excitement; the deal was already signed.

Her mother was well-nigh ecstatic at seeing so many of the strong but neatly built mares she favored in one place. As for her sire, the farther they progressed along the rows of stalls, the quieter and more intent he became; he was completely captivated by the horses.

When they reached the final five stalls, her parents simply stared. They'd run out of superlatives.

Then Toby and Felix found them, and when her mother turned to Pru with an almost-pleading look on her face, Pru grinned and had Deaglan, Toby, and Felix halter the three stallions and lead them to the exercise ring. With her father and mother at her back, she put the three stallions—all of whom now recognized her and were perfectly willing to show off—through their paces.

It was a moment of utter bliss—for her, for her parents, for Toby, and also for Deaglan, looking on with pride, and Felix, hanging over the fence with a huge grin on his face.

When they finally made their way back to the castle, her parents were openly thrilled by the potential of the deal she and Deaglan had struck—and also by the prospect of forging a familial link with Deaglan and his fabulous horses and being an ongoing part of establishing the Glengarah Thoroughbred breeding program.

Cicely met them in the front hall with a wide smile. "Maude and Lady Connaught are in the kitchen, exhorting the cook and her staff to produce a sumptuous dinner in honor of the deal and the engagement."

Deaglan returned Cicely's smile and glanced at Pru. "We do, indeed, have a lot to celebrate."

That set the tone for the evening. The staff were on their mettle, and the dinner was, indeed, worthy of every superlative bestowed.

Toasts were drunk in champagne and fine claret, and laughter and delight captured them all.

Later, when the men had finished a bottle of fine whiskey between them and rejoined the ladies in the drawing room, Deaglan found himself cornered by his father-in-law-to-be.

Rather more serious than he had been, Demon met Deaglan's eyes, then, standing shoulder to shoulder with Deaglan and ostensibly watching their ladies, who were sitting side by side on a sofa, their blond heads together, Demon sipped his tea, then said, "Just so you know, we are aware of your reputation."

"I hadn't imagined you weren't," Deaglan smoothly replied. "However, that particular reputation is well and truly in my past. Since I returned here"—he lightly shrugged—"I've lived a life not noticeably removed from that of a monk."

Demon nearly spluttered. "You sure?"

"Quite. My sole focus since coming back has been to improve the estate and make it strong again."

"Which, I gather, you've done."

Deaglan dipped his head and sipped his tea.

After a moment, Demon went on, "I admit that your reputation—past or present makes little odds—gave me pause, but then my dear wife reminded me that my own reputation prior to our marriage wasn't all that different."

Slowly, Deaglan nodded. "So you know that men do change."

"Indeed. And more to the point, I've observed that of all men, rakes are, in fact, the men most avidly searching for happiness. We try this, then that, all in pursuit of that ultimate goal. Then we find it—or more correctly, love finds us, and we recognize it for what it is, for the happiness it all but guarantees—and we seize it, cling to it, and become equally intent on never letting it go."

Deaglan considered the notion and found nothing with which to disagree. After a moment, he said, "In the interests of having all clear between us, I would marry Pru regardless of you giving your permission. She's her own woman—and she's mine." He drained his cup and set the cup on its saucer with a soft, quite definite clink.

After a moment of staring at his wife and eldest daughter, Demon sighed. "I've always believed that a certain degree of disapproval of one's son-in-law is all but mandatory. However, in your case, I believe I'll make an exception. I would have to wrack my brains too hard to find anything to grumble about."

Deaglan chuckled. "No need to overtax yourself."

"Exactly." Demon thrust out a hand. "Welcome to the club."

Puzzled, Deaglan shook his soon-to-be father-in-law's hand. "Which club?"

Demon looked across at his wife and his daughter. "Why, the Cynster Club of Reformed Rakes." His eyes twinkled as he shot Deaglan a challenging look. "It's general female wisdom in the ton that we make the best husbands, and I can tell you now, you have a lot to live up to."

Deaglan laughed and replied, "I'll consider that a challenge."

"Do." Demon nodded. "Because it is."

Deaglan looked across at Pru—who had heard his laughter and had raised her head and was looking his way, a question in her eyes—and decided that the Cynster challenge was one he would happily spend the rest of his life meeting. Aside from all else, the rewards would be worth it.

That night, when Deaglan and Pru, being the last of the company to retire, reached the top of the main stairs, instead of making their way down the long visitors' wing, Deaglan tugged Pru the other way—to his apartments.

"Now that we have your parents' blessing..." He drew her through the large door, then set her free and turned to shut it.

"Oh."

She was curious; he could see that in her face. He watched as she explored, touching and examining this and that, by stages, making her way into his bedroom.

He followed and closed that door, too.

Eventually, she returned to him, to his arms.

They kissed, and the moment spun out and stretched, filled with all that rose between them.

They came together with single-minded focus, with commitment and demand, worshipping and claiming, surrendering and sating.

This was passion.

This was joy and delight.

Until it became pleasure unimaginable.

This was life.

This was love.

Together, they reached out and caught hold of the comet's tail and clung as the glory seared them.

Leaving them wracked and at peace, shattered yet whole.

Complete in a way they were only just coming to fully know.

Later, they lay side by side, hand in hand, and stared up at the silken canopy and contemplated a joint future that was now very real.

"When should we marry?" he asked, then added, "And where?"

After a moment, she replied, "Do you have a preference on either score?"

"On the second, not really. Your choice. But as for the first, obviously, I'd prefer sooner rather than later."

"Well, that's a relief, because I think we should marry as soon as we can reasonably arrange it. That said, we'll need banns read, and four Sundays from now should give my mother and aunt and the other Cynster wives enough time to organize, as they will. So that lands us marrying somewhere in the middle of May—which sounds fairly perfect. As for the where..." She turned on her side and looked into his face. "I've never been conventional, so I don't think anyone would be surprised if I opted to marry in the chapel here—if that's agreeable to you?"

He blinked at her. "Entirely agreeable, but we are on the far west coast of Ireland."

She smiled. "I know—that's the great advantage. I'm certain the vast majority of the family would welcome an excuse to get away from London, especially then, given the Season will be winding down. In addition, all the males and many of the females would love to stay at a real Irish castle and look over the horses. They may not all be as horse-mad as our branch of the family tree, but almost to a man and woman, they appreciate fine horses. It's in the blood."

"I see." He tugged on the golden curls caressing her temple. "If the thought makes you happy, and I can see it does, then that's what we'll do. As long as you let me put my ring on your finger and you agree to spend the rest of your life here with me, I'll be entirely content."

She laughed softly. "You're easy to please."

"For you, yes." He was reminded of Demon's words of wisdom. In truth, happiness was what he'd always sought, and he'd found it in her.

And the final twist was that he found his greatest happiness in ensuring hers.

That, he'd realized, was the crux of the Cynster challenge.

Through the soft, moon-caressed shadows, she stared into his eyes, then softly said, "I vow, here and now, that I will marry you, that I will be your countess with your ring on my finger, and I will, indeed, spend the rest of my life here with you—and your horses—and together, we will be entirely content."

He smiled and kissed her gently, then settled her against him.

As she relaxed and slid toward slumber, still smiling, he closed his eyes.

He'd finally found what he needed to make his life complete.

His ultimate lover. His countess and helpmate.

His partner in all things forevermore.

His wife—his one true love.

EPILOGUE

MAY 17, 1851. GLENGARAH CASTLE, COUNTY SLIGO, IRELAND.

*N*ot quite five weeks later, Deaglan stood, impatiently and with a degree of nervy anticipation, before the altar in the chapel of Glengarah Castle and waited for Pru to join him.

He fought to quell his restlessness; if he jiggled and shifted, one of the numerous grandes dames seated in the pews at his back might misinterpret and draw an entirely false conclusion.

In an effort to distract himself, he sent his mind skating back over the events of the past weeks.

Pru's parents had initially remained at Glengarah for a full week, discussing and freely dispensing advice regarding the changes necessary to transform the Glengarah stable into an active breeding establishment, before taking Pru and Toby with them and returning to Newmarket.

The following weeks had been a whirl of activity for Pru; they'd been the same for Deaglan. Maude and Esmerelda had flung themselves into the preparations for his wedding with giddy abandon and had recruited several of their cronies to assist. He and Felix had barricaded themselves in the library while he'd grappled with deciding what to do about the now-vacant position of steward. In the end, he'd elected to put off any decision until after the wedding, when he would have ready access to Pru's insights as well.

Pru, Toby, and her parents, as well as her other two siblings, Nicholas and Margaret, had returned to Glengarah four days ago—the first in a long line of arrivals.

Pru's prediction that her family would seize the chance to visit had proved correct; all the various branches of the ducal family tree were well represented, from the parents of the renowned Bar Cynster down. Deaglan owned to having been somewhat wary of meeting the duke and his cohort of cousins—the original members of the club Demon had said Deaglan was joining—but his reservations had proved unfounded. As Demon had, the other five all seemed to regard him as a recognizable entity—a man much like themselves. Deaglan had subsequently met several other gentlemen who had married Cynster ladies—the Earl of Dexter, Viscount Calverton, the Earl of Glencrae, and the Marquess of Winchelsea to name but a few—and indeed, the similarities were striking.

The Cynster Club of Reformed Rakes was a thriving fraternity.

From Winchelsea and Pru's married second cousins, Sebastian, Michael, and Marcus, Deaglan had learned that the members of the family he truly needed to be wary of were the wives—from the ancient Dowager Duchess of St. Ives, who was Pru's great-aunt, down.

It hadn't taken him long to confirm that, within the Cynster family, the ladies were a force to be reckoned with—never taken lightly and never underestimated.

The organ had been playing an inconsequential air; now, the music changed to the introduction to a stirring anthem.

Deaglan straightened. Beside him, Felix shot a glance over his shoulder. Toby, beyond Felix, was Deaglan's second groomsman and had been thrilled to be asked. Deaglan realized both men were now unabashedly staring up the aisle.

He couldn't resist the compulsion. Slowly, he turned and looked up the aisle.

At the vision who had paused beneath the ornate arched entrance to the chapel.

He, too, stared.

The music swelled, and Pru started walking down the aisle—to him.

Beneath her fine lace veil, Pru felt her lips curve as she drank in the look on Deaglan's face. While the bodice and sleeves of her delicate gown were fitted and cut to resemble the tight jacket of a riding habit, the skirts and train were created from bunched layers of silk gauze over a heavy satin underskirt, with the gauze caught and looped to form a rippling cascade of fabric that nevertheless held echoes of a riding habit.

The crystals liberally scattered over the gauze, winking, blinking, shimmering, and shivering with every tiny move she made, transformed the gown into a magical sight.

As she progressed down the aisle, with Antonia and Catriona—her oldest, closest, and dearest friends, now married themselves—following as her matrons of honor, Pru heard the excited gasps and whispers and felt the avid gazes of her younger female cousins as they took due note of her gown.

On her father's steady arm, she neared the altar steps and inwardly admitted that Antonia had been correct; the expression in Deaglan's eyes was worth every last hour she'd spent at the modiste's salon.

Deaglan offered his hand. Her father squeezed her fingers, then placed them in Deaglan's palm.

His eyes held hers as he closed his hand, firm and strong, about hers.

Smiling into his emerald eyes, she raised her skirt and stepped up to join him.

Then Reverend Phillips, smiling delightedly, stepped forward, and she and Deaglan faced him, and the service began.

"Dearly beloved, we are gathered together here in the sight of God, and in the face of this congregation, to join together this man and this woman in holy matrimony—"

The words rolled on. He, then she, gave their responses in clear, firm voices. They were set on their course, committed to their future, and ready to embark on this next stage of their lives.

Then, with a whispered "At last" that nearly made her giggle, Deaglan slid an ornately worked band of Irish gold onto her ring finger.

A minute later, a beaming Reverend Phillips pronounced them man and wife, and she went into Deaglan's arms, and he bent his head, and while both were aware the kiss had to remain within bounds, the brief caress conveyed so much—a veritable ocean of promise.

Then they parted and turned to greet their now-united families.

They were mobbed in the aisle—not just by family but by many of the staff and estate families who had crammed into the rear pews or stood shoulder to shoulder around the chapel walls, all to see their lord marry a lady they'd taken to their hearts.

It was a moment of shining joy—one of many Pru and Deaglan encountered throughout the day.

After what must have been half an hour or more, Maude waded into the melee, clapped her hands, and directed the guests to repair to the ball-room or the front hall—which, for the occasion, had reverted to its former glory as a great hall and had been set up to house a banquet for all the staff and the estate families.

Mrs. O'Shaughnessy had put aside her sorrow and, although still in mourning, had, with Bligh and Mrs. Bligh, taken on the role of directing the estate celebration.

Before joining their families and their other guests in the ballroom, Deaglan and Pru lingered in the front hall, then Deaglan, with Pru by his side, took up a stance a few steps up the stairs and delivered a rousing speech to those assembled, thanking them for their felicitations before expressing his and Pru's joint wishes and hopes for the future of the estate, then recommending them all to address themselves to the celebratory meal being ferried out from the kitchen.

They left the gathering on a roar of approval. Laughing, bumping shoulders, flown on sheer happiness, they wended their way through the corridors to the ballroom, which occupied one corner of the ground floor.

There, familial joy and delight embraced them.

Later, once the wedding breakfast was reduced to empty platters and the speeches, some uproarious, others more poignant, had been delivered, and Deaglan and Pru had circled the ballroom floor in the wedding waltz, they took to ambling around the huge room, chatting with those who had braved the Irish Sea to see them wed.

Deaglan found he couldn't stop smiling; not even the scariest and most unsettling of their encounters—with the Dowager Duchess, flanked by Pru's grandmother, Lady Horatia, and the pair's even more ancient and formidable bosom-bow, Lady Osbaldestone—could dim his mood.

Who had known contentment could be this deep—could reach so profoundly into his soul?

Through the last weeks, Demon's wisdom had, again and again, risen in Deaglan's mind.

Rakes search most avidly for happiness.

And once we find it, we never let it go.

This, then, was the beginning of his happiness—the happiness he'd married to secure. Her beside him, on his arm, his ring on her finger as they faced the world side by side. His estate was prospering and would prosper even more, well into the future as, together, they created and established the Glengarah Thoroughbred breeding program.

Joy, love, life—now he had her as his wife, he had everything he needed to meet any challenge as they moved forward into their future, one they would craft and mold.

It was there, waiting—and together, they would seize it.

As if sensing that welling, swelling resolution moving through him, Pru looked up, met his eyes, briefly searched them, then smiled. "This has been the most incredible day. No dramas—or at least, only the good kind."

He smiled and lightly squeezed her hand. "Today has been perfect."

Pru read the truth of that in his emerald eyes, and her heart sang. She felt so deeply anchored here, at his side, in his castle, at Glengarah, she—who had always thought herself wedded to the downs of Newmarket—was at a loss to explain it.

Her little finger rubbed lightly against the worked gold band that was her wedding ring. It was quite heavy, even weighty, surprisingly substantial given the delicacy of the filigree work, yet that weight felt right, as if the ring belonged exactly where it was.

And that was it, wasn't it?

Her being here felt right—fundamentally right—because this was her rightful place, her own true home.

The understanding, the simplicity of it, rolled through her—and settled inside.

An anchor, a new foundation, acknowledged.

She looked up at Deaglan; he was presently looking across the room at her brothers, who were talking to her cousin Christopher.

She seized the moment to, with her eyes, trace Deaglan's face, his features, now beloved, imprinted on her heart.

She'd found her home. It was here, with him. He was her lodestar, her anchor, her place.

He was the home of her heart.

From one side of the large ballroom, flanked by his cousins Nicholas and Toby, Christopher Cynster watched as Deaglan—Glengarah, Christopher's latest connection—looked at Pru and, after exchanging some comment, steered her toward a gaggle of ladies who had been attempting for some time to catch their eyes.

Inside Christopher, something stirred—quite what, he wasn't sure. Envy, perhaps, possibly tinged with a mild sense of betrayal. Of being left behind.

He'd always thought Pru would be the other member of their generation who would remain unmarried, yet there she was, thoroughly besotted by the previously wicked Earl of Glengarah, who, according to Christopher's mother, was now reformed and entirely acceptable—indeed, something of a prize that Pru had snaffled.

Not that Christopher thought Glengarah any less besotted than his bride. When the Cynster curse struck, it took no prisoners.

Unnerved by the direction in which his thoughts were leading him—unsettled just by the thought of the Cynster curse—Christopher shoved his mind to a different subject. "Your father hasn't stopped grinning. I suppose there can be no better way of ensuring that Glengarah's interests align with those of the Cynster Stables."

Somewhat dourly, Nicholas snorted. "You know Pru better than that. Now she's married the man, she'll fight for Glengarah's interests, even over ours. Not that I imagine it'll ever come to that, and she'll always support us as far as she can, but henceforth, her loyalty will lie with that bastard beside her, and I wouldn't wager a groat on Papa's chances of succeeding in any move that isn't in Glengarah's best interests."

Christopher returned his gaze to Pru, once again taking in the way she looked at her husband. His lips moved before he'd thought. "It must be nice, being the recipient of that degree of devotion."

"That type of devotion," Toby stated, "only works when it's mutual and given from the heart."

Christopher huffed. "You sound like Great-aunt Helena."

Entirely unperturbed, Toby smiled—as if the words were a compliment. "Hardly surprising. The time I spent at her knee, I spent listening." With that, he wandered off.

Christopher watched him go, then said to Nicholas, "Your brother is an irritatingly smug bastard."

"Yes, he is," Nicholas agreed. "Unfortunately, he's rarely wrong." With that, Nicholas, too, ambled off and was soon swallowed up by the smiling, laughing, giddily happy crowd.

Christopher remained where he was, clinging to the shadows. Happiness—in the broadest and widest sense, effervescent and alluring—swirled before him; the laughter, the sheer exuberant joy, the unrelenting good humor contrasted harshly with the emptiness that yawned inside him.

Would he ever fill it?

He didn't know.

Eventually, he slipped out of the door, leaving all reminders of what he didn't have—and believed he never would have—behind.

* * *

Dear Reader,

I always knew Prudence Cynster would go her own way—thatshe would opt to spend her days in a stable rather than haunting the ton's ballrooms. Even when, years ago, she popped up as a child in Dillon Caxton's romance, I suspected that, while she would always remain curious about romance, inevitably, a girl so horse-mad would come to see the usual courtship rituals as simply getting in her way, and the accepted structure of married life as too limiting for her.

It was fun devising a hero strong enough and possessed of the right character and attributes to change even Pru's stubborn mind! I hope you found observing the internal tussles and external challenges Pru and Deaglan face and overcome on their road to their happy ever after as much fun as I did.

As I'm sure you've realized from the last scene in this book, the Cynster Next Generation will return with Christopher Cynster's romance, scheduled for release in early 2020.

Meanwhile, the rest of 2019 will see the release of the second in The Cavanaughs series, *The Pursuits of Lord Kit Cavanaugh*, scheduled for release on April 30, 2019.

That will be followed by a special release on July 18, 2019, of the third volume in The Cavanaughs, *The Beguilement of Lady Eustacia Cavanaugh*, in which Kit's sister, Stacie, tangles with a nobleman, manipulating him into doing something he'd stubbornly refused to do, only to have him skillfully turn the tables on her.

Then to round out the year, we'll have the third volume of Lady Osbaldestone's Christmas Chronicles, *Lady Osbaldestone's Christmas Puddings*, for you to enjoy in the lead-up to Christmas.

As ever, I wish you continued happy reading!

Stephanie.

For alerts as new books are released, plus information on upcoming books, exclusive sweepstakes and sneak peeks into upcoming novels, sign

up for Stephanie's Private Email Newsletter.
http://www.stephanielaurens.com/newsletter-signup/

Or, if you don't have time to chat and want a quick email alert, sign up
and follow me at BookBub https://www.bookbub.com/authors/stephanie-
laurens

The ultimate source for detailed information on all Stephanie's published
books, including covers, descriptions, and excerpts, is Stephanie's
Website www.stephanielaurens.com

You can also follow Stephanie via her Amazon Author Page at
http://tinyurl.com/zc3e9mp

Goodreads members can follow Stephanie via her author page
https://www.goodreads.com/author/show/9241.Stephanie_Laurens

You can email Stephanie at stephanie@stephanielaurens.com

Or find her on Facebook
https://www.facebook.com/AuthorStephanieLaurens/

COMING NEXT:

The second volume in THE CAVANAUGHS
THE PURSUITS OF LORD KIT CAVANAUGH
To be released on April 30, 2019.

*Bold and clever, THE CAVANAUGHS are unlike any other family in early
Victorian England. #1 New York Times bestselling author Stephanie
Laurens continues to explore the enthralling world of these dynamic
siblings in the eagerly anticipated second volume in her captivating
series.*

A gentleman of means
One of the most eligible bachelors in London, Lord Christopher "Kit"
Cavanaugh has discovered his true path and it doesn't include the

expected society marriage. Kit is all business and has chosen the bustling port of Bristol to launch his passion--Cavanaugh Yachts.

A woman of character

Miss Sylvia Buckleberry's passion is her school for impoverished children. When a new business venture forces the school out of its building, she must act quickly. But confronting Kit Cavanaugh is a daunting task made even more difficult by their first and only previous meeting, when, believing she'd never see him again, she'd treated him dismissively. Still, Sylvia is determined to be persuasive.

An unstoppable duo

But it quickly becomes clear there are others who want the school--and Cavanaugh Yachts--closed. Working side by side, Kit and Sylvia fight to secure her school and to expose the blackguard trying to sabotage his business. Yet an even more dastardly villain lurks, one who threatens the future both discover they now hold dear.

TO BE FOLLOWED BY:

**The third volume in THE CAVANAUGHS
THE BEGUILEMENT OF LADY EUSTACIA CAVANAUGH
To be released on July 18, 2019.**

The tale of how Stacie Cavanaugh's quest to establish a place for herself in the ton as an eccentric spinster noblewoman with a love of music finds her pitting her manipulative wits against those of Frederick, Marquess of Albury, a nobleman Stacie gradually discovers is a great deal more compelling and insightful than she'd bargained for.

PREVIOUS CYNSTER NEXT GENERATION RELEASES:

**The first volume of the Devil's Brood Trilogy
THE LADY BY HIS SIDE**

A marquess in need of the right bride. An earl's daughter in search of a purpose. A betrayal that ends in murder and balloons into a threat to the realm.

Sebastian Cynster knows time is running out. If he doesn't choose a wife soon, his female relatives will line up to assist him. Yet the current debutantes do not appeal. Where is he to find the right lady to be his marchioness? Then Drake Varisey, eldest son of the Duke of Wolverstone, asks for Sebastian's aid.

Having assumed his father's mantle in protecting queen and country, Drake must go to Ireland in pursuit of a dangerous plot. But he's received an urgent missive from Lord Ennis, an Irish peer—Ennis has heard something Drake needs to know. Ennis insists Drake attends an upcoming house party at Ennis's Kent estate so Ennis can reveal his information face-to-face.

Sebastian has assisted Drake before and, long ago, had a liaison with Lady Ennis. Drake insists Sebastian is just the man to be Drake's surrogate at the house party—the guests will imagine all manner of possibilities and be blind to Sebastian's true purpose.

Unsurprisingly, Sebastian is reluctant, but Drake's need is real. With only more debutantes on his horizon, Sebastian allows himself to be persuaded.

His first task is to inveigle Antonia Rawlings, a lady he has known all her life, to include him as her escort to the house party. Although he's seen little of Antonia in recent years, Sebastian is confident of gaining her support.

Eldest daughter of the Earl of Chillingworth, Antonia has abandoned the search for a husband and plans to use the week of the house party to decide what to do with her life. There has to be some purpose, some role, she can claim for her own.

Consequently, on hearing Sebastian's request and an explanation of what lies behind it, she seizes on the call to action. Suppressing her senses' idiotic reaction to Sebastian's nearness, she agrees to be his partner-in-intrigue.

But while joining the house party proves easy, the gathering is thrown into chaos when Lord Ennis is murdered—just before he was to speak with Sebastian. Worse, Ennis's last words, gasped to Sebastian, are: *Gunpowder. Here.*

Gunpowder? And here, where?

With a killer continuing to stalk the halls, side by side, Sebastian and

Antonia search for answers and, all the while, the childhood connection that had always existed between them strengthens and blooms...into something so much more.

First volume in a trilogy. A historical romance with gothic overtones layered over a continuing intrigue. A full length novel of 99,000 words.

The second volume of the Devil's Brood Trilogy
AN IRRESISTIBLE ALLIANCE

A duke's second son with no responsibilities and a lady starved of the excitement her soul craves join forces to unravel a deadly, potentially catastrophic threat to the realm - that only continues to grow.

With his older brother's betrothal announced, Lord Michael Cynster is freed from the pressure of familial expectations. However, the allure of his previous hedonistic pursuits has paled. Then he learns of the mission his brother, Sebastian, and Lady Antonia Rawlings have been assisting with and volunteers to assist by hunting down the hoard of gunpowder now secreted somewhere in London.

Michael sets out to trace the carters who transported the gunpowder from Kent to London. His quest leads him to the Hendon Shipping Company, where he discovers his sole source of information is the only daughter of Jack and Kit Hendon, Miss Cleome Hendon, who although a fetchingly attractive lady, firmly holds the reins of the office in her small hands.

Cleo has fought to achieve her position in the company. Initially, managing the office was a challenge, but she now conquers all in just a few hours a week. With her three brothers all adventuring in America, she's been driven to the realization that she craves adventure, too.

When Michael Cynster walks in and asks about carters, Cleo's instincts leap. She wrings from him the full tale of his mission—and offers him a bargain. She will lead him to the carters he seeks if he agrees to include her as an equal partner in the mission.

Horrified, Michael attempts to resist, but ultimately finds himself agreeing—a sequence of events he quickly learns is common around Cleo. Then she delivers on her part of the bargain, and he finds there are benefits to allowing her to continue to investigate beside him—not least being that if she's there, then he knows she's safe.

But the further they go in tracing the gunpowder, the more deaths they uncover. And when they finally locate the barrels, they find themselves tangled in a fight to the death—one that forces them to face what has grown between them, to seize and defend what they both see as their path to the greatest adventure of all. A shared life. A shared future. A shared love.

Second volume in a trilogy. A historical romance with gothic overtones layered over a continuing intrigue. A full length novel of 101,000 words.

The third and final volume of the Devil's Brood Trilogy
THE GREATEST CHALLENGE OF THEM ALL

A nobleman devoted to defending queen and country and a noblewoman wild enough to match his every step race to disrupt the plans of a malignant intelligence intent on shaking England to its very foundations.

Lord Drake Varisey, Marquess of Winchelsea, eldest son and heir of the Duke of Wolverstone, must foil a plot that threatens to shake the foundations of the realm, but the very last lady—nay, noblewoman—he needs assisting him is Lady Louisa Cynster, known throughout the ton as Lady Wild.

For the past nine years, Louisa has suspected that Drake might well be the ideal husband for her, even though he's assiduous in avoiding her. But she's now twenty-seven and enough is enough. She believes propinquity will reveal exactly what it is that lies between them, and what better opportunity to work closely with Drake than this latest mission with which he patently needs her help?

Unable to deny Louisa's abilities or the value of her assistance and powerless to curb her willfulness, Drake is forced to grit his teeth and acquiesce to her sticking by his side if only to ensure her safety. But all too soon, his true feelings for her surface sufficiently for her, perspicacious as she is, to see through his denials, which she then interprets as a challenge.

Even while they gather information, tease out clues, increasingly desperately search for the missing gunpowder, and doggedly pursue the killer responsible for an ever-escalating tally of dead men, thrown together through the hours, he and she learn to trust and appreciate each other. And fed by constant exposure—and blatantly encouraged by her—their desires and hungers swell and grow…

As the barriers between them crumble, the attraction he has for so long restrained burgeons and balloons, until goaded by her near-death, it erupts, and he seizes her—only to be seized in return.

Linked irrevocably and with their wills melded and merged by passion's fire, with time running out and the evil mastermind's deadline looming, together, they focus their considerable talents and make one last push to learn the critical truths—to find the gunpowder and unmask the villain behind this far-reaching plot.

Only to discover that they have significantly less time than they'd thought, that the villain's target is even more crucially fundamental to the realm than they'd imagined, and it's going to take all that Drake is—as well as all that Louisa as Lady Wild can bring to bear—to defuse the threat, capture the villain, and make all safe and right again.

As they race to the ultimate confrontation, the future of all England rests on their shoulders.

Third volume in a trilogy. A historical romance with gothic overtones layered over an intrigue. A full length novel of 129,000 words.

If you haven't yet caught up with the first books in the Cynster Next Generation Novels, then BY WINTER'S LIGHT is a Christmas story that highlights the Cynster children as they stand poised on the cusp of adulthood – essentially an introductory novel to the upcoming generation. That novel is followed by the first pair of Cynster Next Generation romances, those of Lucilla and Marcus Cynster, twins and the eldest children of Lord Richard aka Scandal Cynster and Catriona, Lady of the Vale. Both the twins' stories are set in Scotland. See below for further details.

BY WINTER'S LIGHT
A Cynster Special Novel

*#1 New York Times bestselling author Stephanie Laurens returns to
romantic Scotland to usher in a new generation of Cynsters in an
enchanting tale of mistletoe, magic, and love.*

It's December 1837 and the young adults of the Cynster clan have
succeeded in having the family Christmas celebration held at snow-bound
Casphairn Manor, Richard and Catriona Cynster's home. Led by Sebastian, Marquess of Earith, and by Lucilla, future Lady of the Vale, and her
twin brother, Marcus, the upcoming generation has their own plans for
the holiday season.

Yet where Cynsters gather, love is never far behind—the festive occasion brings together Daniel Crosbie, tutor to Lucifer Cynster's sons, and
Claire Meadows, widow and governess to Gabriel Cynster's daughter.
Daniel and Claire have met before and the embers of an unexpected
passion smolder between them, but once bitten, twice shy, Claire believes
a second marriage is not in her stars. Daniel, however, is determined to
press his suit. He's seen the love the Cynsters share, and Claire is the lady
with whom he dreams of sharing *his* life. Assisted by a bevy of Cynsters
—innate matchmakers every one—Daniel strives to persuade Claire that
trusting him with her hand and her heart is her right path to happiness.

Meanwhile, out riding on Christmas Eve, the young adults of the
Cynster clan respond to a plea for help. Summoned to a humble dwelling
in ruggedly forested mountains, Lucilla is called on to help with the difficult birth of a child, while the others rise to the challenge of helping her.
With a violent storm closing in and severely limited options, the next
generation of Cynsters face their first collective test—can they save this
mother and child? And themselves, too?

Back at the manor, Claire is increasingly drawn to Daniel and despite
her misgivings, against the backdrop of the ongoing festivities their relationship deepens. Yet she remains torn—until catastrophe strikes, and by
winter's light, she learns that love—true love—is worth any risk,
any price.

*A tale brimming with all the magical delights of a Scottish festive season.
A Cynster novel – a classic historical romance of 71,000 words.*

THE TEMPTING OF THOMAS CARRICK

A Cynster Next Generation Novel

Do you believe in fate? Do you believe in passion? What happens when fate and passion collide?
Do you believe in love? What happens when fate, passion, and love combine?
This. This...

#1 New York Times *bestselling author Stephanie Laurens returns to Scotland with a tale of two lovers irrevocably linked by destiny and passion.*

Thomas Carrick is a gentleman driven to control all aspects of his life. As the wealthy owner of Carrick Enterprises, located in bustling Glasgow, he is one of that city's most eligible bachelors and fully intends to select an appropriate wife from the many young ladies paraded before him. He wants to take that necessary next step along his self-determined path, yet no young lady captures his eye, much less his attention...not in the way Lucilla Cynster had, and still did, even though she lives miles away.

For over two years, Thomas has avoided his clan's estate because it borders Lucilla's home, but disturbing reports from his clansmen force him to return to the countryside—only to discover that his uncle, the laird, is ailing, a clan family is desperately ill, and the clan-healer is unconscious and dying. Duty to the clan leaves Thomas no choice but to seek help from the last woman he wants to face.

Strong-willed and passionate, Lucilla has been waiting—increasingly impatiently—for Thomas to return and claim his rightful place by her side. She knows he is hers—her fated lover, husband, protector, and mate. He is the only man for her, just as she is his one true love. And, at last, he's back. Even though his returning wasn't on her account, Lucilla is willing to seize whatever chance Fate hands her.

Thomas can never forget Lucilla, much less the connection that seethes between them, but to marry her would mean embracing a life he's adamant he does not want.

Lucilla sees that Thomas has yet to accept the inevitability of their union and, despite all, he can refuse her and walk away. But how *can* he ignore a bond such as theirs—one so much stronger than reason? Despite several unnerving attacks mounted against them, despite the uncertainty racking his clan, Lucilla remains as determined as only a Cynster can be to fight for the future she knows can be theirs—and while she cannot command him, she has powerful enticements she's willing to wield in the cause of tempting Thomas Carrick.

A neo-Gothic tale of passionate romance laced with mystery, set in the uplands of southwestern Scotland.
A Cynster Second Generation Novel – a classic historical romance of 122,000 words.

A MATCH FOR MARCUS CYNSTER
A Cynster Next Generation Novel

Duty compels her to turn her back on marriage. Fate drives him to protect her come what may. Then love takes a hand in this battle of yearning hearts, stubborn wills, and a match too powerful to deny.

#1 New York Times bestselling author Stephanie Laurens returns to rugged Scotland with a dramatic tale of passionate desire and unwavering devotion.

Restless and impatient, Marcus Cynster waits for Fate to come calling. He knows his destiny lies in the lands surrounding his family home, but what will his future be? Equally importantly, with whom will he share it?

Of one fact he feels certain: his fated bride will not be Niniver Carrick. His elusive neighbor attracts him mightily, yet he feels compelled to protect her—even from himself. Fickle Fate, he's sure, would never be so kind as to decree that Niniver should be his. The best he can do for them both is to avoid her.

Niniver has vowed to return her clan to prosperity. The epitome of fragile femininity, her delicate and ethereal exterior cloaks a stubborn will and an unflinching devotion to the people in her care. She accepts that in order to achieve her goal, she cannot risk marrying and losing her grip on the clan's reins to an inevitably controlling husband. Unfortunately, many local men see her as their opportunity.

Soon, she's forced to seek help to get rid of her unwelcome suitors. Powerful and dangerous, Marcus Cynster is perfect for the task. Suppressing her wariness over tangling with a gentleman who so excites her passions, she appeals to him for assistance with her peculiar problem.

Although at first he resists, Marcus discovers that, contrary to his expectations, his fated role *is* to stand by Niniver's side and, ultimately, to claim her hand. Yet in order to convince her to be his bride, they must plunge headlong into a journey full of challenges, unforeseen dangers, passion, and yearning, until Niniver grasps the essential truth—that she is indeed a match for Marcus Cynster.

A neo-Gothic tale of passionate romance set in the uplands of southwestern Scotland A Cynster Second Generation Novel – a classic historical romance of 114,000 words.

And if you want to discover where the Cynsters began, return to the iconic
DEVIL's BRIDE

the book that introduced millions of historical romance readers around the globe to the powerful men of the unforgettable Cynster family – aristocrats to the bone, conquerors at heart – and the willful feisty ladies strong enough to be their brides.

ALSO AVAILABLE:

**The first volume in Lady Osbaldestone's Christmas Chronicles
LADY OSBALDESTONE'S CHRISTMAS GOOSE**

#1 New York Times *bestselling author Stephanie Laurens brings you a lighthearted tale of Christmas long ago with a grandmother and three of her grandchildren, one lost soul, a lady driven to distraction, a recalcitrant donkey, and a flock of determined geese.*

Three years after being widowed, Therese, Lady Osbaldestone finally settles into her dower property of Hartington Manor in the village of Little Moseley in Hampshire. She is in two minds as to whether life in the small village will generate sufficient interest to keep her amused over the months when she is not in London or visiting friends around the country. But she will see.

It's December, 1810, and Therese is looking forward to her usual Christmas with her family at Winslow Abbey, her youngest daughter, Celia's home. But then a carriage rolls up and disgorges Celia's three oldest children. Their father has contracted mumps, and their mother has sent the three—Jamie, George, and Lottie—to spend this Christmas with their grandmama in Little Moseley.

Therese has never had to manage small children, not even her own. She assumes the children will keep themselves amused, but quickly learns that what amuses three inquisitive, curious, and confident youngsters isn't compatible with village peace. Just when it seems she will have to set her mind to inventing something, she and the children learn that with only twelve days to go before Christmas, the village flock of geese has vanished.

Every household in the village is now missing the centerpiece of their Christmas feast. But how could an entire flock go missing without the slightest trace? The children are as mystified and as curious as Therese—and she seizes on the mystery as the perfect distraction for the three children as well as herself.

But while searching for the geese, she and her three helpers stumble on two locals who, it is clear, are in dire need of assistance in sorting out their lives. Never one to shy from a little matchmaking, Therese undertakes to guide Miss Eugenia Fitzgibbon into the arms of the determinedly reclusive Lord Longfellow. To her considerable surprise, she discovers that her grandchildren have inherited skills and talents from both her late husband as well as herself. And with all the customary village events held in the lead up to Christmas, she and her three helpers have opportunities galore in which to subtly nudge and steer.

Yet while their matchmaking appears to be succeeding, neither they nor anyone else have found so much as a feather from the village's geese. Larceny is ruled out; a flock of that size could not have been taken from the area without someone noticing. So where could the birds be? And with the days passing and Christmas inexorably approaching, will they find the blasted birds in time?

First in series. A novel of 60,000 words. A Christmas tale of romance and geese.

AND RECENTLY RELEASED:

The second volume in Lady Osbaldestone's Christmas Chronicles
LADY OSBALDESTONE AND THE MISSING CHRISTMAS CAROLS

#1 NYT-bestselling author Stephanie Laurens brings you a heartwarming tale of a long-ago country-village Christmas, a grandmother, three eager grandchildren, one moody teenage granddaughter, an earnest young lady, a gentleman in hiding, and an elusive book of Christmas carols.

Therese, Lady Osbaldestone, and her household are quietly delighted when her younger daughter's three children, Jamie, George, and Lottie, insist on returning to Therese's house, Hartington Manor in the village Little Moseley, to spend the three weeks leading up to Christmas participating in the village's traditional events.

Then out of the blue, one of Therese's older granddaughters, Melissa, arrives on the doorstep. Her mother, Therese's older daughter, begs Therese to take Melissa in until the family gathering at Christmas—otherwise, Melissa has nowhere else to go.

Despite having no experience dealing with moody, reticent teenagers like Melissa, Therese welcomes Melissa warmly. The younger children are happy to include their cousin in their plans—and despite her initial aloofness, Melissa discovers she's not too old to enjoy the simple delights of a village Christmas.

The previous year, Therese learned the trick to keeping her unexpected guests out of mischief. She casts around and discovers that the new organist, who plays superbly, has a strange failing. He requires the written music in front of him before he can play a piece, and the church's book of Christmas carols has gone missing.

Therese immediately volunteers the services of her grandchildren, who are only too happy to fling themselves into the search to find the missing book of carols. Its disappearance threatens one of the village's most-valued Christmas traditions—the Carol Service—yet as the book has always been freely loaned within the village, no one imagines that it won't be found with a little application.

But as Therese's intrepid four follow the trail of the book from house to house, the mystery of where the book has vanished to only deepens. Then the organist hears the children singing and invites them to form a special guest choir. The children love singing, and provided they find the book in time, they'll be able to put on an extra-special service for the village.

While the urgency and their desire to finding the missing book escalates, the children—being Therese's grandchildren—get distracted by the potential for romance that buds, burgeons, and blooms before them.

Yet as Christmas nears, the questions remain: Will the four unravel the twisted trail of the missing book in time to save the village's Carol Service? And will they succeed in nudging the organist and the harpist they've found to play alongside him into seizing the happy-ever-after that hovers before the pair's noses?

Second in series. A novel of 62,000 words. A Christmas tale full of music and romance.

ABOUT THE AUTHOR

#1 *New York Times* bestselling author Stephanie Laurens began writing romances as an escape from the dry world of professional science. Her hobby quickly became a career when her first novel was accepted for publication, and with entirely becoming alacrity, she gave up writing about facts in favor of writing fiction.

All Laurens's works to date are historical romances, ranging from medieval times to the mid-1800s, and her settings range from Scotland to India. The majority of her works are set in the period of the British Regency. Laurens has published more than 70 works of historical romance, including 39 *New York Times* bestsellers. Laurens has sold more than 20 million print, audio, and e-books globally. All her works are continuously available in print and e-book formats in English worldwide, and have been translated into many other languages. An international bestseller, among other accolades, Laurens has received the Romance Writers of America® prestigious RITA® Award for Best Romance Novella 2008 for *The Fall of Rogue Gerrard*.

Laurens's continuing novels featuring the Cynster family are widely regarded as classics of the historical romance genre. Other series include the *Bastion Club Novels*, the *Black Cobra Quartet*, and the *Casebook of Barnaby Adair Novels*. All her previous works remain available in print and all e-book formats.

For information on all published novels and on upcoming releases and updates on novels yet to come, visit Stephanie's website: www.stephanielaurens.com

To sign up for Stephanie's Email Newsletter (a private list) for heads-up alerts as new books are released, exclusive sneak peeks into upcoming books, and exclusive sweepstakes contests, follow the prompts at Stephanie's Email Newsletter Sign-up Page

To follow Stephanie on BookBub, head here https://www.bookbub.com/authors/stephanie-laurens

Stephanie lives with her husband and a goofy black labradoodle in the hills outside Melbourne, Australia. When she isn't writing, she's reading, and if she isn't reading, she'll be tending her garden.

www.stephanielaurens.com
stephanie@stephanielaurens.com